The Mail-Order Standoff

D1167355

4 Historical Stories

ANGELA BREIDENBACH
MARGARET BROWNLEY
SUSAN PAGE DAVIS
VICKIE MCDONOUGH

BARBOUR BOOKS
An Imprint of Barbour Publishing, Inc.

Print ISBN 978-1-64352-244-9

eBook Editions:
Adobe Digital Edition (.epub) 978-1-64352-246-3
Kindle and MobiPocket Edition (.prc) 978-1-64352-245-6

Cover Image: Magdalena Russocka/Trevillion Images

Published by Barbour Books, an imprint of Barbour Publishing, Inc., 1810 Barbour Drive, Uhrichsville, Ohio 44683, www.barbourbooks.com

Our mission is to inspire the world with the life-changing message of the Bible.

Member of the
Evangelical Christian
Publishers Association

Printed in Canada.

Right on Time

by Angela Breidenbach

❧ Chapter 1 ❧

Louisville, Kentucky
May 1883

If you get on that train, Timothy Higgenbottom, I'll write to your father. There will be no further support as of the day you walk out this door!" His mother's thunderous mood covered the sitting room as if a storm gathered, lightning hiding just behind the full skirt of her paisley silk tea gown.

In Timothy's experience, not one soul bucked Lady Higgenbottom's edicts, whether in England or Kentucky. But what would it matter in a few months? "Mother, once I turn twenty-five there is no further support anyway, unless both my brothers die before me." He sat next to her on the damask-covered divan and took her hand. "Neither one of us wishes to lose James or John, and I have no wish to be beholden to either."

"An allowance can be sorted, once your father returns from England, until you marry wisely." She set a stern countenance few dared to cross. Timothy, on the other hand, crossed her regularly without trying.

Not at the level of holdings that required his father to travel from England to America twice each year. Roots in one place seemed less a burden and more a lifestyle to Timothy. He didn't want to leave his family behind constantly. "Regardless, it's not my goal to teach spoiled children to ride ponies or pander to rich heiresses in hopes of a financial windfall."

"One must have a reasonable income as the son of the Earl of Cumberland." Her fan flickered like a hummingbird as further proof of her annoyance. "Not this animal doctor nonsense."

She hid her true feelings well. Few ever saw a moment of weakness in her. He knew better. "Mother, I love you." He didn't want to cause this great woman any pain. But there had to be more to life than saddle-backing his father and brother. "I need to build a life, a home, and name of my own."

"Oh pish, you always have a home here. As for your name, only prized for four centuries. Would you insult your forebears?" She pulled her hand away, closing her fan against it with a slap.

"Do you wish me to remain a poor bachelor living off charity forever? Is that what you want for me?"

Dumbfounded, she leaned forward with a shocked expression. "Poor bachelor? You'd control your wife's income and property as does every other man." Seamlessly sliding into composure, she laid out her plan. "It's my duty to find you the best match, and I've done that for you. The Thompson family have been invited to present their lovely daughter, Althea, to us next week." She tapped his forearm with her folded fan. "Of course, you'll change your mind when you meet her."

"I met her last year at the debutante ball." Memories of stilted conversation during the young lady's debut flooded back. Unable to find common ground, they'd lapsed into silence in an awkward waltz. He shivered at the thought of years in the presence of a woman bored with him and he with her.

"Then you know she's perfectly acceptable for our status." She patted her hair. "Thea's mother has already mentioned her daughter finds you quite handsome."

He narrowed his eyes. "I'm not marrying for social status. I'm definitely not marrying a girl who is merely acceptable." He didn't want to be merely acceptable either.

"Everyone marries for social standing. Even poor—" To her credit, Mariana Higgenbottom bit her tongue. "You must understand there's an expectation in our position. Your duty is to the continuance of your family name."

"Mother, I haven't met anyone's expectations up to this moment." Timothy's voice held reality rather than bitterness. He enjoyed helping mares foal, training them to race, and tending injured stock. He could do without all the human drama—and pretense. "A wealthy wife is not going to solve that dilemma for us."

A little twitch fluttered in the corner of her left eye, known only to the most attuned. Timothy caught the significance. Hurricane Mariana was about to unleash a torrent unless he soothed her first.

"I expect you'll be a dutiful and courteous host to Miss Thompson and her parents."

"I'll be a dutiful and courteous host." He reflected her words back to her.

"I only want the best for you, Timothy. Love has nothing to do with a good match."

"Do you really believe that, Mother?"

"At some point, you're going to have to realize society has rules, and that is precisely why it has worked for thousands of years. Land and beasts are our support and sustenance, not our friends. Your duty is to your family and to live within—"

"Yes, ma'am, I understand rules and duty." He'd reached the end of his patience with that long list of ridiculous rules. Who did they benefit? What was the point? Marrying a high society debutante brought respect and riches for both families through status or finances or both. The same way his mother provided an influx into the Higgenbottom coffers, and his grandmother before her. But he would never say so.

"Good, then it's settled. Your father and I learned to love one another, as you and Thea will." She truly did want the best for her children. Sadly, the limits of societal restrictions seemed more like the flat-earth versus round-earth philosophy he'd learned in boarding school. She took his silence as capitulation. "Right after the Kentucky Derby, we'll enjoy a celebration supper and ball. Your father will draw up the dowry contract when he returns."

"You're already planning a party?" With two older brothers, and James already wed and managing the holdings in England, the family would have plenty of money and status. John would run Cumberland Meadows when it came time. As the spare's spare, and everyone knew it, Timothy had no options except to work under his father and brothers as he'd been doing the last several years. He'd never be his own man unless he left to discover who that man could become. He needed to explore the round earth. "English Fancy is still a hair off last year's winning time." Their first American-born filly from an English-born stud showed great promise. But could she win the Kentucky Derby?

"Both you and your father have worked too hard to fail. I feel it in my bones. And then you'll have every debutante from here to Britain wanting you to sign her dance card." She tapped her fingers on his wrist. "But trust your mother. Althea Thompson is the most suitable match." With that, Lady Mariana Higgenbottom, Countess of Cumberland, swirled her cloudy skirts to change for dinner.

Timothy picked up the ticket the butler had left on the silver tray. The thin piece of paper that had set his mother off. He'd be on that train the day after the derby, regardless of how suitable Miss Thompson or how penniless he'd be on reaching Montana.

He jogged up the stairs to stash the ticket with the letter of invitation from Mister Robert Johnston at the JBarF Ranch near Anaconda, Montana. Through their exchange of letters over the last few months, it was agreed that Timothy would take on the position of ranch foreman and future husband to Miss Tara Johnston. He was, in effect, a mail-order husband. He hadn't mentioned his title. Only that he'd been well educated in animal husbandry and veterinary medicine.

His newly intended bride owned half the thousand-acre ranch. If their marriage worked out, Timothy would own the other half one year later. Together they'd share the ranch. Working toward a common goal. Timothy would be on his way to establishing a future for their children without titles defining them. No more spare-heir ideology, or the sense of being useless unless someone died.

To the Higgenbottoms land meant prestige and wealth. But to him it meant independence and freedom here in America. If he and Miss Johnston were agreeable to one another once they met, they'd marry. If not, he'd find another way to become a man of his own means with a future only he controlled.

JBarF Ranch near Anaconda, Montana

"That's the last of the fencing supplies, Pa." Tara Johnston wiped the back of her wrist across her forehead, leaving a streak from dirty leather gloves. Then she plunked her fists on her hips. "We still got the back to replace and half the side down the O'Connells' before we can let the herd graze this acreage again."

"No reason to worry." He leaned into the long wagon. Grasping the end of the fence roll, he said, "Look at the tall, sweet grass they'll be gettin' since it had time to grow. Sweetest grass in the country." He dropped the end of the roll then stretched his back. "They'll be fat enough to drive to Helena's livestock auction this year and lose very little poundage. They'll gain it back on the grain waitin' on the train."

"You ain't a bit worried?" Hopping into the wagon, she scooted around to push the last of the load forward. "The O'Connells are always worth watchin'. That fence didn't cut itself, now did it? We're lucky no calves got caught up in it."

"I placed an order for more supplies that should be comin' in tomorrow," he drawled out. "Should be a new foreman on that train too."

"How'd you find a man that wants to work horses and cows instead of silver and gold?"

Her father quickly looked away and shrugged as he bent to his work. "I placed an ad and he answered."

"Uh huh." Tara pursed her lips. Pa had something up his sleeve. He didn't have a habit of avoiding her eyes. They had to rely on each other since her brothers died, and he couldn't afford to be soft on her anymore. She'd been working as hard driving cattle, harvesting hay, and building their horse stock as any man.

He kept his attention on his work. "Ain't easy to find one around these parts."

"Till he hears about the Anaconda. I'm bettin' he'll be stayin' long enough to jump in one of those shafts and we'll never hear from him again. Ain't nobody gonna pass up the money Marcus Daly is payin' to work in that mining operation." Two more ranch hands quit last week, leaving them in this fix.

She pushed one end of the barbed wire roll toward the end of the wagon and heaved with all her might as her father pulled. A tine tangled in her skirt and cuff, yanking her with the bale onto the ground. She landed flat out on her side with the wind knocked out of her, skirt torn and twisted around her knees, staring at the barbs that nearly skewered her. Her hat had landed three feet away. She let out a groan and flopped onto her back, staring up at spotty clouds.

"Tara!" Her father raced to help. "Where you hurt?" He lifted her to her feet.

A moment later she could breathe again. But she'd feel that one for a bit. "Not hurt, Pa." Tossing aside her gloves, she hid the bleeding scrape with her hand. She looked up into his concerned eyes. "Just a scratch."

Tara was all he had left of his wife and three children. He and Cookie, an old chuck wagon cowhand, watched her like the last chick after a fox destroyed the henhouse. "Sorry. I shoulda paid better attention. That's what drug-out tired will get you—plus a sore elbow."

"You sure?"

"Yep. Coulda been a lot worse if it weren't for all the grass." She shrugged it off. "Landed on nice, fluffy deer bedding." She quietly dragged in another breath while pressing her arm against her ribs. She needed air in more than the literal sense.

Once he let her be, Tara dabbed the hem of her ankle-length riding skirt against the mouth of her canteen. She cooled the scrape and cleaned it up as he finished unloading. That would sting a few days.

"Need some help with that?"

"No, I got it, thanks." Not the first run-in with a scrape, and not likely her last. She ripped off the torn sleeve, fashioning a makeshift bandage around her elbow to keep the sun and bugs off tender skin while they worked.

They couldn't keep going at this rate. Her body screamed from lack of sleep and aching muscles. Another hand would be a godsend. Even if the new man only helped get the downed section rebuilt, her pa was right to bring on a new foreman. Between fencing, cattle, the hayfields, and horses, the work never ended. They could use eight men. But so could most of the ranches for miles around. As it was, they all combined their crews for cattle drives to markets.

"Be prayin' for no crashes, an on-time arrival, and cowboys that want to be cowboys."

Swiping her hat off the ground, she swatted the dirt off her clothes. "Pa, I'm not sure the Lord can deliver on that." She dropped her hat back on her head. "He seems to be focusing on other things lately, if'n you hadn't noticed."

"Don't lose faith, Mouse. God has a way 'bout Him. He likes to sneak in a surprise when you least expect it."

She quoted her father's familiar words in a deadpan sing-song, "But the good Lord is never not on the job." How could Pa still have faith after all their losses? Even now, enough in their account didn't matter when they couldn't find men to employ. Without ranch hands, their funds would dwindle quickly when cattle didn't get to the train to sell back east. Men outnumbered women nine to one in Montana Territory. Who could afford the Anaconda's three-fifty a day when a cowboy earned twenty-five dollars a month?

Tara scanned the fence line yet to be installed. Her parents homesteaded this land, coming across the country with three small children before the war broke out. Her heart clenched as hard as her teeth. She couldn't bear to be uprooted from the place her mother and brothers were buried. Her only connection to her mother was the land. She didn't remember the woman who'd given her life and then died a few months later. Tara's memories were of the stories Pa and Cookie told.

"It's gettin' dark." Her father put an arm around her shoulders, looking out at the work left to be done. "Don't stare at the overwhelming. That'll get you stuck faster than two bucks locking antlers during the rut. Near impossible to get free. Just do the next thing right and keep goin'. The good Lord will take care of the rest." He didn't force her attention off the terrible task as he slipped from her side and turned toward the wagon. He went about his business leading by example. "Some supper, some sleep, and a new mornin' will set us straight."

She smiled at his familiar manner and followed him. Everything against them. They collected tools and set materials for the next day's needs. No giving up for his daughter either. "I'll get that new fella from Silver Bow, and we'll have him out here by dinner."

"That's the spirit." Pa's expression flickered as if worry might have a home after all. Then he shook it off.

She inherited his work ethics, but not so much his positivity. "Well, that's sayin' the train arrives on time, in one piece, and no cows derail it."

"And the wind don't blow her off the tracks. I know. We gotta keep our minds to what we can do. What we can't, we'll turn over to the Almighty."

The smell of dust clung in her nostrils. The unusual heat on what would normally be a cool May evening stuck to her like milk dried on a pail. She caught the little fox running away with her thoughts. She could focus on happy thoughts, possible outcomes, like her pa. Revel in the small blessings. "Hope Cookie made some mint lemonade."

She tossed the heavy leather gloves on top of a bucket of nails, glorying in the cooler air as the sun tilted behind the mountains. Rain would come soon. A hot week or two slipped in every May, then a cool, rainy June.

"Don't torture me, Mouse. We gotta ride home yet, and I'm parched." He turned the water jug upside down. A couple drops wet his old leather boot.

"It's May, Pa. Watch what you say. We'll get caught in a downpour before we can even see the barn." She handed him her canteen. "Just like you taught me. Don't go nowhere without bein' prepared."

"You're gonna do fine runnin' the ranch once we rebuild a solid crew. Those mines won't last forever. They never do. Our time's comin'." He took a swig, handed the canteen back, then swung himself up onto the buckboard. He waited for Tara to jump up beside him and stow her gear under the seat. "Head on home, boy." He clucked at the horse and flicked the reins.

"Tomorrow's gonna be better." Tara elbowed her father. "Said it 'fore you this time."

"I thought it first."

She laughed. "You still gotta get one up on me."

"There's a day will come when you'll miss it." He gave her a gentle shoulder nudge while a sadness settled in the lines of his face. "Like I miss your mama and brothers."

"Pa, why didn't you ever marry again?"

"Aw, my little Mouse, there's not a lot of ladies out here." The side of his mouth hitched to the right, showing a deep dimple. One he'd passed on to Tara. "I didn't have the heart to go chasin' skirts when I had three little kids and a ranch to run. Cookie's been a blessin' hangin' in with me like he's done. But I won't worry none when the good Lord wants me home."

She bumped shoulders back and teased, "Don't be kickin' the bucket anytime soon. I need the help around here."

"Just another hand for you to boss around." He laughed with her. Then he looked at her dirty brown skirt and stained blouse. "Put on a pretty dress for town, will you? Never know when you'll meet some fine fella and get me some grandsons."

"Oh Pa." She squished up her nose at him. "Get me to that lemonade." She gave him a curious glance. He'd kept his eyes on the land ahead. Was he worried she'd never marry? The other farms and ranches seemed to produce as many children as cattle once they sent back east for wives. She would, one day, have children.

"Just sayin' sometimes it takes a bit for young'uns. Sure be nice to have a passel of strong boys with a tie to the land."

"I know." She leaned against the rough plank, trying to relax into the jostling of the wagon. Her father had asked her every so often the last few years if she had a shine for anyone. Going near Anaconda or Butte had brought out droves of men since she was fourteen. The catcalls to outright proposals from strangers toughened her resolve to ignore nearly every man. They didn't care about her. If she found a husband someday, he'd be able to hold a normal conversation and treat her like lady.

"You gotta have somebody to pass all this down to one day. You're the only one that can do somethin' about that, Mouse. I done had my time." He slapped the reins against the horses' rumps. "Get on now. Graze all you want when we get home, Blaze."

Tara loved the land, loved ranching. But she wasn't yet ready to settle down and be somebody's broodmare either. "I'll keep it in mind, Pa."

"That's all a body can ask."

❧ Chapter 2 ❧

Tara shifted her ten-gallon hat backward and peered down the track. So much for a midmorning arrival. The Utah & Northern Railroad made it to Butte's Silver Bow Depot over the winter. She left the ranch well before sunrise for the six-hour trek. The entire depot was deserted except for her and the agent. Her freight order and new foreman should have been waiting on her, not the other way around. But what if that confounded train didn't make it again? Even if it came now, the sun already showed all the signs of blazing hot this afternoon. The long ride home would not be as pleasant as the brisk ride this morning. Montana had a way with weather. She was as fickle as a stray cat, only friendly when she felt her belly rumble.

"Any word, Mr. Dawson?" she called out to the ticket clerk as he worked down the platform from her. She'd like to be doing rather than standing around wasting good time. But one day would be worth it when they had a skilled foreman, Tara consoled herself.

"She'll be coming up the track any minute, Miss Johnston." He set a crate on the growing stack of outbound freight toward the edge of the wide wooden walkway that doubled for a platform. "Got a wire last night that the Security jumped the track on another busted rail. Had to be pulled off in Dillon again."

"Again? What's that make it, five or six times in the last year?"

He checked his freight then joined her. "Ah, let's see. There's the time it hit the last broken rail and tipped. Those folks were shaken up, but no real injuries. Could've been a lot worse."

She nodded. "I saw that in the paper. They've nicknamed that sleeper car the In-Security. It'd make me laugh 'cept people are getting roughed up and it's costing a bunch of hard-earned money when supplies are dumped too." Off in the distance, a black speck chugged toward them puffing out steam like a grandpa with a pipe. "Honestly, I think folks are braver than me to want to ride one of these ghastly things. I'll stick to my horse, thank you. Steady transportation for centuries."

He shrugged and went on counting mishaps. "The time it blew over and killed that mule, another time or two jumpin' the tracks, and don't forget that cow what took out two engines and the Security."

"I heard 'bout that poor old Bessie." She wandered over to lean against the small one-story building and wait the last few minutes in the shade. "Sure nice of the town to get up a collection for that family. Nobody can afford to lose a milk cow."

"Yep, I think you have it near right—'round about five to six times that car has jinxed the train. They oughta count their losses and replace it." Josiah Dawson headed back to the depot doorway as he called over his shoulder, "But it ain't collided yet like them east-west trains keep doin'." He stopped and checked his watch against the church bell tolling noon before going inside. "Don't know why they can't get their schedules worked out. No sir. Just can't figure it."

The whistle blew, grabbing Tara's attention and alerting the town to the arrival of the tardy train. The platform filled with merchants, delivery boys, and locals as the depot agent continued piling outgoing freight. A little boy ran into town announcing the arrival as if no one had heard the blasts and bells. Excited people crowded in to get their wares and visiting relatives.

Most of the town and surrounding homesteads still showed up to greet the trains for catalogue orders, furniture, and especially fruits like oranges regardless of the day. Men swarmed the freight cars, loading mining equipment, farming supplies, and luggage onto wagons. New homesteaders stared in wonder at the bustling area nestled in the green mountains. How many would stay after their first winter?

Where was that foreman? She could use his help loading up the fence and seed supplies. "Mr. Dawson?" Tara hollered over the remaining crowd, no longer pressed shoulder to shoulder. "You got any clue on passengers? Did they all make it on the train in Dillon?"

He called back, "No, ma'am. Nobody said nothin'. You expectin' someone special?"

"I—" A tap on her shoulder caught her by surprise. She spun around.

"Miss Tara Johnston?" The man's accent didn't sound like an

Irish brogue or Texas twang, and it certainly wasn't Chinese or Italian. More snooty-like, to go along with his high-brow suit. My, my, what a suit! The fabric alone would cost a month's rations before a tailor took a scissor to it. Tara had never seen such finery before, not even at a performance in Butte with Marcus Daly and Conrad Kohrs in attendance. She had to admire the silk of his waistcoat and finely woven summer wool coat.

He held out an envelope toward her as he pointed at the return address, a very nice smile on his handsome, clean-shaven face. "Are you Miss Johnston?"

She suddenly needed a drink of water. "I am." *My, my, what a head turner. Too bad he'd never be staying in the wilds of Montana Territory. By the look of him, Montana would be far too rugged and primitive and fickle. There wasn't a practical thing about him, from his shiny shoes to the gem stickpin holding his fancy cravat's intricate design. The kind of man that came on one train and left on the next with a handkerchief to his nose.*

She scanned past his broad shoulders for a real cowboy. But all the men left were either unloading into wagons or gathering luggage for another party. "I'm waitin' on someone." *Kinda wish it were you.* She forced her attention off him and to the passenger car behind him. But he didn't move on.

"I believe you're here for me." He held out a palm the way a gentleman did for a lady alighting from a carriage. She stared at his hand curiously until he pulled it back and gave a courtly bow. "Timothy Higgenbottom at your service, mademoiselle."

What did he just call her? Her neck warmed, and the sun hadn't even burned her yet. "Mad-ma-what?" She tipped up her chin, taking his measure. *Her father had said to find a Timothy*

Higgenbottom. Was this man a fraud or a jokester? Who would have put him up to it? Then it occurred to her that this could be a carpetbagger here to defraud them. Her eyes narrowed. She'd heard of shenanigans with impostors. This fancy pants had no call to be working as a ranch foreman.

"Mademoiselle. It means—"

"I don't care what it means. What I care about is finding the true Mr. Higgenbottom so we can collect our freight and get back to the ranch. I do not find your joke funny. If you'll pardon me, I have work to do before a long ride home."

He looked confused. "Miss Johnston, I'm truly him. I mean, me. I'm Timothy Higgenbottom." He sounded sincere. "Your intended."

What a funny way to say it, even for a foreigner. "What I intended, Mr. Higgenbottom, was to pick up an able-bodied man to help run my ranch." She looked him up and down. "You sure ain't trained to work cattle and horses and manage cowboys." She again made a point to notice his attire. "Am I wrong? Though you got quite a flare for fashion with that, uh, jeweled thingamabob. Evenin' wear just ain't practical in Montana, sir." Dressed like that, what would he do rounding up the horses? Feeding the cattle? "I think we might well call an end to this charade. Uh. . .good luck." She sighed and turned to leave.

"Miss Johnston, in my hand I hold a proposal telling me to come to Montana. In good faith and at personal expense, I have done so to learn ranching and partner with you. Are you telling me that because of my choice of suit, which for your information is not evening wear, you would not wish to marry me?"

Tara stopped. For a moment she gaped at him, trying for the

life of her to sort out the knot in his yarn. Then the absurdity of the situation struck her. Pa telling her to wear a pretty dress, which she ignored for her common town outfit. This man in his elegantly embroidered silk vest thinking the job offer from Pa was a marriage proposal. The coincidences couldn't have been contrived, as they crashed worse than two engines going east and west. The odd situation was utterly ridiculous. She couldn't hold it in. Tara's laughter burst forth and doubled her over until tears squeezed out. When she gathered her presence of mind, she finally looked up and saw thunder in his eyes.

Was she outright laughing at him? Timothy couldn't believe the rudeness and disdain this woman displayed. Public humiliation was not acceptable. Her father's letter claimed a well-bred young lady. Pretty features held much less attraction when one manifested such disastrous manners. His reckless decision proved nothing but a failure at this point. Mother would plan his wedding to Miss Thompson the moment he walked through the door at Cumberland Meadows.

Timothy straightened his spine and gathered his dignity. He had to figure out what to do now that he'd come this far. "I've made a mistake in coming here. I see that." He tucked the letter in his breast pocket, then picked up the small valise with his most important belongings. "I'm sure there's another train soon. Good day, Miss Johnston." Heading home with his tail between his legs churned his stomach. Perhaps he'd buy a ticket back to Salt Lake City or Denver and try his luck in more established, civilized areas of the country.

She straightened right up. "Hold up, mister." Humor peeked through her words and tweaked the edges of her lips, setting off an intriguing dimple. Her western accent was pleasant, though not her tone. "There's been a mistake, I'm sure. Likely in the translation of whatever you have there."

"It's written in plain English."

"There's English. . ." She hesitated. "And there's whatever you're speakin'." She held out her hand. "May I see that letter, please? Let's figure where all this tangled mess comes from."

She was still the rudest girl he'd ever encountered, but at least she'd sobered. Had he misunderstood something? Highly likely, given her particular vernacular. "Of course."

He handed the envelope to her, noticing the roughened hands of a hardworking woman. No gloves. Nails dirty and uneven as if broken regularly, and calluses covered the skin on her palms. Had he agreed to marry a field hand? Thankfully, they both had the right to change their minds.

Nothing in her father's letters led him to believe he'd misrepresented their standing in society. But to look at her, one could only conclude he had written tall tales. She wore a simple ankle-length brown skirt belted around a red-and-white gingham blouse. A red kerchief was tied at her neck, and one thick, long braid the color of coffee dangled down her back. But the letter had emphasized her education in ranch management and half ownership of the JBarF. "Perhaps you can explain how you interpret it."

Her nose crinkled into cute little wrinkles between lovely brown eyes that danced with curiosity.

Yes, she could be called pretty under the road dust. Too bad she didn't care to dress the part of a landowning lady. Maybe the

23

letter was fabricated. It wouldn't be the first attempt to defraud the Higgenbottom family. Perhaps the most clumsy and poorly enacted. But then he'd fallen for it, if that were the case. Doubt steeped his words. "Are you the co-owner of the JBarF Ranch?"

Irritation sparked in those eyes like lightning in dry grass. "What do you mean, am I the co-owner? Who else would I be?" She looked at him like she might look at a toad. "How would you know—" She ripped the envelope open and unfolded the letter. A few moments later her eyes closed and her head tilted up toward the sky.

"I've got you." He moved close to catch her should she faint. A bit taller than the average girl, Miss Johnston appeared more fit than the high society young ladies that took to fainting at the least provocation. He held out his arms and braced his legs for her weight. Instead, she opened fiery eyes. If it were possible, Timothy knew without a doubt he'd be ablaze.

She crossed her arms, tilting her chin to the side like a schoolmarm. "Exactly what do you think you're doin' back there?"

"Easing your fall." He lowered his arms.

"Oh my word!" Her offense at being considered delicate took their first meeting into disaster. "You thought I was goin' to faint?"

"In my experience, difficult news or a shock to a woman often results in the vapors. I wouldn't let a—" Her eyes flashed, but what else could he say? "—lady fall." Definitely not like any lady he'd ever met.

"Oh my word!" she said again. She drew back her shoulders and drilled him with a dead-on, straight eyeball-to-eyeball glare. "I ain't never had the vapors. The vapors!" Then she pointed at his valise. "Is that all you got?" She didn't leave room for an answer as she stomped away. "Let's go," she tossed over her shoulder. "We need an explanation from my pa. We've both been duped."

Once past his surprise, Timothy caught up to her quickly with his longer stride. "Your pa?"

She stopped for a brief moment. "Mr. Higgenbottom, I'm very sorry that I laughed at you. Well, not really at you. More the situation. But I didn't know Pa wrote that letter offerin' you marriage and a partnership." She took off at a clip that bordered on a run. "In fact, I was told to come and pick up a new ranch foreman. A foreman the JBarF desperately needed yesterday, and the day before that. Are you a foreman?"

"Yes, that's the agreement."

"But not my agreement."

"Obviously not." He planted his feet and took out his pocket watch. "I'll find the depot agent and—"

An exasperated sigh escaped as Miss Johnston again folded her arms like she would for a naughty child. Then she asked, "Can you at least ride a horse?"

"I assure you that I cannot only ride a horse, I train them. I'm capable and quite good at my profession as a riding instructor and animal doctor. I wrote as much in my letters."

"I don't have any idea what"—she grimaced at his finery—"you're capable of doin'. What I'm hopin' is that you're willin' to try, because at this point we're desperate. Are you?"

Willing to try, or desperate? At this point the conversation felt like an untrained pup had broken into the henhouse and feathers were flying everywhere. "Since we're now both unclear about the situation, can you be more specific?"

"More specific? Surely. I need an able-bodied foreman on the

25

JBarF. You say you're a capable worker. Well, I got a fence down, cattle to round up, and horses to work. How's that for specific?"

Animals and land. "I am able and willing." Also desperate not to go home.

"All right, let's see what you can do." She turned toward the end of the wooden walkway. "We got supplies to load and a six-hour ride ahead of us, eight if the wagon's heavy, and I already done six to get here this mornin'."

Relief flooded over Timothy. At least he didn't have to board the train back to Kentucky as a failure—yet. But with such a distasteful misunderstanding already between them, he'd better get a crystal-clear agreement. "Then marriage is not our immediate goal?"

"Oh. My. Word. That's all you men can think about, ain't it? Gettin' a wife to do the cookin' and cleanin' and birthin'. I got no plans to be addin' to my workload." Hands on her hips, brown hair tickling at her dusty cheeks, Miss Johnston made quite the Wild West postcard under her ten-gallon hat. "In case I wasn't specific enough, Mr. Higgenbottom, I ain't ever marryin' you. Now if you want a job, you got one. But you gotta prove you can keep it."

Their eyes locked. "I'll keep it, Miss Johnston."

She put out a hand. Timothy took it and shook, sealing the deal.

"Good." Her words were softer, more melodious, as she glanced back over her shoulder. "Let's get the horses, load up, and get ourselves back to the ranch. Where's your horse?"

"Had to leave him behind for the trip."

She raised her eyebrows and sent a look heavenward. "Of course you did." She walked away quicker than he'd expected, leading him to two magnificently bred chestnut Morgans at the water trough. "Come on, Blaze. Walk on, Biscuit."

She took them to the wagon, hitched them up, and drove them to the offloaded freight. She hadn't blinked an eye or asked for his help.

Timothy took off his suit coat, leaving it on the padded driver's seat. They worked together lifting, piling, and pushing fencing supplies into the long wagon bed with few words between them. She worked as hard as he did, not slowing or watching anyone do it for her.

Timothy's astonishment at her strength and ability set his impression of women on its head, his idea of a capable, interesting woman challenged in that instant. Was a cultured, educated, and socially prominent woman somehow better than a woman with a valuable skill set who worked alongside her man? He stole a glance at her. Yes, definitely pretty under all that road dust. She could be something special. He'd have to watch and see.

Did Miss Johnston's idea of a capable man have a different set of standards than what his pocketbook held or whether she'd have a title to wield? A man working for her and the man she married might be two very opposing interests. But her uneducated slaughter of the English language poked a hole in that theory. Still, she intrigued him.

The depot agent rolled a heavy-laden cart over. "This here's the last of the luggage. Any of it yours before I lock it up?"

"Yes, thank you."

"Yes?" Miss Johnston gave a quick double-take. "All that?" She had an incredulous expression.

"Where ya' from, mister? That's some accent ya' got there," the agent said.

"Kentucky, most recently. Timothy Higgenbottom. But originally England."

"No kiddin', all that way. Well, welcome to Montana Territory. I'm Josiah Dawson. Josiah's fine." He lifted one end of a huge travel trunk. "You go by Tim?"

"No, Timothy, if you wouldn't mind."

"All right, Timothy, let me know when ya need a ticket back home."

"I'm planning to stay." He couldn't avoid Miss Johnston's reaction as she shook her head ever so slightly in disbelief.

"Looks like maybe ya are." He gave a low whistle at the remaining travel trunks on the cart. "Maybe so."

"What if I hadn't brought the wagon?" Shoving some of her supplies hard against the wall of the wagon bed, she said, "Did you bring all of England?"

Best not to bite that bait. Timothy held back the fact that he'd left the majority of his belongings behind.

Josiah helped Timothy load three large trunks and rearrange the other supplies to better balance the load. Miss Johnston carried a smaller trunk to the front, setting it on the passenger's side of the seat. Timothy noted her confident ease. She didn't complain about the work. She simply did the next needed action. In his world, menservants carried and moved anything hefty for the women, regardless of station. A maid thought nothing of dusting under heavy furniture while men moved it here and there. The women of higher station ordered others about while they drank tea. This woman, who waited for no man, who gave as much of herself as she demanded from others, had him mystified.

Josiah watched them for a moment. "Miss Johnston, I think ya mighta got more than you was expectin'."

Her expression was unreadable as she checked the horses and their rigging. "Not sure what you mean, Mr. Dawson."

He tipped his hat. "Good luck to ya, Timothy." He left, chuckling under his breath.

Timothy lifted his coat from the driver's seat. "I think I can fit that small trunk in the back with some twine to hold it."

"No, you need a place to ride."

"You mean ride in the back?" Maybe as a lad, but never since.

" 'Less you want to lose any of those precious trunks? Your choice." She climbed up and took the reins. "Better hop on one way or another—it's a long walk." She snapped the reins above Blaze and Biscuit. "Walk on."

The wagon lurched forward. Timothy swung onto the back, feet dangling a few inches above the earth. She was the boss and, hopefully, a future partner. But did she have to hit every bump and rock in the road?

❧ Chapter 3 ❧

The full moon sent eerie shadows across the yard when they drove into the homestead.

"What took you so long?" Her father lounged in a rocker on the porch, feet up on the railing. "The train late again?"

His expression was as innocent as a baby lamb, and that irked her. Tara marched up to her father and handed him the letter. "How about an explanation, Pa? You tryin' to marry me off against my will?"

"Now why would I do somethin' like that, Mouse?" He stood and handed the letter back without reading it. "I invited Tim to come on out and manage the ranch. If'n things work out between you, he could marry you and the dowry would be my half of the ranch to give him a partnership."

"That's Timothy, sir."

They both ignored him.

"If'n things work out?" She folded her arms. "Things are not goin' to work out. I will choose if and when I want a husband. I got a ranch to run and no time for courtin' and all that nonsense." She pointed at Timothy and back at her father. "Do you two hear me?"

Both men looked at her, looked at one another, and nodded.

"Now we understand one another." She held her gaze steady. "Let's get unloaded so we can get some supper and a good start in the morning on that downed fence." She stomped to the wagon. "I can't believe we lost a day of work on shenanigans." She shot a squinty-eyed glower and a growl at the men from the back of the wagon.

Mr. Johnston offered a hand. "Welcome, Tim. Robert Johnston."

"Timothy, sir." He shook hands with him. "Thank you for, uh, your—"

"Aw, let it go, son. We ain't all that hospitable the way she's fumin'. She's just like her mama. Makes for a good wife, it does."

"It does?"

"You just gotta know when to ease up. Strong women have minds of their own and goals of their own. That's what we need out here, or we can't survive. People who can see what they want and go after it. Think for themselves. Your job, Tim, is to be man enough to be her equal so she'll give you a chance." He spread his hands wide and looked out at a stretch of endless grassland illuminated by the moon's light beyond the farm buildings and corrals, the mountains dark and craggy in the distance on either side of the massive valley. "I need grandsons to pass all this on to. Otherwise, what's it all for?"

Timothy whistled through his teeth. "She's pretty well decided, I think."

"She'll calm down and be rarin' to go at first light." He clapped Timothy on the shoulder. "Cookie's got some corn bread and steak inside once we get all this put away and the horses up for the night. You just keep showin' your best side, and you'll win her over in no time. You hear me, boy?"

"Yes, thank you, sir. That's good advice." Did he want to win her over? Tara Johnston had a sharp tongue to go along with her sharp intellect and work ethic. Not to mention horrendous social skills. But then, who was he to talk? High society didn't care for him either. Though not for lack of dignified manners. He couldn't carry a conversation about fluff, and preferred animals over people. He slid a quick glance at Miss Johnston. Much preferred animals. Animals made sense to him.

If they had to work together, he'd put on his best manners, as advised, so they'd at least get along in one another's company. After all, it wasn't her idea to place an advertisement for a husband. Her father certainly had the right to find her a match. But he might have to hog-tie her to accept some poor sop. Tara Johnston was as unlikely a choice for him as the socialite he'd rejected.

Maybe there'd be a way to earn a partnership without marriage—for both their sakes. A sharp-tongued wife would be as uncomfortable to live with as a dull wife. Either extreme would make a marriage unbearable. He'd learn about running a ranch and buy his own land eventually. The future lay wide open with opportunity out here on the frontier. Maybe he'd advertise for a mail-order bride one day. Though he'd not ever met a woman willing to work the way Miss Johnston did.

The men carried the trunks into the bunkhouse. Mr. Johnston lit a lantern. As the newly hired foreman, Timothy was assigned quarters in a dusty room with a single lumpy bed. A washstand and pitcher stood under a shaving mirror. Two shelves and a few wooden dowels poked into the nearby wall as clothing pegs. Once all the trunks lined the room, there was little space left. "Is there a wardrobe, or should I procure one?"

"We keep things simple here. Pare down a bit, or you're goin' to feel like a corncob in a pigsty once we get a few more bodies in the bunkhouse."

Timothy stood in the square yard remaining, grateful for the privacy from the communal bunk space. "I only brought necessities, thinking to send for the rest later."

Mr. Johnston screwed up his face. "Might want to rethink that plan, son. Let's get that supper. I imagine you're a tad hungry."

"Yes, sir, it's been a long time since breakfast." The dried meat and bread they'd had on the road helped, but he needed a good meal. The Johnstons didn't seem to know about normal courtesies of offering a traveler a day or two of rest. But by the looks of their situation, they couldn't afford the wait. He stifled a yawn. "I'll get changed."

"Those clothes will do."

"You don't dress for dinner?"

"Yep, got a sense of humor, don't you? This is a workin' ranch." A smile crinkled the sun-weathered skin around Robert Johnston's eyes. "We don't have time for all that pomp here."

When he walked into the main house for the late-night supper, the smell of sizzling steak and sweet corn bread set Timothy's stomach to growling. Though not as large as the Higgenbottom eighteen-bedroom country house in Kentucky, and nowhere close to the massive thirty-two-bedroom castle called Cumberland Manor his family owned in England, the Johnstons' place had an attractive, homey atmosphere. Comfortable furniture appeared well made, and possibly home fashioned. A harp rested in its stand near a cushioned stool. Did she play?

"Come on in, son. Cookie, this here is our new foreman, Tim—" Before getting corrected again, Mr. Johnston added, "—othy."

"Hungry?" The cook, who looked more like an old mountain man, speared a juicy, monstrous steak out of the cast-iron frying pan and held it up, dripping juices onto a wooden cutting board. Then he eyed Timothy's silk vest, cravat, and expensive shoes, all a little worse for wear. He clamped his mouth shut and went to work carving the slab of meat into quarters.

Timothy had never felt judged by a household servant before. "Quite. Thank you." But then his servants rarely looked anything like the old bearded man in denim and frayed suspenders.

The cook plunked a piece of meat onto each pewter plate. A bowl of mashed potatoes with gravy, corn bread cake, a crock of butter, and a pie covered the table. As Tara came to the kitchen, still dressed in her simple homemade skirt and blouse, Timothy stood and held a chair for her.

Astonishment lit up her freshly washed face while her father shared a conspiratorial wink with him.

"Thank you." Tara said. "You ain't got to be such a gent all the time. It's goin' to get near impossible when we're out runnin' fence and roundin' up herds. Appreciate the thought."

Her sweetness, after the day they'd had, caught him off guard.

"My pleasure, Miss Johnston." He took his seat, stealing a casual glance at her. No ten-gallon hat, her hair pulled back in a ribbon, cheeks scrubbed clean and pink, and reasonable table manners had him rethinking his first impression.

"Dig in." Cookie slid out a chair and sat down. As soon as grace ended, he scooped potatoes onto his plate and passed the bowl to his left. "Well, you gonna eat, boy?"

Servants ate with them? "Yes, thank you." That would take some getting used to for Timothy. Not one would dare overstep at the Higgenbottom household or in any other society home. Then again, the family rarely stepped foot in the kitchen. Now he was an employee. The only difference between Cookie and himself had to be that his own future held potential partnership. Cookie, at his advanced years, would always be a servant. As uncomfortable as he felt, was there truly anything wrong with people eating together? No one had told him Cookie's relationship to the Johnstons. For all he knew, Cookie could be family. Holding his tongue and observing would be prudent.

"Got some less fancified duds?" Cookie asked him.

Miss Johnston giggled. "Could be a challenge."

"I'll find something." Timothy focused on loading his plate.

Cookie grunted his disbelief while chewing. He flicked his knife in Timothy's direction. "He know how to ride?"

"Says he can." Miss Johnston buttered her corn bread. "Guess we'll find out."

Mr. Johnston rubbed his chin thoughtfully. "Did you bring any tack with you?"

"Yes, sir. My saddle and tack are in one of my trunks."

"Good. We'll pick out a horse for you right after supper.

We got a good bit of mendin' fence to knock out in the next few days."

"I'll be ready, sir."

"I give 'im a week," Cookie grumbled. "Look at them hands. Ain't used to hard work."

Miss Johnston piped in, "I don't know. He did all right loading and unloading." She tapped her fork against her lips, contemplating. "I give him the benefit of good intentions. Maybe two weeks."

He could be invisible, except they kept assessing him as they wagered opinions like a horse at auction. Would they check his teeth next? "I assure you, Miss Johnston, I'm up to the task." He could see the doubt in the eyes around the table. "Your ad requested a hardworking, God-fearing man with a willing heart and a sense of humor. I'm a man of honor, and I will stand by my word."

"That's how you advertised for a foreman, or was that for a husband?" She plunged her fork into her steak and glared at her father.

Mr. Johnston ignored her. "Sure you are, son. You're young and strong." He reached for the potatoes. "Why don't we see how you feel in a month? Maybe this life is for you and maybe it ain't. In the meantime, we all go by our first names here. Gets to be close quarters for all that highfalutin business."

"Yes, sir."

"Robert is fine, son." He scooped a helping of gravy over his potatoes. "You prove Tara and Cookie wrong for me, ya hear. I'm thinkin' you got more spirit in you than they're givin' you credit for."

"I don't know, Pa. You're goin' off his word. Maybe he can ride. But I want to see him really work if we're gonna turn over big responsibilities to him."

"He'll do that tomorrow. Fencin' all day will show his measure right off."

"We've got cattle to brand. If Timothy knows how to work with livestock, he can show us how to cut and rope a calf after we've closed up that gap next to O'Connell's place."

His steak stuck in his throat. He'd be let go right here and now. But he had to tell the truth. "Uh, Miss Johns—Tara, I've never rounded up cattle before."

She didn't look a bit disturbed. "Now why doesn't that surprise me?"

"I know it sounds bad, but I train riders and horses for the steeplechase, hunting, and racing. The cattle are not huge herds such as you have out here. They're kept in barns and paddocks where I'm from." Wouldn't his skills translate with a little training? After all, he could outride most men.

"So, you got no useful knowledge of ranchin'?" Tara groaned, pushed her plate away, and gave her father an I-told-you-so look while Cookie harrumphed through his food.

Timothy winced at her reaction. "I didn't say that." He set his silverware on the pewter plate. Hungry or not, he needed to prove he'd be a benefit to the JBarF. "I'm not just a trainer and instructor. Animal husbandry is crucial for racing and showing horses and for family survival. I'm educated in caring for horses, cattle, and sheep as well as crops and land management."

Tara's voice held a new respect. "That says somethin'. All right, Pa, thirty days it is." She put her chin on her fist, elbow on the table. "If you can do all that, you could still be very helpful. But you gotta learn to round up and brand cattle. There's no way around it, or no self-respectin' cowboy will follow your orders."

"Willing and ready, Miss—" He caught himself. Losing the societal rules he'd rebelled against could be harder than he thought. "Tara. You name the day, and I'll be your best student. Though, could you let my backside recover from today's wagon ride first?" He grinned and reveled in the sound of her unexpected laughter.

A mysterious twinkle in Robert's eyes remained after the humor settled. He watched Timothy and Tara converse together as if he knew something they didn't. "Come on, Timothy, let's get a horse picked out for you."

Thirty days to prove he wasn't a greenhorn and learn the day-to-day duties of a working ranch without servants to do the menial tasks. Timothy needed to learn all he could from the enigma, Tara, as he trained with her. Her father saw her as an equal in all financial and business decisions. A very curious arrangement indeed. He'd prove himself to all of them for as long as it'd take to fit in around the JBarF.

He hauled his saddle out to the barn. By the door, he plucked a small handful of long, sweet grass. "Hello, Freckles, remember me? We met last night." He stood close to the Morgan mare's stall, hung his saddle on the short wall, and blew gently in small puffs near her nose. The beautiful fifteen-hand roan snuffled near his cheek as she familiarized his scent.

"Here you go, girl." He held out the green grass. She took it with gentle lips and chewed the treat while he eased himself into her stall. Finding her curry brush on the shelf, Timothy gave her a good going-over, watching for any sore spots or burrs while she munched on hay. He swept the finishing brush over her, following with his hand. Last, he checked her legs and hooves. Satisfied with Freckles's excellent condition, he gave her oats to fortify her. Then he worked fast, mucking out her stall and throwing clean bedding, before moving to the next horse. He had three done and three to go before anyone else arrived.

"Mornin', son." Robert moved into a stall nearby, preparing his horse for the day.

"Sir." He patted the neck of Socrates, a Standardbred colt. "You have some excellent horses. They're well tended and quite well bred."

"That yearling came by way of the esteemed Marcus Daly himself in trade for some beef cattle. Mostly I like the Morgan for their versatility on Montana's hills. Real sturdy, fast pace, and lots of endurance." He brushed his fingers against Socrates's nose. "But Daly wants to focus on his thoroughbreds and racing stock. Thinks he can breed one to win the Kentucky Derby, he does."

"That's a near impossible goal. But this fellow has good lines even if he's not for the flat racetrack. You could still train him to harness race."

"He isn't as popular a breed out here. Been thinkin' of sellin' him for a fancy carriage or some such. He'll take some trainin' yet." Robert gestured at the already thrown hay. "Gotta say, you show initiative to beat a man to his own barn chores."

"I want to earn my place here, sir." He shot a grin to Robert. "And help you win that bet."

Robert folded his arms on the top of the stall rail and watched Timothy curry the next mare. "You sure do wear fancy duds for dirty work." Then he spied the saddle. "Let's get some breakfast under our belts before Tara gets an eyeful of your getup—" He waved a hand over at the saddle and Timothy's outfit.

"What are you plannin' to do with that thing around a herd of cattle?" Tara stood at Freckles's stall door, pointing at Timothy's saddle.

Too late.

"Ah son, now you done it."

Would he see a day he didn't set her off first thing? "I realize you have western saddles. But this is how I ride."

"Maybe out to do the fencin'." She gave a slow shake of her head. "But you're gonna need a decent saddle to rope calves and such."

"It's more than decent, I assure you."

Tara examined the difference in size and seat in her western and his English saddles. "How do you stay in your seat when you gotta cut a cow or jump a creek?"

"With my legs." He walked out of the stall to stand by his saddle. "You'll see. I can better feel a horse's movement, especially jumping." With all his horsemanship awards, he'd be fine in any situation. But again, he had to prove it.

"Gonna need somethin' to tie off a rope."

Tara and her father, and for that matter, the men who would work under him, did not know his expertise. Day by day, he'd show them and win their trust.

Her voice broke into his thoughts, incredulous. "Those your only boots?"

He followed her gaze down to his highly polished and stylish black leather riding boots, a little dusty from the morning's work, but the quality showed. "They'll do, won't they?"

"They ain't gonna look like that when we get back." She measured out some oats and dumped them into Queenie's manger. "I'm not sayin' you can't do the job in all that finery." She sent a doubtful look to her father. "But if you were to dress more like a cowboy, people might think you were one."

He'd brought his savings, but that didn't amount to a reason to buy a new saddle and clothing on the whim of someone's judgmental opinion. He'd fence and ride circles around her and change that opinion.

Robert tossed a flake of hay into the feed bin. "Mouse, he's bitin' off a whole new life. Let's give the man a chance."

She looked about to say more but turned to her horse's care.

Mouse? Her hair was a dusky brown. But to call a young woman a mouse? There had to be a story, and Timothy wanted to know it. Miss Tara Johnston was anything but a mouse. More like a lioness.

"Tell you what, son, on Sunday we all head into Anaconda for services. After church we'll see if we can find at least four wranglers, but maybe you're wantin' a crack at fillin' out our crew yourself."

"Yes, sir, I'll have some thoughts about that once I know the running budget, the lay of the land, scope of work, and size of herd." A stable boy would ease their burden by giving them back hours each day. "Possibly a lad about thirteen or fourteen could muck out the stalls, rub the horses down, and keep a feeding plan. If it fits in the funds, sir."

"We've never had a stable boy." Robert threw straw in the last stall for clean bedding. "Not against it, mind you."

"For a few dollars a month, we'll get more productive work

when skilled men"—he saw Tara's scowl as she looked up from brushing her horse—"uh, people, are freed up to do their jobs. We'll end up saving money while making more money from higher productivity."

"The books is Tara's business. I'll let you two chew that to bits on the ride out today." Robert opened the stall for Tara to join them. "She's been a real blessin' since she graduated eighth grade."

"Eighth grade?" Now he had doubts about her abilities. He foresaw disastrous accounting.

Tara beamed at her father's pride. "Aw, thanks, Pa." She slid an indiscernible glance his way before checking Timothy's care of the rest of the animals.

"Get a list going," Robert suggested. "You can pick up whatever you need while we're in town."

"I'll keep it in mind, sir." After the early hours spent preparing horses before breakfast, his first priority would be to train a stable hand. Then acquire a rope. Definitely a rope. He'd go to great lengths to have that on hand before Tara saw that he didn't.

❧ Chapter 4 ❧

Early Sunday morning Cookie had a steaming basket of biscuits and a bowl of sausage gravy on the table with eggs frying. A hamper for lunch stood ready for the afternoon church social.

Tara loaded a plate for her father then for herself. "I know he done good this week."

"He had the barn near spotless, horses fed, and nary a falter." Her father seemed to be enamored of Timothy's good qualities, as if the greenhorn was the snake oil elixir their ranch needed. "We got more finished on that fence in the last few days than we got all the week before. Yep, he's a good addition to the JBarF."

"He works hard and sure cleans up good." She hid her admiration for a man who could ruin expensive shirts daily without complaint. "But the problem is he's always cleaned up and he still don't know how to ride like a cowboy." She ladled gravy over a biscuit. Pointing the spoon at her father, she said, "If I had a hard time believin' he could do the job, what hand is gonna follow a man so gussied up? You tell me that."

"All they gotta do is take his orders. They don't have to stand for a portrait with him."

"All right. I'm just sayin' we can't keep the bunkhouse full as it is."

"I hear you." He swallowed a good amount of fresh milk. "But I sense things are headin' in the right direction."

"I'll give you that he's all-in and seems to know his stuff. But he ain't gonna make it lookin' like some high and mighty prince or somethin'." Though his blond hair and blue eyes caught her attention more than she wanted to admit.

The kitchen screen door squeaked open. Timothy gave them all a nod. "Sorry I'm late to breakfast." He took a seat. "Had a little extra work on the horses. They've had a long week."

Had he heard their conversation? Tara passed the fluffy baking powder biscuits, watching him closely.

He met her eyes. "Thank you." Splitting one open with his fork, he added, "You win. I'll get some clothing worthy of my new position when we're in town."

Her father cleared his throat and sent a not-so-subtle message through his glare.

She couldn't take her words or the way she'd said them back. But she could own up to her slight. "Forgive me, Timothy. I meant no hurt."

The sparkle in his eyes didn't diminish. "I'm down six shirts in as many days."

"That's true." He'd ripped voluminous sleeves and lace cuffs and turned white shirts the color of their soil. She lifted the platter of eggs.

"By the end of my trial period, I'll be working shirtless if I don't get something more suitable."

Shirtless? Her gaze dipped to his chest and quickly back up to his face. The platter shook in her hands, all the eggs sliding toward the table before she righted it.

"I'll take those, please." He said it with a wide grin, like he knew he'd affected her.

Her father took the platter and quirked an eyebrow at Cookie, nudging him to notice Tara's awkward response. "Can't have that around womenfolk, now can we?" He handed the platter off to Timothy. "Might cause a stir with the church ladies."

Cookie joined the banter. "Nope. Them ladies got genteel sensibilities, they do."

She tucked into breakfast without another word. Might be time to break Socrates and test both man and beast. Or the beast might wipe that smug grin off Timothy's handsome face!

"Looks like Jeremy is going to be an excellent stable boy with a little more training." Timothy rode Freckles alongside the wagon. "He seems to be a natural with the horses."

"He's gonna be a big help around the ranch," Tara agreed. "You know, we still need men or be run ragged tryin' to get all those horses and cattle to the auction this fall." She reined in her horse. "Whoa now."

"With this section closed up, I'll head in tomorrow and try again." He dismounted and tied his horse loosely to the wagon, letting her graze.

She held back a teasing grin as she met him at the back to pull out tools and fencing. "Least you won't scare 'em off this time in your finery."

"You noticed my duds, did you?" Timothy added western words to his vocabulary. His mother would have the vapors.

"I like this new getup. It's almost believable." She lifted the bucket of nails and tossed a mischievous smile over her shoulder.

"Couldn't have done it without your sage advice, thou wisest of women."

"Oh my, the sweet talkin' is too much for me." She laughed, blushing. "Help me with this wire?"

"My pleasure, ma'am." He touched the brim of his brand-new ten-gallon hat. He'd picked the light gray one when Tara seemed pleased with the look on him. This morning she seemed pleased with everything. How could he keep that going?

Together they measured, unrolled barbed wire, and hammered the galvanized nails until dark clouds drew close and the wind picked up. A clap of thunder threatened in the distance. Suddenly Freckles spooked and yanked free of the wagon, then took off at a gallop toward home. "I'll get her," Tara yelled. "Finish out that post. We gotta get out of here before the lightning hits!"

Tara jumped into the wagon, scooped the reins, and released the brake. "Haw!" The horse lurched forward.

Then as another rumble rolled across the miles, Freckles switched direction, toward the last few feet of unfinished fencing. Tara caught the change and drove to block her escape. A few minutes later she'd managed to soothe Freckles and tie her to the wagon.

Timothy bent to his task, hammering as fast as he could. The buffeting gusts grew colder, blowing stronger with each blast. Wind whooshed over him, and then a searing pain pierced the entire length of his back as if an enormous wasp hive had hit from behind. His agonizing howl was lost in the savage storm as the end of the barbed wire roll wrapped around his shoulders and arms. "Tara, help!" The more he struggled, the deeper the barbs bit. He couldn't fight both the wind and the twisted wire roll. The dark, encroaching clouds flashed with lightning. A couple seconds later he heard the thunder. Not long, and he could be electrocuted. "God, help me! Please bring Tara back."

Moments later he heard the wagon. She used it to block him from the wind as best she could.

"Timothy, I'm here!" She was at his side with wire cutters. "Hang on."

With each clip, he felt the fence dig in then pull away. He could smell the rain on the air. "You have to go, Tara. Go now before the lightning hits us both," he rasped out.

"I ain't leavin' you even if the Lord decides to strike us down. It ain't what we do out here." She took both hands to the cutters and worked her way through the rest of the wire until she had him free. Jagged fire zipped through the sky above them and large droplets sprinkled over them. "This is gonna hurt. I ain't got time to do it nice. Grit your teeth now!"

She tugged the last of the barbs out all at once. A flash blew up the sky around them. Timothy couldn't tell if he'd been lit on fire or if it was the hot agony of torn skin. The horses' high-pitched whinnies matched the fear in his heart. Then he felt Tara's arms lifting him.

"Come on, get on up. You can do it." Her voice was strident

with urgency and effort. "Timothy! Don't go passin' out on me now. We gotta go!"

Fighting for consciousness and footing, he pushed off the ground. Once up, he managed, with her help, to stumble to the wagon through the whipping rain.

She grabbed a wool blanket and threw it over the wagon bed. "Just lay down." He crawled up and lay down belly first. Then she folded the blanket over him, anchoring it between his calves against the building storm. "We got a half mile home and we're gonna run for it. Keep your head on your arms, or you're gonna have a headache on top of all that."

She hollered from the buckboard as hail drilled down on them, "Haw, get on, Blaze!" The sky belched white fire, illuminating the prairie for miles.

Chapter 5

Tara watched while the doctor dipped the last strip bandage into the bowl and finished applying the poultice to Timothy's shoulders and back. "Change these several times a day. You'll dip them in this mixture of bitterroot, honey, and whiskey until I can get back with a bromide solution." He swished his hands in a bowl of water then picked up the towel as he gave instructions. "Keep giving him a lot of fluids, especially bitterroot tea with a little more honey. If he doesn't get infected, he has a fighting chance."

"I can do that." Tara said. "But Pa, what about the fence and the cattle if'n I'm here?"

"Don't worry about that, Mouse. I'll find more men." He put his arm around Tara. "Anything else we should do for him, Doc?"

"Someone should be watching over him the next several days around the clock. If a bad fever sets in or if his muscles lock up. . ." He shook his head. "Well, there'd be little I could do, but call me over and I'll try."

"He can stay here in my son's room. We can take turns watchin' out for him through the night," Robert said.

"Give him a spoonful of this for pain so he sleeps through the worst." The doctor set a small bottle of laudanum on the bed stand. "Watch out for a red, creeping rash from any of those cuts. That barbed wire did a nasty number on him. He's lucky to be alive. Quick action, young lady, probably saved your man's life."

"He's not—" Then she realized the doctor meant employee, not suitor. "Thank you, Doc, for your help."

Tara stared down at Timothy sleeping fitfully on his stomach. When he was awake, he grimaced each time he moved his head, but with the wounds down his back and arms, there'd be no way for him to sleep comfortably in any other position. She gently covered him with a lightweight sheet and then a heavier quilt for his lower body. The cool nights could set him to shivering. But for now, the sedative seemed to ease him enough he no longer flinched at every touch.

Over the next few days, Tara nursed Timothy while the extra hands her father found in town helped on the ranch. So far she hadn't yet met any of them and only caught a glance now and then when she saw them in the yard. Cookie fed them out in the courtyard, or on rainy days they ate in the bunkhouse. Anything to keep Timothy's healing undisturbed.

She'd taken to reading passages from Psalms out loud to comfort him and playing hymns on her lap harp to entertain him. Cookie came in to assist with needs too personal for an unmarried woman. But Tara waited outside the door, cringing at each groan from any movement. Two weeks in and clear of fever, Timothy sat up in bed waiting for her.

Carrying in a tray of chicken and vegetable soup, Tara stopped in surprise. "Look at you sittin' high like a rooster on a fence." A sense of relief flowed over her. "How's that feelin' to your back?"

"I have a new understanding of what the scourge might have been like for Jesus."

The comparison struck Tara's soul with conviction. Jesus went through all that punishment unto death for her. The wounds Timothy bore were horrible. How much more the Son of God's? *Lord, forgive my grudge against You for the deaths in my family. I see what You done for me now.*

His smile still seemed a bit strained. "And I think my neck has a new shape to it."

"I'm sorry. I'd've hurt you more if'n I tried to do anything about it."

"I'm better for sitting up." He inhaled the aroma as she set the tray on the nightstand. "Eating face down has not been ideal."

"Nor for the floorboards," she teased. "You're a sloppy slurper."

"My apologies, dear lady." He placed his hand over his heart. He winced and drew in a quick breath. New skin replacing deeper cuts hadn't fully regenerated, tugging painfully across his shoulder.

She caught his hand in both of hers and lowered it gingerly to his lap. "Stop all that whippin' your arms about. You want to break all them wounds to pieces?" She leaned over his shoulder and peeled the light cotton nightshirt away, checking for damage. She braced her hand on the edge of the bed so she wouldn't lean on him or cause him pain in any way.

"I'm not whipping my arms, Tara. I was just—"

She cut him off with a gentle, admonishing tone. "You can use any excuse you like, but I saw what you did." His hand slid off his leg and covered hers, catching Tara off guard. She didn't move. Instead, she whispered close to his cheek, "That's my hand there, cowboy."

He turned his head and looked deeply into her eyes. "I know. I'm grateful for your care. And you called me cowboy."

She couldn't tear her gaze away from his, though their noses were near touching. The shaving cream scent still clung to his skin from Cookie's work. Should she let him kiss her? She held her breath, waiting.

"Would you—"

"Would I what?"

"Help me with the soup?" He gave her a lopsided smile.

She sprang backward, plopping into her chair. Heat raced to her cheeks. Turning away from him, she said, "Yes, of course." She took a little extra time to gather the tray into her lap. How foolish of her to think he might want a kiss when he still had so much recovering to do. Tara forced herself to pretend she'd felt nothing. But his eyes never left her face, unsettling her even further.

"You know, Timothy, I think you're 'bout able to feed your-self now."

"Oh no, I need your help." His smile nearly curled her toes. His voice lowered and held the allure of romance, if she wasn't imagining it. "Maybe for a while yet."

"So that's how you get a pretty gal 'round here-abouts." A gruff cowhand leaned against the doorjamb, holding a bunch of wildflowers. "Guess I'll have to go and break a leg."

Timothy's face darkened at the intruder.

"I'll take care of this." She rose, set the tray on the stand, and hurried toward the man. "You know you can't be here, uh. . ."

"Jesse, ma'am."

"Jesse." She met him at the door. "Timothy needs to rest and heal. I'll put those in a jar for him."

"Miss Tara, I ain't here for him. These here buds are for you."

She shooed Jesse out of the way and closed the door behind her, leaving Timothy to feed himself for the first time. Except she wanted to be in there with his blue eyes and not out here dealing with yet another man who wanted a washwoman and grub maker. *Ain't there someone, Lord, that wants me for me?*

Timothy could kick himself, except he couldn't get out of bed yet. Now that burly cowhand brings Tara flowers? He had to get well before he lost his chance for good. Hadn't he honored her wishes? He should have kissed her. But what woman wanted her first kiss to be from an invalid who could barely move his arms? When he kissed her, Timothy wanted to be able to hold her close. Show her she could rely on his strength and protection. No matter what it took, he'd figure out a way to prove he was the best choice to be her husband.

He could see and hear enough through the cracks in the door planks to tell this Jesse fellow's intentions—to woo a wife!

"I heard ya say ya liked these here wild roses the other day when you was out by the creek."

"Thank you, Jesse, I do. But you don't have to pick them for me."

"Yes, ma'am, I do if I want ta show ya how I feel." He cleared his throat. "I'm hopin' ya'll will accompany me ta the Independence Day party over ta the Gregson Hot Springs next week.

They got a band, a potluck, and such."

Fuming, Timothy pounded a fist on the mattress then squelched a groan. The effort sent sizzles through the tender skin of his shoulder.

Another man's voice joined the conversation outside his door. "Hey, I asked her first. You cain't go hornin' in on another man's territory!"

What? There were two of them? Timothy closed his eyes and shook his head. He'd have to manage these new cowboys, show himself worthy of leadership. But right now he wanted to throttle both of them.

"Thank you for the invites, but I ain't nobody's ter—"

Her stern tone was interrupted by yet another interloper. "Hey, I got business here with boss lady."

Timothy hung his head. Three men vying for her attention? What could he do about it from a sickbed? With great effort, he rolled to his stomach. His only hope would be to heal as fast as possible. That meant rest and prayer. Desperate prayer!

A few minutes later the third man warbled out a love song. Timothy shoved his head under the heavy feather pillow to drown out the caterwauling coyote and prayed like he'd never prayed before.

❧ Chapter 6 ❧

July 4, 1883

Cookie held open the bedroom door. "He ain't yet good as new, but the boy dressed hisself and is standin' all on his own." The gruffness in Cookie's voice belied the fondness he'd built up for Timothy doing the things only a man could do for him over the last few weeks.

He looked so handsome in one of his expensive shirts. Simple pleats showed above his waistcoat rather than ruffles. His tall, starched collar folded back into small, sharp wings decorated solely with a thin black tie—western-style. No cravat and expensive jeweled stickpin. Even better, he'd put on a few pounds since he could sit up to eat at the table, and his color had improved mightily.

"I can't wear a coat just yet," he apologized. "Too much pull across my shoulders. But your father loaned me a more appropriate tie. I hope I'll draw less attention now."

"Right fine." Did her quick response give her away?

"Besides, takin' the waters at the hot springs is more important for your health than wearin' a jacket in public. Not a soul will worry themselves about it. Right, Cookie?"

He shrugged. "Leastways I ain't gotta shave him no more and the boy can put on his own swim costume. There's a limit to my charity."

"If we were back in Kentucky, I'd be in peril for my life." He flicked a hand over his attire. "Or give my mother the vapors for walking out the front door improperly dressed."

"Good thing you're recuperatin' here." She patted Cookie's arm. "You've been God's hands in all this, from your cookin' to all the rest you did."

"Learned to take care of cowhands on the trail is all." He answered with nonchalance, but the old cook's chest puffed out more than usual at her praise. "Might as well use it when it's needed. Chicken soup cures a world of problems."

Timothy moved with painstaking slowness after three weeks stuck in bed. "She's doing my talking for me, Cookie. I truly am indebted to you." He held out a hand. "One day I hope to return the kindness, but I don't think I can ever manage nearly as well." As they shook on it, he said, "Please know I'll try."

"Aw, I ain't done nothin' but what was right. Golden Rule and all." In his humble manner, he left without allowing another word. He turned up next weaving past them, a large picnic basket in his hands, heading out to the carriage. "Time's a wastin'." He disappeared out the front door, letting the screen clatter behind him.

"We're coming." Tara tied on a straw sunbonnet, fixing the red ribbon to the right of her chin. She wore a matching red sash circling her waist with a fluffed bow at the small of her back and her Sunday boots peeked out beneath her hem.

"You make quite a fetching vision, Tara." His voice held a husky tone.

She flushed. How should she respond to such a romantic notion? The other cowboys doused her in compliments. But they all seemed insincere, as if an underlying selfishness hid like a tick in weeds. A body didn't find it until the parasite had a good, long feast first. Timothy meant what he said, and he said it in a way that she believed no other girl had heard before.

"Shall we?"

She took Timothy's proffered elbow. "That hurt?"

"No. It feels right."

Cookie opened the door, letting them pass through to the porch. "Young'uns," he said more to himself than to them. "Well, let's get on the trail." He rushed off into the kitchen for another load.

"I think this is Cookie's favorite holiday besides Christmas. You might catch him tappin' a toe at the bandstand. Then you'll know he's extra happy," Tara mused. "Wait till you see the feast he prepares each year. Fried chicken, apple pie, cider, all sorts of goodies. I know he made gingersnaps too."

"Gingersnaps. Your favorite?"

"Those or snickerdoodles."

"He seems capable of anything. I've never known a man to be so versatile with food and able to help around the ranch. Our ser—" He stopped talking as if he needed a moment.

"Too much too fast?" She moved an arm around his waist. "Am I botherin' any of your wounds if I help you? They were still a bit pink this mornin'."

He dropped his arm around her shoulders.

One of the new cowhands shot a grumpy look at them. The poor fellow drew the short straw. The others would go to the picnic. Her father would spell him halfway through the day, and she would bring everyone home after a soak in the hot spring plunge and the fireworks.

"No, I'm fine. But I do like the way you're helping me." His lips turned up at the corners.

She enjoyed the shine in his blue eyes when he looked into hers. She didn't care whether he really needed her help or not. "You were sayin'?"

"Where did Cookie learn to cook so well?"

"In the army." She matched his pace as they eased down the front path. She kept talking to keep his mind off the effort of his first outing. "Pa was on a cattle drive comin' up from Texas in sixty-six. Cookie was drivin' the chuck wagon. Together they decided to go in on raisin' cattle in Montana. That's how we got this land. Pa says there ain't no way we'da managed without him, and I know he's right. They're brothers bonded by the best and worst experiences."

"So he's been with you your whole life?"

"Well, he moved into the kitchen after my mama passed on. I was pretty small. Pa took to workin' the ranch, and Cookie took over mannin' the house and barn animals. He'll go on the short cattle drives still, but he's on in years."

"He never had a family of his own?"

"A wife once. He lost her to typhoid before the war ended." She glanced up at him. "He says the Lord knew she was too good for this earth."

"He must have loved her very much to not marry again."

Tara searched his face. *Will you love me like that if I marry you?* "There's not many womenfolk around, in case you hadn't noticed."

"I've picked up on the amount of men around lately." Somehow one of the new hires seemed to show up just about every spare moment. "You're the belle of the ball."

"I ain't got a desire to be."

"Most of the young ladies I know would love being the center of attention."

"I ain't got time for all those shenanigans. If I wanted—"

"Wait right there." Her father called out to them from the four-seater carriage as he finished hitching up the horse by the barn. "I'll come around."

Thank goodness her father interrupted her thoughtless prattle. She nearly told Timothy the silly daydream that'd run through her head these last weeks.

"We're going in style." He reached for the gate latch.

"Pa and I thought you'd like more cushion than the last time," she teased.

Jesse came hoofing it across the courtyard from the barn as soon as he spied them. "Miss Tara, you're looking fine this morning." He snatched open the picket gate right out of Timothy's hand. "May I help you up?"

Jesse wasn't shy about his intentions. Though Tara didn't seem bothered by him much, and that bothered Timothy. When the hands weren't out working, one or the other of them found a reason to be underfoot. Jesse most of all. Timothy couldn't even open a gate for her to pass before one of them beat him to it. When he'd answered the advertisement, sent letters back and forth confirming both parties' agreement, and come to Montana Territory, the last thing on his mind was competition. What gallant gesture would prove his worth to Tara with these three bumpkins edging him out at every turn?

The ride over to Gregson Hot Springs went well with Robert driving the carriage. Cookie rode with Tara and Timothy, keeping an eagle eye on them when he wasn't dozing. The other men rode alongside, trailing an extra horse for Robert to ride home later and relieve the cowhand on duty. The two-story Gregson Hotel housed up to sixty guests, while the lawns and grounds could hold many more. Quilts spread out like little islands in the deep, green grass. Children squealed and played, running circles around adults picnicking or listening to music.

People came from all over, sharing food, swapping stories, and catching up on news. Another train collision caused by poor timing made headlines. Everyone wanted to know how they'd solve the safety issues plaguing the new form of transportation.

Tara stayed with Timothy as if she wanted to keep company, not simply watching out like a nurse. After changing into swimming costumes, they spent time lounging in the hot springs plunge chatting with other bathers. He had no problem visiting with anyone. Without the barrier of his title, conversation came easier. Or maybe Tara's easy way made all the difference.

They met outside the changing rooms to walk their wet costumes and towels to the carriage boot.

Tara looked lovely with her braid spun and pinned low beneath her bonnet. "It's nice to see so many families. I made new friends." Her features lit up as she waved to a mother leading her dancing little girl out to the lawn where the brass band played a jaunty march.

"Sam met a new lady friend as well." Timothy referred to one of their newer ranch hands, directing her attention to the fledgling couple. "You may have lost a suitor."

"Good for him." She seemed genuinely pleased. "Now, what did you think about the railroad news?"

The fact Tara wasn't crestfallen at Sam's new pursuit buoyed his spirits as much as the healing waters eased his body. He'd never felt as relaxed as at this moment. And, perhaps he was down to two competitors. "All the train schedules on one system would simplify travel."

She accepted his elbow as they strolled toward the livery. "Fixin' the tardy trains would be a good start. Nobody ever knows what time to expect one."

"I understand." Her fingers were on his arm, and he covered them with his own, enjoying the intimacy. "I had to decipher several schedules on the way from Kentucky to Salt Lake City, then more from there to Silver Bow in Butte. Did you know the railroads publish eighty or so? Thankfully, I didn't have to read them all, just a handful."

"Eighty?" she scoffed. "That's ridiculous."

"The news is all the railroads are sending delegates to another General Railroad Time Convention set for October in Chicago. Maybe they can finally agree. I thought the preliminary report from the April meeting sounded promising."

"Really. What did you hear?"

"Some plans about dividing up the country on the meridians."

He remembered a quote. "Something like fifty-six time zones now could change to five, if they ever institute the idea."

"Will it work?"

He thought for a moment. "Maybe. I changed my watch at each depot. Gets downright confusing."

"I think the waters and walkin' are workin' wonders for you." She smiled up from under the brim of her bonnet at him as he dropped their things in the wagon bed. "Should we continue our stroll?"

He didn't care where they went since he had Tara all to himself. A horse whinnied and then a dog yelped. The poor dog's whining worsened as they searched for it. Finally, near the livery, they found a young, skinny Collie-mix lying on her side and panting in pain.

A group of men debated what to do with the dog.

One said, "He was kicked by that horse yonder and drug himself far as he could."

"Oh no." Tara's eyes welled up, and she whispered, "That's our team. I'm so sorry." She searched the men's faces. "Who owns the pup?"

Several of them shrugged until another man said, "Must be a stray. Not much worth anything now."

"Yep, better just shoot the pitiful thing," another added.

Timothy grit his teeth. "No. I'll check him over."

"You gonna find what we did. That horse whacked him a good one." The man took out a pistol. "Better take the lady aside."

Instead, Timothy moved in next to the dog and knelt. "Go on, gentlemen, I'll take responsibility. By the way, he's a she."

"Suit yerself. Coulda been a good herdin' dog, but he ain't

gonna be no good to nobody now, no matter what it is."

Holding his hand low and curved, Timothy offered his fingers and spoke to the dog. "I'm here to help, girl." The dog snapped at him and then cried because of the pain from her sudden motion. She dropped her head to the ground, whining.

"I've got an idea. Tara, could you stand there and see if you can draw her attention toward you. Get her to look up and away from me." Timothy pulled a handkerchief out of his pocket and tied it loosely into a circlet with a sliding knot. As the dog warily watched Tara, he quickly slid the handkerchief around her muzzle and tightened it.

Now that the dog was no longer able to snap at anyone, Timothy asked for a light blanket. Tara found her towel in the carriage boot and gave it to him. He lowered it around the dog's upper body then asked a bystander, "Can you gently place your hands here and here. I'm going to examine her. Don't let her fight. Just hold her down with the material, especially around her neck and shoulders so she doesn't struggle."

"All right."

Timothy spoke soothing words as he ran his hands over the dog's back and legs. "A broken front leg. At least it's not her hip or ribs."

"What'd I tell ya?" the man with the pistol proclaimed.

Timothy looked him square in the eyes. "I can splint this leg. She'll be fine in a few weeks."

A small, curious crowd had formed. Sam and Jesse pushed toward the front.

Tara called them over to her. "Sam, please go get Cookie. We're heading home. And Jesse, go ahead and hook up our team."

Jesse looked confused. "We're leaving early for a dog? Why

don't you just put it down?"

Before Timothy could say anything, Tara's eyes narrowed. "I said ready the carriage. No one is killing this animal."

Whispers skittered around the edges of the crowd. "What's going on?"

"What did she say?"

"Are they going to put it out of its misery?"

Tara held her parasol above Timothy and the dog, shading them from the afternoon heat. "What can we do?" she asked him.

"I need some bandage strips, a thick stick about this long"— he held out his hands for the length—"and a bowl of water." Various people passed forward the items as they arrived. Some of the crowd dispersed for more interesting entertainment while others stayed watching him work.

"He's a horse doctor," said the shooting advocate. "They're all quacks." He walked off.

Timothy breathed deeply, ignoring the barb from an ignorant soul. Wrapping the dog's leg, taking care the splint fit, Timothy finished. He made eye contact with the man helping him. "We're going to keep the blanket tight to her body so she doesn't try to move while we shift it down so we can offer a little water." The man nodded.

Tara set a small bowl near the dog's muzzle, causing a wiggle in her overly dry nose.

Cautious of the dog's reaction while she snuffled around the water, Timothy shifted the blanket slowly, freeing a soft, puppy fuzz-face. "There we go, girl. Be nice now."

The dog wriggled but failed against her trappers holding

the blanket tight across her ribs and rump. Her big brown eyes darted around, sad and scared. Timothy reached out and stroked behind the pooch's ear, causing her to push her head into the kindness. She closed her eyes. "You're going to be fine, girl. Just fine."

Timothy kept soothing the dog. Glancing up at Tara, he saw an expression of admiration that caused his heart to lurch. Then she lowered herself, skirts bunching at her feet, to pet the dog. She didn't seem to mind her skirt and sash dragging in the dirt one whit.

"Do you think it's safe to take off the kerchief?" she asked, mimicking the gentle tone he used.

"Once these folks disperse. I don't want to spook her while she's in pain."

Tara stood slowly, careful not to cause the injured animal alarm, as Jesse returned. "Folks, we're goin' to take her on home. Go enjoy the festivities, please." Then she directed Jesse to collect some sort of crate.

"Still don't get why we're takin' that peg leg instead of puttin' her down." He shook his head. "Women."

To her credit, she said nothing, though her eyebrow raised disdainfully. There was an elegance to her disapproval. Though Timothy had no desire to be on that side of her again, she may have eliminated one more suitor.

"The crate's a good idea. We can transfer her into it to keep her as comfortable as possible on the ride home."

"Well, I remember bringing you home with no way to ease the trip on your body."

The assisting man's eyes went wide at them.

"I had an accident a few weeks back," Timothy told him. "Still sore."

"You're doing better than this little girl," his helper acknowledged. "But I see you know what you're doing."

"I'm a veterinarian." He tipped his head in the direction the pistol-waver left. "Not everyone thinks animal medicine is valuable. I believe in stewarding God's creatures."

"You think she'll survive?"

"Undoubtedly. She'll be a working dog yet, with some healing and training."

Tara added, "We need a good cattle dog."

With everyone but their helper finally gone, Timothy freed the dog's muzzle. "Easy now. That's it, relax." He pushed the bowl of water toward his patient again. "What are we going to call you, huh?"

Jesse returned with a crate from the livery. "Found this. I figured you'd want these here burlap sacks for padding."

Tara broke into a grin. "How thoughtful, Jesse, thank you."

The dog growled, voicing the silent sound in Timothy's head. "I know how you feel, girl." He lowered his voice and rubbed her ear.

"How old do you think she is, Timothy? She looks so hungry." Compassion tinged Tara's every word. "I can see all the bones in her body."

"Maybe six months? A lot of growing up to do yet, but that means she should heal fast. If I set her leg right, this pup might be knit up in a matter of weeks." After sniffing at the bowl, the puppy lapped sideways at the water. Timothy lifted her slightly to help her drink. Water dribbled out all over the ground, muddying the dirt beneath her.

Jesse laughed. "That mutt ain't more than a mess. Probably gonna be more trouble than it's worth. But since he cain't walk, that little peg leg will be a right fine lapdog!" He chuckled at his own joke.

"Interestin'." Tara's brow crinkled and her eyes narrowed again. "I've always wanted a lapdog."

Suddenly Jesse clapped his mouth shut. "Yes, ma'am."

Timothy bit back a laugh, but he wanted to let it loose badly. "Pack in as much padding as you can. Then we'll muzzle her again before we lift her with the towel into the crate."

Cookie arrived with Sam, a quilt folded over his arm. "Heard you got yourself a situation." He took a look at the dirty, patched-up collie, scratched his head, and said, "So we're finally gettin' a ranch dog, heh?"

Tara nodded and gave him an affectionate smile. "Guess so."

"She got a name?" Cookie asked while he spread the quilt in the box, creating cushy bedding on top of the burlap.

Timothy looked at the puppy, and a grin spread across his face. "I'm leaning toward Peg."

Tara's giggle solidified it. "I like it."

"Well, Peg, got some chicken for ya." Cookie opened the picnic basket Sam held, then turned to Timothy. "What you waitin' on? Git the dog in the crate so she can have her reward."

Slipping his hand under the dog's neck, Timothy rubbed under her chin until he slid the kerchief back on. Then, with Cookie's aid, they wrapped Peg to keep her as still as they could and gently lifted her into the wooden box. Once in, Timothy let Cookie dangle the chicken in front of her nose as he released her mouth. She went for the chicken like she'd been starving.

"A little now. Too much at once and we'll be cleaning it up." He held out his hand to the man who'd stuck by them. "Thank you. Timothy Higgenbottom."

"Pastor Paul Chell. We're building a new church down the road. The Anaconda parish is overflowing." He returned the handshake. "Let me know if she needs more than prayers. She's God's creature, and as you said, He's given her into your care." He turned to Tara and offered a handshake to her while he looked between them. "Looks to me like God's trusted them both into your care, young lady."

Tara blushed. "I'll do my best, Pastor. Thank you for your help."

"I'll be eager to hear how she fares. We should have the new building up in a few weeks." He continued around the group shaking hands and introducing himself to each one. "Come for services soon."

Cookie took off his hat. "We'll be by, Pastor. Thank you kindly for the invite." He elbowed Jesse, who grabbed his hat off his head.

Timothy and Jesse each took a side of the crate and gently slid it onto the carriage floor.

"Your pa's sure gonna be surprised." Cookie climbed up and took a seat. "Hand me that chicken, Jesse. I'll feed her a little now and then to keep her happy. Then stow that basket."

Timothy asked Cookie, "Can you cook up a bone broth with willow bark? It'll help to ease her pain."

"Sure can." Cookie fed Peg a bite of chicken, and the dog gazed up at him expectantly. "Gonna be a rough ride for the poor mite."

"You two deserve your time off," Tara said to Jesse and Sam. "Stay on. We'll be fine."

Timothy never saw more exuberant men.

"Thank you, Miss Tara," Jesse said.

"Ma'am." Sam nodded and hightailed it as quick as he could back toward the pretty girl by the bandstand.

"My pleasure," she replied to Jesse. "We'll see you back at the JBarF later." She turned to climb into the driver's seat.

Timothy stopped her with a hand on her elbow. "I'll do that, Tara."

"Oh really? You're still tender from a fence whippin', and Peg might need your expertise." She gave him a look that said, *Are you really that daft?* then hoisted her skirts and stepped up. "I'll go as easy as I can."

She'd sent the men away, commented on his expertise, and cared about a small dog. Beyond her abilities to work alongside him, Timothy recognized Tara had chosen him all day above the others. She could have stayed behind and had someone bring the carriage back. But she didn't. He leaned down to the crate, petting Peg as he whispered to her, "We have a fighting chance, girl."

They pulled out to the strains of "My Country 'Tis of Thee" sung by the schoolchildren. He breathed in the fresh Montana air and felt at home for the first time.

❧ Chapter 7 ❧

Gold Creek, Montana
September 8, 1883

Standing on a small rise with Timothy, Peg sleeping at her feet in the noonday heat, Tara could see over the huge crowd of local settlers, miners, Crow Indians, and railroad workers waiting for the moment the golden spike connected the entire country. "Who could have thought all those politicians would want to come way out to Montana to pound a piece of iron?" she said. "There must be hundreds of 'em." She almost felt guilty leaving everyone else back at the ranch on this historic day. But Pa, with his list of chores, insisted he didn't want to come. Cookie refused, saying his rheumatism was acting up, but he managed a right proper feast to send them on their way.

Cookie had outdone the Independence Day feast, even sending along a special meal for Peg of her favorite chopped chicken. She went everywhere with them now that she could walk instead of hop. Timothy worked with her on obedience training and her fear of horses when he wasn't out with his men working.

Timothy slid the *Daily Independent* out of the picnic basket's handle, which kept the paper from blowing away in the breeze. "This article says that besides the two hundred politicians expected from every state in the Union, the United States President Chester A. Arthur, General Sheridan, and General Grant, there are journalists and dignitaries from Europe. The man expected to drive the final spike is the president of the Northern Pacific, Henry Villard. He invited all these people to show them the wonders of the West." Refolding the paper, he added, "I'm sure he's counting on the word to spread and keep those trains filled. The amount of money the Northern Pacific has to recoup is astounding."

"Yet they haven't solved the time schedules." Tara shook her head. Her gaze followed the length of the temporary wooden grandstand built to hold a thousand. There hadn't been room for all the people who came from every corner of Montana. Many sat on the hillside as Timothy and Tara did or in their wagons and carriages. Elaborate decorations of pine boughs and draped bunting on the grandstand turned the south side of the river into a spectacle like a county fair. Flags from England and Germany fluttered in the wind, friendly neighbors to the United States flag. Trains lined the track in the distance, waiting to carry their passengers all the way to the Puget Sound on the cross-country extravaganza. "But five trainloads? I think they just doubled our population."

Timothy sputtered then gave in to the laughter.

She gave him a resigned glance. So much for sarcasm. "I know there's more than a thousand people in Montana. There's more than that in Butte alone." The Fifth Infantry Band struck up a march, drowning out any response from him. She didn't need to be laughed at as a dumb girl. She could out-cipher any man. Her ledgers proved it.

He leaned into her ear. "Tara, I think you're brilliant."

She turned, their lips so close she could feel the warmth of him. "Oh."

Timothy touched her nose lightly with his then held out his elbow for her to take. She slid her hand into the crook of his arm, looked up into his eyes, and a smile passed between them.

Throughout the afternoon, the generals and other dignitaries gave speeches interspersed with music until the finale. The honored dignitaries half-circled the tracks for a momentous photograph. The historic joining of East and West on the northern line changed the concept of travel as much as the 1869 event, maybe more. Tara's western world collided with Timothy's eastern. Every time she snuck a peek at him, he snuck one right back. She hardly heard a word from any of the speakers over the thumping of her heart. Peg forced her nose into Tara's palm. Grateful for the distraction, she sat for a moment and gave the devoted dog her attention.

Timothy broke into applause with the throng, jolting Tara to follow suit. Peg jumped up, tail wagging. She looked almost regal, full of health and energy, as Timothy ruffled her rust-and-white fur. They were both the picture of health and energy. Happiness pinged around inside Tara's heart. Coming at Timothy's invitation, without her father or Cookie, gave the impression of courting. She liked the idea of courting Timothy. Would she remember anything of the historic day other than how she felt right now?

President Arthur stuck out his hand, clamping onto the Honorable William M. Evarts's as he raised his voice for the crowd. "Sir, a mighty oration worthy of this historic moment. Thank you."

General Ulysses S. Grant received the sledgehammer. Instead of raising it, he presented it to Henry Villard. "The honor, Mr. Villard, is yours for being the man who believed it possible to traverse our great country from sea to sea. There's no greater symbol of unity than this today."

At the moment the hammer struck the spike, the one hundred guns thundered a salute. Peg barked to her heart's content while the band roared into a rousing celebration mixed with thousands of cheers. Tara couldn't for the life of her figure out what song played over the raucous noise. They'd come to see history made and a continent opened to the world. Now the world would come to, and through, Montana. Would they be better off for it?

"Been a long day. We shouldn't be too late to the Kruegers's."

Timothy folded the quilt while Tara gathered the basket. "Kind of your friends to let us stay tonight."

She grinned. "You get the barn loft."

They walked together down the grassy embankment, Peg trotting alongside, to the winding river where hundreds of horses lined the bank, resting through the afternoon. The cottonwoods showed the early signs of autumn, turning from deep to lime green with some already tinged yellow.

September's warm days were Tara's favorite. Rarely a bad day in the month as the leaves turned to a glowing gold better than any mine could produce. The next few weeks would be glorious. Tara soaked in the blue sky, thanking God for the beauty around her.

Finding the JBarF Morgans, they dodged others preparing to leave while a newsie circulated specially printed leaflets.

"The next endeavor, miss." He handed the news page to Tara. "See where the train goes next." He wandered off, calling, "Big news! Get your copy!"

"Next?" She scanned the printed ad. "Oh no!"

Timothy halted the horse he led next to the carriage. "What? What's wrong?"

Peg leaped inside, nose in the air sniffing at the wind and waiting for her people.

She shoved the flyer into his hands. "We have to get home now!"

The carriage ride home took long, grueling hours. Tara paced each time they rested the horses, unable to do so herself. What if the newly created Montana Railway succeeded in their plans to build from Butte to Helena? The proposed route would run west and then north right through the JBarF and several other ranches. Now the mechanical beast that revolutionized transporting their cattle and horses could destroy everything!

"Pa!" Tara hitched up her skirt and jumped from the buckboard. The longer skirt she normally saved for Sundays hampered her speed. "Pa?" she called again, Peg right at her heels, barking their arrival.

Her father swung open the front door. "What's all this ruckus?" He slid a suspender over the shoulder of his long johns.

"We're in trouble." She shoved the leaflet at him. "Big trouble."

"Calm down." He hugged her, the paper crinkled in his hand.

"Take a deep breath and tell me the problem, Mouse."

"Pa, they're gonna take our ranch!" Tears coursed down her cheeks. "The railroad has plans to cut right through our property to connect Anaconda up to Helena, and then all the way down to California. They're callin' it eminent domain. Even if they buy our land, it's gonna be at rock-bottom price."

"Hold on." He smoothed the page out and read. Worry lines deepened on his forehead. Finally, he raised his head. His words were measured. "We'll fight it."

Timothy turned the horses over to a groggy Jeremy. Hopping up the two porch steps, he asked, "How, sir?"

"We go to this hearin' in Helena and present our case."

Her father ushered them into the kitchen where Cookie already had a pot of coffee boiling on the wood-burning stove. They'd managed to wake them all.

"How are we supposed to do that?" Tara folded her arms. "Even if we go, nobody will listen to one rancher, Pa." She sat heavily in a kitchen chair. "And what about the livestock auction? We got a lot of horses and cattle that need sellin' if we're gonna make it through the winter."

Peg curled up in her box by the back door. Her long fur ruffled in the light breeze that blew through the house. Crickets chirped as if singing with the occasional hoot of an owl.

"What if we form a protest?" Timothy spoke up as he turned his chair backward. "Let's circulate a petition." He straddled the chair. "We won't be the only ranch affected."

Her father looked at his pocket watch. "Two." He shook his head. "Gonna be a short night. After church, we talk to as many families as possible."

Cookie slid a coffee cup in front of each place. His quiet way added a solemn, unifying presence.

Pa nodded, taking a chair beside Tara. "If we organize and make sure everyone knows, there's some potential in makin' a stand. Might mean somethin' if the hearin' is packed with land-owners."

"Then I'll ride out this week and talk to as many others as I can before the roundup. We can ask them all to go to the hearing."

Tara disagreed. "No, Timothy. It's a good idea, but I need to be the one to ride to the other homesteads and ranches. People know me. They'll listen. With the cattle drive comin', you need to keep charge of our men."

Cookie added, "Peg ain't gonna train herself to herd them cows." He served up rhubarb custard pie.

"We have enough ranch hands for the time being to hold the roundup, Timothy, thanks to you findin' a few more." Her father leaned one elbow on the table, reaching for his slice. "But Tara is right. The men are just gettin' used to takin' your orders." He tapped his fingers on the table, emphasizing his words. "Now that you are up and about, we need that expertise here more than run-nin' around the county. How's Peg's training comin'? She gonna be useful?"

Timothy lifted a cup of coffee to his lips then lowered it. "Peg will be riding with Cookie for her first drive and guard-ing at night. She's too young and inexperienced for the whole run. Next year we'll have a herding dog fully trained." He took the swig.

Her pa nodded. "Guardin'. That'll do." He nodded a satisfied approval. "We'll call a plannin' meeting. Mouse, you go out by the

Carlson and O'Shea ranches, and keep headin' that direction. I'll go by way of the O'Connell and Burke places and get some of them to spread the word with us." He nodded again, "No matter what happens, we need to get our herds to auction. That, above all else, is how we survive."

Tara agreed. "Maybe that'll bring the O'Connells around. They work with us or lose part of their ranch too."

Pa nodded. "And, everybody, pray us through. Ain't nobody gettin' nowhere without the Lord on our side."

"We'll have so many agreeing as one, it'll be louder than that hundred-gun salute today." Buoyed by the plan, Tara savored the sweet-tart flavor of Cookie's dessert. A protest from the whole county would surely force the railroad to build through unclaimed land in the territory rather than steal from those already established. Though they'd have to survey another stretch. She closed her eyes and sent a prayer heavenward.

Chapter 8

Two weeks later Cookie drove the chuck wagon out ahead of the team as Robert, Timothy, and the rest of the cowhands saddled their horses. Jeremy rode out, driving the spare herding horses behind the chuck wagon. They'd meet up with several other ranchers to combine efforts and herds, then join the other ranch owners at the Helena stockyards after the cattle drive.

"Check in on the trail from time to time in case we need a fresh mount." Timothy waved Jeremy off. "We'll see you and Cookie at the camp, hungry for a hearty supper."

Robert watched the boy handle five sturdy, spirited Morgans. "You done well with that kid, Timothy. He's gonna make a right good wrangler."

"He's a quick study and suited for it."

Tara met them on the porch steps with something wrapped in brown paper. "Don't want you to starve, boys." She grinned as she held out the packet to Timothy.

"I thought I smelled something good in there." He brushed her fingers with his as he took the package. Lifting the top layer of paper, he found four turnovers still cooling from the oven. "Smells almost as good as you do."

She blushed at the compliment. "They have apple filling from our trees."

The words were out before he could capture them. "I didn't know you could bake."

"'Course I can bake." Her matter-of-fact response tinged on indignant. "Had Cookie for a tutor."

"Can't wait to taste them." His eyes focused on her lips.

"Just don't go flashin' them around out there. You might cause a stampede." Her voice lowered. "I made 'em special for you." Her eyes darted to an amused Robert. "And Pa." Her cheeks deepened in color.

"I'll take one right now." Robert held out a hand. "Thank you, Mouse."

Timothy obliged him. Then he turned back to Tara, lowering his voice as Robert left the porch for his horse. "I'll keep mine for later and think of you on the trail."

She dropped her gaze. "I'd like that."

Robert mounted up for the weeklong ride ahead of them. "You're sure about leavin' Tumbleweed and Socrates out of this auction?"

Loath to leave Tara, Timothy stashed the packet in his saddlebag. "Yes, sir. They're top-quality yearlings." He checked his cinch, looking over his new western saddle at her. By her expression, he finally looked like a real cowboy in her eyes.

"If you and Tara trust my horse sense." He turned to her. Did she trust him?

Her peaceful countenance encouraged him. He gave her a long, thoughtful look that ended in a contented smile. He could spend his life with her. "Those two will bring you more at auction in Kentucky than you can get in Montana, especially if they show good times at a special viewing." He'd have to leave her a second time to secure the sale later this fall, unless he convinced her to come with him and her father. Would she ever get on a train?

He circled his arm in the air and pointed forward, signaling the men to release the corralled stock.

Robert kept his eyes on the cattle. "How do you know they'll be contenders, Timothy?"

Dust swirled in the air around them, almost pink as early morning rays stretched ahead of the dawn. The lowing of cattle grew louder as they complained and pushed for freedom.

"Because I'm working them the same way I did Cumberland Meadow's winner, English Fancy. She may not have won the Kentucky Derby, but she's made a name in other prominent races. You have my word they'll be ready by the time we take them to Kentucky in November, sir. We'll get ahead of winter and give the new owners training time before the next season."

With one last lingering look at Tara, he whistled to Peg. "Let's get to work, girl." He'd let her run off some nervous energy for the both of them before putting her in the chuck wagon. The sooner they made it to market and the Montana Stockgrowers Association meeting with the railroaders and the politicians, the sooner he could come back to Tara. He turned in his saddle and waved to her.

She stood in the courtyard, a wrap warding off the chill of the morning over a simple work dress, tendrils of her hair flickering across her cheek. She lifted a hand and waved back then tucked the errant lock behind her ear. He'd never seen a more beautiful sight as the sun broke across the mountains, bathing her in its light.

With a chuckle, Robert called out to Timothy, "All right, she'll be here when we get back, son. Let's get on the trail." Robert nudged the flanks of his gelding, catching up with him. "You do what you do best, and when you say they're ready, we'll load 'em up." He rode alongside Timothy. "Then we'll maybe have a talk about my daughter."

"Yes, sir!"

"We'll send word before heading back to the hotel." Robert tapped Timothy's arm and pointed toward the short line at the telegraph office. "Tara will appreciate knowing things turned out well for us."

Dismounting, Timothy tied off Freckles as Robert tied his mount. "That's quite a splurge."

Robert patted his pocket. "With what we earned selling the cattle and the ease it'll give 'er, it's worth the extra."

"She'll be tickled pink," Timothy agreed.

"After the horses are transferred tomorrow, you'll have a bonus. I think it's time I had an adventure." He rubbed his chin. "Let's take that train ourselves and let the men head back with our mounts and the chuck wagon. Gotta live 'fore the livin' is done. Feel like keepin' me company?"

"A few hours versus a few days in the saddle?" Timothy thought of how quickly he'd see Tara. "Absolutely."

Robert gave him a sly glance. "I'm sure that's the reason."

They moved to the telegraph clerk's window. Robert nodded a hello and said, "Please send a message to Miss Tara Johnston, care of Silver Bow Depot."

"Saved the ranch at the meeting too, did you?" The clerk adjusted his spectacles.

Both Robert and Timothy gave him a surprised glance. "Yes, sir." They answered in unison, faces lit with satisfying success.

"Been a theme today. Sounds like they're thinking of going the opposite direction, down to Copperopolis, next spring instead." He looked up expectantly. "Message?"

Robert answered, "JBarF saved. Stop. Home on next train. Stop. Plan a big party Saturday. Stop." He turned to Timothy. "Maybe we'll have another reason to celebrate soon."

The clerk's attention was still on his pencil and paper. "Stop?"

Robert laughed. "No, siree, leave that last line out, or she might have my hide."

Timothy leaned against the counter. "I'd rather you don't set any more hurdles in my way, sir." They laughed together. But Robert's suggestion gave Timothy the feeling it was time to move forward, if Tara was willing. Her special care while he healed, the easy time together at the spike ceremony, and the apple turnovers she'd made just for him. . . If those apple turnovers didn't say she cared, what did? He hadn't been able to get her out of his mind since he met her. But now his favorite dessert would always be apple turnovers.

Not a crack in his demeanor, the clerk said, "That'll be seven fifty."

"Worth every penny." Robert handed over the money. "You know she'll embroider the words and frame it, right?" He clapped Timothy on the back as they walked out of the telegraph office on their way to the booking office.

"She knows how to embroider?" Run a ranch, ride herd, and rope and tie a cow was more than any woman he'd ever met before could do. But he'd just learned she could bake, and now this? What else could she do? "How?"

Robert looked at Timothy as if he were daft. "Every girl has to learn." He untied his horse.

"Did you or Cookie teach her?"

Shock registered on Robert's face. "The women's circle at church."

"Of course, I just thought since Cookie taught her to bake—"

"You thought I know how to embroider? Not 'less it's done with rawhide." He busted up into a chuckle. "Timothy, son, you lighten my load."

Two tickets to the Silver Bow Depot handled, they rode out to the stockyards for the JBarF's final auction. They spent the afternoon working transactions for fifty head of Morgans fit for ranching, riding, and breeding. With their plans in place for their men to head out the next morning, the trolley dropped them steps from the downtown hotel. A quick bite to eat and Timothy was asleep the moment his head hit the pillow.

The next morning an easy walk to the depot had them on the train in the well-appointed dining car, ordering mutton chops for lunch.

"Ain't never seen a menu with such grand eats as this before." Robert admired the elegance of the print on his menu.

"Wait until we take the two horses back to Kentucky. My mother is quite proud of her dinner parties." His thoughts of home brought mixed feelings. He'd grown quite fond of the Johnstons. To the point of feeling more at home with them, even Cookie, than with his family.

"That'll be somethin'. Imagine you come from good stock."

"Well, sir, my father is the—" The waiter arrived with their mouthwatering meal. Steam still rising from the mutton carried a peppery aroma, the vegetables in a huge pile with butter pats melting down, mingling with the meat juices, and a roll on the side baked fresh that morning, from the flaky looks of it.

The train chugged through the mountains as they ate, nearing the track change at Whitehall.

"Good as Cookie can make, but don't be tellin' him I said so." Robert winked. "I'll let on you're spreadin' tales."

Timothy chewed a bite of his chop and swallowed with a grin on his face. He relaxed, ready to tackle the future. He had no reason to believe Robert had changed his mind, or would when he learned of Timothy's family background. After all, his children wouldn't likely inherit any title.

Time to ask permission to court Tara properly—no matchmaking letters or unexpected surprises. This time they'd approach it the old-fashioned way. When he saw her next, Timothy planned to ask her to accompany him to the celebration, with everything out in the open. This time he'd have the jump on Jesse, since the men, extra horses, and chuck wagon wouldn't be home for another two days. And, if things went well, he'd have Robert's blessing on his intentions. "Sir." He cleared his throat as his heart sped up.

Robert looked up from his plate. "What's on your mind, son?"

"I'd like to be up front about my qualifications and intentions for courting your daughter."

"Got qualifications, do you?" Robert put down his fork and knife. "Been wonderin' if'n you'd get 'round to it one of these days 'fore one of those other fellas lassoed your filly." He shrugged. "Never know what a gal sets her mind to." He leaned back in his chair and crossed his arms. "All right, let's hear it."

Timothy's hands had suddenly gone clammy. He rubbed them on his denims under the table. "Well, I haven't been as forthcoming as I should about my family."

"There some kind of problem?"

"No, sir. Except maybe you'd like to know my full name before I say anything more?"

"It's not Timothy Higgenbottom?"

"Yes, sir, but. . .I'm also the Lord of Cumberland, third son of the Earl of Cumberland." He cringed at the officious sound the words made all strung together.

"I see. That's quite a mouthful." He searched Timothy's face, spending a long moment in thought. "Does that somehow change how you feel about my daughter?"

"No, sir." He swallowed before admitting the truth. "I love Tara completely. What I think you should know is that my family has a belief in societal conventions."

"Uh huh." His lips pressed together as he seemed to assess Timothy again. "If I'm hearin' you right, your family won't be approvin' of Tara."

"Sir, it's not an issue for me. But I wanted you to know they might be less than enthusiastic."

"I've learned to take a person on character, not wealth. Don't know nothin' about titles." He lifted his coffee cup and drank. "But if you're wantin' my permission to court Tara—"

Screeching metal and the sudden jerk of the slowing train flung them forward then back. Coffee from Robert's cup splashed everywhere. Instead of coming to a halt, the car careened sideways off the track, folding into other cars bucking the rail. Dishes, silverware, and serving carts flew through the air, smashing into windows, ceiling, and floor. Passengers screamed, grabbing for anything to anchor them, to no avail.

Seconds later people lay crumpled over the ripped wreckage like the broken fine china they'd been served. Timothy pressed his ribs, gathering his feet beneath him. Other than a few cuts and bruises, he seemed fine. The car had been shorn into jagged shreds with wood splintered everywhere. He couldn't find Robert anywhere through the dust and smoke.

"Fire!" someone yelled over the mayhem. "Get anyone out that you can!"

Timothy shook his head, trying to regain a sense of equilibrium. "Robert? Robert Johnston?" He tested a table, pulled himself up, and saw the disaster. In the curling dust and smoke, Robert lay under another table broken from its base, with a blockade of five mangled chairs.

"I see you. Hang on. I'm looking for how to free you." Then he saw the devastating situation. No matter what he did, Tara would lose her father to the massive injuries riddling his body. But Timothy had to try.

Wrenching twisted furniture piece by piece out of his way, Timothy managed to get to Robert. Shooting a glance at the black smoke, he gathered his gravely injured friend and picked step-by-step through the wreckage. His arms burned from the strain as much as his lungs burned from the smoke. It'd be much easier if he could use a shoulder carry. But he couldn't, not with the damage to Robert's chest. He'd smother before they were safely out.

Muscle-heavy from long years of physical work, Robert slid a little in Timothy's grasp. Timothy fought to hold on as he lowered to the edge of the dining car—what was left of it—until he could lean against the edge to hop the rest of the way to the ground.

Robert groaned at the jolt, though Timothy did his best to soften the landing without falling over. Then he scanned the area for a safe place. Exhaustion shaking his knees, he managed to make it to the shade of a tree. He sank against the trunk, holding Robert tightly to him for fear of another jolt.

Breathy, his mouth foaming with blood, Robert fought to open his eyes. "Marry." He dragged in a jagged breath. "My girl." His eyes fluttered.

"I will."

With all the strength he had left, he added, "Love her. She nee. . ." The pain in Robert's face smoothed into serene peace.

"I will." Timothy's words were too late. He dropped his head against the rough bark, banging it a few times in helpless frustration. He lifted his eyes to God and choked out, "Receive Robert's spirit, Lord. He's been a good and faithful servant." Then he closed his eyes and let the ragged loss flood his soul. Today he'd lost a man he admired and a friend who'd accepted him in a way Timothy had never known.

A cold shiver ran through him. He'd have to tell Tara her father's last words and hope she believed him. "God, what am I going to say to her?"

Tara waited at the Silver Bow Depot wearing her prettiest Sunday-go-to-meeting dress. She'd pinned a pretty brooch at her throat that had belonged to her mother, tied a new satin sash around her waist, and given her hat a saucy tip to the side. Wouldn't Pa crow like a rooster that she'd taken his advice? But she hoped to spark a light in Timothy's eyes when they arrived.

"Why, Miss Johnston," Josiah Dawson proclaimed. "I ain't seen you look so pretty since the Easter cantata. You must be expecting someone special this time. Or are ya sweet on that English fella?"

Tara felt the heat rise to the roots of her hair. Everyone would know soon. Though for a short time longer, she'd keep and savor her secret. "We're havin' a celebration party, Mr. Dawson, down to our place this Saturday. You heard the railroad changed their mind on cuttin' 'cross all our ranches."

"Heard they was goin' to build a short line to Anaconda instead. Worth a genuine celebration if there ever was a reason."

"Bring your missus. Spread the word for the barn dance and potluck, will you?"

"Sure will." He seemed about to say something more when the telegraph clerk ran out onto the dock. After reading the message, he paled as if suddenly ill. They spoke for a moment. The telegraph clerk hurried away.

She didn't like to interfere, but things looked serious. "Somethin' I can help with, Mr. Dawson?"

Rather than holler back and forth as they commonly carried on, the depot agent trudged toward Tara with a solemn air. "Miss

Johnston, please sit with me a minute." He held out an elbow.

Worry gathered crinkles at the bridge of her nose. "Someone take ill? You don't look so good." She sat with him on the wooden bench as the church bell began a mournful litany. The bell tolled through their conversation, calling the community together for an emergency.

"There's been a telegraph." He looked down the track toward the east. "The train coming north and switching east hit the train coming west. I don't have more information yet on survivors. Since you was waiting for your pa and your sweetheart, I thought it best to tell you."

"Where? Where did it happen?" The shaking started in her hands, crawled a cold line raising chills along her arms, and crashed into her heart. Her father and Timothy, the two men she loved most in the world, could be lying dead in a tangle of debris.

"Outside of Butte. I'll know more soon."

"I'll go now."

"They'll bring everyone in as they clear up the site. Best wait here."

"How long will that take? How long until I know if my people are alive or dead?"

He breathed in and out, releasing the air in a slow stream. Then he gave a minute shake of his head. "I surely don't know that. I'm sorry."

"I understand, but I'm not waitin' around twiddlin' my thumbs when I can be where I'm needed." She popped off the bench, the need to take action sizzling through her veins. She had to know they were all right. "I—" She blinked back tears. "Thank you, Mr. Dawson."

"I know you're upset. I got no gripe if you stay or go. But—"

She laid a hand on his arm. "I know. I have to go to them, whatever I find."

"God go with you, Miss Johnston." He took off his hat. "I'll be sending help as they come in."

Tara ran from the depot, hitched the horse to the carriage, and hightailed it toward Butte. She'd follow the tracks until she found the train then follow her instincts. With the wilds of her imagination howling at her heels, Tara prayed with all her might, shouting to God as she drove. "Good Lord, send Your angels to minister to the poor souls needin' Your help right now. Give heed to my words. Help my father. Help Timothy. Grant them safety or grant them peace. Your will be done." She repeated the words over and over. What would she find? Her heart pounded in her throat like the beat of the horses' hooves. Would God answer her desperate pleas?

❧ Chapter 9 ❧

The new, bigger church held all the funerals together as the whole of the area held one another up in the following days. All in all, they'd lost fifteen loved ones throughout the county. They also prayed for the five strangers whose hastily crafted coffins went back east in the days after the tracks were cleared. Twenty souls went up yonder, leaving tears to those left behind. Then each family took their dearly departed either to the churchyard or to private family graveyards.

The Johnston family cemetery held four graves now, each covered with a layer of stones to protect the sanctity of the resting places from the ravaging of wild animals and elements. A newly carved memorial stone matched the weathered markers of Tara's mother and brothers.

Tara brushed the dirt from her leather gloves as Timothy finished stomping down the fill around the headstone.

Peg lay on the ground in front of the arched wooden gate in the picket fence that surrounded the family plot, guarding her people, nose sniffing at the air and floppy ears alert. A gopher crawled out of his tunnel twenty yards away and sat on his haunches, staring at the dog. Peg rumbled a low growl and sat up.

Timothy caught the standoff. "Peg, hold." The puppy in her responded with shivers of anticipation. She kept her eyes on the gopher but didn't budge though her head lowered a smidge.

"Thank you for visitin' with me and doin' all this work," Tara said. "I can think of all of them together now. They won't be forgotten."

"It's an honor to help install your father's marker and pay my respects with you." Timothy stood with her, looking down at the grave. "I'm glad you trust me enough to let me be a part of your troubles." He walked her to the wagon. They tossed in their shovels.

"I hate those demon trains." Tara's pain welled up inside as if it would blow like the gas inside a mineshaft. "They mar the land, slam into our livestock, and kill our families. They're like a plague of locusts that leave destruction in their wake."

"Losing your father isn't fair." He offered a palm to help her climb into the wagon. "I hope now that they've set up standard times, there'll be no more accidents. I know it doesn't stop what you're feeling."

She placed her hand in his, stepped up, and plunked herself on the buckboard. "One month." She hunched over on the bench seat. "This whole disaster could have been avoided by one month."

"It makes no sense," he agreed. "I'm sorry, Tara."

"Thank you."

He called the dog. "Up, Peg."

As Timothy gave Tara his nonjudgmental ear, her courage built to share what had taken seed in her heart as she grieved. "Maybe God is really just rolling dice. Why else would He so blithely let people die for the tick of a clock?"

"I can see how it feels that way."

Their shoulders bumped as they swayed over the rough road. Tara remembered her father's words the last time she'd gone this same trail over their land. "He was right." Her lips trembled. "Almost prophetic."

Timothy gave her a curious glance. "Who was prophetic?"

"My pa. He said, 'Mouse, there'll be a day you'll miss it.' He was talkin' 'bout our funny ways of laughin' off hard work and worries. He taught me to focus on good things and laugh at trouble. I can't laugh at this." She pressed her heart as if she could ease the boulder off her chest. "I miss it. Him," she whispered and lowered her head, dropped her hands, and stared at them in her lap. "I miss him."

The bare and dreary trees waved bony arms in the brisk chill like goblins come to steal away all the joyous color in Tara's world. Timothy drove the team with one hand, reached out and covered Tara's hand with his, squeezing with gentle comfort.

His touch, the strength of his hold, enveloped her in warmth. A warmth that flowed toward her heart, easing the chokehold of grief.

"Can I ask a question, if it's not too difficult?"

She searched his eyes. Still kind. Still compassionate. Still trustworthy. She nodded. "Go ahead."

"I've always wondered why your father called you Mouse."

The black clouds dampening her spirit broke as her father's loving ways came to mind. A reminiscent sweetness came over her. "That came from when I was born."

"Would you tell me?"

Her shoulders lifted. "My mother died from giving birth to me too early. I guess she hung on a few months. Then Pa had to feed me goat's milk with a bottle. But he says—"Tara closed her eyes for a second and took a deep breath. "I mean, *he said,* that I made funny squeaky noises for the longest time when I drank and sometimes when I slept. He said I was so tiny and delicate, I was like a little baby mouse. Said I was as bald as a baby mouse too." She chuckled.

"Look at that. Your father can still make you laugh." He squeezed her hand again.

Tara finished her story. "As long as I was makin' noise, he knew I was alive." A wistful smile crossed her lips. "He promised my ma that he'd name me Tara Joy, but all my life I've been Mouse to him."

"It's a miracle from God that you survived."

"He used to tell me he prayed that God would send angels to guard my cradle. That my squeaks must be an angelic language, 'cause they kept me safe." She wiped an errant tear. "For so long, as a little girl, I believed in God and guardian angels."

"You don't believe in God now?"

Anger crackled in her, snapping like static electricity through her very being. "Why would I? I've lost everyone. My mother, both of my brothers, and now my father."

Timothy listened and drove. "And Cookie? You said he was there all along."

She relaxed a little again in Timothy's easy presence. "He says we were already his family by then 'cause he had no other left. We've been so blessed to have him." She paused. "They were like brothers. Pa said they were brothers born on the trail of adversity."

"Tara, I miss your father too." He let the horse take the lead toward home. "I'd like to tell you his last words." His forehead wrinkled as if he struggled with something deep down.

Was he worrying how she'd respond or that he'd hurt her? She pressed him, promising herself not to weep. "Go ahead. I'm fine." Tara heaved a sigh. "Guess I'm just workin' through my feelin's."

He glanced at her and then at the ranch ahead. "I know. But it's hard to get out. Maybe I'm not ready yet. Will you give me a little time to sort through my thoughts?"

Peg popped up from the wagon bed, paws on the back of the seat. Timothy reached back and ruffled the fur on her neck. Her body wiggled from how hard her tail wagged. He slowed enough to let her jump down. "Okay, girl, go home." The dog was off and running.

Tara searched his face, his eyes, and sought the inexplicable. She found no deception or cause for distrust. She nodded, content to leave well enough alone for the moment. Pa had taught her to give people the space to think. She needed a little of that herself. She could honor her father's memory by honoring his teachings.

Cookie clapped Timothy on the back. "Well, I done my part. Let's see ya get our girl onto a train." He stood back and admired the special chicken dinner, roasted vegetables, sourdough bread, and chokecherry jelly. "I got all 'er favorite foods. Don't be messin' it up. She cain't go through the rest of 'er days scared of progress. Ya fall off a horse, ya get back on. Works with anything, even a train."

November's crisp weather did nothing for the nervous sweat Timothy had built up. He changed into a "fancy" shirt, as she called them. Cookie left to deliver dinner to the ranch hands. At least that was Timothy's plan to get Tara alone for a long talk. With Cookie's help, he'd lay out Robert's plan for their future. . .and convince Tara to take a train with him to sell the two horses and meet his family. But he had to help her overcome her very valid fears.

He stood in the kitchen with a plate of gingersnaps as he heard the porch door open and close. He quickly rubbed one palm, and then the other, on his denims.

Her bewildered smile set his heart thumping.

"What's all this?"

He held out the plate. "I had Cookie help me set up a nice dinner and dessert so we could converse privately."

At first her quizzical look was just shy of comedic. Then she took the ugly cookies with grace, lifted her eyes to his, and said, "You had him make my favorites?" She lifted one. "They're a bit off his usual."

He cleared his throat. Cookie had been stunned but partnered up in approval. "I, uh, I asked him to teach me how." Though the partnership produced an uneven, crispier than usual offering.

"You made these?" She had a look that said, *Now that makes all sorts of sense,* while holding back merriment with pursed lips and dancing eyes.

"Probably not the best you ever had, but I couldn't pick you flowers at this time of year."

Her expression softened. "This is better. Flowers are overrated."

"Maybe not after you taste one of these." He loved the sound of her laughter.

She set down the platter, keeping the one, and tasted Timothy's first-ever attempt. "Mmm. You'll be first in line if Cookie ever decides to quit runnin' our chuck wagon."

He never aspired to bake anything before. But suddenly he wanted to do anything to provide for Tara. "You are a bad liar," he teased.

She giggled and cupped a palm over sputtering crumbs. Her appreciation and praise of a simple treat drove home to him why this woman would be his perfect mate. She inspired him to open his heart to a simpler life too.

After seating her at the table, Timothy carved the chicken and served supper. He sat with her once their plates were filled. "One of your father's wishes was to take Socrates and Tumbleweed to Kentucky for a sale. They're special."

"I know." She answered while spreading the cranberry-colored jelly on fresh bread.

"It would mean taking the horses by train." He watched her flinch and so badly wanted to ease her fears.

"I don't like trains." She handed the chokecherry jar to Timothy.

"I don't blame you. But it's too late in the year and too far to ride them across country and keep them healthy for the sale." If he let her think on his points, maybe she'd come around.

"I know that too." While they ate, they reasoned through the issues. The horses might be trusted to an agent. But then no one would be there for important decisions or emergent situations. "You go with a letter from me as my agent," she suggested. "Then wire me if you need somethin' important."

He scooted his chair a little closer. "You've never seen other parts of the country. How can you let fear rule your choice? God is not a God of fear." Timothy meant every word. He wanted to rejoice with Tara when she conquered this overwhelming internal battle. But he had his own fear too. He wasn't stepping foot back in Kentucky as an available man. The woman he wanted to spend his life with sat in a large country kitchen in the middle of the Wild West enjoying a chicken dinner. Wherever he went in the world, he wanted Tara by his side.

"Please come with me and be part of the sale as the owner. Don't let fear take over and choose your future for you, or for us."

Worried eyes flashed between her plate and his face until finally she capitulated. A tiny nod, then she whispered, "I don't want to be ruled by fear anymore."

They ate and then finished with another gingersnap, splitting one that had cracked to pieces already.

"The crunchier the better," she said as she brushed away the crumbs. "Will you tell me Pa's last words now?"

He swallowed some coffee to fortify himself. Based on her reaction to his last marriage proposal, this could go either way. "When your pa and I were on the train, I was about to ask permission to court you when the wreck happened." He spared her the details. "I think he knew how I felt about you."

"How you felt?" Mixed emotions flickered across her face.

Too far in now. He had to say what he had to say and live with the consequences. "Your father, your pa—" Timothy dropped his native formality. In a moment she'd say yay or nay. *Man up, Lord Cumberland.* "Tara, he said, 'Marry my girl,' and 'Love her.' Those were his last words."

Tara's nose turned rosy and tears gathered in her eyes. "You're not makin' that up, are you?"

He shook his head. "I don't know that he heard me, but I told him I would do as he asked." He laid his palm on the table, open to her. "But I also told him I do love you."

Her gaze dropped to his palm. She stared at it for what seemed a hundred years. Timothy held his breath. Right before he thought he'd turned blue, she placed her hand in his. "I accept."

He exhaled with such relief they broke out in nervous laughter.

She looked from their hands to his face. "I'm thinkin' maybe God is workin' things out after all, and it's time I let 'im."

Then he realized what she hadn't said—and what he hadn't yet told her.

❧ Chapter 10 ❧

Timothy, true to his word, held her hand until she relaxed during the train trip. A full day passed before she settled into the rhythm of the tracks. When she did, the beauty of God's earth and her awe of His handiwork took over for the rest of the journey.

Tara enjoyed the carriage ride from the train station. They passed rolling lawns fading to brown and fenced paddocks that went on for miles and miles in all directions. "It must be gorgeous here in the spring."

"Different from Montana, but yes. Quite lush."

The front door of the plantation at Cumberland Meadows stretched as tall as the whole first floor of the Johnston ranch house. The glossy black door and shutters all contrasted with the classic white building. Grecian columns marched around the porch as if they were soldiers standing guard. She'd never seen anything so grand. Not even Marcus Daly's mansion.

Timothy opened the door of the carriage, stepped down, and turned to assist Tara. She took his hand, thrilling to the potential of their future. Taking in the elegance of the residence and surrounding grounds, she'd chosen her new blue traveling gown well. The more stylish attire was a good choice to meet his family. She felt smart, fashionable, and confident. She'd brought one work dress, should she need to care for her horses. She didn't dare let it be seen here. Her two good dresses, including her Sunday dress, would be more appropriate.

"Why didn't you tell me you lived in a castle?"

Timothy laughed. "This is just a house. Our castle—" He sobered.

"Your castle what?"

"Our family home in England is a three-hundred-year-old castle." He appeared uncomfortable at her astonishment. He moved in front of her, blocking anyone's view of their conversation. "A small one, really, because my father is the Earl of Cumberland."

"An earl? I don't understand." She poked a finger into his chest. "Are you hidin' it for some reason?"

He flattened her hand against his heart and held it there. "Well, yes. When you laughed at me for not being a real cowboy, I wanted a chance to prove myself to you. All this—it wasn't important." He lifted her hand and set it in the crook of his elbow. "You and I are what's important. Our future. Not the past or what place I come from."

"I still don't understand." She let him lead her up the porch stairs to the wide veranda. "You come from a castle and your pa is an earl?" She tugged back on his elbow to stop him. "What does that make you?"

The double doors swung open. A man dressed in a black swallow-tailed coat, black waistcoat with a starched white shirt, and gray trousers, held out his hands. "Welcome home, Lord Cumberland."

She looked at him askance. "Lord? Am I supposed to call you that here?"

"No." He winked as he lowered his lips close to her ear. "I like the way you say my name."

She smiled and loved how he lit up in response.

Timothy dropped his hat into the waiting servant's hands. As he slid out of his overcoat, he said, "This is Charles, our butler. He'll take care of your outerwear. Charles, this is Miss Johnston. Please give her our best guest room. She's very special to me."

Charles eyes warmed, but he remained stoic. "Miss Johnston, pleased to make your acquaintance." He gave her a sharp bow.

"Thank you, Charles. Just call me Tara." She untied her belt and removed the navy blue waist jacket.

"It wouldn't be appropriate, Miss Johnston." He held out a hand. "Your hat?"

She felt like a six-year-old being chastised by her teacher. "Oh. I didn't know." She slipped her hat pin loose, letting her long braid unroll from where she'd stuffed it. What else could she do? Handing over her velvet travel hat, pin stuck back through, Tara couldn't avoid ogling the room. "I can't believe this is your home. How could you stand mine?"

He leaned in to her ear again, sending a shiver down her neck. "I prefer yours. It's full of life and love." A shiver she quite liked.

"Really? This is magnificent, and mine is a bird's nest in comparison."

"I've come to feel at home with you unlike any other place in the world. I wouldn't trade it for the queen's palace." He tucked her hand into his elbow again then addressed Charles. "We'll say a brief hello and then freshen up."

"Very good, sir, I'll see to the baggage. Lady Higgenbottom will accept you in the sitting room." He left them with a smart nod that bordered on a bow.

"My, he's formal," she said as they walked the long hall past the curving staircase. The wood was polished to an almost mirror sheen. She trailed her fingers along the flared balustrade, marveling at the workmanship.

"That's the way it is here."

"Those flowers!" She stopped in front of the floral spray that had been hidden by the curving staircase. "They're enormous!" Lavender and white silk flowers mixed with velvet and satin greenery filled a fine porcelain vase three feet above the credenza. "I wish I could grow some flowers instead of only vegetables and fruits. These are so pretty even bein' not real." She took his offered hand. "Those white ones are similar to our bitterroot, but our flower is pink."

"Those represent bloodroot, and the purple ones are supposed to be bluebells. My mother loves them."

"I think your mother and I are going to get on really well."

They rounded the corner where an ornate door opened into the family's sitting room that could easily accommodate thirty people. An imposing figure of a woman lounged on a chaise near the sunny window. Brocade chairs, velvet settee, marble fireplace, and gold-etched burgundy wallpaper overwhelmed Tara's senses. She hesitated at the doorway. How did one greet an earl's wife?

Was she supposed to curtsy or shake hands? Did they shake hands differently?

"Timothy!" The woman wore a day dress in a floral pattern with a bustle. She rose to kiss her son. "Who is this you've brought? Isn't she lovely." Her tone was uninterested as she perused Tara's appearance.

"Lady Higgenbottom, Countess of Cumberland, I'd like to introduce Miss Tara Johnston of the JBarF Ranch, Montana." He tugged Tara forward and squeezed her hand.

"I don't understand." With another glance over Tara's new traveling suit, Lady Higgenbottom asked, "Is she in need of employment?"

His face darkened. "Tara is my intended, Mother, as I said in the wire." He tightened his grip on Tara's hand as she tried to pull away.

"Your. . .intended?" Her eyes opened wide. "Who are your people, Miss Johnston?"

"My people?" Tara felt like an ant whose trail had been disrupted.

Timothy looked his mother in the eye. "She's from a family of very good people who are beloved and respected in Montana. Her late father was Mr. Robert Johnston of the JBarF Ranch."

Encouraged by his warm answer and the strength he exuded, Tara turned to Lady Higgenbottom. But her newfound confidence plummeted at the skeptical coldness in his mother's demeanor.

"I see." She stretched out the tips of her fingers. "Welcome, Miss Johnston." Her expression showed the opposite.

Tara took hold of the countess's fingertips and gave a small shake. Did she do it right? A good, strong handshake felt complete. This dancing with fingers seemed more like the grand lady avoiding the touch of a mangy stray cat.

"I'm sure you're exhausted from your journey. I'll have Charles take you to your room."

"Yes, thank you."

A moment later, as if he'd hovered nearby, Charles ushered Tara out. They couldn't have been three steps away when Lady Higgenbottom's disapproval carried after them.

"I don't know what you're playing at, Timothy, but you are not marrying a poor nobody from a no-name family. Goodness, she's straight off one of those show posters like that Annie Oakley. I've already invited the Thompsons and their lovely Thea for a dinner party tonight to welcome you home."

Stricken, Tara's face flushed with heat. Did he have another intended? She turned around, unsure if she should reenter and let Lady Higgenbottom know she'd been overheard, or go back to the train station immediately.

Charles touched her arm, compassion in his words. "Miss Johnston, opinions of others have no bearing on who we are." He picked up his pace, drawing her with him. "If you'll please follow me."

But the lady had more to say before they'd cleared earshot. "Goodness, you nearly gave me a heart attack. She doesn't even know how to dress or greet her superiors properly. Has no one taught her. . ." Her words faded as Tara followed Charles up the staircase.

"Take heart, Miss Johnston. Trust that all will work out as it should."

Tara's stomach churned. She choked back embarrassed tears. How could anything be worked out? Timothy's mother hated her, hated her pretty new traveling suit, and thought she was a poor nobody. Surely there'd be a room available nearby where she could stay. Somewhere she wouldn't feel unwanted. Then she could go home on the first available train after the sale. There'd be no need for a talk about their future plans. What man would go against his family for an uncouth Wild West gal like her?

Timothy knocked. "Are you ready for dinner?"

She opened the door, still wearing her travel clothes. "I think it's best if'n I head back toward town." She handed him her overnight valise. "Would you call a carriage for me?"

He knew right away she'd heard the heated exchange with his mother. "Tara, no. You don't understand." He set her woven carpetbag inside the room but didn't enter. Under no circumstances would he endanger her reputation.

She placed a palm on his cheek and said with a raspy hitch in her voice, "I think I do, dear Timothy. I do." She turned to the rest of her luggage, never unpacked. "I'll find an inn until the horses sell. Then I'm goin' home."

"My mother doesn't know you yet. She didn't recognize your family name. Please give her a chance."

"I think you have it backwards. An unwanted guest is an unwanted guest." She picked up the bag. "I'll handle my things. Thank you."

A vise gripped his chest. "I've already smoothed things over. She knows and accepts that I have no interest in any other woman as a wife but you."

"Didn't you wire ahead?"

"I did." He stepped aside as she moved into the lush hallway where Victoria's England ruled. Portraits of ancestors, silk potted plants in between each bedroom, and a thick Persian runner drew the eye to a massive coat of arms display in an alcove at the far end. Timothy saw the overwhelming centuries of aristocracy through her eyes. The rules he strained against, societal pressures, and family names that defined one's past and future. How foreign to a girl from the land of the free whose people defined themselves based on their faith, dreams, and personal achievements.

"Then this is already settled." She lifted a palm and gestured at his history on display. "You have a life here. I don't."

"Except one thing would always be missing for me."

"What?"

"You." He moved a little closer. "I can't live without you."

She wavered. The tiniest flicker of love hinted in her eyes.

He could see he had a chance. He lifted her fingers and pressed them to his lips. "Let me help you sell Tumbleweed and Socrates as we planned. Then we'll go home. We can marry there with Cookie and our friends as witnesses. Where we both feel loved." There. He'd said his piece. He let go of her while he silently prayed from the depths of his soul.

The grandfather clock's mechanism ticked a full minute, echoing off the walls.

She swallowed. "Give me a few moments to change."

❧ Chapter 11 ❧

"since Leonatus won the Kentucky Derby last spring, he's going to be high in demand as a stud in the next few years. That could mediate the auction today." After a final word with the jockeys, Timothy strolled with Tara from the Churchill Downs stables on their way to the grandstand area. "He's won all ten of his starts. And he did it in just seven weeks."

"What an amazing horse," she said.

"He promptly ate the roses presented with the trophy," he informed her with a silly grin.

She laughed and added, "Smart horse too."

He led her toward the fence at the racetrack. A select crowd gathered by invitation for the special sale of Socrates as a harness racer and Tumbleweed for flat racing. They'd witness the warm-ups and two timed training runs, one per horse. "Many owners will be vying to have him cover their mares, hoping to get a winner foaled."

"Do you really think someone will buy Tumbleweed, hoping to get a foal from Leonatus?"

"They'd be foolish to pass her up. She'll add to the pool of available broodmares with her stellar lineage." He stopped her out of earshot of their guests, Churchill Downs club members, and others. The luncheon brought many inquisitive high society investors. "But Tumbleweed belonged to your father. We can board her and manage her from my family's stables if you want to keep her. Are you ready to sell her?"

"Once the buyers see what she can do, yes." She touched his lapel and set his heart racing when she raised her eyes to his. "I know you're watchin' out for me. But I'm a rancher, not a racehorse owner. Seein' her run in trainin', I think my Pa would be real happy with my decision."

"Then let's see her run one more time." He signaled for the warm-up.

A short time later Tumbleweed's time impressed everyone enough to create a bidding frenzy. Socrates had his warm-up then his timed run. He too sent a ripple around those who came to see the novelty of Montana-raised horses challenging their way into the elite racing world. Rather than merely a lark of an afternoon's entertainment, the horses set an air of excitement. With several months yet to prepare them, their new owners would fare well.

Timothy congratulated Tara at the end of the auction. They watched as the horses were led away. "Both sold for excellent profits. That, on top of the Montana livestock successes, sets the JBarF for a long, long time." Shadows lengthened and a crisp fall breeze sent scattered leaves past their feet as they walked to the carriage house.

"You were wonderful, Timothy." She closed her parasol, no longer needing its shade as the sun sank. "Thank you for seeing me through the Kentucky business. I'd have no trouble in Montana. But I wouldn't have known who to even talk to out here."

"I was asked more than once when you plan to bring more horses."

She looked a little taken aback. "I don't."

"I know." He took her gloved hand and helped her into the carriage, the satin material blocking the warmth of her skin. He much preferred her bare hands, so different than his first impression, though his mother had been wise to suggest covering Tara's rough skin in polite company, for her sake. He followed her into the passenger box. "I've never seen a horse auction go so well. Socrates will race for the Cranston Stables and Tumbleweed for Maple Farms. We'll have to watch the papers next season."

"Weren't they surprised at how well you trained them? Imagine, a Standardbred and a thoroughbred from Montana taking top dollar in Kentucky! All thanks to your hard work." Her praise sang in his ears. Others could shout his skill from here to the ends of the earth, but it was Tara's opinion that could crush or set him to soar on the heights.

"When Socrates proves himself on the track, I predict he'll sire a line of great champions. Any other animal there couldn't stand next to him for fear of being overshadowed. The JBarF made a name for itself today right along with its lovely owner. If you do choose to bring more horses, I'll be proud to be here with you." She'd charmed everyone because of her genuine interest in each person and her true knowledge of the horses in her care. No airs. No pretense. Never mind how pretty she looked in her new striped walking dress. Though he loved the soft curls swept up under her hat that the maid fashioned, and the femininity the flowers brought out around the brim of her hat, Timothy missed the ease of their everyday life back in Montana. How naturally beautiful she was here, but in her own space the West gave her purpose. Tara looked a tad out of place and rather bored during long days with little to do compared to her normal pace. She'd be miserable wending through party after party.

She lifted her reticule, patting its contents. She looked so happy planning their return home, and she'd shed the reserved demeanor of the last few days. "I'm gonna bring Cookie a new wingback chair with those fancy cushions everyone here has. Can you imagine how it'll help his rheumatism? Our wood chairs are too hard on his old bones."

Timothy caught the singular. *Didn't she mean we?* "We've been invited to a ball this Friday. I can't wait to share a dance with you." He lifted her gloved fingers and kissed them. His lips yearned for the touch of her warm skin. "Would you do me the honor of accompanying me?"

She dropped the playful tone for a more serious one. "I over-heard your mama talkin' about my lack of fashion and social skills."

Timothy's mouth turned down as his eyes darkened. "I'm very sorry. But I don't happen to agree with her at all. I've told my mother that her opinions are not welcome."

"I don't want to be the cause of a rift between you and your mama. I couldn't." She turned in her seat to look at him directly, tears shimmering in her eyes. "I know what we said on the train. I know you're a man of your word. But I'd understand completely if'n you need to honor your parents." She whispered the next words. "I would've married you if Pa had made me. I was just blessed he let me choose you instead. Your mama, she wants someone else for you."

Taking her in his arms, Timothy held her close in the privacy of the closed carriage. "Tara, no one is coming between us now." He touched her cheek and lowered his lips to hers. Lifting his head, he asked again, "Will you accompany me to the ball?"

The sparkle came back to her eyes. "It'd be my pleasure, Lord Higgenbottom." She mimicked the ladies she'd heard. "I think I like callin' you by your name better too."

His heart pumped hard. "I love the way you say my name. I want to hear it from you for the rest of my life." He kissed her again.

"Timothy," she whispered against his neck as she snuggled next to him for the remainder of the ride to Cumberland Meadows.

Tara sat forward on the brocade settee. Wearing a bustle for the first time had its challenges. Buying this dress for the trip had been a wise decision. The pink color complemented her complexion beautifully. She couldn't wait to show Timothy and see his reaction after tea with his mother.

The maid passed her a teacup. A tiny spoon balanced on the delicate plate.

"You understand, dear, don't you?" Lady Higgenbottom's tone was so sweet she could ice a cake with it. "I'm not saying your choice of clothing is unacceptable." She dipped her fingers and motioned Tara to look at herself in the full-length mirror near the settee. "But if you were to dress with style, more like a society lady, people might think you were one." She sent a doubtful look to the maid.

The very words Tara had said so cruelly to Timothy when he'd first arrived in Montana. The Lord used her own thoughtless speech to convict her. How uncomfortable she must have made him feel. Shame washed over her. She'd forced him to buy new clothing to fit into her ideals of Montana life. To look like a real cowboy in order to be acceptable regardless of his true self or abilities. How could she hope to fit into his world unless she was willing to do the same? At the very least, she'd give her best effort to eat humble pie so as not to embarrass the man she loved or his family. She owed him an apology for the way she had prejudged him. If Montana dressmakers weren't up to date, she could easily fix that problem. Oh how she loved this dress though.

So be it. "If'n you have a dressmaker, I'll be happy to buy a gown or two." She smiled with the genuine desire to please and respect her future mother-in-law. "I need one for the ball."

"Such a sweet thing you are." Lady Higgenbottom added, "I can see why you turned Lord Higgenbottom's head."

"I don't want to attend the ball lookin' poorly when representin' your name. No, ma'am. My pa taught me better than that."

"If it were so simple, child." Timothy's mother sipped her tea from the finest porcelain. "Unfortunately, the moment you speak, we're all undone." She set her teacup off to the side. "The truth is, Miss Johnston, my heart breaks for my son. You'll never manage society successfully without having been trained in the graces. I say this not to harm you. I find you sweet and lovely. It is for both of you. The world is cruel. You must see that Timothy needs a wife worthy of his position."

Her blood froze, and then shards of glass scraped through her veins. "You think I'm unworthy?"

"No, dear, no. I haven't explained it well." She patted Tara's hand with genuine compassion. "Your position is unworthy, not you, of course."

Tara yanked her hand away. "Of course." Her cheeks heated as her heart pounded a rhythm like the sound of the train on the rails, louder and louder approaching the station.

Lady Higgenbottom looked distressed. "It may be that you can't understand what I meant. Your education level and lack of funds—"

She couldn't buy a dress fancy enough to dress the pig in the sty this woman saw in front of her. "Oh, I believe we understand one another." Tara breathed deeply and bit her tongue, holding back the words she wanted to release as loudly as a steam whistle. Her wealth could never amount to enough no matter how large her accounts.

"Trixie, get the salts. I'm afraid Miss Johnston may have the vapors."

Her eyes went wide. "I ain't never had, nor will I ever have a vapor!" She rose from the settee. "Oh my word!" Tara clamped her lips closed while she gained control of the anger rampaging through her. She took a deep breath, and said, "Lady Higgenbottom, I understand you too well. I think my dog, Peg, could understand what you're sayin'." She swirled around, skirt and petticoat flaring. She'd been so proud to dress for tea in a fashionable outfit that Timothy's mother would approve. Now all Tara wanted was to go home.

She quirked an eyebrow at the maid who seemed especially

flustered until she finally opened the door to let Tara out. "Appreciate it." She couldn't bring herself to be rude to one who hadn't caused all the hurt.

"Miss Johnston, dear, do wait. You misunderstand me."

The maid bobbed a curtsy, not taking her shocked eyes off the Montana pig in the Kentucky mud.

Tara scooted down the entry hall, lifted her skirts at the stairs, and took them two at a time. She'd be out of this place before the dinner bell.

Chapter 12

Tara finished packing her new collection of dresses and shoes then had second thoughts. Should she just leave it all behind? She had to go, and he had to stay. Maybe one day she'd need them for a trousseau, but not likely, not with her heart crushed to crumbs. She could always sell the clothes if she needed money for feed in a pinch. The question settled, she called for a footman to load her baggage in the carriage. "I'll be leaving for the train station immediately."

"Yes, miss." He picked up the heavy trunk. "I'll be back for the rest in a moment."

She stood at the window, taking in the view for the last time. So beautiful, the welcoming courtyard. So deceiving. Tara lifted her chin and stiffened her back. She belonged back at her own ranch in Montana, not here. Not at a fancy ball. Not where she lost sight of herself, succumbing to the poor and judgmental treatment of others. But should she at least say goodbye?

Instead, she chose to write a thank-you note addressed formally to Countess Higgenbottom expressing appreciation for her stay in the beautiful suite. This room gave her some grand ideas for improvements on the JBarF. Her home could do with a sprucing up. Not nearly as grand as all this, but some fluffy covers on a new mattress, a little paint in a cheery yellow would be lovely, and practical updates in general. She could take home good from this experience. *See, Pa? I found the positive side.*

Her mind steeled to focus on the future she could control, Tara gathered the small valise and a wrap she'd need for the long ride home. She would say a quick farewell to Timothy. He deserved more than a note. She owed him her blessing on his future, even if he should marry the ever-so-perfect Miss Thea Thompson. Tara nearly missed the top stair at the thought of Timothy married to the silly girl she'd met at the first dinner party. She clutched at the balustrade and steadied herself before taking the next step.

She found Timothy in the breakfast room absently eating while reading, completely unaware of what was about to happen.

He looked up from the newspaper. "Green suits you." He stood and offered her a chair. "It's very becoming."

Meaning to simply say goodbye and flee, she faltered. He wanted to be with her. She couldn't let him. As he bent to kiss her cheek, she blurted out, "Timothy, stay in Kentucky. Your home is here, where you're used to the comforts and have your family." She couldn't look at him. "You'll have a better life with prospects of a more"—the last two words came out in a whisper—"suitable wife."

He touched her cheek, turning her to face him. "I thought we'd put all this nonsense away."

"It doesn't matter." She fought against the deep sadness gripping her chest. "We both know this won't work."

"No, we don't know it won't work. We agreed we would work." His face darkened. "I've never known you to go back on your word."

"I have to do this for both of us." His mother's words clanged in her heart.

He lifted her hand and held it between both of his. "I love you, Tara, and I want to marry you."

"I can't." She focused on the buttons of his shirt. She'd capitulate if she let herself make eye contact. She tugged her hand from his. "Let me go. It's best." She swallowed the tears, her voice cracking as she said, "It's what I want."

The color drained from his face. "What do you mean, 'it's what you want'?"

She turned and hurried from the room, past Timothy's mother, who was just entering.

Lady Higgenbottom swept her skirts aside, avoiding a collision. "Wait, child, I came to speak with you. I—"

"Tara!" The sound of his voice, like an injured wolf, rasped after her as she ran out the front door.

The footman, a little confused at the situation, held out a hand to help her into the carriage. "Do we drive, miss?"

"Yes. Right away, please." She pulled her traveling skirt up after her.

"Yes, miss." He closed her in.

She saw Timothy with his mother on the porch as the

carriage rolled away. Both had deeply serious expressions. They were not her problem now.

Tara pulled her wrap tight and slid away from the window. A tear slid down her cheek as she silently prayed. *God, if You really mean good for me and really love me, why have I lost everyone I love? Couldn't You show me how all this is supposed to work out for my good?*

"Are you sure she's on board?" Timothy strained to see if Tara waited anywhere in the station. He'd thrown basic necessities and his grandmother's heirloom ring in a rucksack slung over his shoulder. Six months ago survival subsistence was something he'd never have considered.

"I sold her the ticket. Yes, I'm sure." The agent stamped Timothy's ticket "Lexington to Silver Bow" when the whistle blew. "You'd better run, mister, if you're going to catch that girl. The train's leaving any minute."

Grabbing the ticket from the agent's outstretched hand, he took off. The last departure whistle blew. As he rounded the corner, the engine eased forward. He leaned into his dash, dodging those waving at their loved ones leaving. Then he caught a glimpse of Tara in the fourth passenger car. He launched himself at the steps in a daring effort. One foot dangled inches from the ground, only one thought in his head. She couldn't leave him.

Gripping the handle on the last car, Timothy heaved himself up and aboard. The danger suddenly struck as he watched the rails and rocks speed away beneath the stairs. The brisk breeze grew into a strong wind with the velocity of the train. Exhausted, he opened the door, to the surprise of the occupants. Timothy caught his breath. He made it!

But the train jerked on the rail, sending him sprawling in the middle of his official, third try at a proposal. He looked up at Tara. "I probably could have timed that better."

Relief flooded through Tara. God had not withheld good from her. He'd given her the desire of her heart. She laughed. "No, you were right on time."

He rose to his knee, catching the rhythm of the moving train. "Tara Johnston, I told you once I could not live without you. I then told you I love you. Now I'm here to prove I will follow you wherever you may go, because I choose you. Will you please stop running away and marry me?"

She folded her hands around his. "I will never run away again."

"After you left, I told my mother that she would have to stand before God and explain her behavior. I reminded her of Mary, the mother of our Savior. She did not hold a position in society and yet God chose her to bring His Son and forgiveness into the world. I told her I couldn't be a part of a family who didn't know how to love one another."

"You said that?"

"I did."

"What happened?"

He slipped onto the bench beside her. "I've never seen her cry before, Tara. She truly thought she had the best of intentions. But as we talked, my mother understood how some of those best intentions can blind us to what God intends for us. She realized how awful she'd been to you and how deeply she'd hurt me. Enough to drive me away permanently."

"I think I've been blind to how God works in our lives too. I judged you when we first met. Then I blamed God for losing everyone in my family. Then I left instead of working through the problem with your mother."

He stuck his hand inside the rucksack and pulled out a small wooden box. "My mother gave me this for you." He opened it, revealing a beautiful ruby set in gold. "It's my grandmother's ring."

"She accepts me?"

"She does, if you'll forgive her."

Tara swallowed. "I need her forgiveness. And I need God's." She bowed her head.

They quietly prayed together.

Tara lifted her eyes to his. "I'll send a letter from our next stop."

"Let's also wire ahead to have Cookie meet us with the pastor. I'm not taking another chance with our future. I want to put this on your finger as soon as possible." He ducked his head and touched her lips with his to the sighs of two young girls behind them.

"I'll be sure to thank your mother for the ring."

"Maybe invite her to visit us." He grinned. "I think she'd be surprised to see what the ranch has to offer."

"You mean because your mother thinks you're marrying a pauper?"

He shrugged. "It crossed my mind."

Two days later Cookie met them at the Silver Bow Depot, wearing new suspenders for the occasion. "Good to have you both safe home." A very excited Peg ran around them as they loaded the luggage. He drove them straight to Pastor Chell's church near Anaconda.

"Pastor, you'll remember my intended, Timothy." Tara wore the pink gown at Timothy's request.

"Welcome home, Timothy." The pastor extended his hand.

"Sir, please call me Tim."

They celebrated the first wedding in the new church with the pastor's wife and Cookie for witnesses as the clock struck high noon, Mountain Standard Time, their future before them.

Angela Breidenbach is a bestselling author of eighteen books and hundreds of articles. She's also a professional genealogist, radio personality, and president of the Christian Author Network. And yes, she's half of the fun fe-lion comedy duo, Muse and Writer, on social media. Note from Angela: *"I love hearing from readers and enjoy book club chats. To drop me a note or set up a book club chat,* contact me at angie.breidenbach@gmail.com. *Let me know if you'd like me to post a quote from your review of this story. If you send me the link and your social media handle, I'll post it to my social media with a word of gratitude including your name and/or social media handle too!"*

For more about Angela or to set up a book club chat, please visit her website: www.AngelaBreidenbach.com

Facebook/Instagram/Pinterest/Twitter/MeWe:
@AngBreidenbach

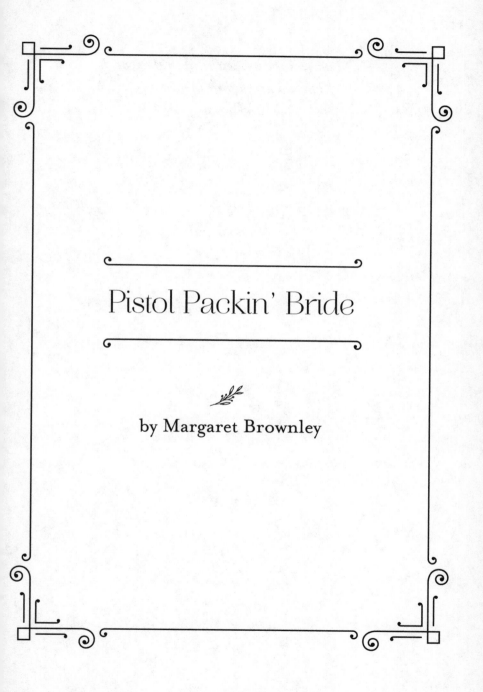

Pistol Packin' Bride

by Margaret Brownley

Adam was the luckiest man in the world.
He had no mother-in-law.
Mark Twain

❧ Chapter 1 ❧

Prickly Pear, Texas
1885

The stagecoach rocked like a ship on a stormy sea, and it was all Elizabeth Colton could do to keep from being tossed from her seat.

The constant rattles and groans gave her no confidence in the stage's integrity. She feared it would fall apart or, at the very least, the wheels would fall off. Her fear only increased when the coach hit a deep rut in the road and leaned precariously to the side.

Jarred to the bones, Elizabeth sprawled across the seat like a gangly colt and held on for dear life.

As the lone passenger, she made no attempt at decorum. Her feathered hat had tumbled off her head three hair-raising turns ago and now skittered across the floor like an inebriated chicken. The skirt of her blue traveling suit was in disarray, and strands of auburn hair had come loose from her bun.

Just as she thought she could hold on no longer, the coach

mercifully straightened. Taking advantage of the reprieve, she pulled herself upright and gasped for air. Hand on her chest to calm her racing heart, she moved the leather curtain aside and peered out the window. Miles of desolate landscape stretched out for as far as the eye could see.

Every horror story she'd ever heard about Indians and outlaws came back to haunt her. While still at home, it was easy to discount such tales, but here in the wilderness she imagined danger behind every bush and rocky outcrop.

Her fiancé had assured her in his letters that such tales had been greatly exaggerated, but then he'd also described Texas in glowing terms. That alone put his credibility in question. The spacious skies and wide-open spaces he'd written about held no appeal for her, and already she missed her hometown of Dayton, Ohio.

Elizabeth dropped the leather curtain in place with a sigh. Never had she imagined herself a mail-order bride. But at age twenty-four, it was either leave her hometown or remain single. Most of Dayton's eligible bachelors had answered the call of the wild and traveled west. The few men left behind were either already married or old enough to be her grandfather.

She opened her purse and pulled out the last letter written from the man she agreed to marry. His name was Ben Heywood, and he was a lawyer.

She studied the photograph he'd sent. He really was a good-looking man—handsome even. He was clean shaven and had nice eyes. He also had strong cheekbones, a straight nose, and a firm chin. Though he looked serious, she imagined he also had a nice smile.

It worried her that he'd written so highly about his accomplishments. Nothing she hated more than a braggart, but maybe he had just been trying to impress her.

She really had nothing to complain about. His last letter had included money to pay for her journey. He'd sent enough to pay for a train ticket, but her thrifty mind opted to travel by the more economical stagecoach. After seventeen days of misery, it was a decision she now regretted.

Included in the letter were implicit instructions on what to do upon reaching Prickly Pear. She only hoped the town was friendlier than it sounded by name. She also prayed her intended was as kind and good-hearted as his letters suggested.

Such were her thoughts, that it took a moment before she realized the stagecoach had slowed.

A male voice shouted, "Halt!" and the stagecoach rolled to a stop.

She stuffed the letter back into her purse and peeked through the window. A single man on horseback was talking to the driver. She couldn't see his face or tell if he was wearing a mask. Nor could she hear what he was saying.

All she knew for sure was that the man sat tall and assured in a saddle, his shoulders seeming to strain the seams of his shirt. From the back, he looked like a force to be reckoned with, and her mind leaped to a startling conclusion: he was a highwayman come to rob them. Gasping, she drew away from the window.

Who else would stop a stage in the middle of nowhere except someone meaning to do harm?

Heart pounding, she unsnapped her purse and pulled out the derringer hidden inside. It was a good thing she had thought to carry a weapon. A woman traveling alone out west couldn't be too careful.

Swallowing hard in an effort not to panic, she straightened her skirt and held her cocked weapon pointed at the door, finger on the trigger. Trying to still her shaky hands, she whispered a silent prayer. God wouldn't have brought her way out here to meet with an unpleasant end, would He?

Nerves taut, she sat frozen in place. She didn't have much of value on her person, but it wasn't her jewels that worried her; it was her virtue.

The door of the stage suddenly flew open. With a cry of alarm, she jumped, and her gun went off. Though the small pistol delivered a low recoil, it was enough to make her drop the weapon and rear back in her seat.

The man's startled blue eyes met hers. Their gazes locked for a moment before he gripped his upper arm and pulled his bloody hand away. He tried to speak, but nothing came out of his mouth. Instead, he grimaced and sank ever so slowly to the ground.

❧ Chapter 2 ❧

Ben Heywood groaned as he tried sitting up in bed. Of all the dumb things that could have happened. Getting shot by a woman he didn't know—didn't care to know.

Doc Evans told him he was a lucky man. The bullet had hit him in the upper arm. Although it had hit an artery, causing him to lose a lot of blood, he could just as easily have been shot in a vital organ. Still, Ben didn't feel all that lucky.

The day had gone from bad to worse, starting with his parents' confession that they had meddled with his life—yet again!

Until that morning, he had no idea that he was betrothed, let alone to a mail-order bride. He had been furious upon learning that his parents had written letters on his behalf to a woman—a stranger, no less—they'd expected him to marry. He still couldn't believe it.

All he'd done was stop the stage to tell his so-called bride-to-be that there had been a terrible mistake and he had no intention of marrying her. To pay her for her trouble, he'd purchased a train ticket so she could travel back home in style.

A bullet to his arm changed all that.

"Take it easy," Doc Evans said as he straightened the pillow behind Ben's back. "With all the blood you lost, you're lucky you survived. You can thank the stagecoach driver for that. Fortunately, he was a medic during the war."

"I'm much obliged to him. To both of you," Ben said. After being shot, he remembered nothing until waking up at Doc Evans's medical infirmary. "I still can't believe what happened."

The doctor chuckled. "You're not the first of my patients to have female troubles, but you're the first to have been shot by one."

"Don't remind me," Ben said with a grimace.

The doctor stepped back and tossed a nod at the door. "Are you up to receiving visitors?"

Ben groaned. "Are they all here?"

The doctor's eyes crinkled at the corners as if amused by the question. "You know they are. It's not every day that Prickly Pear's favorite son gets himself shot."

Ben laid his head back on his pillow and shifted his legs, but trying to get comfortable was out of the question. The doctor had to remove broken bone pieces before stitching Ben up, and every move sent pain shooting through his bandaged arm.

What the doc said about him being the town's favorite son was no exaggeration. Ben had been left on the church steps as an infant, and three childless couples had taken it upon themselves to adopt him. He didn't know what was worse: the hole in his arm or what awaited him behind the door.

As grateful as he was for the love and care showered upon him through the years, it hadn't been easy growing up with three sets of parents.

Everything he did or had wanted to do in his youth had been debated at length and decided by parental committee.

His parents weren't happy with his decision to accept an apprenticeship with a lawyer, and that was putting it mildly.

Pa Baer had wanted to teach Ben his family blacksmith trade, but Pa Edwards had insisted that banking was a nobler profession. Then there was Pa Norton, who had his heart set on Ben taking over the Norton General Store. The raging arguments that had followed Ben's announcement had his adoptive mothers in tears. All except Mama Baer, who never cried.

Ben had hated to disappoint his six parents, but there comes a time when a man has to stand on his own two feet and follow his heart. He couldn't explain it, but he'd always been fascinated by the law.

"So, what do you want to do?" the doctor asked, breaking into Ben's thoughts.

Ben sighed. His head ached, his arm hurt, and his brain felt like mush. All he wanted to do was sleep. "Might as well get it over with," he muttered.

"Whatever you say." The doctor braced himself with a deep breath before reaching for the doorknob. He barely managed to keep from getting trampled as Ben's parents stormed into the room.

As sure on foot as she was in her opinions, Ma Baer reached his bed first. "Oh you poor dear," she said in her thick German accent. Clucking like an old hen, she leaned her bulky form over Ben, the feathers of her three-story hat brushing against his face.

"You gave us quiet a scare."

"You most certainly did," Ma Edwards said, wringing her hands. Her small size and modest demeanor were deceiving. A former schoolmarm, Ma Edwards ran her house as rigidly as she had run her classroom and had taught Ben to read even before he'd been old enough to attend the town's one-room schoolhouse.

Pa Norton thumbed his suspenders. "I knew you'd regret becomin' a pettifogger."

Ben clenched his jaw. It wasn't the first time Pa Norton had used the derogatory term to describe Ben's chosen profession, but it still stung.

"I'll say," Pa Baer said. "All those criminals—"

Ma Norton leaned on her cane and nodded. "You should have listened to your pa and worked at the shop with him."

No sooner were the words out of her mouth than the other two couples protested. The argument that followed made Ben's head spin. He lifted his one good arm to gain his parents' attention.

"My being a lawyer had nothing to do with this," he said. "I was shot by. . .the woman you wanted me to wed."

Six pairs of rounded eyes stared at him, and a stunned silence filled the room.

Ma Edwards was the first to recover or at least find her voice. "Good heavens!" she exclaimed, her face as full and round as a powder puff. "What did you say to make her shoot you?"

Ben blinked. "Say?" The memory of being shot was foggy, at best. All he could remember with any clarity was the alarm in the woman's big blue eyes after she'd fired her gun. He'd blacked out soon after.

"I didn't have a chance to say anything. She shot me before I could open my mouth."

Ma Norton tutted. "Well, I do declare," she said in her southern twang. "And to think she claimed to be a fine Christian woman."

Pa Baer made an impatient gesture with his arm, and his thick nose flared. "I told you that sending away for a bride out of a catalogue was a bad idea."

Ma Baer glared up at him, arms folded across her ample chest. "Our son is about to turn thirty and has yet to find a suitable wife. I don't see you coming up with a better plan."

Pa Edwards stroked his graying beard and sniffed. "I still don't know what's wrong with the local girls." He went on to name several who'd earned his favor as a possible daughter-in-law.

Not to be outdone, Pa Norton added, "And don't forget the pastor's daughter."

Ben had no argument with any of them. All the women came from fine families and would probably make some men fine wives. Unfortunately, no woman in her right mind wanted to marry a man with six parents. If Miss Mail-Order Bride had known what she was getting herself into, she probably wouldn't have wanted to marry him either.

"Did she know that you contacted her behind my back?" Ben asked. The silence that greeted his question made him groan. "She didn't know."

Ma Baer stared at him from beneath the stack of feathers on her head. "When she got here, we intended to tell her that we wanted to surprise you."

"That's right," Ma Norton said with a nod of her head. "How were we supposed to know she'd come gunning for you before we had a chance to tell her about the surprise?"

Ben furrowed his forehead. "What made you think I would marry a complete stranger?"

"She sent a photograph," Ma Baer said. "And she's very pretty."

Ben's frowned deepened. "That's it? You expected me to marry her based solely on looks?"

"She also cooks and sews," Ma Norton said, looking at the other two women for confirmation.

Pa Baer glanced at his wife with a look of impatience. "There's no sense rehashing this. What's done is done. The question is, where do we go from here?"

The lively discussion that followed made Ben's head hurt as much as the wound in his arm.

Pa Baer stopped the discussion with a wave of his arms. "If you ask me, Miss Cotton needs to be prosecuted to the fullest extent of the law." He looked at his son. "You tell them, Ben. You're the lawyer."

"Colton," his wife said.

Pa Baer's eyebrows drew together. "What?"

"Her name is Colton. Elizabeth Colton."

"So where do you suppose she is now?" Pa Norton asked.

Ma Baer crossed her arms, and the lines on her face deepened. "If she knows what's good for her, she's on the way back to Ohio."

Doc Evans cleared his throat, drawing all eyes in his direction. "According to the sheriff, she's in jail."

Ben stiffened. Until that moment he'd not thought of the legal ramifications of Miss Cotton—Colton's—actions. Now that he had, his mind went to work. Shooting an unarmed man could get her some serious cell time.

Ma Norton scoffed. "If you ask me, it serves her right."

Miss Colton's punishment seemed to be the only thing his six parents agreed upon. Nodding heads circled Ben's bed.

While Ben wasn't feeling particularly sympathetic toward the woman who'd shot him, he couldn't ignore the fact that she appeared to be as much of a victim as he was.

Doc Evans checked the bandage on Ben's shoulder. "Our patient needs to get some rest," he said.

Ma Edwards clasped her hands to her chest. "Will he be all right?"

The doctor cast a meaningful glance at Ben. "We have to watch for infection, but I expect him to make a full recovery. Providing, of course, that he follows my orders."

Ma Norton took Ben's hand. "You heard what the doctor said."

Not to be outdone, Ma Baer reached for Ben's other hand. "I'll bring you some riffle soup," she said.

Her German riffle soup was an old family recipe, but right now the thought of eating made Ben feel sick to his stomach. "Much obliged," he said. Declining an offer of food would only subject him to one of Ma Baer's lectures on keeping up his strength.

Ma Norton said she'd make his favorite berry pie. Not to be outdone, Ma Edwards told him she'd whip up the brownies he liked so much.

"And I'll make Bauernbrot," Ma Baer quickly added, calling the bread by its German name and signaling the beginning of round two of *Can you top this?*

Pa Baer rolled his eyes and yanked open the door. "After you, ladies," he said in a voice meant to discourage further discussion or argument.

After the other five had filed past him, Pa Baer lifted his gaze to the ceiling and muttered something beneath his breath that sounded like, "Why me, God? Why me?" He then followed the others out the door.

❧ Chapter 3 ❧

E lizabeth brushed her hair until it was almost dry. Oh, how she wished her jail cell had a mirror. Earlier the sheriff had accompanied her to the local bathhouse and stood guard outside while she bathed.

Washing her long tresses while in handcuffs had been no easy task, but never had soap and water felt so good.

It had been three days since she'd shot the man she was supposed to have wed, and she had yet to see the judge or even a lawyer.

After arranging her hair into a tidy bun at the back of her neck, she smoothed out the wrinkles of her blue calico dress and dabbed perfume behind her ears. The Texas heat had made her woolen traveling suit unbearable, and she appreciated the sheriff's wife for insisting on her being allowed to bathe and change into something more comfortable.

Returning the perfume and hairbrush to her valise, she reached for her sketchbook. Normally when she felt sad or lonely or just plain scared, her sketchbook and watercolors gave her solace.

Today, however, her feelings were bottled up, and for once in her life, she had no desire to draw or paint.

Sighing, she returned her sketchbook to her valise and wrapped her hands around the iron bars. The door to the sheriff's office stood open, and she could see him sitting at his desk. Bracing herself for another confrontation, she called to him.

Sheriff Farley tossed down his pen and jumped to his feet. Muttering, he stormed into the cell room and planted himself outside the iron bars, his fleshy red face suffused with impatience. "Now what?"

Elizabeth drew in a seething breath. "I still haven't seen a lawyer," she said. Back home a prisoner would have had access to a lawyer within hours, not days. "It's not fair to keep me locked up like a common criminal."

Hands at his waist, Sheriff Farley glared at her, his mustache seeming to droop more than usual. "I don't know where you came from, but here in Prickly Pear, shootin' an unarmed man is serious business. That makes you a criminal whether you like it or not!"

Elizabeth gritted her teeth. Back in her hometown, a person was innocent until proven guilty. Apparently that wasn't true of Prickly Pear. "I told you it was an accident."

The sheriff scoffed. "Yeah, well, that's what they all say. Like I explained, the judge won't hear your case if you don't have proper legal counsel, and Mr. Livingstone is out of town till next week."

Elizabeth chewed on her bottom lip. "Are there no other lawyers?"

"Only the one you shot," Farley said. "Since I doubt the victim would be willin' to defend you, it looks like you'll have to hold yer horses till Livingstone returns from his trip."

"Is Mr. Heywood all right?" The sheriff's daily reports on the man's condition left much to be desired, but still she had to ask.

"Far as I know he is, no thanks to you. Now, if you'll excuse me, I have other criminals to catch." He glared at her. "The Madison gang held up the bank again," he said, as if it were her fault. With that he spun on his heel and returned to his desk.

She stared after him. Now wasn't that just dandy? Like it or not, she was stuck in jail for who knew how long. And what if the judge didn't rule in her favor? So far no one she'd talked to believed that she'd shot Ben Heywood by accident.

The stagecoach driver hadn't even let her near Mr. Heywood after she'd shot him, for fear she'd do him further harm. Instead, the guard had tied her up while the driver worked to save Mr. Heywood from bleeding to death.

Pushing the memory aside with a shudder, she paced the width of her cell and tried to think. It wasn't in her nature to sit around and do nothing. But without a lawyer, it looked like she had no choice in the matter. As for Mr. Heywood, all she could do was hope and pray that he made a full recovery. Not only for his sake, but for hers as well. The last thing she needed was to be tried for murder.

Her thoughts were interrupted by raised voices. Several people had entered the office and were now gathered around the sheriff's desk, everyone talking at once. Finally, the sheriff shot up from his desk and led the way to her cell.

"You have visitors," he said, indicating the six people crowding through the doorway behind him.

"You have five minutes," the sheriff said and stomped back into his office.

The woman wearing a mile-high hat was the first to speak. "I'm Mrs. Baer, and I have to say, you're as pretty as your photograph."

"You. . .you saw it?" Elizabeth asked, not having the slightest idea who any of these people were.

Mrs. Baer nodded. "Yes, and I could tell that you weren't one of those awful women who use face paint and bosom enhancers to fool a man."

One of the other women nudged Mrs. Baer with her elbow. "Now, Agnes, you're embarrassing her."

Behind her, the heavyset man scoffed. "She should be embarrassed. She shot our son."

Elizabeth's eyes widened. "Ben. . .Mr. Heywood is your son?"

"Indeed he is," Mrs. Baer said with another emphatic nod of the head.

"I'm Ben's mother too," said the woman next to her with a thump of her cane. As an afterthought, she added, "I'm Mrs. Norton."

"And you can call me Mrs. Edwards," added the small birdlike woman. "I'm also Ben's mother."

Elizabeth stared at the three women. "All three of you?"

Mrs. Baer indicated the men with a wave of her hand. "And these are Ben's fathers," she said, introducing them by name.

The man she now knew was Mr. Edwards met her gaze with a scowl. Dressed in a frock coat and matching trousers, he looked important, like a banker or politician. "What do you have to say for yourself, young lady?" he asked.

"I–it was an a–accident," Elizabeth stammered. "I didn't mean for the gun to go off."

"You didn't mention a gun in your letters," Mrs. Norton said, sounding peeved.

"You read my letters?" Elizabeth gasped.

"Well of course we read your letters," Mrs. Baer said, as if they were talking about something as innocuous as the weather. "You didn't think we'd allow our son to marry a *complete* stranger, did you?"

Elizabeth didn't know what to think.

Mr. Baer threw up his hands. "I told you that whole catalogue business was a mistake. Just like coming here was."

Mr. Edwards shot him a look of exasperation before turning his gaze to Elizabeth. "You shot our son, and I aim to find out what you intend to do about it."

Elizabeth winced at the tone of his voice. She wasn't sure what he was asking of her. She had no money. She didn't even have a dowry. "Like I said, it was an accident."

Mrs. Norton tutted. "I don't know how you can shoot a man by accident." She sniffed. "Don't you have to physically point a gun or something?"

Elizabeth explained the stories she'd heard back home about the Wild West. "So, you see, when your son stopped the stage, I thought—"

"Time's up," the sheriff called from the doorway.

"We're not finished," Mrs. Baer said.

"We're finished," her husband said, taking her by the arm and practically dragging her out of the cell room.

Mrs. Baer didn't go quietly, and her protests could be heard even after the three couples had left the building.

Elizabeth covered her face with her hands, her mind in a muddle. What a fine pickle she was in, and she didn't have the slightest idea what to do about it.

Prickly Pear had turned out to be a strange place in more ways than one. Not only did it lack a full-time judge, but it also had some odd ideas about family. How does someone come to have *six* parents?

She was still pondering this question moments later when a male voice floated into her consciousness.

Someone else had entered the sheriff's office, and he sounded just as determined as the people who had claimed to be Ben's parents. A quick glance through the open door made her catch her breath. The man heading her way was not only the man she'd come all this way to wed. He was also the man she'd shot.

She gripped the iron bars and braced herself for his wrath.

❧ Chapter 4 ❧

Ben Heywood had visited many clients and would-be clients in jail, but never had he witnessed a more fetching sight behind bars than Miss Colton.

It was hard to imagine that such a small, delicate woman could cause him so much trouble. She didn't look large enough to hurt a fly, let alone bring down his six-foot-tall frame. She barely came up to his shoulders, and her waist appeared small enough to circle with his hands.

Hair the color of polished mahogany was caught up in a neat bun, and little tendrils curled around her full, rosy cheeks. Today her eyes were more violet than blue. She even smelled good—like lavender, and it offered a welcome relief from the normal musty jailhouse smell that usually greeted him whenever he visited a client.

"I'm Ben Heywood," he said, though judging by the wary look

on her face no introduction had been necessary. "I understand you're without a lawyer."

She glanced at his arm in a sling and lowered her lush lashes beneath his steady gaze. "The sheriff said that Mr. Livingstone is gone till the end of next week."

"I'm aware of that." He'd wanted to break the bad news without causing alarm, but there was no way around it. "The judge is due in town Monday and will only be here for a couple of days. There's no telling when he'll be back. Could be as long as a month."

Miss Colton's lashes flew up and her eyes rounded in alarm. "You m—mean, I might have to stay here for a month?" she stammered.

He nodded. "Unless Livingstone comes home early, though I doubt he will." He let that sink in a moment before adding, "Meanwhile, I'll be happy to represent you in his absence. That is, if you have no objection."

Her fine eyebrows drew together in a frown. "The judge might object to the victim representing the accused," she said.

"The judge won't be the problem," he said. He shuddered to think what his parents would say should he represent the woman who'd shot him. But Miss Colton appeared to be as much a victim of circumstances as he was, and he felt compelled to help her.

Her gaze clung to his. "I want you to know I never meant to harm you," she said softly. "The gun went off by accident."

He studied her for a moment. "Didn't anyone ever tell you not to point a loaded gun unless you mean to shoot?"

She lifted her chin and, despite her small size, looked like a force to be reckoned with. "Oh, I meant to shoot, all right," she said. "But only if you were worth shooting."

He regarded her with tilted head. "And what would have made me worth shooting?" he asked.

"If you intended to rob me or do me bodily harm." Beseeching him, she continued. "Before coming to Texas, I'd heard awful tales about outlaws, and I had no idea who you were."

Now that he thought about it, his stopping the stage must have seemed scary to a woman traveling alone. "I had no intention of harming you. I stopped the stage to tell you there had been a terrible mistake."

"A mistake?"

He rubbed his chin as he considered how to answer her. "I had no prior knowledge that my mothers had arranged for us to wed."

She stared at him. "Mothers? So those couples who came to visit me. . . ?"

He stiffened. "They were here?"

She nodded, and anger flared inside him. He should have known his parents wouldn't leave well enough alone. "My mothers took it upon themselves to contact a marriage broker without my knowledge."

She frowned. "Are. . .are you saying that you didn't write to me?" she asked, her voice incredulous.

"Write to you? No. I didn't even know about you until the day you were scheduled to arrive." He clenched his jaw. "It seems like we were both duped."

Her mouth fell open and she appeared to be speechless.

"I'm just grateful you're such a bad shot," he said, breaking the silence and hoping to relieve the tension that stretched between them as well. "So, what do you say? Do you want my help, or don't you?"

A shadow of indecision fleeted across her forehead. "Why. . .why would you want to help me?" she asked.

He arched an eyebrow. "Why? Because I blame my mothers for what happened. They meant no harm but. . ." Torn between loyalty to the three women who had loved and cared for him through the years and the need to help a woman whose trouble they'd caused, he let out his breath. "I guess you could say they were trying to help."

She stared at him with blazing eyes. "Put their noses where they don't belong is more like it," she muttered.

She had every right to be angry. He was angry too. In the past his parents' attempts to run his life had been nothing more than a nuisance. But this time was different. Their actions almost cost him his life and had landed a young woman in jail.

"So, what do you say?" he asked. "Do you want me to represent you?"

She chewed on the question a moment before asking, "What exactly does that mean? I've never been arrested before, and I don't know how the legal system works here in Texas."

He couldn't blame her for being cautious. "For starters," he began slowly, "I'll post your bail, but you won't be able to leave town until you've appeared before the judge. I'll ask him to drop the charges."

"You can do that?" she asked.

Ben hesitated a moment before answering. Judge Riley wasn't known for leniency, not even when children were involved, but there was no sense worrying her more than she already was.

"I can," he said. "Meanwhile, you can stay at the hotel until then."

She considered his offer with a worried frown. "As I wrote in my letters, I have very modest means."

He discounted her concern with a wave of his hand. "I'll take care of any expenses," he said. It was the least he could do to make up for the trouble his parents had caused.

Rather than relieve her mind, his offer seemed to cause her more consternation. "I won't be able to pay you back," she said, her cheeks turning red. "That is, unless I get a job with the newspaper."

He arched an eyebrow. It suddenly occurred to him that he'd offered to help someone he knew nothing about. "You're a journalist?" he asked.

She shook her head. "An artist. I drew illustrations for the *Dayton Press*."

"That's impressive," he said and meant it. It seemed that Miss Colton was full of surprises. He doubted that the *Prickly Pear Gazette* was progressive enough to use illustrations, but he kept the thought to himself. "You don't have to pay me back," he said instead.

Rather than relieve her mind, his generosity only made her more suspicious. "How do I know you aren't trying to get back at me for shooting you?"

It was a fair question. Had he been in her shoes, he might have wondered the same thing. "As I told you, I blame my parents. Not you." He tilted his head. "So, what do you say?"

"I'm thinking."

Feeling he was about to drown in the depths of her expressive blue eyes, he asked, "Do you want me to come back later?"

"Yes, no, I mean. . ." Her eyes narrowed as she studied him, her face still filled with distrust.

"I mean you no harm," he said. "My only motive is to right a wrong. Nothing more."

He couldn't tell by her face if she believed him, but after much thought she relented. "I'd be most grateful for any help you can give me."

He nodded. "Stay here," he said, as if she had a choice. Walking away from her cell, he had a feeling that he'd taken on more than he'd bargained for.

❧ Chapter 5 ❧

Elizabeth gripped the iron bars and watched Ben Heywood walk away with long purposeful strides. He looked like a man on a mission, a man who knew how to get things done. A man not easily swayed.

Watching him, she wondered how she could have mistaken him for an outlaw.

He was taller than she'd recalled by at least several inches, and his dark hair was shorter than it had been in his photograph but still neatly combed to the side. He also had the bluest eyes and longest lashes she'd ever seen on a man. For someone who had been recently shot, he looked surprisingly sturdy and strong. Surprisingly healthy.

Since he matched the likeness in his photograph, his good looks came as no surprise. But the question was not if he was the most handsome man she'd ever set eyes on. The question was, could she trust him?

She'd thought she knew him through his letters and was shocked to learn he'd not written them. The letters she had read by candlelight and carried close to her heart had been written by his mothers. That made him a stranger in more ways than one, and she could no longer think of him as Ben, but rather Mr. Heywood.

She couldn't hear all that was being said, but the expression on the sheriff's face told her that he wasn't happy with Mr. Heywood's decision to represent her. Still, after much discussion, Farley walked into the cell room, keys jingling, and unlocked her cell.

"This ain't gonna go over well with your parents," he said. "Or the town."

Mr. Heywood shrugged off the sheriff's comment. "Let me worry about that." He grabbed one of her two valises. "I'll come back later for the other one," he said.

"Thank you, but I can manage it." Elizabeth didn't want to put him out any more than she already had. Lighter in weight than the first valise, the second travel case held her wedding trousseau, which she now had no use for.

Without another word, Mr. Heywood led the way out of the cell, through the sheriff's office, and outside.

Blinking against the glaring sun, Elizabeth hurried to keep up with his long strides while lugging her valise by her side.

Walking with Mr. Heywood was like walking with President Cleveland or someone of equal importance. Everyone they passed stopped to inquire about his arm and cast curious glances at Elizabeth. Greeting each person with a polite nod, he apologized for not having time to talk and kept going.

"Thank you," she said catching up to him when he stopped at the street corner to wait for a horse and wagon to pass.

"I haven't done anything yet," he said, as if getting her out of jail or protecting her identity as the woman who'd shot him from curious onlookers was no big deal.

He led her across the street to the Prickly Pear Hotel. It was still morning and the lobby was empty when they entered. Mr. Heywood strode up to the reception counter and asked for a private room.

The clerk looked up from his newspaper and shook his balding head. "No private rooms left," he drawled with a glance at the board of keys. "But Room 201 still has two unoccupied beds."

"I only need one bed," Mr. Heywood said. "And it's for the lady."

The clerk squinted up at Elizabeth. "If she doesn't mind sharing a room with two men, it's hers."

"Much obliged," Mr. Heywood said, "but we'll pass." With that, he spun around and led the way back outside.

"Now what?" Elizabeth asked, hurrying to catch up to him.

"We'll try Mrs. Hampton's boardinghouse."

Located two blocks from the hotel, the boardinghouse was a two-story house with gabled roof. An elderly woman answered the door to Mr. Heywood's knock, and her face lit up as she greeted him with a warm smile.

"Ben, how nice to see you!" The smile died when he told her what he wanted.

Rheumy eyes regarded him through a lorgnette. "Colton, Colton," she muttered to herself as if trying to recall where she'd last heard the name. Finally, a light dawned, and she stared at Elizabeth aghast. "You're the woman who shot him!" She shifted her gaze to Mr. Heywood. "Why would you want to help someone who tried to kill you?"

"Miss Colton claims it was an accident." He glanced at Elizabeth before adding, "And I believe her."

Elizabeth felt something catch in her throat. He believed her? Ben Heywood believed her? For the first time since coming to Prickly Pear, she didn't feel quite alone. It had been wrong of her to suspect him of revenge when apparently all he wanted to do was help her.

Mrs. Hampton broke into her thoughts with a harrumph. "That's not what your parents said." She lifted her lorgnette and stared straight at Elizabeth. "You should be ashamed of yourself, young lady. Shooting a good man like Ben."

"Oh, but I didn't mean—" Elizabeth began, but Mrs. Hampton would have none of it and slammed the door shut in their faces.

Turning away from the door, Mr. Heywood's gaze met hers, his eyes filled with the soft lights of sympathy. "Sorry," he said.

Biting back tears, Elizabeth forced a smile. "Now what?"

"We'll try the other two boardinghouses in town." Without another word, he started down the walkway.

When they had no better luck at procuring a room at the second boardinghouse, Mr. Heywood checked his pocket watch. "It's noon. Let's get something to eat."

Moments later they found a corner table at the Prickly Pear Restaurant. After quickly perusing the bill of fare, Elizabeth looked up to find Mr. Heywood's gaze on her.

"Do you really believe what I said?" she asked. "About shooting you by accident, I mean?"

Mr. Heywood folded his bill of fare and set it on the table. "Doesn't matter what I think. All that matters is what the judge will think. So far I haven't done a very good job of persuading anyone of your innocence."

Elizabeth chewed on her bottom lip and suddenly lost her appetite.

The restaurant proprietor made a big fuss over Mr. Heywood when she came to take their order. "And who do we have here?" she asked, with a pointed look at Elizabeth.

"This is Miss Colton," Mr. Heywood said.

"Colton?" The woman's eyes widened. "Isn't this the woman who—?"

"I'll have the beef stew," he said abruptly, his expression dark and forbidding.

To her credit, the owner took the hint and wrote down their order without further comment.

"Thank you," Elizabeth said, after the proprietor had left.

Mr. Heywood studied her. "Like I said, you have nothing to thank me for."

She rearranged her utensils and put her napkin in her lap. "You got me out of jail."

"That was the easy part." He reached for a sourdough roll. "The hard part will be keeping you out of jail."

The thought of going back to that horrible place made Elizabeth shudder. Pushing the thought aside, she studied him as carefully as he appeared to be studying her. "How did you come to have three sets of parents?" she asked.

He finished buttering his roll before replying. "As an infant, I was abandoned on the church steps."

"That's awful," she said.

He shrugged. "Fortunately, I don't remember any of it. All I know is that the town has been good to me. So have my parents."

"And you don't know who your real parents are?"

He shook his head. "This was a main stagecoach stop. Still is, even with the train. We think I was left by someone out of the area."

She considered that a moment. "Your name, Heywood. . ."

He set his knife aside. "I guess you're wondering how I got that name. My adoptive parents couldn't agree on which of their surnames to give me. So they named me Heywood, after the manufacturer of the baby carriage they found me in."

She laughed. She couldn't help it. But instead of looking annoyed or offended, he laughed too, and his sudden mirth made her heart do a flip-flop. She had always been aware of his good looks, but never more so than now.

"Not too many babies named after their baby carriage." She tapped her chin. "Let me guess. Your first name. Ben. . .you were named after a baby rattle. Am I right?"

"Not quite," he said, the humor still in his eyes.

"A teething ring?"

He dimpled, and his crooked smile made her heart pound a second time. "My parents' last names are Baer, Edwards, and Norton. The first initials of their names spells Ben."

"Ah." Having lost her own parents at a young age, Elizabeth was both intrigued and envious of his parental excesses. "What about living arrangements?" she asked. When he didn't answer right away, she sat back in her chair. "Don't tell me you all live together?"

"Hardly," he said. "Growing up, I spent a week at a time at each house. Every Friday I had to pack up and move."

"That must have been hard," she said. She still remembered how difficult it was to move into her aunt's house after her parents had died.

He shrugged. "At the time, I didn't know any better. Now I have a place of my own over the gunsmith shop." He chuckled. "Funny thing though. Every Friday I have the urge to pack up my things."

She laughed.

He regarded her thoughtfully for a moment, his eyes crinkling at the corners. "But enough about me. I'm curious. Why would you take a chance on traveling all the way out here to marry a stranger? What's wrong with the men in Ohio?"

"Nothing's wrong with them," she said. "Except that most of the eligible bachelors have left for the West." She paused for a moment. "What about the women here? Why did your parents decide to send away for a bride?"

"Long story," he said, his voice and manner putting an end to the subject. "What about your parents? Did they agree to you traveling out here alone?"

She hesitated. Even after all these years, it still hurt to talk about her loss. "They both died during a yellow fever epidemic," she said. "I was raised by my widowed aunt until she passed."

"No other family? Siblings?"

She shook her head. "No."

His eyes filled with sympathy. "It can't be easy. A woman alone."

She dipped her head in a wooden nod. It hadn't been easy. What little money she was able to earn with her artwork barely covered her expenses. "What's going to happen next?" she asked.

"I'll try to get the judge to drop the charges. If that doesn't work, you'll appear before him and plead not guilty. If things go right, you'll be free to go home."

She knew he was trying to make her feel better, but there was nothing for her back in Dayton and even less for her here in Prickly Pear. Her future looked bleak indeed. "And if things don't go right?" she asked.

"Let's hope they do," he said just as their food arrived.

After leaving the restaurant, Mr. Heywood led the way to the third and last boardinghouse in town. A matronly woman with cotton-white hair and bright rosy cheeks opened the door. Upon seeing Mr. Heywood, her face lit up.

After introducing Mrs. Culpepper to Elizabeth, he explained the need for a room, using enough charm to talk the bark off a tree.

Since the boardinghouse owner couldn't seem to remember anything for more than a moment or two, he had to repeat himself several times.

"So what happened to your arm?" Mrs. Culpepper asked.

"I had a little accident," he said.

Mrs. Culpepper tutted. "Oh, that's too bad," she said, and her gaze drifted away as if distracted by something only she could see.

Mr. Heywood cleared his voice. "About that room. . ."

Seemingly startled by his voice, Mrs. Culpepper's hands fluttered to her side. "Oh yes, you want a room."

"Not for me," he explained again, his voice and manner patient. "For Miss Colton here. You said you have a room available."

Mrs. Culpepper looked momentarily flustered but then

nodded. "Of course." This time she invited them into the house and led the way up the stairs to the second floor. She flung open the first of two doors, startling a man dressed in his long johns, before finding the room she was looking for.

"Oh, it's lovely," Elizabeth said, setting down her valise. The walls were painted a bright yellow, and the canopy bed was piled high with pillows. After spending three days in that horrible jail cell, the room seemed like heaven.

Mr. Heywood placed her traveling bag next to the chifforobe and tugged on the brim of his hat. "I'll leave you to get settled," he said.

Elizabeth moistened her lips. "Thank you." Though she'd only known him for a short time, she hated seeing him go.

"I'll see you out, Ben," Mrs. Culpepper said in her British accent. She started for the door. "So tell me, luv," she asked again. "What happened to your arm?"

Chapter 6

Elizabeth met Mr. Heywood the next day at his office. He rose from his desk to greet her and took her hand in his, sending warm ripples down her spine.

"Are you okay?" he asked. "Is Mrs. Culpepper treating you right?"

"Yes, thank you," she said.

He released her hand and indicated a leather chair. "Have a seat."

With a quick glance around, Elizabeth sat and smoothed her skirt. She wore a pretty blue skirt with yellow flowers and matching shirtwaist. The outfit had always been her favorite, but today it felt out of place in a room as serious as this one.

The furniture, including the oversized desk, was made of dark polished wood, and one entire wall was covered with bookshelves. Never had Elizabeth seen so many books in one place.

Mr. Heywood took his seat behind his desk and shuffled through some papers. Though his arm was still in a sling, he looked every bit as serious and polished as his office. "I met with the judge, and I'm sorry to say I was unable to get the charges dropped."

She frowned. "What does that mean, exactly?"

"It means you will appear before him at Monday's hearing."

She moistened her lips. "I've never appeared before a judge."

"You needn't worry. I'll do all the work. The only thing required of you will be to state a plea of not guilty."

"You make it sound so easy."

"Nothing about law is easy," he said.

She leaned forward. "Mr. Heywood—"

"Ben."

"Excuse me?"

"Call me Ben."

She sat back. "Is that the proper way to address one's lawyer?"

"Proper or not, I need you to look relaxed on Monday. Dropping formalities might make you feel less anxious. Nothing says guilt like nerves."

"All right," she said. "Ben it is. But you must call me Elizabeth."

"I'll call you whatever you want. As long it takes that worried look off your face."

She smiled. "I'll do my best."

He studied her. "It won't be easy. The prosecutor will do whatever he can to prove his case."

"But how?" she asked. "What could he possibly say or do to hurt me?"

Ben hesitated as if weighing his words. "He could say you

were a woman. . .scorned. He could say that you shot me simply because I broke off our betrothal."

"But that would be a bald-faced lie," she said, aghast.

"I'm afraid the circumstances of my birth have made the town overly interested in my welfare. For that reason, there are many who might be swayed by the lie."

"I see." Suddenly feeling hot, she pulled her handkerchief out of her purse and dabbed her face.

"There's also been a series of bank robberies in the area," Ben continued. "People are upset, and that's never a good thing, especially before elections. Those running for reelection might want to prove they're cracking down on crime in Prickly Pear. So you might get the brunt of it."

As he continued to outline the possibilities they faced, she suddenly burst out laughing.

Regarding her as if she'd lost her mind, he arched a dark brow. "What's so funny?"

"You told me not to worry," she said, "and then proceeded to tell me all the reasons why I should."

Shaking his head, he laughed too. She liked the hearty sound of it, the deep rich tone. She liked it a lot and could have listened to it all day, but all too soon he grew serious again.

"I just want you to be prepared," he said. "There's no such thing as a good surprise in court."

She smiled politely and stood. "There's always a first time."

❧ Chapter 7 ❧

Ben tried to discourage his parents from being present when Miss Colton made her appearance before the judge. Still, they showed up in full force, along with practically everyone else in town.

Prickly Pear didn't have a courthouse, so the hearing was held at the Jolly Cork Saloon. It was hardly the place for a lady like Miss Colton, let alone his mothers, but Ben had no say in the matter.

Inside, the saloon was packed to capacity, and a throng of spectators crowded outside to peer through the dusty windows and push against the batwing doors.

"I didn't know there would be this many people here," Elizabeth whispered by his side.

He thought she looked especially young and vulnerable today, and more than a little scared.

It was the first time a woman in Prickly Pear was scheduled to appear before the judge. That alone was enough to bring out the crowds. But the fact that the defendant was charged with shooting the town's favorite son made the proceedings that much more newsworthy, and people had traveled from all over the county to watch.

He reached over to cover her tremulous hand with his own. "Hold on," he said softly. "It will soon be over."

Judge Riley entered through a side door behind the bar. Ben rose to his feet and motioned for Elizabeth to do likewise.

With barely a glance at them, the judge took his place behind the bar. His black robe and long pointed nose made him look like a crow sitting on a telegraph wire. Light glancing off his bald head, he stared at the crowd in front of him.

"Quiet," he shouted with a scowl and banged his gavel. He waited for silence before addressing Elizabeth. "You're charged with shooting an unarmed man," he said. "How do you plead?"

"It was an accident," she said.

Ben leaned sideways to whisper in her ear. "Remember what I told you?"

Her blue eyes met his, and her pale cheeks colored slightly. Turning to the judge, she corrected herself. "I plead not guilty."

This brought an immediate response from spectators in the way of hisses and boos.

"Nonsense!" Ma Baer called, pushing her way through the mob. All six of his parents had objected to his defending Miss Colton, but Ma Baer had been the most vocal. "She shot my son clear in the arm," she said in her thick German accent. "Show them, Ben. Show him where she shot you."

Clenching a hand by his side, Ben fought for self-control. As if the judge couldn't see for himself that his arm was in a sling. "Ma, please. Let me handle this." He turned back to the judge. "Yes, Miss Colton shot me, your honor, but, as she told you, it was an accident."

The judge stared down his pointed nose. "Accident or not, I want to hear what her lawyer has to say."

"Mr. Livingstone is out of town," Ben explained. "Meanwhile, I'm representing Miss Colton."

Judge Riley shook his head. "You can't represent her. You're the victim."

"Right now, I just want to be known as her legal counsel."

The judge scoffed. "First you asked me to drop the charges. Now you're acting as her legal counsel. That tells me the bullet did more than graze your arm. It looks like it scrambled your brains." He picked up his gavel and gave the bar another good whack. "This case is recessed until Mr. Livingstone's return." Ignoring the cries of protest from spectators, the judge peered at Miss Colton with a stern expression and wagged his finger. "Don't leave town."

❧ Chapter 8 ❧

The following morning, Elizabeth sat in her room at the boarding-house with her sketchbook on her lap. Mrs. Culpepper's lush English rose garden reminded Elizabeth of home and was a welcome sight.

She'd intended to sketch a picture of the garden and present it to Mrs. Culpepper as a way of thanking her for renting her a room when no one else would. But instead of the garden, Elizabeth was surprised to find herself absentmindedly sketching a portrait of Ben Heywood.

She drew back and studied the charcoal sketch. She'd captured his likeness from memory down to the crinkly lines around his eyes and mouth, and indented chin. She'd prided herself on having a good eye for detail, but never had she drawn such an accurate picture of someone from memory.

Staring at the sketch, she imagined the feel of his mouth on hers. She'd been kissed only twice. Once at a dance under the watchful eye of a chaperone, and once at the county fair. Neither kiss had left much of an impression. Somehow she knew that wouldn't be true of Ben's kisses.

Not sure what to make of her sudden obsession with Ben Heywood, she stashed her art supplies and sketchbook in her valise.

The smell of bacon wafted through her open window from the kitchen below. Stomach growling, she left the room.

Two people were already seated at the long oak table in the dining room. Mrs. Culpepper sat opposite the boarder who had been caught in his long johns.

A little boy who looked no older than four sat on the floor playing with his blocks.

Mrs. Culpepper looked up as Elizabeth entered. "Sorry, luv. I don't have any rooms available."

Elizabeth introduced herself again. "I already have a room, remember? Ben Heywood brought me here."

Ben's name brought a smile to the old woman's face. "You know Ben?" she asked.

"Yes." Elizabeth stooped to place a block on top of the little boy's tower, earning a smile in return. Dressed in knee-length pants, the child had blond hair and big blue eyes.

"And who do we have here?" she asked.

"His name is Luke, and he's my grandson," Mrs. Culpepper said, her face and voice filled with pride. "His mum is staying here for a couple of days."

"Hello, Luke." Elizabeth stooped to pick up a second block and handed it to him before helping herself to the generous display of eggs, bacon, and sweet rolls on the sideboard. Balancing her plate in one hand and a cup of coffee in the other, she sat across from the male lodger.

"What did you say your name was again?" Mrs. Culpepper asked.

"Elizabeth," she said. "Elizabeth Colton."

Mr. Long Johns lowered his newspaper. He had a bushy mustache and sideburns and wore his long hair tied back at his neck. His eyes grew round behind his thick-rimmed glasses as he studied her. "It says here that an Elizabeth Colton tried to kill Ben."

Miss Culpepper gasped. "You killed Ben?"

"Tried to kill," Mr. Long Johns said. "Tried."

They both stared at her. "I would never. . ." Elizabeth cleared her throat. "It was an accident."

"That's not what it says here." Mr. Long Johns tapped his newspaper with his finger and read the section aloud.

The editorial left little doubt as to her guilt and called for her immediate and swift punishment.

Elizabeth's temper flared. "That's. . .that's terrible," she stammered. The writer hadn't even given her the benefit of the doubt.

"I'll say!" Mrs. Culpepper exclaimed, tutting. "Anyone who tried to kill our dear Ben should hang." The horrified look on her face lasted for only as long as her memory, and she soon returned to her plate of bacon and eggs as if no such discussion had occurred.

Following her lead, Mr. Long Johns shrugged and returned to his paper, leaving Elizabeth to stew in silence. She no longer felt like eating. Instead, she pushed her plate away and said a silent prayer. *Oh God, what if my new lawyer can't save me? What do I do then?*

Mrs. Culpepper looked up from her plate, a puzzled look on her face. "Who are you, again, luv?"

Elizabeth didn't have a chance to answer before little Luke looked up from his building blocks and lisped, "Her name is Lithabeth Coton, and she twied to kill Ben."

❧ Chapter 9 ❧

Ben arrived at Elizabeth's boardinghouse later that morning with the news that Livingstone had returned to town early and was waiting to see her.

"I was able to reach him by telegram," Ben explained, "and he arrived on the morning train." When she failed to respond, he arched a brow. "I thought you'd be happy to hear that."

She thrust the morning newspaper at him. "Have you read this?"

Sighing, he took the paper in hand and tossed it on an upholstered chair. "Elizabeth—"

"They want me to hang," she said, her voice breaking. Tears sprang to her eyes and trickled down her cheeks.

He reached out with his good arm and pulled her close. Careful not to press against his injured arm, she laid her head on his chest and sobbed. Her tears soaked his shirt, and his manly scent filled her head. He let her cry it out before dabbing at her cheeks with his handkerchief.

"Nothing's going to happen to you," he said softly. "I won't let it."

She wanted so much to believe him, but could one man alone—even one as popular as Ben—really fight an entire town?

She pulled away from him, but only so she could gain control of her senses.

"Are you all right?" he asked.

"Yes. . .I'm sorry. It's not like me to—"

"Don't apologize," he said. "Anyone in your shoes would be upset." The tall clock in the corner chimed the hour. With a glance at it, he tossed a nod at the door. "We'd better get going. I want you to meet with Livingstone before facing the judge again."

"Give me a moment," she said.

Before she left the room, Mrs. Culpepper entered, her face melting like butter upon seeing Ben. "What happened to your arm?"

While Ben explained, Elizabeth ran upstairs to fetch her bonnet, gloves, and purse, stopping only long enough to say a quick prayer.

Livingstone's office was only a block away from the boardinghouse, but they were forced to take the long way around to avoid Ben's many curious friends and acquaintances.

They finally arrived at their destination. Bookended by the undertaker on one side and the feed shop on the other, the modest adobe office was offset by an impressive sign reading J. A. LIVINGSTONE: ATTORNEY AND COUNSELOR AT LAW.

Ben hustled her inside. After locking the door and drawing the window shades closed, he made the introductions. He then stood at the back of the cramped room. Elizabeth sat in the chair facing Livingstone's desk and waited while he perused her file.

Livingstone was dressed in dark trousers and white shirt, the sleeves rolled up to his elbows. Hair the color of black shoe dye was brushed back from a widow's peak.

Elizabeth didn't have a good feeling about him. He just didn't seem as forceful or as commanding as Ben Heywood. Nor did he seem to have Ben's confidence in her innocence.

As if he guessed her thoughts, Livingstone set the file aside. Folding his hands on his desk, he regarded her with a frown that made his blunt mustache twitch.

"If you'd shot anyone else, I could get you off like that," he said, snapping his fingers. "But Heywood. . ." He sat back in his chair and rubbed his chin. "And the editorial in this morning's paper didn't help."

Reminded of the harsh words used against her in the *Prickly Pear Gazette*, Elizabeth felt a searing pain in her heart. Of all the people she had to shoot, why did it have to be the town's favorite son?

Ben moved to the side of her chair. "As I explained, Miss Colton shot me by accident."

"So you said." Livingstone shuffled the papers on his desk. "Tell me again how the. . .incident occurred."

Ben shrugged in exasperation. "My mothers sent away for a mail-order bride without my knowledge." He went on to explain how he'd stopped the stagecoach. "I was afraid that once Miss Colton arrived in town, my parents would overwhelm her, and she wouldn't know what hit her."

Livingstone checked his notes. "Okay, so you opened the stage door, and she fired her gun."

"By *accident*," Elizabeth said, emphasizing the word. "I thought he was a bandit out to do me harm."

"By accident," Livingstone repeated, underlining something on his writing tablet.

"I'd heard a lot of scary stories about outlaws," Elizabeth explained. "A woman alone can't be too careful."

Ben nodded. "That's got to be her defense."

"Yes, but it may not be enough." Livingstone stuck his pen in the penholder and steepled his hands beneath his chin. "As I'm sure you know, it's gonna be hard to convince the townsfolk of Miss Colton's innocence."

Ben made an impatient gesture with his good arm. "I don't care a fig what the public thinks."

Livingstone pushed out his breath with a whooshing sound. "You know as well as I do the judge's opinion can be swayed by public opinion."

Elizabeth looked from one man's grave face to the other, and she felt what little hope she had fade away. "So, what do we do?"

The two men exchanged a glance. "We pray for a miracle," Livingstone said. "That's pretty much all we can do."

Ben hardly slept the night before Elizabeth was due in court. He couldn't help it. He felt partly responsible for what had happened.

He didn't doubt that Livingstone would do his best to plead Elizabeth's case, but a lawyer could only do so much. And with the whole town against her, things sure as blazes didn't look good.

Sitting on the edge of his bed, he rubbed his forehead and tried to think. But a vision of Elizabeth's big blue eyes and bright, pretty smile kept coming to mind. He remembered all too clearly how she'd felt when he held her, her head against his chest. Even now he could smell the faint scent of her perfume, as if it had become a permanent part of him.

He grimaced. What was wrong with him? It wasn't like him to obsess over a woman.

He just wished he had a better feeling about the outcome of her case. It didn't help that she was a stranger in town. The citizens of Prickly Pear tended to look after their own. Livingstone was right; nothing short of a miracle would save her.

Closing his eyes, he thought of all possible legal defenses he could and discarded them one by one.

Finally, he did what he always did when a task seemed impossible: he prayed for help. *God, I know there's got to be a way to save Elizabeth, but I need You to lead the way.*

After taking care of his morning ablutions and dressing in his usual dark trousers and frock coat, he donned his wide-brimmed hat and made himself a quick cup of coffee. Anxious to talk to Livingstone and discuss possible defenses, he grabbed his attaché case and left his apartment over the gunsmith shop without bothering with breakfast.

The sound of church bells filled the air as he stepped outside, and the street was lined with revelers.

Stopping in his tracks, he craned his neck to see over the heads of the crowd. A horse-drawn carriage headed his way, carrying a newlywed couple. The groom was the mayor's son, and Ben remembered with a start that he had been invited to the wedding, along with what looked like half the town.

Cheers rose as the carriage passed by and the couple waved to their well-wishers. Then something strange happened. Something totally unexpected. Ben caught a glimpse of the bride, and for one crazy moment in time, he imagined that she was Elizabeth.

Blinking, he shook the vision away. With a clearer head, he realized the dark-haired bride looked nothing like Elizabeth. Then why. . . ?

Irritated by such thoughts and even more annoyed that the wedding had held him up, Ben headed for Livingstone's office on foot, only to find he was too late. The office was closed and a sign in the window read IN COURT.

❧ Chapter 10 ❧

Elizabeth was seated in the front row of the Jolly Cork Saloon. Glancing at the hostile crowd behind her, she felt very much alone and afraid.

Livingstone did his best to reassure her, but nothing he said had eased the fear in her heart or stilled the butterflies in her stomach.

Even Ben's arrival couldn't do that. Still, for some reason, his presence and reassuring smile did make her feel less alone.

He sat next to her and leaned over to talk to Livingstone. "I thought court wasn't supposed to start till eleven," he said, his voice low.

Seated on the other side of Elizabeth, Livingstone whispered back. "The judge has been called out of town and wanted to hear the case before leaving. I didn't have time to contact you."

Both men fell silent and rose to their feet when the judge

entered the saloon and took his place behind the bar. "This court is now in session," he said with a bang of his gavel. He peered over the top of his spectacles at the prosecutor. "What say you, Mr. Hamilton?"

Hamilton rose from his seat and did his best to persuade the judge of Elizabeth's guilt. "Don't let this young woman's appearance fool you," he said, his voice booming over the hushed crowd. "Behind that pretty face is a woman who was furious at Ben Heywood for refusing to marry her."

"Objection," Livingstone said, and was quickly overruled.

The prosecutor kept going. Mincing no words, he put Elizabeth in the same league as the outlaw Belle Starr.

Elizabeth glanced at Ben's profile but couldn't tell from his rigid expression what he was thinking.

She turned to Livingstone. "Nothing he's said is true," she whispered.

"Shhh," Livingstone said. "We'll have our turn."

Livingstone was finally allowed to get up and speak. Elizabeth listened with growing dismay. His defense of her seemed mild compared to the vigorous case staged by the prosecutor. But that wasn't the only problem. He kept getting shouted down by spectators.

This forced the judge to bang his gavel repeatedly and yell, "Order in the court," but his efforts to control the crowd were futile. It was only after Livingstone called Ben as a witness that the room grew silent.

In a low and controlled voice, Ben asked the court to imagine how it must have felt for a young woman traveling alone to a strange new place. "Imagine the stories she must have heard about the Wild West," he said.

He cited the recent crime spree committed by the Madison gang as an example. "Their robberies have been covered in newspapers across the country. Can you blame Miss Colton for fearing for her life?"

Elizabeth gazed about the room as he spoke. She couldn't tell by the passive expressions if anything Ben said had changed anyone's mind, but at least they were listening.

After Ben finished his statement, one of his fathers—Elizabeth didn't remember which one—jumped up. "That's my boy," he exclaimed. Thumbing his suspenders, he added, "Always willing to give people the benefit of the doubt."

One of Ben's mothers frowned beneath a tall hat that looked about to topple. "*Harrumph!* If you ask me, there's no doubt to give," she said in a German accent. "Everyone knows the woman shot him."

Ben tried to silence his mother. "Ma Baer, please. . ."

His voice was drowned out by someone yelling from the back of the room. "If she wasn't a woman, she would have already swung from the gallows for shootin' an unarmed man."

"That's right," shouted another. "And Ben deserves justice. We all do."

This brought nods and shouts of approval, and not even the judge's gavel could restore order.

Elizabeth stared at the enraged faces around her and bit back tears. Clutching her hands to her chest, she closed her eyes. *Where are You, God? Where are You?*

Aware of a sudden silence, she opened her eyes. Ben was once again addressing the crowd, his voice so quiet people had to lean forward to catch his every word.

"I wish to thank you all for your concern on my behalf," he said. "I also thank you for the consideration and care you've shown me through the years. I especially want to thank my parents."

His statement brought vigorous applause from the crowd, and Ma Baer clapped so hard her hat fell over her eyes.

Ben waited for the applause to die down before stating how lucky he felt at having been left as an infant in a town like Prickly Pear. He went on to talk about his growing-up years and how everyone had watched over him.

"I couldn't get away with anything," he said to amused laughter.

The judge gave an impatient bang of his gavel. "We are here to determine Miss Colton's guilt or innocence. You can save the trip down memory lane for another time."

"I apologize, Your Honor," Ben said. "I just have one more small statement to make."

The judge made a face. "Well, get on with it so we can get back to business."

"Much obliged, Your Honor," Ben said, and sought Elizabeth's gaze. "As I stand before you today, I ask that the same kind regard you've shown me through the years be extended to Miss Colton, whom I hope to make my bride."

A collective gasp rose from the stunned spectators. Elizabeth's mouth fell open and her breath rushed out of her. Had she really heard what she'd thought she'd heard?

Ben froze, his face mirroring her own shock. The tense silence seemed to stretch unbearably long before the room came alive again with broken murmurs. With a start, Ben shook his head and cleared his throat.

"That is, if Miss Colton will kindly do me the honor of agreeing to be my wife."

Before Elizabeth could find her voice, Ma Baer jumped up from her seat. "Of course she'll agree," she shouted. Her tall feathered hat teetered from side to side as she made her way to the front and threw her arms around her son. "She'd be crazy to turn you down."

Following her lead, others murmured in agreement and burst out in applause. Before the judge could declare his decision, the crowd moved in to congratulate the couple.

Ben dropped down on one knee in front of Elizabeth and took her hand. "What do you say?" He had to raise his voice to be heard. "Will you marry me?"

Elizabeth stared at him and glanced at the well-wishers in bewilderment. Apparently all was forgiven when marriage was involved. "I—"

Before she could get the rest of her words out, the judge banged his gavel.

"Case dismissed," he called out, but hardly anyone could hear him amid the cheers.

❧ Chapter 11 ❧

The well-wishers followed Ben and Elizabeth down Main Street, his three mothers in the lead.

When it appeared that their supporters had no intention of leaving them alone, Ben took Elizabeth by the hand and pulled her into the gunsmith shop. With a wave at the owner behind the counter, Ben led her through the storeroom and out the back door.

Giggling like two schoolchildren, they raced up the alley and didn't stop till they reached Mrs. Culpepper's boardinghouse.

Hand on her chest, Elizabeth collapsed on the steps of the porch and tried to catch her breath.

"You okay?" Ben asked, seating himself by her side.

She studied him and wondered how, after everything that had happened that day, he could ask such a question. "That was some escape."

He chuckled. "When you live in a town like this, you learn all the tricks. It's called self-preservation."

"Doesn't all that attention bother you?" she asked, glancing toward the end of the street to make sure they hadn't been followed.

"It used to," he said. "When I was about twelve or thirteen, I hid in the church to get away from it all. Pastor Carr found me and read some verses from the Bible that said not to be influenced or distracted by others. He told me to keep my eyes on God and His plan for me, and everything else would fade away. I've followed that advice ever since. And you know what? It works."

She moistened her lower lip. "And you think God's plan is for you to marry me?"

Ben locked her in the depths of his eyes and pushed back his hat with a tip of his finger. He hesitated a moment before answering. "I'm convinced it is."

Elizabeth rubbed her hands up and down her crossed arms. "I'd rather go to jail than marry someone who—"

He arched an eyebrow. "Someone who what?"

She dropped her hands to her lap. "Feels sorry for me."

He reared back. "Is that what you think? I feel sorry for you?"

"What else can I think? You had no intention of marrying me. You didn't even know I existed until—"

"I admit I came late to the party, but as much as I hate to admit it, my mothers are right. It's high time I settled down and got myself hitched." He studied her so intensely, Elizabeth felt her cheeks grow hot. "I'm willing if you are."

When she failed to respond, he reached for her hand. "You came out here to marry me. In that regard, nothing has changed."

She pulled her hand away from his, but only so she could think. Something had changed. It was true she'd been willing to settle for a marriage of convenience, but that was before. Now for some reason she couldn't understand, she wanted more.

Much more.

"Marry me," he said. "Like I said, I'm convinced it's what God wants."

Her gaze dropped to her lap. "How do you know that?"

"This morning I asked God to show me the way to help you, and He did."

She chewed on her lower lip. Nothing irritated her more than people using God to justify their acts. "So, what did He do? Send you a telegram?" she asked, her voice edged in sarcasm.

"Not quite," Ben said, his voice as serious as his expression. "This morning when I walked outside, I was held up by a wedding procession. That's why I was late. The bride—"

"What about the bride?" she asked.

He shook his head. "Nothing. I was just annoyed that the wedding made me late. But after thinking about it, I realized the wedding was the answer to my prayer. God showed me the way to save you should all else fail."

She stared at him. "I. . .I don't know what to say." His unexpected proposal had shaken her to the core, and she could hardly think straight. He'd graciously asked her to marry him. Given her circumstances, she'd be a fool to turn him down. Still, she hesitated. As much as she appreciated what he was trying to do, she didn't want him to feel obligated.

"It's God's will," he pressed. "There's no other way to explain it."

Elizabeth stared at him in astonishment. If only she had his faith. "How can you be so sure?"

Ben pressed his hand to his chest. "I feel it here," he said, looking at her with such tenderness it took her breath away. He then pointed to his head. "I know it here."

She'd thought it was God's will for her to come to Texas, but so far things hadn't worked out the way she'd hoped. She lowered her gaze. *Please, God, help me make the right decision.*

Since Ben gazed at her so intently, she smiled. "You said no good surprises ever occurred in court."

"If you think my proposal was a good surprise, can I assume your answer is yes? Or do you need time to think about it? Pray about it?"

After a moment she shook her head and lifted her gaze to his. "I don't need to think about it," she said. "I would be happy to marry you. And. . ." Her heart was pounding so fast, she could hardly speak. "I want you to know that I'll make you the best wife I possibly can."

He grinned. "Well then. . ." He glanced at the deserted street. "I guess we should seal this with a. . ." He paused.

Holding her breath, she felt her heart practically leap out of her chest.

"Handshake," he said.

Her mouth dropped open. "A h–handshake?" she stammered.

He shrugged. "It's the usual way to seal a deal."

Since he appeared to be serious, she offered her hand. He clasped it between his own, sending ripples of warmth up her arm. She recalled how comforting his strong chest had felt and wished she was brave enough to lay her head there again.

"It's been a hard day." He released her hand and stood. "I'll let you get some rest."

She stared up at him in utter confusion. "We just made a decision that will change our lives completely. How can you be so calm?"

He lifted his eyes to the heavens. "I told you. It's God's will."

With that, he turned and walked away, whistling a tune. Watching him, Elizabeth felt an odd combination of disappointment and relief.

Relief because she was now a free woman. She only wished she had been exonerated because of her innocence and not because the town's favorite son had agreed to marry her.

If only his marriage proposal had been by choice. But it hadn't been, and that was the source of her disappointment. Instead, he'd asked her to marry him only to save her from going to jail or worse.

Still, she couldn't deny that marrying Ben was what she'd wanted to do all along. It was the very reason she had traveled here to Texas. Now that she'd met him in person, she considered herself a lucky woman indeed. Maybe, given enough time, he'd come to care for her as she had come to care for him.

She only wished their agreement hadn't been sealed by a cold, businesslike handshake. What she'd wanted, hoped for—hard as it was to admit even to herself—was for Ben to have kissed her.

That would have told her that something existed between them that they could build on. Something special. Something that would last a lifetime.

It was a foolish thought. Theirs wasn't the kind of marriage that required moonlight and roses. Love wasn't involved. How could it be? She hardly knew him. But even as her mind said one thing, her heart said another. It said she knew enough.

❧ Chapter 12 ❧

Ben's proposal was the talk of the town. People were shocked that he would marry the woman who shot him, but no one was more shocked than he. His proposal had simply popped out of his mouth, just like that. In a courtroom no less, where he was known for his eloquence of speech and careful planning.

Never one to act on the spur of the moment, he still couldn't believe he had agreed to marry someone he hardly knew. But it felt right, and that was the strangest thing of all. If it wasn't God's will, what in tarnation was it? And why did the vision of Elizabeth in a bridal gown keep popping into his head?

Well, what was done was done. Now he just wanted to learn everything he could about his future bride, starting with the letters she'd written.

With that in mind, he arrived at the Baer house and found all six of his parents gathered there. He should have known that his upcoming nuptials would require a family meeting.

Ma Baer greeted him with a big hug. "We were just talking about you," she said.

"Really?" he said, as if that was a surprise.

"Yes," Ma Norton said, thumping her cane for emphasis. "We're so excited. We knew that Miss Colton—Elizabeth—was the perfect woman for you."

Pa Baer raised his eyes to the ceiling. "Have you all forgotten that Miss Colton shot a bullet into our son?"

Ma Edwards's waved his question away with a flick of her hand. "I prefer to think of it as Cupid's arrow."

This brought groans from all three of Ben's fathers and smiles from his mothers.

Ben rubbed the back of his neck. It was amazing how quickly his mothers changed their tune about Elizabeth once wedding bells were involved.

"So, what are you doing here?" Ma Baer asked.

"I came to fetch the letters."

Ma Baer looked at the others. "Letters? What letters?"

"The letters that Miss. . .that Elizabeth wrote," he said.

"Oh, of course." Ma Baer moved toward the rolltop desk that occupied a corner of the parlor and pulled a stack of letters out of a drawer. "I think you'll be as impressed with her as we were," she said, handing over the letters.

He glanced at the flowery handwriting on the top envelope. "Much obliged," he said, stepping toward the door.

"Must you leave so soon, son?" Ma Norton asked. "We wanted to discuss your wedding plans."

He grimaced. Anything that required family planning led to

endless discussions and arguments. "Sorry, but I have work to do."

He left all three of his mothers looking disappointed, but it couldn't be helped. He shuddered to think of the elaborate ceremony they no doubt had planned. His mothers seemed to believe that anything worth doing was worth overdoing.

After arriving at his office, he sat at his desk, eager to read what Elizabeth had written before his first client of the day arrived. After reading each page, he studied the sketches included with every letter.

Elizabeth had told him she'd illustrated for her hometown newspaper, but he had no idea how good she was.

Her letters were charming and sometimes even funny, but her sketches of animals, flowers, and children told him more about his future bride than anything she'd written. How odd that none of his parents had mentioned that his soon-to-be wife was an artist.

He folded the last of the letters and slipped it into its envelope. The more he knew about Elizabeth Colton, the more he wanted to know.

For the next couple of weeks, Elizabeth saw Ben every day, but wherever they went they drew a crowd.

On Sundays they attended church together and then shared a family dinner at one of his parents' homes. The only way they could talk in private was to take a carriage ride.

During one moonlit ride she shared an idea she'd been tossing around for a while. Ever since being turned down by the local newspaper, she'd tried to think of a way to earn money. "I'm thinking about giving art lessons," she said.

"Art lessons?" He made it sound like he'd never heard of such a thing.

"You and your family have done enough for me. I can't keep depending on you."

"We're betrothed," Ben said. "It's only right that I look out for you."

"Yes, but—"

"If you want to give art lessons, that's fine with me. But do it because you want to. Not because you feel obligated to me."

Elizabeth felt her heart soften around the edges. Many men objected to a woman working or following a passion, but apparently that wasn't true of Ben. His mothers had described him as traditional in the letters they'd written, but he was apparently more progressive than they knew.

He pulled the carriage over to the side of the road and turned in his seat to face her. Suddenly it felt like the world stood still, and her pulse pounded. Maybe now, at long last, he would put his arms around her and kiss her. Maybe then she would feel like they were really betrothed and not just playing a role.

In the glow of the full moon, Ben's eyes shone like bright new pennies as he held her in his heated gaze. Holding her breath in anticipation and hoping to be crushed in his embrace, Elizabeth moistened her lips and waited.

"I've been meaning to bring this up," he began slowly, "but I wasn't sure you were ready." He cleared his throat. "I think we ought to set a wedding date."

Her breath caught in her throat.

Apparently taking her silence as agreement, he continued, "I was thinking maybe the end of the month or early August." He waited a moment. "So, what do you think?"

"The end of the month sounds good," she said, wishing with all her heart that she felt better about the marriage. Better about his family. Still, she was committed to going through with her plans. The end of the month was only three weeks away, but it gave her ample time to prepare for the simple wedding she'd set her heart on.

With a nod of his head, he took up the reins again. "I'll let Reverend Carr know."

She stared at his profile and tried not to feel hurt that he still hadn't kissed her or showed affection. If marrying Ben really was what God wanted, why did things feel so unsettled between them? Why was she constantly questioning God's will?

❧ Chapter 13 ❧

Elizabeth left her room at the boardinghouse on that hot July day, carrying her mother's wedding gown over her arm.

Two days had passed since she and Ben had set a wedding date, and things had been hectic ever since. Word traveled fast in Prickly Pear. Everywhere they went people had stopped them to inquire about the wedding plans.

The more she knew about Ben, the more she liked, but she wasn't used to all the attention they received. In truth she hated it. Hated how it seemed to be driving a wedge between the two of them. They could hardly have a conversation without someone interrupting, preventing any sort of meaningful discussion between them.

She'd grown up in a small town. After her parents died, it had been just her and her aunt. Living in Prickly Pear was like living in a glass house. It felt like everything she did was on public display, and she wasn't sure she'd ever get used to it.

Still, she'd known what she was getting into when she agreed to marry a man as popular and beloved as Ben. There didn't seem to be any way around it but to learn to live with it.

Sighing, she hurried down the stairs to the parlor where Ben's three mothers waited for her. They had come to help her plan the wedding and had asked to see the gown.

Entering the parlor, she proudly held the wedding gown in front for all to see. Six horrified eyes stared back, and Ma Norton let out a gasp.

Mrs. Baer was the first to break the stunned silence. "B–but it's purple," she exclaimed. "Purple!"

Elizabeth lowered the gown and hugged it close. Actually, the dress was more lilac than purple. "It was my mother's," she explained. "She wore it to marry my papa."

Mrs. Norton held her hand to her chest. "Lordy, who ever heard of getting married in such a color?"

"Who indeed?" Mrs. Baer gasped.

Elizabeth looked from one to the other. "Mama got married during the war. Some brides wore purple to honor a dead soldier."

Even as a little girl, Elizabeth had always wanted to marry in her mother's gown. Not only did she love the beaded bodice, puffy sleeves, and short train, but she loved what the color stood for. Not many brides would buck tradition for such a noble cause.

"Mama wore it in remembrance of her brother who died on the battlefield," she said.

"That's very nice, dearie," Ma Norton said in a placating tone. "And I'm sure the gown means a lot to you."

"Yes, yes it does," Elizabeth said.

Mrs. Norton looked to the other women. "But the war's been over for a long time. . ."

"Yes, yes," Mrs. Baer said with a vigorous nod of her head. "And wouldn't you rather wear something a bit more. . . fashionable?"

Elizabeth blinked. "Fashionable?"

Mrs. Edwards patted Elizabeth's arm. "Ben is a very successful lawyer," she began tentatively. She hesitated as if searching for the right words. "People might not understand why his bride is dressed in something so, so—"

"Purple," Mrs. Baer blurted out, having no apparent need to choose her words.

Mrs. Norton tutted and wrinkled her nose. "And look at the skirt." She stretched the fabric out for all to see. "It's so full you'd have to wear a hoop skirt, and I don't know where you'd find one in this day and age."

"But it's my mother's wedding gown," Elizabeth said, biting back tears. "And I plan to gather the extra fabric in back."

Mrs. Norton shook her head as if she couldn't imagine such a thing. "People around here are what you might call. . ." She looked to the others to supply the needed word.

"Traditional," Mrs. Edwards said.

Mrs. Norton brightened. "Yes, that's right. Traditional. A lawyer can't be seen breaking with tradition."

Elizabeth tried not to let her dismay show. She'd wanted to marry in her mother's gown, but not enough to chance harming Ben's reputation.

Mrs. Edwards patted Elizabeth's arm again. "Don't feel bad.

I'm sure if your mother were alive, she'd understand."

"Of course she would," Mrs. Baer said and, apparently thinking matters had been settled to her satisfaction, slipped on her gloves. "I'll speak to Abigail Stewart tomorrow. Now don't you worry about a thing, you hear? She's a wonderful seamstress and makes all my clothes. She'll know exactly what to make for you."

Elizabeth's gaze drifted from Mrs. Baer's sky-high hat to her dowdy floral frock, and her heart sank.

That night, while having supper with Ben, Elizabeth described the meeting with his mothers. At least she tried to, but she kept getting interrupted.

They were seated at a corner table of the Prickly Pear restaurant where a long line of people stopped to congratulate them on their upcoming nuptials.

Ben patiently thanked each person, and Elizabeth was acutely aware of how charming he was, how handsome. If his height and good looks didn't make him stand out in a crowd, his attire surely did. His arm no longer in a sling, he wore a black frock coat and matching trousers, whereas most of the other men were dressed more casually in canvas pants and checkered shirts.

Doing her best not to show annoyance at the interruptions, Elizabeth smiled and tried not to wilt under the constant attention.

"Sorry," Ben said when the last of the well-wishers had left them to finish their meal in peace. "You were telling me about your wedding gown."

Fearing that they would be interrupted again, Elizabeth got

right to the point. "I wanted to wear the same dress my mama was married in, but your mothers don't approve."

Ben set down his fork and gazed at her with raised eyebrows. "Why wouldn't they approve?"

Elizabeth explained.

"Purple, eh?" he said, dabbing at his mouth with his napkin. He looked more amused than sympathetic.

"The dress means a lot to me," she said.

He studied her for a moment, and the amusement vanished from his eyes. "I'll talk to them."

"No, no, please don't do that." The last thing she wanted was to cause a problem between Ben and his mothers. "They mean well." As much as she hated to think it, maybe they were right. Ben's status in town seemed to require certain standards and considerations.

"Are you sure?" he asked.

She wasn't sure of anything, but still she nodded and blinked back the tears that threatened to undermine her composure. Ben was willing to make concessions for her. The least she could do was meet him halfway.

"You said you wanted to talk to me about something," she said, changing the subject.

Nodding, he placed his napkin on the table. "I thought we should discuss where we'll live after we're married."

She drew in her breath. So much had happened, she hadn't thought much beyond the wedding. Now that she did, the thought of sharing the same roof with him—sharing the same bed—made her heart practically turn over in her chest.

When she failed to respond, he continued. "There's a small

house for sale outside of town. I thought we could ride out tomorrow and have a look. It has two bedrooms, and the parlor is large enough for the piano you always wanted."

Her eyes widened in surprise. "Now how do you know I always wanted a piano?"

He gave her a crooked grin that made her senses spin. "I read your letters," he said. "They were addressed to me, and I thought it was a good way to get to know you better."

Impressed that he'd wanted to read what she'd written, she smiled across the table at him. "What else do you know about me?" she asked.

"Well, let's see." He tapped his chin, drawing her attention to the intriguing indentation there. "I know that you're an artist."

Her breath caught. She loved to draw, but no one had ever called her an artist, and the fact that he did meant a lot. "And?" she asked, her voice choked.

"I know that you like to read and are a terrific cook."

"I never said terrific," she said, though she did know her way around the kitchen.

"Can't a fella read between the lines?" he asked.

"Maybe," she said, smiling. "So, what else?"

"Your letters included sketches of birds and flowers. That tells me you're a nature lover. I also know that your church was important to you, as is your faith in God." He grinned. "You also like the color purple."

"Not bad," she said.

He studied her. "So, what did I write in my letters? Or rather, what did my mothers write?"

She thought for a moment. Oddly enough, she knew more about him now than she had learned from the letters. "I know that you're adored by everyone in this town."

"Not everyone," he said. "If the town prosecutor had his way, your bullet wouldn't have just grazed my arm."

"He sounds like a poor loser," she said.

He shrugged. "What else?" he asked.

"Let's see." She pretended to think. "I know that you're a braggart."

He reared back in his chair. "What?"

"In your letters, you bragged about being the most brilliant lawyer that ever walked the face of the earth," she said, teasing him. Had she met him before reading his letters, she would have immediately known he hadn't written them. He would never be so brazen as to brag about his accomplishments.

He laughed. "And you still agreed to marry me?"

"Actually, it was the part that said you were also the handsomest man alive."

He laughed again before growing serious. "I hope my parents aren't going to be a problem."

They had already posed a problem, but she didn't want him to worry. "Your parents care for you very much," she said. Having no family of her own, she couldn't help but envy him that.

"My parents will come to care for you just as much," he said.

She doubted that, but she let the comment pass.

"Thank you," he said.

"For what?

"For understanding. Most women wouldn't." He pulled out his money clip to pay the check.

She couldn't help but wonder how many women he was talking about, but wasn't about to ask.

"So, what do you say?" he asked. "Want to take a look at that house tomorrow?"

She nodded. "Yes, but I promised to meet your mothers at the dressmaker's in the morning. I should be done by noon."

"Noon it is then."

After leaving the restaurant, he walked her back to her boardinghouse. It was a balmy night and a full moon rose over the distant hills, blanketing the town with a golden glow.

Upon reaching her boardinghouse, he leaned over and pecked her on the cheek. It wasn't much of a kiss, but it set her body on fire and caused her knees to tremble.

"See you tomorrow," he said, his voice strangely hoarse.

Nodding, she forced a smile. "Tomorrow," she whispered.

Chapter 14

The following morning Elizabeth found Ben's three mothers waiting for her when she arrived at the dressmaker's shop.

A counter was centered in the middle of the shop, and shelves laden with bolts of fabric adorned two walls. A Singer treadle sewing machine stood in one corner, an ironing board in another.

Mrs. Baer took charge as was her usual habit and made the introductions. The seamstress, Miss Stewart, was as round as a pin cushion. Black hair pulled back into a severe bun at the back of her head emphasized a nose as pointed as a needle.

As Elizabeth shook Miss Stewart's hand, she could see the dressmaker was already mentally measuring her.

"I have some designs I think you'll like," Miss Stewart said. Reaching for a portfolio on the counter, she pulled out several sketches.

Everyone crowded around the counter to look at the designs.

While Ma Baer and the others oohed and aahed over each of the sketches, Elizabeth felt her heart sink.

"Glory be," Mrs. Norton exclaimed. "I do believe these are the best wedding gowns I've ever seen." She lifted her gaze to Elizabeth. "What do you say?"

Elizabeth didn't know what to say. Never had she seen such an abundance of ruffles, pleats, and feathers. "Well. . ." She cleared her throat. "They are all very. . .nice, but—"

"I think this one is perfect," Ma Baer said, pointing to the gaudiest gown of all. Layers of cream-colored feathers adorned the skirt, and the bodice was draped in miles of ruffles with hanging tassels falling from the waist. The pleated mutton sleeves and scalloped neckline seemed rather plain compared to the skirt.

The dressmaker nodded in agreement. "And I have the perfect fabric." She pulled a bolt of cream-colored taffeta off a shelf and held it up for all to see. "I just got a new shipment of ostrich feathers," she added, and pointed to a large wooden box next to the sewing machine.

"Perfect!" Mrs. Baer exclaimed, the stuffed bird on her hat seeming to nod in agreement.

"Beautiful," Mrs. Norton said.

Mrs. Edwards eyed Elizabeth with a raised eyebrow. "So, what does the bride think?"

Elizabeth bit her lower lip. Think? What *could* she think? The bell-shaped skirt looked like a tarred and feathered pickle barrel, but of course she couldn't say that.

"The fabric is beautiful," she said. At least that much was true. "As for the dress. . ." She cleared her throat. "I'd prefer something a bit less—" *Garish* was the word that came to mind, but she didn't want to hurt anyone's feelings. "Ornate." Since everyone was staring at her, she went on to explain. "I prefer a plainer look."

"Plainer?" Mrs. Baer said, peering down her nose. "Oh, that will never do. Embellishments show status and success. You can't marry a man as important as Ben in a plain gown."

The dressmaker seconded what Mrs. Baer said with a nod. "Absolutely not. Why, that would be like the queen of England marrying in muslin."

This brought shocked murmurs from Ben's mothers.

"You're also small in size," the dressmaker continued, indicating Elizabeth's tiny waist, narrow hips, and small breasts. "The ruffles will fill out the places that you lack."

Elizabeth stared down at herself. *Lacked?*

Mrs. Norton took her hand and patted it. "Miss Stewart knows what she's talking about. You'd be wise to take her advice."

Elizabeth took another look at the sketch. She knew they did things differently here in Texas, but the thought of walking down the aisle in such an atrocity made her feel sick. Still, if it was what Ben's family wanted. . .

Seeming to accept Elizabeth's silence as consent, Mrs. Baer busied herself planning accessories. "And I saw the perfect hat," she said, addressing Mrs. Norton. "You know the one I mean. The one in your husband's shop window."

Mrs. Norton let out a little squeal. "You mean the wide-brimmed hat with the peacock feathers?" She raised her arms over her head and spread them wide to indicate the hat's enormous shape.

"That's the one!" Mrs. Baer exclaimed.

Elizabeth stared at the towering mass of feathers on Mrs. Baer's head, and her spirits dropped another notch. She felt a flicker of hope when Miss Stewart insisted that only a proper veil would do. But her hope was dashed a moment later when the dressmaker pulled out a hideous mile-long veil that made the gown look almost plain in comparison.

Gulping, Elizabeth battled back tears. She realized with a start that it hadn't been only her mother's gown she'd given up; she was about to give up a large part of herself.

❧ Chapter 15 ❧

Elizabeth fell in love with the house the moment she saw it.

"It's beautiful!" she exclaimed after Ben had shown her around. The house was like a blank canvas begging to be filled, and her mind whirled with ideas on how to decorate each room.

She was especially eager to get started on the dull kitchen, which overlooked a small yard. Like the rest of the house, the garden had been neglected, but Elizabeth had no trouble picturing the yard filled with flowers, a vegetable garden, and a swing hanging from the large sycamore tree.

Ben wiped a finger across the dust-covered kitchen counter. "The house needs work," he said, sounding apologetic. "A lot of work."

"But that's what makes it so special," Elizabeth said, her head filled with ideas for curtains and rugs.

Together they left the kitchen and walked back into the drab parlor. A stone fireplace took up one wall, and Elizabeth imagined sitting in front of a blazing fire, rocking a cradle or reading while Ben worked on his legal briefs.

"I think the piano should go there," Ben said, indicating a corner of the room.

Elizabeth squealed with delight at the thought of owning a piano. "And my easel will go there," she said, pointing to the corner by the window where the north light was best for painting. "And. . ." She studied the single bare wall opposite the fireplace. "I plan to paint a garden scene on the wall with trees and birds and maybe a rabbit or two." On and on she went, describing the winding stream and sun-filled woods the mural would include, her excitement growing by the minute.

Ben laughed at her enthusiasm. "I would expect nothing less than an entire national park from my artist wife."

He did it again; he called her an artist, and she felt her heart melt with pleasure. No one had ever called her an artist. Not even the editor of the newspaper where she'd previously worked.

"And what artistic endeavor do you plan for the nursery?" he asked.

The question brought a flush to her face. The mere mention of a nursery implied a physical side to the marriage that made her heart pound in anticipation.

"If it's a boy," she began, but before she could finish her thought, the front door burst open. Much to her dismay, Ben's three mothers came rushing in, filled with decorating ideas of their own.

Mrs. Norton brandished a roll of floral wallpaper. "It's a pre-wedding gift from your father and me," she said. The paper had a brown background with bright orange and yellow flowers.

Not to be outdone, Mrs. Baer showed them swaths of fabric for curtains that matched the wallpaper.

Mrs. Edwards volunteered to make them a quilt.

Ben tried his best to curb his mothers' enthusiasm without hurting their feelings. "Elizabeth has some great decorating ideas of her own," he said kindly but firmly.

"Well, of course she does," Mrs. Norton said, and then proceeded to tell them about her ideas for the garden.

"We'll take your ideas into consideration," Ben said, showing his mothers to the door.

"Oh, you'll need this," Mrs. Norton said. She pressed the roll of wallpaper into his arms. "There're plenty more where that came from."

Ben looked about ready to decline the offer, but Elizabeth stopped him with a hand on his arm. "We appreciate your help," she said, not wanting to hurt anyone's feelings.

"Wait till you hear our ideas for the wedding," Mrs. Baer said.

"Can't wait," Elizabeth said, swallowing her misgivings.

After the three women left the house, chatting all the while, Ben closed the door and stood the roll of wallpaper against a wall. "Sorry about that." He heaved a sigh. "I asked the land company to keep things quiet, but—"

"Don't apologize," she said, not wanting to worry him. "Your parents are just trying to help."

He studied her. "Are you sure you don't mind?"

She smiled, though her heart wasn't in it. Everything from her gown to the house and even the wedding ceremony required a battle, and she felt bad that Ben constantly had to take sides. "I'm sure," she lied.

Chapter 16

Elizabeth fled the church in tears. The meeting had been a disaster. She and Ben had planned to meet with the pastor alone. But Ben had been detained by a client, and his three mothers showed up in his stead.

Elizabeth had wanted a simple but meaningful ceremony. Since she couldn't wear her mother's wedding gown, she'd hoped to read a poem her mother had written, but her idea was immediately discounted.

"Poetry simply has no place at a wedding," Mrs. Baer had said, sounding like an authority on the matter.

Elizabeth didn't even have a say on the time. In Ohio, afternoon weddings were favored over the more traditional morning ones, but that was deemed improper.

"Weddings are always held in the morning," she was told. "To signify new beginnings."

One by one, her ideas were overruled. Again she was reminded that Ben was an important man and his wedding had to reflect his lot in life.

Feeling as if she wanted to scream, Elizabeth stopped a distance from the church to catch her breath and found herself in front of Norton's General store. She gazed at her reflection in the window and hardly recognized the tear-streaked face staring back.

"Dear God," she whispered. "Ben is so sure You mean for us to wed. But if that's true, why do I feel so uncertain? Is marrying Ben really what You want for me? Tell me, God. I'm listening."

Eyes closed, she held her breath hoping for an answer, but all that could be heard above the sound of a passing horse and wagon was the long, lonely whistle of a train.

Ben knew that something was wrong the moment Elizabeth stepped into Mrs. Culpepper's parlor where he'd been waiting for her.

She looked beautiful, as always. Her blue frock hugged her feminine form in all the right places. But the eyes gazing back at him lacked their usual sparkle, and a vertical line separated her delicate eyebrows.

He stood to greet her, hat in hand. She'd agreed to have supper with him as usual, but it was obvious that she had something far more serious on her mind.

"What's the matter?" he asked.

Sighing, she looked away for a moment before answering. "It's. . ." She stopped and started again. "It can wait until after supper."

He studied her. In the short time they'd been together, he'd come to know her every mood. But this time he sensed something different. Something he couldn't put a name to. Something that couldn't wait.

"Tell me now," he said. "Are you having second thoughts about the house? If you are, we can find another. One that needs less work or is larger. Whatever you want."

She lowered her eyes. "It's not about the house."

He frowned. "Then what?" His mind scrambled for an explanation. "Are you upset because I missed the meeting with the pastor?"

She shook her head. "No. You explained that you had to meet with a client."

"Then what is it?" he asked.

She looked at him long and hard before answering. "I—I can't marry you."

The words hung between them for several moments before he could make sense of them. "Why not?" he asked, his voice sharper than he'd meant. Her change of heart had shocked him, but so did suddenly realizing how much he wanted the marriage. Wanted her. "Is it something I said. Did? Tell me, and I'll make it right."

She shook her head. "No, it's. . ." She moistened her lips. "The reason doesn't matter."

"It matters to me," he said. When still she hesitated, he clenched his jaw. "It's my mothers, isn't it? Did something happen at the church?" When she failed to respond, he groaned. "I told them not to meddle."

She lifted her eyes to his. "I don't think they see it as meddling. They see it as helping, but. . ." She sighed. "The large wedding they've planned is not the one I envisioned. The parade and fireworks make it seem more like a circus than a wedding."

Ben frowned and knotted his hands by his side. His mothers

had managed to scare away every woman he'd ever had the slightest interest in, but nothing they'd done in the past compared to this.

"I'll talk to them again," he said.

She shook her head. "It won't do any good. You know it won't." Her voice broke, and he could see her struggling for words. "They care for you very much," she said at last.

"And they care for you too," he said.

He heard her intake of breath. "I'm sorry, Ben, but I don't think our marriage will work."

He stared at her. "You don't mean that."

"I'm afraid I do," she said.

He clenched his jaw. After what had happened at the house, he'd talked to his parents, both individually and as a group and had made it clear that he would not stand for any more interference. But apparently his warning came too late. Blast it all. He should have taken a stronger stand earlier, but he hadn't wanted to hurt his parents' feelings.

"Please," he said, reaching for her hand. "Let's talk about this. We'll work it out."

She shook her head and pulled her hand away. "There's nothing to talk about."

"Nothing?" He arched a brow. Had all their long discussions meant nothing to her? Did he only imagine how close they'd become? How they'd started to finish each other's sentences. How every hour spent with her had seemed like only a brief moment in time?

"I believe we've come to care for one another," he said. "I thought you wanted to marry me."

"I did. I do, but. . ." She closed her eyes as if trying to gather her thoughts. After a moment she opened her eyes again and wiped away a tear with her finger.

"I feel like I'm not just marrying you. I'm marrying the whole town, and everyone is trying to turn me into something I'm not."

He grimaced. "Then we'll move. Go where I'm not known."

She frowned. "This is your home. This is where you belong."

"I belong with you, Elizabeth. I know we had a rocky start, but I've come to love you." Stunned at how easily the word *love* had fallen from his lips, he stared at the surprised look on her face.

"Don't say that," she whispered.

"Why not? It's true." He wished it hadn't taken the prospect of losing her for him to realize how deeply he'd come to care for her. "I know God means for us to be together. He'll show us the way. I know He will."

"I don't see how that's possible," she said. "Not unless I give up who I am and become someone I no longer recognize."

"That doesn't have to happen. I won't let it happen."

"It's already happened," she said and flung out her hands in despair.

He hated seeing her so upset and reached out to hold her hand, but she pulled away. "I've talked to my parents and made it clear that the house is yours to decorate as you please."

"It's not just the house," she said, her voice filled with regret. "I have no say in the ceremony, the dress, the reception. . ." She sighed. "I hate coming between you and your parents. I hate that you have to take sides."

"Please, Elizabeth. We can work this out. I know we can."

She shook her head. "I'm sorry, Ben, but I've thought about this long and hard. I've also prayed about it." He started to say something, but she held up her hand to stop him. "I'm leaving in the morning." She beseeched him. "Please don't try to stop me."

Chapter 17

Saying goodbye to Ben last night was the hardest thing Elizabeth had ever done, and she'd hardly been able to sleep.

Ben had said he loved her, and that had made it even harder. His words of love had triggered a rush of feelings inside that she could no longer contain. And those feelings all added up to one undeniable truth. She loved Ben too. Loved him more than words could say.

Oh, how she wished she didn't. How she wished she could walk away and never think about what she'd left behind. She'd worried about losing herself if she stayed. Now she knew she'd already lost more than she could ever regain; she'd lost her heart.

Pushing aside her thoughts, she reintroduced herself to Mrs. Culpepper, who never failed to act like they were strangers meeting for the first time. After saying goodbye, she hauled her two valises to the train station.

As much as she hated spending the last of her savings for a train ticket, she had no intention of enduring a miserable stage-coach ride for a second time.

Though she was early, already the open-air train station was buzzing with activity, and she was stunned to spot Ben's three mothers in the crowd.

Waving madly, Mrs. Baer rushed up to her, the feathers on her hat bopping up and down. "Ben told us the news," she gasped, looking as anxious as a new mother.

Mrs. Norton rushed to join them and hooked her walking cane over her arm. "You can't possibly want to leave."

Elizabeth gritted her teeth. She should have known Ben's mothers would try to stop her. "I'm afraid it's best."

Mrs. Baer stared at her in disbelief. "But. . .but why?"

"It's the wedding gown." Mrs. Edwards walked up to them with a smug look. "I knew it!"

A look of relief crossed Mrs. Baer's face. "Well, if that's the reason you're leaving, we can take care of that." She looked to the others for confirmation before continuing. "Nothing's set in stone. There's still time to make changes. Mrs. Stewart is very understanding and has several other designs you can choose from."

"I personally favored the bell-shaped dress with the winged-shaped sleeves and the ruffled train," Mrs. Norton said.

"It's not just the dress," Elizabeth began, but before she could explain that her decision to leave was out of concern for Ben, she was stopped by a woman's scream.

Three masked men hurried across the platform brandishing guns.

"Don't move!" yelled the tallest of the three.

Mrs. Baer looked more indignant than afraid. "Of all the nerve—"

She would have said more had one gunman not pointed his gun directly at her. "Your jewels or your life."

Glaring at him all the while, Mrs. Baer pulled a silver bracelet off her arm, but the gold wedding band remained on her finger.

Elizabeth glanced around to see if any help was available. But all she saw was the other two bandits quickly and efficiently relieving men of their wallets and women of their jewelry, and no one looked inclined to argue.

"The ring!" the masked man yelled, drawing Elizabeth's attention to the problem at hand. Mrs. Baer didn't like being told what to do, and she looked determined to fight her assailant.

Fearing for the older woman's life, Elizabeth clutched her purse close, the pistol inside hard to the touch. She wished she'd thought to carry her weapon in her pocket for easy retrieval.

After Mrs. Baer handed over her ring, the bandit's gaze swept over Elizabeth's valises. "What have you got there?" he asked.

Elizabeth's hand froze. "J–just clothes," she stammered.

He held out his hand for her purse, but not wanting to part with it, she held on tight. A tug-of-war ensued, which ended with his grabbing her, pulling her into his arms, and holding his gun to her head.

"Don't move, anyone," he shouted. Then, with a nod at his partners, he backed away, dragging Elizabeth with him.

That's when pandemonium broke loose. Mrs. Baer pulled off her hat and flung it at him. Her aim as precise as her opinions, the hat hit him square in the face, stuffed bird and all.

Momentarily distracted by the onslaught of feathers, the man lowered his guard. Elizabeth pulled free and grabbed the gun out of his hands. All three of Ben's mothers came rushing up to attack him, Mrs. Norton swinging her cane.

Falling to his knees, the man held his hands over his head to ward off the blows. One of his cohorts came running over to rescue him, but Elizabeth pointed the gun at him and made him drop his.

Mrs. Baer tossed him a warning look. "You'd better watch it, mister. She's already shot one man."

Refusing to heed Mrs. Baer's warning, the man reached out and tried to grab the gun out of Elizabeth's hands. Refusing to let go, Elizabeth held on tight. Just as it looked like the masked man was about to claim victory, the gun went off.

Everyone at the station froze, and a hushed silence fell over the crowd.

"Oh, dear God," Mrs. Baer exclaimed when the smoke cleared. "You shot Ben!"

Chapter 18

Elizabeth paced the floor of the doctor's waiting room. Never had she prayed so hard in her life—or felt so awful.

Two times! Two times she'd shot Ben. If he never wanted to see her again, who could blame him? She had done nothing but cause him trouble. This whole trip to Texas had turned into a nightmare.

She didn't even know what to say to his shaken parents. No one felt like sitting, and all six of them paced the floor with her. To keep from bumping into each other, Elizabeth and the three couples circled the room like ducks in a row.

For the longest while, no one spoke. But that changed when Mr. Baer stopped to pull out his watch, causing the three people behind him to collide. "What's taking so long?" he asked.

Pulling herself away from his back, Mrs. Baer straightened her hat. "Now calm down, dear."

"How can I calm down?" Mr. Baer spun around to face his wife. "None of this makes sense. How can someone get himself shot two times? And what in blazes were you doing at the train station?"

"I told you," Mrs. Baer said, standing practically nose to nose with her husband, "we were trying to prevent Elizabeth from leaving."

Mrs. Norton nodded and thumped her cane on the floor. "And that's when those masked men showed up."

Mrs. Edwards pressed her hands against her chest. "And the one bandit tried to kidnap Elizabeth," she said.

The memory made Elizabeth shudder. "If it hadn't been for the three of you, I don't know what would have happened."

Mrs. Baer patted her on the arm. "That's what family is for, dear. To protect one another."

Elizabeth stared at her in astonishment. *Family?* It had been a long time since she'd had a family to call her own. And to think that Ben's mother. . . A lump rose in her throat, and she suddenly couldn't breathe.

"B–but," she stammered when she could finally find her voice, "I shot your son. Twice!"

"I know, dearie," Mrs. Baer said. "But don't feel bad. It could happen to anyone."

Her husband threw up his hands. "It only happened because you sent away for a bride out of a catalogue. I told you it was a mistake!"

"I told you the same thing," Mr. Norton said, glaring at his wife.

Elizabeth watched in bewilderment as all three couples started talking at once. Tempers flared and harsh words flew back and forth like uncaged birds.

The door to the operating room suddenly opened, and everyone fell silent.

"You can come in now," Doc Evans said.

Springing forward, Elizabeth shot past the doctor and reached Ben's bed even before his three mothers.

It did her heart good to see Ben sitting up. Before he had a chance to speak, Elizabeth reached for his hand and her eyes filled with tears. "Oh Ben, I'm so sorry. I never meant to—"

"I know, I know," he said, squeezing her hand.

"Is he going to be all right?" Mrs. Baer asked, leaning over the foot of the bed.

The doctor nodded. "This time the bullet just grazed his arm."

Elizabeth pulled her hand away from Ben's to wipe away a tear. "Will you ever forgive me?"

"Of course he'll forgive you," Mrs. Baer said. "Tell her, Ben."

"Let him speak for himself," Mr. Baer said.

Ben glanced around his bed. "What were you all doing at the train station?" he asked.

Mr. Baer grunted. "They were putting their noses where they don't belong, as usual."

Mrs. Edwards glared at him before turning to Ben. "We were there to talk the woman you love into staying," she said with an indignant toss of her head.

Ben locked Elizabeth in his gaze. "That's why I was there."

"Well, you took your own sweet time," Mrs. Baer said, the feathers on her hat seeming to bristle.

"I'll say," Mrs. Norton said.

Ben held Elizabeth's gaze, and for a moment it seemed as if they were the only two people in the room. "I went to your boardinghouse, but you'd already left. I looked for you at the stagecoach stop, but when I didn't find you, I went to the train station." His gaze softened. "I'm glad you're still here," he said, his voice hoarse.

"You can thank the Madison gang for that," Mrs. Edwards said. "She was bound and determined to leave till they showed up."

"I guess we have God to thank for that," Ben said and, in a softer voice, added, "Don't go."

Elizabeth's heart felt like it was about to burst with emotion, and she could hardly catch her breath. So much had happened that day, it was hard to sort out her feelings, but one thing was clear. She loved this man. Loved him with her whole heart and soul. If she hadn't known it before, she knew it now.

"I'm not going anywhere," she murmured.

Ben tightened his hold on her hand and gazed deep into her eyes. "Do you mean that? My family—"

She touched his lips with a finger and glanced at Ben's three mothers, who were straining to hear every word. "Your mothers put their lives at stake to save me," she said. "How can I walk away knowing how much they care?" Her voice broke. "How much you care."

She heard his intake of breath and felt him shudder, but before he could speak, Mrs. Baer's voice rang out.

"Does that mean you're going to marry Ben?" she asked.

Elizabeth's gaze never wavered from the face she'd come to know so well. The face that she could draw with her eyes shut. "If he'll still have me."

"Well, of course he'll still have you," Mrs. Baer said. "Tell her, Ben."

Mr. Baer tried to steer his wife away from the bed. "This is between the two of them," he said. "We should leave them alone."

"Horsefeathers!" Mrs. Baer exclaimed, and pulled her arm away from her husband's hand. "If it wasn't for us, Ben wouldn't even know Elizabeth existed."

Mrs. Norton gave a satisfied smile. "We knew she was the right woman for him the moment we read her first letter."

"And her photograph didn't hurt," Mrs. Edwards added.

"This calls for a proposal, Ben," Mrs. Baer prompted. "So, what do you say?"

Elizabeth's heart pounded. "I say yes," she said, not waiting for Ben to speak up. "I'll marry you."

Mr. Baer threw up his hands. "Confound it, she won't even let the boy speak. She's getting to be as bad as my wife."

Ignoring his father, Ben had eyes only for Elizabeth. "Not so fast," he said, his voice as serious as the look on his face.

Elizabeth pulled her hand from his, and her heart sank. "Are. . .are you saying you don't want to marry me?"

"Oh, I want to marry you, all right, but only under three conditions."

Elizabeth stared at him in dismay. "Conditions?" This was beginning to sound like another business deal.

Ben nodded. "One, you must promise that when you walk down the aisle, you'll wear a purple gown."

Elizabeth gasped. "Oh Ben—"

He held up his good arm, his gaze as soft as a caress. "Two, you agree to decorate every wall in our house with gardens. Lots and lots of gardens."

Elizabeth covered her mouth with her hand, and fresh tears sprang to her eyes.

Pulling his gaze from hers, Ben directed his attention to the others. "And three. . .my lovely mothers promise to offer help and advice only when it's asked for."

Mrs. Norton started to protest, but Mrs. Baer elbowed her. "You want him to marry her, don't you?" she said. "If all it takes is a purple gown and gardens, then so be it."

Mr. Baer gave an exasperated toss of his head. "And don't forget the third condition. You gotta stay out of Ben's affairs."

Mrs. Baer made a face at her husband but, for once, kept her thoughts to herself.

Not knowing whether to laugh or cry, Elizabeth hugged her before turning back to Ben, her heart filled with love not only for him but for his whole crazy family.

"Just a minute," Mr. Baer said with a booming voice, and all heads turned his way. "I think it only right that a fourth condition be added. I think Miss Cotton here—"

"Colton," Mrs. Baer said.

He corrected Elizabeth's name and continued. "I think it only right that she agrees to stop shooting Ben."

"That I gladly promise," Elizabeth said. "I no longer have a need to carry a gun." With Ben, she felt as safe as a babe in a cradle.

"Whoa. That's a relief," Doc Evans said, wiping his brow. "As Ben has now run out of arms."

Ben chuckled as he gazed at her. "Well?" he asked. "What do you say? Will you marry me? Do we have a deal?"

"Deal," Elizabeth said and offered him her hand.

Laughing softly, he took her hand and, moving his bandaged arm aside, pulled her onto the bed next to him. Mindless of the crowd around them, he proceeded to kiss her like she'd never been kissed before.

She quivered at the sweet tenderness of his lips. But when he deepened the kiss, her heart nearly burst with joy. Cupping his face in her hands, she returned his kiss with equal fervor. Pressed against his strong chest, she inhaled his manly scent and felt like she had found a home. A refuge. A safe harbor.

Had she not suddenly recalled that they weren't alone, she might have stayed in his arms forever. Feeling flustered, she pulled away, her lips still moist from his kiss, her body still flushed with heat.

Surprised at how easily she'd forgotten his parents' presence, she stared deep into Ben's eyes before slipping off the bed. He had been right all along. Loving and being loved by him could only be part of God's plan. As long as she stayed focused on that, nothing, not even his well-meaning mothers, could come between them.

Looking at his parents with new, appreciative eyes, she couldn't help but smile. All six of them looked like they had just discovered a pot o' gold.

Mrs. Edwards beamed with pleasure, and Mrs. Norton's smile practically reached her ears. Mrs. Baer, who Ben said never cried, dabbed at her eyes with a handkerchief.

Then all six of Ben's parents and the doctor burst into applause, and for once, Elizabeth didn't mind being the center of attention.

New York Times bestselling author **Margaret Brownley** has penned more than forty-five novels and novellas. She's a two-time Romance Writers of America RITA finalist and has written for a TV soap. She is also a recipient of the *Romantic Times* Pioneer Award. Not bad for someone who flunked eighth-grade English. Just don't ask her to diagram a sentence.

The Bride Who Declined

by Susan Page Davis

❧ Chapter 1 ❧

Boston, Massachusetts
May 1885

Rachel Paxton carefully wrapped the lustrous silk gown in brown paper, tied string around it firmly, and handed the package to Mrs. Winston's maid. Mrs. Winston handed her a crisp ten-dollar bill.

"Thank you, ma'am," Rachel said, her eyes downcast.

"You're welcome, Miss Paxton. I'll see you at my house next week for a fitting on that travel ensemble."

"Very good," Rachel said. She walked with the customer to the door. Once Mrs. Winston and her maid were outside, she closed it and let out a quiet, "Thank You, Lord!" She would be able to pay her month's rent, buy a few supplies for her business, and eat reasonably well for a while.

She went to her worktable and took out the pattern she would use for the next customer's formal ball gown.

The street door swung open, and she looked up, smiling

225

as the postman entered.

"Mr. Bailey, good morning."

"Good day to you, Miss Paxton." He handed her two envelopes.

"Thank you very much." Rachel waited until he left, and opened the first one. Her account at the yard goods store had accumulated a bit more than she'd remembered. She hoped another customer would pay her this week. Even though she was constantly busy with her sewing for Boston society women, Rachel sometimes found it hard to get by. With a sigh she opened the second envelope.

Her heart lurched then raced as she read the heading. The letter was from an attorney she had never heard of, a Mr. Donald McClure, Esquire, of Fort Worth, Texas. What on earth would a lawyer two thousand miles away want with her? She held her breath and skimmed the letter, which was written with a clear, bold hand.

> *Dear Miss Paxton, This letter is to inform you that you are the heir of Mr. Randolph Hill, deceased March 23 instant. . .*

Stunned, Rachel plunked down onto the stool she used when pinning up ladies' hems, the letter dangling limply from her hand. This communication made no sense to her.

Mr. Hill's name she recognized. He was the man whose ad in the newspaper's matrimonial column she had answered a year ago. They had corresponded for a few months. Rachel had received a total of four letters from him. He sounded like a nice man, sincere and hardworking. But after he told her about the rough life he lived on his ranch, she had decided that she was not really made for that kind of life. She was a city girl, and she thrived on contact with other people.

It was true, she didn't like having to earn her living or having to share a small boardinghouse room with a woman who cooked at a nearby restaurant. She and Rhoda got along all right, but both of them longed for homes of their own and, God willing, families to love and nourish.

A small part of Rachel's heart longed for adventure—and love—but she didn't think the ranch in wild and distant Texas was the right place for her. She'd written to Mr. Hill apologetically, telling him she regretted taking up his time. She advised him to look elsewhere for a bride. Someone less timid and fearful than she was would be better suited for the role.

Now he was dead. How? Why?

She read the first part of the letter again, but Mr. McClure didn't divulge that information, only that Randolph Hill had named her sole heir to his estate.

Rachel couldn't imagine why Mr. Hill had done that after she'd turned him down. She read the rest of the letter carefully, her dismay growing line by line.

One provision of the bequest was that Rachel must live on Mr. Hill's property for at least a month to inherit it. Was this his way of forcing her to go to Texas, even though he was no longer there? Was it some warped revenge for her rejection?

Her mind whirled. She would have to write to the attorney this evening. She didn't want to leave her business and strike out for Fort Worth. In fact, she couldn't. She barely had enough money to cover her month's expenses, let alone train fare all the way to Texas.

The door opened and two ladies came in, smiling and chattering as they walked.

Rachel crammed the letter into the cupboard where she kept extra lengths of cloth. She would deal with it this evening. Meanwhile, it could simmer in the back of her mind. As of that moment, she was inclined simply to tell Mr. McClure that she wasn't coming and didn't want Mr. Hill's ranch.

"Hello, Miss Simpson," she said to one of the women, a debutante who was an occasional customer.

"Good morning." Miss Simpson held out a hand toward her companion. "Miss Paxton, this is my cousin, Cynthia Bowman. She's interested in a couple of summer day dresses."

Rachel quickly assessed the fashions the two women were wearing. She put on her best smile, relegating the attorney's letter to the far recesses of her mind. "Welcome, Miss Bowman. I see you like the new, longer bodice."

"Not necessarily," Miss Bowman said. "Is that the fashion in Boston now?"

"Let me show you some of the newest patterns I've received from New York and Paris."

Rachel turned to her pattern boxes, determined to end this interview with a sizable new order.

Three weeks later Rachel was taking measurements from Mrs. William Stafford, a new mother whose wardrobe needed adjustments.

"I'm certain I can let out the gray worsted and the striped silk. I'm not so sure about the muslin." She slid the measuring tape around Mrs. Stafford's hips. The lady had certainly retained some of the weight gained during pregnancy, but mostly in the area of her waist. Her bust was also a little larger, but since she had decided not to nurse her infant, Rachel was sure that would soon decrease. Mrs. Stafford was one who would restrict her diet, no matter what.

"I can't believe that green dress won't button," the woman said in an aggrieved tone.

"I'm sure you'll be back into it in a few weeks," Rachel said. "Sometimes it takes ladies awhile to get their figure back, but I know you can do it."

"Hmm, yes. Well, in the meantime, it's so hot this summer; I suppose I will need another dress. Something loose and flowing, perhaps?" She arched her eyebrows.

Rachel nodded. Some women saw her as their last hope to retain a fashionable silhouette. "Of course. And I'll stitch it up so that it carries a wide sash at the waist and you can adjust it as your weight changes. Or perhaps an empire waist would flatter you." She ruffled through the pattern sketches. "What do you think of this?" She pointed to a dress that would allow for a weight loss—or gain—of five or ten pounds.

The door was flung open, and a boy of about twelve stood panting on the step, peering in at her.

"Telegram for Miss Rachel Paxton."

Rachel opened her mouth and then closed it. Telegrams meant bad news. Tragedy. She'd never had one before in her life. Slowly she stepped toward the boy. He handed her an envelope but lingered. For a moment she wondered if he was waiting for her to read it and send a reply, but then she realized he wanted a coin for his service. She hurried to a cupboard and took a copper from the tin box within.

"Thank you, miss." He tipped his hat and scooted out the door as soon as he had pocketed the coin.

"I hope it's not bad news," Mrs. Stafford said.

Rachel stuck the envelope in the cupboard with the tin.

"Don't you want to read it?"

She turned to face Mrs. Stafford. "I'm sure it can wait until we've finished."

"But, my dear." The customer walked over and laid a gentle hand on her shoulder. "Surely it's important. If you'd like privacy, I can come back later."

"No." Rachel didn't want to take a chance the customer wouldn't return, meaning she would lose the sale. She managed a smile. "If you'd like, I can give you a cup of tea and take just a moment to look at the message."

"That sounds like a good plan," Mrs. Stafford said.

Rachel kept the teakettle on the back of the small stove's flat top in the room behind the shop. In five minutes she'd brought it to a boil. She prepared tea and took the cup and saucer on a tray out to the shop. Mrs. Stafford was sitting on her stool and eyeing two sketches that she held, one in each hand.

"Thank you." She accepted the cup and laid the sketches on the worktable. "I'm hovering between these two. Perhaps I'll be extravagant and have you make one of each."

"I'm sure you'd put two summer dresses to good use, ma'am."

Mrs. Stafford sipped her tea. "Mm, that's very good. Now read your telegram, dear. Take all the time you need."

Glad for such an understanding customer, yet dreading what she would read, Rachel moved slowly to the cupboard and took out the envelope. Her parents were dead, and she had only one sibling, a much older brother who had moved to Connecticut ten years ago. Had something happened to Gideon? She certainly hoped not, even though they weren't close and she hadn't seen him in a decade.

Her hands shook as she forced the flap open and drew out the slip of paper. Of all things! It was from that lawyer. It took her a moment to absorb the full import of the message.

ESTATE WILL SEND FUNDS FOR YOUR TRAVEL AND INCI-DENTAL EXPENSES *Stop* PLEASE ADVISE SEND BY MAIL OR BANK TRANSFER *Stop* SINCERELY D MCCLURE ESQ.

She stood staring at the words and feeling very stupid. Did the man expect her to reply by telegram? That would take her entire savings. She was inclined to go into the back room and throw the telegram into the firebox, but she couldn't do that.

Mrs. Stafford stood and walked toward her. "Is there anything I can do, Miss Paxton?"

"No, no." Rachel slid the paper back into the envelope and laid it on the cupboard shelf. "It's something I can attend to later."

"Not bad news then?"

"Not really. Just. . .business, of sorts. Now, what did you decide?" She went over and picked up the fashion sketches. For a half hour she retained a cheerful attitude and showed Mrs. Stafford fabric samples and discussed hemlines, tucks, and pleats. As she worked, a vague plan formed in her mind. Rhoda Sinclair, her roommate at the boardinghouse, was a practical soul. Rhoda knew about Rachel's correspondence with the rancher but not about the bequest. Rachel had kept that to herself, feeling slightly guilty, as though she must have somehow offended Mr. Hill. But she and Rhoda could discuss the telegram tonight. If anyone could make sense of this, it was Rhoda.

"Of course you should go! Think, Rachel." Rhoda shook her head and studied Rachel as they ate together that evening in their third-floor room. "The poor man has left you valuable property. If you go out for a month and hate it, you can still take possession and sell the ranch. Surely that would give you enough money to hire an assistant and maybe even set up a fashionable dress shop."

Rachel hadn't considered that. For several years her dream had been owning her own clothing store, but she'd never had funds to even expand the sewing business. Maybe now. . .

"But I've got several orders pending." She eyed Rhoda helplessly. "I can't run off and leave my customers without their new gowns. I'd never get any more business in this town."

"*If* you decided to come back and resume your dressmaking."

Rachel caught her breath. "You don't think I'd really start raising cattle on some dusty ranch in the wilds of Texas, do you?"

"I don't know what you'd do." Rhoda smiled and patted her shoulder. "Think about it. If nothing else, it's a free trip. A change of scenery. You'll meet all sorts of people, and maybe even meet some people you'll find helpful in your business, even if you decide to come back to Boston. And you might come back richer. Certainly not poorer. The attorney said the estate will fund your incidental expenses. I say finish up the orders you have, don't take any more for now, and head west."

The idea frightened Rachel. But why not? Rhoda was right.

Taking the trip in itself would be an adventure, and perhaps advantageous. She'd been on her own since her father died—nearly twelve years now. She'd been fifteen when he passed away, leaving her only enough money to survive for a few months. Necessity had forced her to move into the boardinghouse and scare up enough dressmaking to keep her alive. It had taken her two years to afford rental on the shop where she now took orders and did her sewing. What if she got a thousand dollars out of this venture? Or even a few hundred? It would make a huge difference in her future.

"How long would it take you to fulfill the orders you have right now?" Rhoda asked.

Rachel did some quick calculations. "A month at least."

"What if you hired a girl to help you? Someone to do the hems and straight seams. The buttonholes, maybe. Don't you know someone who can do the plain work?"

"Yes," Rachel said slowly.

"How long would it take with help?"

"Three weeks, maybe."

"That gives you time to write the lawyer, or send him a telegram with your travel date. He'll send you the money for your ticket."

"I don't know." Rachel's stomach was already fluttering, and she hadn't decided yet.

"Honestly!" Rhoda jumped up and paced to the window, where she whirled in a cloud of calico skirt that Rachel had sewn for her. "Listen to me. This could be the biggest opportunity of your life!"

Rachel pulled in a slow breath and straightened her shoulders. "You're right. I think I'll walk over to the Smiths' house and see if Emmy would like to do some sewing for me."

❧ Chapter 2 ❧

Jack Callen listened to the lawyer with dismay. It had already been more than two months since the boss died. Mr. McClure had let go several of the ranch hands, but he'd kept on Jack, who was Mr. Hill's foreman, and three cowpunchers. The men were uneasy, wondering if they should look for jobs on other ranches or stay put. Right now the work wasn't too hard. They had plenty to eat and no one but Jack looking over their shoulders.

But a woman for a boss?

"She says she's leaving Boston on June twenty-eighth," Mr. McClure said. The wind ruffled his graying hair as they stood in the yard before the bunkhouse. "That gives you time to redd up the house and make sure things are in order. I expect she'll arrive here around the Fourth of July."

Two weeks. Jack and the men had two weeks to get things ready for the owner. Not just any owner—a woman who knew nothing about ranching.

"So we should go in the house and clean it up?"

"If it needs it. We checked the kitchen and pantry after Mr. Hill died, you recall. I expect all that's needed is a little dusting and making up the bed fresh. Leave his things as they are. Make sure she's got fresh eggs and milk the day she arrives. Can you handle that?"

"I guess." Jack didn't exactly feel comfortable about making a lady's bed up with clean linens, but he supposed it had to be done. A thought struck him. "Could I maybe hire the neighbor's wife to come over and do that?"

McClure considered for a moment then reached into his pocket. "I guess so. Here's two dollars. Give her that if she spends a day here working."

Jack accepted the money with a nod. Kate Stanno would likely be glad to make a couple of dollars. Her husband's ranch was scraping along.

"Just my opinion," he said, watching the lawyer's face closely, "but this is no place for a lady. We've got that bull coming that Mr. Hill sent for right before he died, and we need to hold the roundup in August."

McClure's eyebrows drew together. "Be that as it may, Callen, we have to follow the particulars of the will. Miss Paxton is coming, whether you like it or not. I sent her money for her train ticket this morning. Now maybe it would be wise for the estate to sell off that bull. What do you think?"

"No, sir." The boss had been adamant about his plans for the ranch, and Jack would honor them so long as he had the chance. "That animal was what Mr. Hill saw as the future of his herd. He sank a lot of money into that bull, and he figured next spring we'd have a fine crop of beef calves kicking around here. If you sell the bull now, what will happen to his dreams? You might as well sell off the whole herd and auction off the ranch."

McClure sighed and looked out over the pasture. "It may come to that if Miss Paxton won't stay. She may want to sell the place outright. But maybe she'd sell it with the stock, as a working ranch. Then you and the other hands might keep your jobs."

"But she has to live here for a month before she can sell it, right?"

"That's correct. If she doesn't come, or if she won't stay a full thirty days, she inherits nothing but a train ticket back to Boston."

"Then what would happen to the Hill ranch?"

McClure's mouth twitched. "I would be forced to sell it. Half the proceeds would go to Mr. Hill's aunt in St. Louis, who doesn't really need it, the other half to a cousin believed to be living somewhere in California."

"You don't even know where he is?" Jack asked.

"Not for certain. My letter to his last known address came back unopened."

Jack shook his head. He wasn't sure which he hoped would happen—the sale of the property and probably having to find a new job, or a new lady boss who would flounder through the trials of learning to run a ranch. He wished he had enough money to buy the ranch, but that was a pipe dream. Over the last seven years, he'd only been able to put aside a hundred and fifty dollars, nowhere near the price the ranch would bring.

"Didn't you say she's some kind of seamstress?" he asked.

"That is my understanding—a dressmaker."

Terrific. Just what they needed. Jack couldn't imagine she would stay.

McClure cracked a smile. "Cheer up, Callen. It's possible she might pocket the money I sent and never leave Boston."

Rachel's nerves kicked up as the train approached Fort Worth. Mr. McClure had sent her a telegram about the financial arrangements and said he would meet her at the depot and escort her to the Hill ranch. When she'd gone to her bank to withdraw the money he'd wired, she was shocked at the amount. It was well over the amount she needed to buy her ticket. For incidental expenses, he'd said. She had immediately given Rhoda enough to pay her share of the room for another month and paid for the shop's rental a month in advance. Then she'd bought new shoes and stockings.

The rest she had squirreled away. Who knew what she would need on the journey? Food, of course, perhaps a hotel room for a night or two if her connections were complicated. And she supposed she might need some new clothing once she reached the ranch. A riding habit, perhaps, though the idea of riding mustangs appalled her. Still, one never knew what lay ahead. She left Boston with twenty dollars in her purse and nearly two hundred sewn into her hems. She wrote to her brother the day before she left, explaining about her change in fortune but leaving him no time to protest about her upcoming journey. Rhoda had waved her off, and Rachel immediately felt nauseated. What was she doing?

Now she had nearly reached her destination, hurtling across the plains in a train laden with grain, building materials, and cattle. When they paused at depots along the way, she could hear the cows lowing in the boxcars behind the two passenger cars.

She'd gotten off the train a few times, but the last stop had frightened her. It seemed a rough town, with the depot a quarter mile from the businesses and houses. A man had brought sandwiches to the platform for travelers to buy if they didn't want to venture into town, and she'd bought one and scurried back onto the train. It sat there for nearly an hour while the workers took on coal and water and the other passengers walked to a small restaurant for lunch. And the cattle bawled and thudded about.

Now she was nearing Fort Worth. As the train slowed, she looked out the window. Paddocks everywhere, teeming with cattle. She shuddered. Would she have to walk among the stockyards?

To her relief, although the train paused at the stockyards for half an hour, with odorous, dusty air sifting into the cars, the conductor informed Rachel that she should wait. Soon the train would move on to another depot nearer the business district, where most passengers usually disembarked.

Such a relief. She hoped Mr. McClure knew at which depot she would arrive. By the time she stepped down onto the platform, her heart was pounding with anxiety. She brushed back an errant strand of hair and looked about the seething, noisy, dusty platform. For a few seconds, she feared Mr. McClure wouldn't find her and she would be left on her own to find lodgings and try to contact him.

"Miss Paxton?"

She turned toward the sweetest sound she'd ever heard. A stately middle-aged man in a black suit was hurrying toward her. He might have been a senator.

"Miss Rachel Paxton?" he asked.

"Yes." She extended her hand, and he took it.

"Donald McClure. Welcome to Fort Worth."

"Th–thank you."

"You must be tired. Would you like to join me for a late luncheon? There's a respectable hotel just around the corner."

"That would be nice, thank you."

A young man came up beside him, tall and rugged, with a tanned face and unruly dark hair. His brown eyes appraised her quickly, and he nodded, tugging at the wide brim of his hat.

Mr. McClure glanced at him. "Miss Paxton, may I introduce Mr. Jack Callen? He was Mr. Hill's foreman and is still filling that position for the estate."

"How do you do," Rachel said.

"Ma'am."

"I will drive you out to the ranch after we eat," Mr. McClure said. "I wanted you to meet Callen first, but he and two of the other ranch hands will be collecting a bull that Mr. Hill ordered shortly before his death. They will take it from the stockyards to the ranch for us. For you, I should say."

Rachel's face flamed at his mention of a bull. Back in Boston, nice people didn't speak of such things in polite company. However, she realized this wasn't Boston. Instead of dwelling on the embarrassment, she seized on McClure's last sentence.

"But the ranch is not mine, Mr. McClure."

"No, not yet. Forgive my slip. I spoke as if you were the new owner. As you will be at the end of thirty days, I trust."

She swallowed hard. "We shall see."

"If you'll excuse me, miss," Callen said, "I'll get on over to the stockyards."

"Of course," she said. "Thank you for coming."

He lifted his hat briefly and strode off. Rachel wondered about him. He was the man she'd have to deal with from day to day. She'd noted his keen assessment of her.

"He's a good man," Mr. McClure said. "If you choose to keep him on, he will be of immeasurable help to you. He knows every aspect of managing a ranch."

Would he resent answering to a new owner? A female owner? Rachel could see that she would have a lot to think about, and she might need to nurture some diplomatic skills in the next month.

Mr. McClure smiled. "Let's secure your luggage and get something to eat, shall we?"

"Yes, thank you."

A good lunch of fried chicken, mashed potatoes, gravy, and featherlight biscuits went a long way toward calming Rachel. She only wished for some green vegetables and hoped the ranch had a kitchen garden. Mr. McClure talked about the Hill ranch, and her head whirled. He gave her a list of places in town where Mr. Hill had established accounts—a bank, a mercantile, a feed store, and a haberdashery.

"You can charge any purchases you make for the ranch or for your use during your stay to the ranch's accounts at these stores."

Rachel gulped and tucked the list into her purse. She'd never imagined that Mr. Hill had such resources. When she dared ask the value of the property she might inherit, his reply staggered her.

On the way to the ranch, which was several miles out of town and took an hour's travel in Mr. McClure's buggy, he talked at length about Mr. Hill's vision for the ranch.

"This new bull will be the foundation of his breeding program. That is, of course, unless you decide to go a different direction once you take possession. But he's got some fine breeding cows ready and was quite enthusiastic about what he had planned."

Rachel felt as if her face was on fire. How could he talk so casually about those things? She had never heard men talk about their livestock in such intimate terms. She supposed they had to, but farmers probably excused themselves from mixed company when doing so. Ought she be offended? Surely Mr. McClure was a gentleman. Or was he trying to get a reaction from her?

"I suppose I'll have to settle in at the ranch and see what the life is like before I make my final decision," she said without looking at him.

"Of course." He turned the conversation to the sights and conveniences of Fort Worth. Rachel tucked away a few things he mentioned, but she couldn't help wondering if she had made a huge mistake.

After he'd talked nonstop for ten minutes, she said, "Excuse me, but may I ask you how Mr. Hill died? Was it an accident?"

"Oh no, not at all," he said. "It was very sad. A lingering illness. He knew for several months what was coming."

Rachel frowned. "Some kind of wasting disease?"

"Yes, I believe his doctor said it was a cancer." Mr. McClure shook his head. "So tragic in a man so young."

She thought back to the letters they had exchanged.

"He never mentioned it to me in our correspondence," she said. "How long ago did he know?"

"It was about two months before he died, I believe. At least that's when he came to me and asked me to draw up his will."

Relief washed over her. He hadn't known at the time she had sent her refusal. His illness had struck last winter, after their correspondence ended.

"Did he say why he chose me to inherit his property? We hadn't had any contact since September, I believe."

"No, not specifically. He did tell me that you were a woman he admired and wanted to do something nice for, that's all."

She thought about that as he drove along. Something nice. That was an understatement, considering Mr. Hill's assets. Her feelings of guilt resurfaced. That poor, thoughtful man! She'd turned him down, and then he'd learned he was dying. How awful.

When they at last turned off the main road onto a dirt lane, Mr. McClure looked at her with a smile. "This is your land now, on both sides of the road. Your home, if you decide to move permanently to Texas."

She looked around with a sense of wonder. The hills spread out around them, fenced in with barbed wire, and in the distance she saw several clusters of cattle. And they were hers, or they would be in thirty days.

"How many acres?" she squeaked out.

"A thousand, more or less."

Her chest squeezed. In Boston people owned house lots if they were lucky, or suburban houses on plots of a few acres if they were wealthier. Of course this land wasn't prime real estate. The grass looked brownish for the first week of July, and for the most part no improvements had been made.

They rode into a hovering dust cloud, and she coughed. It was so hot that she'd almost shed her shawl, but perhaps it would keep some of the grime off her dress.

"I imagine this dust was stirred up when the men brought the bull in," Mr. McClure said.

There it was again. She had the feeling she wouldn't be able to dodge the topic forever.

"I suppose Mr. Callen and the other workers can tend to that end of the business," she said with hesitation.

"Well yes, for the most part." He pulled up and turned toward her with a wide smile. "There's the home place, up ahead."

The larger structure, she quickly realized, was a barn. She could see hay through the open loft door above the main entrance. Around it were rail-fenced pens, and in some of them she could see a few horses. To one side was a one-story addition with several windows along the front.

Mr. McClure pointed across the driveway. "That's the house." On a slight rise about a hundred feet from the barn was a small dwelling. Mr. Hill had been a bachelor, so she supposed he didn't need a big house. She swallowed hard. It looked very plain, with board siding and a chimney built of rocks. Modest, but what had she expected? And she had never lived in a fancy house. For the past several years, she had shared one room in an inexpensive boardinghouse. She would not complain about having a roof over her head and the privacy of a dwelling to herself, no matter how spartan.

She stirred and gathered her shawl and handbag. Mr. McClure climbed down from the buggy, but before he could go around to her, another man appeared at her side. Startled, she looked down into Jack Callen's sober brown eyes. He held up a calloused hand.

"Help you, ma'am?"

"Thank you." She hit the ground awkwardly and stumbled. Callen's grip on her arm was like steel, and she quickly recovered.

"All right, ma'am?"

"Yes."

He nodded. "We put the new bull in a reinforced corral out back of the barn. Would you like to see it?"

"Oh, the, uh, the new ox. Not now, I think. I'm rather tired from the journey, Mr. Callen."

"Sure," he said, "but call me Jack if you don't mind, ma'am."

"Oh." She eyed him closely to be sure he was serious. "You are the foreman."

"Yes, ma'am, but we don't stand on ceremony here."

"All right." *I'll try,* she added mentally. In her eastern life, she was on a first-name basis with very few men.

Mr. McClure had reached her side. "Let me show you the house, and the men can bring in your baggage. Then I'll head back to town." He offered her his arm.

"Thank you." Rachel went with him into the little house, where he pointed out the large kitchen and sitting room, which were really only one room, and the bedroom, which she was glad to see was firmly partitioned off.

"There's a pantry here." He opened a door in the kitchen, near a small icebox. "I had Callen lay in supplies for you, but I'm sure there'll be other things you want. You can just ask him. Make a list, and he'll send one of the men to town for your wants, or you can ride in yourself."

"I don't ride horseback." Rachel tried to keep the rising panic from her voice.

"Oh well, Mr. Hill has a wagon. Maybe two. Just get one of the boys to harness it up for you."

"Boys?"

"The ranch hands."

She nodded, wanting to scream, "I've never driven a wagon either." But she kept quiet.

The front door opened, and a young man she hadn't seen before came in carrying her two large satchels.

"Howdy, ma'am. I'm Rusty. You want your bags yonder?" He nodded toward the bedroom door.

"Out here is fine," Rachel said.

"Awright then." Rusty set down the two bags, smiled at her, and disappeared out the door.

Rachel certainly hoped the men weren't in the habit of entering the house without knocking. She would have to check the locks on the doors.

"Now, the necessary's out back." Mr. McClure opened a door off the sitting room, and she stared outside, across an expanse of grass to where a rough privy stood. A clothesline was strung to one side.

"Er, thank you."

He nodded and closed the door.

"What about laundry?" she asked.

"Oh, I'm sure there's a washtub. Ask Callen."

She would if necessary, but she'd take a good look around first. Rachel was used to doing her own laundry and generally looking out for herself.

"Now, you'll want to sit down with Callen soon and go over the books for the ranch. I've had him keep track of expenses and income."

"Oh." Rachel hadn't supposed he'd know a ledger from a branding iron. She would certainly ask him about the ranch's finances, but she didn't really want to discuss Mr. Hill's breeding program with him. If the men would leave her alone and tend to the livestock without her direct supervision, she was sure she could survive here for a month. That was all she needed to do—survive.

❧ Chapter 3 ☙

Jack stood in the barn doorway, watching Miss Paxton wave off the lawyer. To his relief she had said nothing about a chaperone or society, though he supposed she might have given McClure an earful. She looked fragile somehow. Uncertain. Lost even. What had ailed Randolph Hill, leaving his ranch to a woman like her? She wasn't capable of bossing this outfit.

As he was about to go into the barn and check their gear for the next day's work, she raised a hand and stepped in his direction.

Jack clenched his jaw and walked toward her. They met in the middle of the yard.

"Can I help you with something, ma'am?"

"Yes, I hope so. Mr. McClure said I should ask you about the daily operations of the ranch and the finances. He said you've kept the books since Mr. Hill died."

"Yes, ma'am. Since before he died, actually. He put me in

charge of it about three years ago, once he learned I had some talent in arithmetic."

Her eyebrows shot up as if she hadn't expected that. "I see. Well, whenever is convenient for you."

"I could give you a few minutes now."

"Fine. In—in the kitchen?" She looked confused, as though she wasn't sure it was proper to invite a man inside her house.

"I'll fetch the books." He turned toward the bunkhouse.

Inside, he took a glance in the small mirror that hung above their washbasin. He was glad none of the others were there to see that. What did it matter if his hair was combed? But it did, somehow. Miss Paxton may not be rich, but she was certainly a lady. Anyone could tell that just by looking at her. She wasn't stunningly beautiful, but there was something fine about her. And those blue eyes. They could look right inside you.

Those thoughts weren't helping him think about the ledger. He snatched it from the shelf over his bunk and hurried outside. When he got to the house, he knocked, and sure enough, he heard her call, "Come in."

She was bent over the cookstove, peering into the firebox. In this heat, she wanted a fire?

He set the ledger on the table. "Can I help you, ma'am?"

She lowered the lid onto the stovetop and turned toward him. "Sorry. I was thinking perhaps I could offer you coffee, but I guess it would take too long to get the stove going and heat it."

"We've got coffee in the bunkhouse, ma'am. We leave the pot on the stove all day. I could bring some over for you."

"Oh, not for me, no. But thank you."

Jack nodded. "Well, I'm fine without."

"Good. Let's get to work, shall we?" She pulled out a chair and sat down.

Jack took a seat opposite her. "If you want a fire later to cook your supper, one of us can start it for you."

"I can light a fire myself," she said. "It's so warm, maybe I'll just. . ."

"Well, Rusty started a stew simmering in the bunkhouse," Jack said. "If you'd like, we can bring you a bowl of that, and you can eat some of the biscuits we left in your pantry with it."

"You left biscuits for me?" Her eyes widened in surprise. They were right pretty.

"Yes, ma'am. Abe had a baking spree yesterday, and we all thought it might be good to leave you a little something cooked, so we put half a dozen biscuits and a piece of cake in your breadbox."

"How kind."

She sounded sincere. Jack nodded and nudged the ledger. "What do you want to know first, ma'am?"

"Is the ranch on a sound footing financially?"

"Oh yes, ma'am. Mr. Hill made a profit the last two years."

"Good to hear. And how many cattle are there?"

"About five hundred. Most of the cows and calves are up in the far pasture. It's been awfully dry this summer, and we've spread 'em out since the grass is poor. It seems a little better in the hills, so we turned most of them up there on what we call the range—but it's all fenced. You can be sure of that. We ride the fences pretty much all the time to make sure they stay in good shape."

She nodded almost mechanically. "Well, I assume that you and the hands take care of the livestock, and I won't have to do much there."

"We do, mostly," he said. "Mr. Hill liked to keep his hand in. He'd ride out with us most days. Put in a day's work on things like fencing and branding too."

"Oh." A hint of dismay clouded the vibrant blue eyes. "And when do you brand the cows?"

"When we round them up in August, before we sell off the yearlings, we'll make sure all this year's calves are branded. Mostly it's the young stock that needs it." She wouldn't be here for the next roundup if all she wanted to do was claim the land and sell it. "You don't need to worry about that, at least not right now."

She smiled then. "Good. Let's hope that if I do ever take part in a roundup, I'll be more prepared than I am now."

"Yes, ma'am."

Jack opened the ledger and went through the most recent expenditures—payday, feed, groceries, fencing materials, leather, blacksmith's services.

"You seem to have done a thorough job," Miss Paxton said.

"Thank you. If you'd like, I can go all the way back to when Mr. Hill died, or even to when he put me in charge of his books."

"That won't be necessary at this time," she said. "Perhaps later."

He nodded. "Mr. McClure had somebody go over the ledger in April to make sure things were in order for the—the estate. He said everything was as it should be."

"I'm sure he would have told me if it was otherwise."

"Yes'm. Now, Miss Paxton, if you'd like to talk about Mr. Hill's plans for the breeding program—"

She sat bolt upright, her cheeks flaming. "No. I would not."

"Oh." Jack frowned. "It was dear to his heart, ma'am. A very important part of his plans for the ranch."

"I'm sure it was." She sounded as if she had something stuck in her throat. "But I'm not prepared to discuss the—the gentleman cow he purchased, or any other aspect—"

Jack couldn't help laughing, and she stared at him. If possible, her face got even redder.

"I'm sorry, ma'am," Jack choked out. "It's not an ox, it's a bull, and there's nothing gentlemanly about him."

"I only—" She gulped and closed her lips firmly, not meeting his eyes.

"Sorry." Jack managed to hold in his laughter. "I didn't mean to make fun of you. It's just that bulls can be mean and ornery. Sometimes they're downright dangerous. If you're going to run this ranch, you need to learn how to behave around stock and how to keep yourself safe when you're working with them. Part of that is using the correct terms for things so we're clear on what we're talking about."

Her hand clenched and unclenched at her neckline. "Forgive me, Mr.—Jack. I mean no disrespect, but this is not the kind of discussion I would—" She stopped and cleared her throat. "I do want to learn about ranching, but it may take me some time to become accustomed. . ."

She shoved back her chair. "Perhaps we can continue this discussion tomorrow."

"Sure." He stood and picked up his hat. "Would you like to tour the ranch in the morning?"

"Well. . .yes, I suppose that would be nice."

"I'll have our horses saddled at seven thirty."

"So early?"

"Before it gets too hot."

"Oh." She hesitated.

Surely, Jack thought, she isn't balking at getting up at a decent hour.

"There's one other thing that perhaps you should know."

"What's that?"

"I've never ridden a horse before."

Of course she hadn't. Jack gritted his teeth and gave a curt nod.

"Riding lesson at seven then. Don't worry, I'll give you a gentle horse."

He strode for the door before she could call it off.

Rachel nearly panicked, but she reminded herself to take three deep breaths and pray. *Lord, what do I do? I don't have any riding clothes.*

When a knock came at the door, she had all five of the dresses she'd brought spread out on Mr. Hill's bed—*her* bed. She wouldn't think about how it had been her suitor's bed and how she might be Mrs. Hill right now if she'd accepted his marriage proposal. Then she would have a right to be here. And no doubt she'd know how to ride a horse by now.

She went to the door and opened it. A cowboy stood there holding a tin tray. He was older than either Jack or Rusty, his hair and beard nearly white.

"Howdy, ma'am. I'm Abe."

"Oh, you're the baker."

He beamed. "Yes'm. Brought you some vittles."

"That's very kind of you." She stepped back to let him in. "I confess I ate one of the biscuits that was left in my pantry earlier, and they're very good."

"Thank you kindly." He moved past her and lowered his tray to the kitchen table. On it were a steaming bowl and something wrapped in a limp cotton napkin. "Beef stew and gingerbread." He straightened and smiled at her.

Rachel found herself liking Abe. He reminded her a little of her uncle Tobias, God rest his soul. "Why, thank you. You didn't need to make gingerbread. You already left me a piece of chocolate cake."

Abe shrugged. "It's a special day, ma'am. We've all been a little blue since the boss died, and with you coming—well, I thought we could all use a little celebration. So, welcome, and enjoy the gingerbread. They's some thick cream in your icebox, if you're partial to it."

"That sounds lovely. Uh, Abe. . ." She peered up into his faded blue eyes.

"Yes'm?"

"Mr. Callen says I'll have a riding lesson in the morning. Do you have any idea how I should prepare?"

"Just head on out to the barn after you eat breakfast, I guess."

"Oh. Well, I. . .don't suppose there's a sidesaddle for me to learn on?"

Abe frowned. "I don't reckon there is, ma'am." His face brightened. "Mrs. Stanno, she doesn't use a sidesaddle."

"Who?" Rachel asked.

"Cleet Stanno's wife. She wears an old pair of Cleet's britches. Rolls up the bottoms and jumps in the saddle."

"Oh." That sounded a bit daunting. First of all, there was no way on earth Rachel would wear trousers, and she was certainly not going to jump onto a horse's back. She was not an acrobat, thank you.

"Don't worry, ma'am," Abe said. "We boys won't hang around to watch. We've got to ride fence in the mornin'."

Taking that as small comfort, Rachel saw him out and threw the bolt on the door. Then she sat down to her supper. Rusty's stew and Abe's gingerbread exceeded her expectations. She looked longingly at the slice of cake but decided she'd better save that for tomorrow. She'd have a bellyache if she ate any more tonight, and she had a lot of work to do.

She spent an hour agonizing over whether to alter a dress into a riding outfit. Her oldest, plainest calico might not have enough fabric to form the loose, billowy trousers she imagined. She remembered what Abe had said. With some misgivings, she opened Mr. Hill's wardrobe. A few shirts and two jackets hung to one side. There was plenty of room for her dresses.

She walked over to the dresser and pulled out one drawer after another. In all, she found four pairs of pants. Three looked like everyday working trousers, and the fourth was probably his Sunday best. She sighed. These clothes could surely be distributed to the ranch hands, who could get some wear out of them. She supposed Mr. McClure hadn't removed anything, awaiting the disposition of the estate. If she inherited, she would certainly give away Mr. Hill's clothing. Meanwhile, did she have a right to use some of it?

She whirled back to the bed and picked up the skirt of her travel ensemble.

Jack stood by the corral fence, gazing across at the house. A thin stream of smoke issued from the chimney, but other than that, he saw no signs of life.

Both the horses were saddled. He'd picked Brownie, his favorite mount, for himself, and Patch, a steady old gelding, for Miss Paxton. Should he go knock on the door to see if she was ready? Surely the smoke meant she was preparing her breakfast. He'd give her a few more minutes, but he sure wasn't going to stand around here all morning when the men were already out riding fence and moving a few cattle.

He ducked between the rails of the larger corral, where they kept half a dozen remuda horses. Might as well do something useful. He approached each horse quietly and lifted its hooves one at a time. They all looked in good shape, their shoes tightly nailed on. He patted the last one's flank and turned away as the door to the house closed.

There she was. He tried not to stare. She walked—or waddled—toward him, looking rounder than she had yesterday. How many layers of clothes was she wearing?

He spotted rolled up cuffs as her dark blue skirt swirled around her ankles. He strode back to the two saddled mounts, hiding his face until he could control his amusement. Must be the dungarees and the belt under her skirt that made her look plumper and walk strangely.

"Good morning, Jack." Her direct gaze was almost a challenge.

"Morning, miss." He felt his lips twitch and looked down.

"Might be you'll need some boots if you're going to ride much." Her laced walking shoes would be all right, but boots would be better.

"We'll see."

He nodded and lifted Patch's reins. "This here's Patch. He'll go easy on you."

Miss Paxton's eyebrows rose. "Indeed? And what do I do first?"

"Well, ma'am, you come around to this side. Always best to mount on the horse's left side."

"Why?"

He blinked. "I dunno. It's just the way they're trained."

"Huh." She turned sideways to ease in beside him, between the two horses.

"Put your left foot in the stirrup," he said.

She eyed the stirrup with skepticism. "Isn't that rather a reach?"

"Well, I can run the stirrup down the leather if you want and adjust it once you're in the saddle."

"Is that how most people do it?"

"No, ma'am. And you'll have to learn to do it with the leather at the right length for you. But this being your first time and all—"

"Stand back," she said firmly.

Jack stood back.

She swung her leg, and on the third try, skirts flailing, she made contact with the iron. She paused and then worked the toe of her shoe farther into the stirrup. Her smile was triumphant.

Jack pushed his hat back and said slowly, "That's a good effort, ma'am, but that's your right foot."

"My. . . ?" She stared at the stirrup as she stood there on one leg, stretched out. He could see in her eyes the moment she made the connection and visualized herself plopping backward into the saddle. "Right." She lowered her foot to the ground. "Left foot."

Watching her was painful. Jack longed to pick her up and hoist her onto the horse's back, but she had to learn. If she didn't grow confident in something as simple as this, she'd never stay on the ranch. And if he laughed—well, she could be out of here on the next train. Then where would he and the other men be? Out of work, that's where.

Finally, she managed to get the correct foot into the stirrup.

"Now what?" she asked, panting a little.

"Gather yourself and jump," he said. "Put your weight on the stirrup and shove yourself right up there. Swing your right leg over the horse's rump and sit down. Then we'll see if we need to adjust the leathers."

"Hmm."

"Just don't jump so hard you go over the far side." He'd seen it happen once, when a tenderfoot mounted a fidgety colt.

Her jaw set in determination. She paused. She tensed. She leaped. And landed with a soft thud in the saddle, her skirt settling gently around her and the denim legs of Mr. Hill's old dungarees exposed to the knee.

Miss Paxton smiled down at him.

"I did it!"

"Yes'm, you did. That's fine. And this stirrup looks about right. How's the other side?"

She looked down the horse's off side and wriggled in the saddle.

"Got your foot in?" Jack asked as he walked around to the other side.

"Almost." Her brow furrowed and she hunched down. "There." She sat up straighter, proud as a peahen, then gasped as Patches lifted a foot to kick at a fly.

"Steady, ma'am," Jack said. "You're doing fine." He checked the leather. "Let me put this one up a notch."

She cringed away from him as he grabbed the strap, loosened the buckle, and ran the leather up to the next hole.

"There you go."

She quickly spread her skirt as far as she could over her pant leg. He looked up at her. Her cheeks were flaming, and a lock of her fair hair had escaped her bun and fluttered in the wind. Jack's chest tightened. He didn't know if he'd ever in his life seen a woman so attractive, and that was when she was wearing his boss's old pants. He didn't presume to think about how she'd look in a fancy dress.

"Are we ready?" She didn't quite meet his gaze.

He picked up the reins and held them in front of her.

"Take these. No, in your left hand."

"Why?"

"Because that leaves your right hand free for other things."

"Like what?"

He frowned. "Anything. A lasso, a gun. . ."

Patches shifted, and she grabbed the saddle horn with her right hand.

"But not that."

"What?"

"Don't hold on to the horn."

"Then what's it for?" Her blue eyes looked slightly panic stricken.

"That's for snubbing your rope."

"I don't have a rope."

"That's true. I'll have to teach you to rope, I guess. But for now, try to ride with the reins in your left hand."

"What do I do with this one?" She lifted her right hand and wiggled her fingers.

"Put it—put it—" He gulped. "On your leg." He was suddenly sure that gentlemen in Boston never said anything implying that ladies had limbs beneath their skirts, denim-clad or otherwise.

Gingerly, she rested her right hand on her thigh. "Like that?"

"That's fine, ma'am. You should only hold on to the horn in a crisis. Now, I'll mount up and we'll take a nice, slow ride around the pasture. Just turn Patch around, and—"

"Turn him? How do I turn him?"

Jack realized what the day ahead would be like and let out a big sigh.

❧ Chapter 4 ❧

Rachel's first riding lesson turned out to be less trying than she'd imagined. Once she learned the basics of directing the horse, she and Patch got along fine. She and Jack walked the horses about the nearest pasture and, from a distance, examined the cattle grazing there. She actually found herself laughing at the antics of the calves. They leaped about and butted each other then chased each other around, like toddlers at play while their mothers placidly watched.

"Should we try a jog now?" Jack asked.

"A jog?"

"Put your weight on your feet and lean forward just a little. Now loosen the reins a bit and squeeze Patch with your legs."

She didn't have time to consider that Jack knew what her limbs were doing. As Patch lurched into a languid trot, she almost pitched out of the saddle and, deeming that moment a crisis, grabbed the horn.

"Weight on your feet," Jack snapped. "Think how heavy your legs are. Send all your weight down to the stirrups."

He jogged along beside her on his brown horse, looking as if his pants were basted to the saddle, while she flopped and thudded about in hers. After she had ridden a short distance, her teeth jarring with each step, he let her slow Patch to a walk.

"There," he said. "How do you feel?"

"Very jostled."

He laughed. "You'll get used to it. And when you're ready for a lope, you'll find that much smoother."

"A lope? Is that faster?"

"Yes, but smoother."

"How can that be? Are you trying to trick me?"

"I wouldn't do that. I promise."

She frowned and rode along sedately beside him for a minute. "And then do we gallop?"

"Oh, so you do know about a horse's gaits."

"Well. . ."

"A lope is what they might call a canter in the East."

"Oh." She gazed over at him. "Why do they have different names for things out here?"

"Like what?"

"Well, I heard Rusty call his horse a pony. It was as big as this one though."

"I'm thinking you say things in Boston that we don't say out here," Jack said.

She thought about that. "Probably so." Her father had said woodchuck, while their neighbor called the same animal a groundhog. What Rhoda called a veranda, she called a porch. She supposed there were many regional differences in speech, just as there were different accents. Her diction probably sounded odd to Jack and the other men. Did they think she was snobbish because she had a Boston accent?

They returned to the fence near the barn, and Jack said, "Come on. I'll teach you to open the gate without getting off the horse."

She stared at him. "Really? Is that possible?"

"Yes, ma'am, and a very handy thing to know."

She looked ahead toward the gate where they'd entered the pasture. Two russet-colored cows grazed complacently just this side of the gate.

"Oh."

"What?" Jack asked.

"Those cows." She glanced at him self-consciously. "They *are* cows, aren't they?"

"Yes, ma'am. All our cattle have horns, if that's what you mean. Cows and steers both."

"Why is that?"

Jack shrugged. "Just the nature of the beast."

"Ah. Well, how do you get them away from the gate?"

"Just yell at 'em. Tell 'em to move."

"And they'll do that?"

His smile made her stomach flip, and she looked away.

"You scared of cows?" he asked.

She hesitated and then nodded.

"Look, Miss Paxton, you and Patch together are bigger than those cows. As long as you act firm and confident around them, you've got no problems. Show 'em who's boss."

"But I—" Patch stopped walking, his nose almost touching one of the cows' furry hides. Rachel swallowed hard.

Jack pushed his horse forward and swatted his hat at the nearest cow. "Go on, you!"

The two bovines ambled a few steps away and resumed grazing.

"There. You see?"

She nodded. "What if you're afoot though?"

Jack put on his hat and adjusted it. "I try not to be among 'em too often without my horse, but it's the same thing. Stand your ground. Look 'em in the eye. Make yourself big and loud. And don't run."

Rachel gulped. Those cows must weigh six or eight times what she did. She doubted she could convince them she was bigger and stronger than they were. She vowed inwardly never to put herself in that situation.

Over the next week, Rachel got to know the ranch. She took long, slow rides with Jack, Rusty, Abe, and the fourth cowpuncher, Goldie, who was somewhere in age between Rusty and Abe. She thought his name was odd, since his hair was almost black. Then she learned that his real name was Ernst Goldenshue, and it made sense. He had a slight accent, which she supposed was German, and she occasionally heard him speak to the animals in a foreign language.

The men varied in their willingness to converse with her when they rode. Abe was always pleasant and polite but only explained things when necessary. Rusty was more garrulous, and it was from him that she learned a bit about the others' backgrounds. He even told her stories about when Mr. Hill was alive and nearly twenty ranch hands were employed. A few of his tales were funny, about odd things that happened on roundups or out on the range. It sounded exciting, even fun. She didn't spend much time with Goldie, but he was mostly smiles and nods, and she wondered how well he spoke English.

Jack was the source of most of her information. He pushed her to learn more about horses and cattle, to master the jog and then the lope, and to toss a loop of rope over a fence post. He even shared with her Mr. Hill's plans for the ranch.

"He loved animals, and he wanted to build a herd of really good cattle. He ordered that new bull, even though it cost a lot, because he knew it would make his herd better. Other ranchers have crossed Herefords with their range stock, and they've done well. They make a better beef animal."

Rachel cleared her throat, doing her best to ignore her sensitivity to the topic. "In our correspondence he seemed like a very intelligent man."

"Oh, he was. He was studying up on ways to provide better feed for his herd too. I don't know if you were aware, but last winter was really hard here. More snow than usual and low temperatures."

"No, I didn't know that." She should have watched the papers for reports on conditions in Texas, she thought. But then, why should she? She had made up her mind well before the onset of winter that Mr. Hill wasn't the man for her.

Jack looked out over the range. They'd ridden to the highest spot on the ranch, a hill overlooking the pastures and the languid stream that wound through them, only a trickle right now.

"Well, it's dry now, like a lot of our summers. The boss was hopeful that the extra snow would mean we'd have a better summer—more water. But it doesn't look that way now."

"What will you do about the cattle?"

Jack eyed her closely. "I expect the new owner will lay in extra feed, maybe buy up some hay. It'll cost though. The crop isn't likely to be very good this year."

His brown eyes seemed to be measuring her.

"Jack, I don't know anything about ranching or agriculture in general. If I kept the ranch, I'd probably make a lot of mistakes. It might be better to sell it and let someone who knows these things come in and take over."

He rode along for a minute then halted Brownie. Patch stopped of his own accord.

"You've got people who can help you," Jack said.

"You mean. . .you?"

"Me and the other hands. You'd have to hire on more men at roundup time, but that wouldn't be a problem. We'd send—I mean, you would send a couple hundred steers to market."

"On a cattle drive?"

"Just into Fort Worth. It's not like the old days, when it took months to drive the herds to the railhead. It's a matter of one day's work to get them from this ranch into town. We'd set it up ahead of time with the stockyards, so's they were expecting us. I mean, *you* would set it up."

She nodded slowly. "What else would need to be done?"

He huffed out a breath. "Lots of things. We've let some things go a little because Mr. McClure didn't think he should keep a full outfit until he knew if you would claim the estate. Until your thirty days is up, I guess we just keep on like we've been doing—getting by until someone really starts working again and making this ranch what Mr. Hill wanted it to be." He sighed. "Too bad you couldn't have known Randolph. I bet you would have liked him."

"I'm starting to think I would have." Rachel gazed into the distance, where she could barely see the roof of the barn and bunkhouse. "If Mr. Hill were still here, what would he be doing now?"

Jack's eyes lit, and he launched into a list of things his former employer had planned for this summer: laying in feed, stringing new fence, building a stout enclosure for the bull, culling the herd, adding new breeding cows, constructing a line shack at the farthest reach of his land, and training new horses for the remuda.

"But you're not doing any of that?" she asked.

Jack's shoulders sagged. "Mr. McClure said there wasn't any sense adding more stock or getting horses ready for a bigger outfit until we knew who the new owner would be, and what he—or she—wanted to do. If we prepared for twenty hands being on the job this fall, and then the new owner sold off all the cattle, that would be money wasted from the estate."

"I see."

Mr. Hill wouldn't care what she did with his ranch, now that he was dead. But would she dishonor his memory if she didn't carry out his vision?

Rachel's thoughts troubled her for the rest of the day. She took a lesson from Abe on saddling and bridling horses until she managed to outfit even a rather stubborn mare who hated to open her teeth for the bit. Then she practiced her infantile roping skills, and before sundown she rode out with all four men to watch them move a band of about thirty cattle into the highest pasture. She even felt she'd been a bit useful, blocking a few of the yearlings from veering away from the bunch.

But that evening, alone in the ranch house, she sat with the lamp low and her beans and corn bread barely touched. She would never be as capable as these men. What would it matter if she stayed the rest of the month and then sold out? It would mean she could have the business she'd always dreamed of. Back in Boston, of course.

She sighed. If she sold the Hill ranch, it would change more lives than her own. Would a new rancher come in with his own crew and displace the men who worked here? Would Abe, who wasn't elderly, but was well past his prime, be able to find work on another ranch? What would become of young Rusty, and of Goldie, the German man? She was sure Jack could find other employment, but he probably couldn't step into another job as foreman. He'd go back to a dollar a day as a cowpuncher, no doubt. But he had such wisdom and skill, he really deserved to manage a ranch. She wondered if he dreamed of having his own spread someday. Probably they all did. But a man like Jack Callen could make a go of it.

Jack sat at the small desk at one end of the bunkhouse, looking through the ranch's ledger. They'd pared expenses to the bone for the past few months, as Mr. McClure had requested, but they really needed to spend some money now if they were going to be ready for the roundup in August. He would send Abe to town tomorrow for the supplies they needed.

"You playin' tonight, Jack?" Abe called from the small square table where they took their meals and played poker in the evenings.

Jack looked over his shoulder. "No, count me out."

"I wonder what Miss Paxton's doing," Rusty said.

Abe riffled the deck of worn cards. "Prob'ly writin' letters to her friends back east."

"Maybe we should see if she wants to join the game."

The others laughed, but Rusty had sounded serious.

"Ladies don't play poker," Jack said.

"Why not?" Rusty turned around in his chair to look at him.

"She probably doesn't know how," Abe said. "Anyway, it ain't fittin'."

Rusty frowned. "How come?"

"Ladies do not play poker," Goldie said in clipped, precise words.

Before Rusty could say, "Why not?" again, Jack shoved back his chair.

"I'll mosey over and see if she's got everything she needs." Abe could be right—she might have letters she wanted mailed. And they hadn't been into town and checked the mail since the day she arrived. There might be mail for her waiting at the post office—or for him or one of the boys, for that matter. Jack heard from his mother and brother now and then, and Goldie got occasional letters from down Victoria way, where a lot of the German folk had settled. Rusty's sisters and grandma sent him cheerful notes from Missouri. So far as he knew, Abe had never gotten mail so long as he'd been at the Hill ranch, but that didn't signify much.

He put on his hat and ambled across the yard and up the steps of the house. She came to the door almost at once. She looked surprised and a little disheveled—her hair was down around her shoulders, and her cheeks had a slight flush. She looked pretty that way, almost beautiful, or Jack's idea of beautiful.

"Hi. Sorry to bother you, ma'am."

"You're not bothering me." Her eyes were downcast, and she ventured a glance up at him through her long lashes.

"I'm going to send one of the boys into town in the morning," Jack said. "I thought maybe you had some letters you'd like to send, or maybe there's something you'd like from the store."

"Oh thank you. I'll write a letter or two this evening, if you or whoever's going into town would kindly stop to get them in the morning."

"Of course."

"Are you going to see Mr. McClure?" she asked.

"Well, I don't know, ma'am. We *could* see him, if you want. Would you like to send a message for him?"

"Oh, I. . ." She hesitated and turned her face away.

"Would you like to go to town and see him yourself, ma'am?"

"That would be a lot of trouble, wouldn't it? I wouldn't like to hold up your man."

"No trouble at all," Jack said. "In fact, if you'd like, I can drive you there myself, right to his office. And you could do any shopping you want to afterward." He was sorry he hadn't thought of it before. Some women actually enjoyed shopping, and Miss Paxton was used to living in the city, where a wide variety of shops were close at hand.

"It wouldn't interfere with your work?" she asked.

"No, it's fine." He was starting to like the idea. Maybe they could eat lunch in town. He didn't usually splurge for stuff like that, but it seemed worthwhile. Or maybe Mr. McClure would offer to pay for her dinner. Somehow that thought didn't sit right with Jack. He didn't want the lawyer treating Miss Paxton. He wanted to spend the time with her—by himself.

"Good," he said. "I'll send the men out to work after breakfast, and then I'll hitch up the wagon. I'll let you know when I'm ready."

"Sounds good." She closed the door with a smile that made Jack's stomach flip. But maybe she was just happy that she wouldn't have to ride Patch all the way into town.

He paused halfway to the bunkhouse to look up at the stars. They were extra brilliant tonight. Better not care too much for Miss Paxton, he told himself. She'd stated soon after her arrival that she would probably stay the required month and then sell the ranch. She'd be gone in a few weeks, and besides, he didn't want her to think he only liked her because she owned the ranch, or soon would.

For the past week and a half, he'd helped her in every way he could think of, hoping she'd change her mind. Randolph Hill hadn't wanted to die when he did, but when he knew it was coming, he'd set things up this way on purpose. He wanted Rachel to have the ranch that he loved. Could she learn to love it the way he had? Randolph had been his boss, but Jack was also proud to think of him as a friend. They'd had many a long conversation on balmy nights like this, sitting on the porch of the ranch house and gazing at the stars.

Randolph had confessed his disappointment when Miss Paxton turned down his proposal. He'd begun to hope that he'd found the woman who would share his life with him. Jack hadn't seen their letters, but he hadn't expected to like her. The laugh was on him. In his short acquaintance with the young lady, he was beginning to see why his friend had been drawn to her. She was earnest, and she was a hard worker. She wanted to do things right, and she wanted to see the ranch succeed, even if she didn't stay on as its owner. If she decided to claim it and then sell it, she wanted it to be in good shape for the buyer.

Jack hoped she would stay. He'd never imagined he'd wind up working for a woman, but the reality wasn't so bad. Not if she was willing to ask for help and listen to reason. Rachel seemed open to both. But would it be harder to work for a woman he admired? Because he was definitely starting to feel that way about her, and it seemed wrong somehow. There was no room for romance in a working relationship. Maybe he should have one of the men take her to town, but he'd told her he would take her. He couldn't see a good way out of it without insulting her.

❧ Chapter 5 ❧

"Good to see you again," Mr. McClure said, shaking Rachel's hand. "How are things at the ranch?"

"Going well, I think." She smiled. "Perhaps you should ask Mr. Callen."

"Oh?" McClure shot a questioning glance at the foreman, who stood behind her in the doorway to the attorney's office.

"She's doing great," Jack said. "She's putting in several hours every day, learning to ride and getting to know the ranch."

"That's wonderful." Mr. McClure looked decidedly relieved, and he gave Rachel a playful smile. "You've lasted this long, young lady. Can I assume you plan to stay out your month?"

"I don't have any plans otherwise," she said. "If Mr. Callen and the other men can put up with me that long, I guess I'll stay at least another nineteen days."

McClure's smile faded. "But not longer?"

"I haven't decided yet," she confessed. "There's a lot to consider."

"Of course."

"But I wondered if you would think it appropriate to hire a few more men at the end of this month? Mr. Callen tells me they'll be needed for the roundup in August and getting the cattle to the stockyards."

Jack held out the book he'd brought. "I took the liberty of bringing along the ledger. I thought you might like to have a look at the numbers before answering that question."

"All right." McClure took it. "Will you be in town long?"

"We're going to the post office and then to the general store," Jack said. He glanced at Rachel. "We might get some lunch before we head back out."

"Fine," McClure said. "Stop in before you leave, and I'll set aside a few minutes to talk about the ranch. I'll try to look through this in the meantime."

"Thank you," Rachel said, and Jack nodded.

As they left the office, a boy ran up the walkway and pounded on the door. Mr. McClure opened it almost at once, and the boy said, "Telegram for Mr. McClure."

Rachel arched her eyebrows at Jack.

"I s'pose he gets a lot of those in his business," Jack said. "Post office?"

"Yes, thank you."

Rachel accepted his hand to help her onto the wagon seat. Jack climbed up on the other side and took the reins. She enjoyed driving through the town with him.

At the post office, several items were in the box earmarked for the ranch. Jack glanced through them.

"I see Rusty's got a letter from his sister." He tucked two envelopes into his shirt pocket. "My mother," he mumbled.

"How nice that you hear from her," Rachel said.

"I don't write to her often enough, I s'pose." He handed her the last envelope. "That's addressed to Mr. Hill."

"Oh. Have there been others?"

"Yeah, mostly business."

"What do you do with them?"

"I usually take them to McClure," Jack said.

She nodded. "Then that's what we'll do, when we go back to pick up the ledger."

They went on to the store, and Jack told her to pick out whatever she needed for supplies or to make her stay more comfortable. Rachel chose a few items to supplement her food, and a teapot and a pound of tea. She browsed the yard goods and housewares but didn't buy anything in those departments. If she stayed and owned the ranch one day, there would be a few things she would want. She would sew a riding outfit that would replace Randolph's old dungarees, for instance, and buy a wide-brimmed hat that wasn't too big. Randolph's hat wouldn't stay on her head when her mount started to jog, and Rusty had poked holes in the brim and fitted a cord through them to keep the hat in place. It would be nice to have one that fit properly, without the cord. But for now the limited wardrobe she'd brought with her and the few things she'd borrowed met her needs.

Jack needed to pick up some salt blocks and several sacks of grain at the feed store. Rachel went in with him and met the owner. She was fascinated by the bins of different grains and the vast stacks of bagged feed.

They ate lunch at the same restaurant where the lawyer had taken her the day she arrived, and Rachel found the food tasty and filling. She ought to do more cooking at the ranch, but it seemed silly to prepare full meals for herself while the men cooked their own food in the bunkhouse.

"Where did Mr. Hill eat his meals?" she asked Jack when they were back in the wagon.

"Mostly with us."

Rachel frowned. It wouldn't be appropriate for her to eat in the bunkhouse.

"Reckon you could hire someone to cook for you if you stay," Jack said slowly.

"Oh, I don't need a cook," she said quickly. "It just seems odd to cook meals for just me."

"Still, you ought to eat well. I noticed you didn't ask for any meat, other than what the boys and I have brought over."

"What about the chickens?" she asked. "Do you ever eat them?" The small flock was kept penned behind the barn, and one of the men fed and watered the birds. Rusty brought her a couple of eggs every other morning.

"We ate all the roosters but one, and after the boss died, I wasn't sure we should ask for more. There's a few young ones that will be big enough soon."

"I'll speak to Mr. McClure. Maybe we can get a dozen more—a few eating birds and some hens. If he lets us hire more men, you'll need extra eggs in the bunkhouse for sure."

"That'd be good. I should have asked him sooner. The hens don't lay very well in this hot weather."

When they arrived back at Mr. McClure's office, he showed them in and invited them to sit. He went around the desk and took a seat.

"Well, did you have a successful shopping expedition?" he asked after Rachel handed him the letter.

"Yes, sir," she said. "We wondered if we could buy a few chickens."

"Live chickens," Jack added.

"I don't see why not." McClure nudged the ledger toward the edge of the desk. "I looked over the accounts. You haven't spent much this month, Jack."

Jack shrugged.

"You need to keep yourself and the men healthy, not to mention Miss Paxton."

"Yes, sir," Jack said.

"By all means, stop at the mercantile or wherever you can get them and pick up some birds. Anything else you need?"

"Well, if we're going to hire more men to help with the roundup. . . ," Jack said, and left the sentence dangling.

"I suppose we won't know exactly what will happen until Miss Paxton makes her decision, but in any event, you'll need a full crew to drive some cattle." McClure settled his gaze on Rachel. "Even if you decide to sell the whole ranch and its stock, some of the cattle will probably be sold in August or September."

Both men's eyes were fixed on her, and she knew she had to say something.

"I'd like another week or two to decide," she said.

"Of course. Meanwhile, there's another matter I should bring to your attention."

"Yes, sir?" she said.

"A telegram arrived for me earlier, shortly after you left."

"We saw the boy," Jack said.

McClure nodded. "It was from Randolph Hill's cousin."

"His cousin?" Jack sounded awestruck.

Rachel had heard mention of the cousin when Mr. McClure went over the will with her, but she hadn't expected to hear more about him.

"I thought his whereabouts were unknown," she said.

"They were, but I sent several letters in an attempt to locate him. It was my duty, as executor of the will."

"Even if he's not getting anything?" Jack asked.

Rachel was surprised that he seemed to know the contents of the document, but maybe Mr. McClure had told him when he asked him to stay on as foreman. Or maybe Mr. Hill had told him in person when he had the will drawn up. After all, he and Jack had been friends.

"I just wanted you to be aware, in case he shows up here," McClure said. "His name is Andrew Hill. I think he would come to see me first if he does travel here from San Francisco, but if he shows up at the ranch, send him to me."

"We certainly will," Rachel said, and Jack nodded. She found it comforting to have someone like Jack, who understood the circumstances fully, at her side.

McClure smiled. "All right then. I found the accounts in order. Just carry on as you are until you're ready to make a decision, Miss Paxton. I'm here anytime you want to discuss any aspect of the ranch business."

"Thank you," she said.

She and Jack bought a dozen chickens and some extra feed. Jack loaded the two crates that held the birds into the wagon, and they headed for the ranch. On the way, Rachel thought about everything she'd learned since her arrival in Fort Worth.

"Jack, I think I need to know more about the operation of the ranch," she said about halfway home.

"Sure. Like what?"

"Like how the hiring will work, for one thing. We'll need to take on more men before my month is up. Will you handle that, or should I?"

"I can do it if you want. I know a lot of people around here. I have a few men in mind, ones who've worked for the ranch before. If you decide not to stay, we'll take them on just long enough to get the necessary chores done. After we sell off the cattle we've got earmarked for the stockyards, we can let them go."

"And if I'm staying on?"

His eyes flickered to meet her gaze, and then he looked ahead at the dusty road. "Then I'd say keep on at least three more men. I'll handpick them, if you think that's best. Hard workers who won't drink a lot or cause trouble in town."

She nodded slowly. "Perhaps when you begin hiring, you can tell those few that the job might become more permanent?"

"Sounds like a good plan." His face was like stone, and he stared forward. Rachel wished she could read his mind, about the men for the outfit and several other things.

"Now, about the stock to sell," she said. "I take it this is something Mr. Hill did every year?"

"Yes, ma'am. That's the purpose of the ranch, to raise beeves to sell to the meat market."

"So this fall roundup is the main source of income for the ranch."

He hesitated then nodded. "There's other things, other times, but mostly, yes. This is important to the well-being of the ranch."

"Can you tell me more about the roundup? I'd like to know more before it gets here."

Jack smiled then, and the rest of the way home, he talked about the job he loved.

Jack tried to figure out what was right. He wanted to be there for Rachel if she needed him, but he was afraid he was beginning to care about her too much. He answered her many questions on the way home from town, but the next day he asked Abe to take her out with him when he rode fence. Abe later reported that she asked him a lot of questions too, about Mr. Hill and about ranching in general.

"So long as she's not asking questions about me," Jack said.

"Oh no, not much," Abe replied. "She really wants to learn though." He grinned. "Smart lady."

"I think so too."

Jack went into town alone to spread the word that he'd be hiring a few hands at the Hill ranch soon. The day after that, he let Rachel watch Goldie shoe a couple of horses while he was busy elsewhere. Then he sent her with Rusty to herd a small bunch of cattle in from the range.

"Take your time," he told Rusty. "Let Miss Paxton learn how to get them moving and keep them going in the right direction. They don't have to get here fast, but you all have to get here in one piece."

"Sure thing," Rusty said.

After they left, Jack wondered if he should have sent Abe or Goldie with them. But they arrived a couple of hours later, safe and sound, with all the critters accounted for.

Rachel looked terrific. She'd made some kind of divided skirt out of a dress she'd brought with her, and her skin was starting to bronze from all her time out in the sun. He recognized the made-over cotton work shirt she wore, and he admitted privately that it looked better on her than it had on Randolph. Of course, he would never hint at such a thought.

Beyond that she had gained an assured air when it came to sitting in the saddle. Not overconfident but no longer afraid. And it seemed she'd learned a bit from Rusty about heading and driving the stock. A little pride welled up in him at the progress she'd made in two weeks.

But he'd best keep avoiding time alone with her. Her fair hair seemed lighter than it had when she arrived—he ought to have insisted she get herself a good hat in town. Next time. But that hair was pretty. Real pretty.

The next day, Jack took Goldie and Rusty with him to move a bigger band of cattle.

"Can't I go?" Rachel asked when she heard what they were going to do.

"Aren't you sore from yesterday?" Jack asked. "You spent several hours in the saddle."

"I'm getting over that." She gazed up at him with those hopeful blue eyes. "Please? Rusty said I did well yesterday."

"Yes, he told me." Jack looked out toward the far pastures,

frowning. He couldn't deny that the idea of having Rachel nearby for half a day appealed to him. And it wouldn't be like they were alone. "All right, but—"

"Thank you!" She whirled and ran to the corral gate before he could finish. She seemed so happy. He felt good inside for having given her that. But he had fully intended to issue some strict warnings. Well, there'd be time on the trail.

She came out a couple of minutes later leading Patch.

Jack smiled. "Saddle him yourself?"

"I sure did."

"Better check the cinch one more time."

Her brow furrowed, but she halted the horse and flipped up the stirrup leather. She worked at the knot in the leather strap and tugged.

"Holding your breath on me?" she asked in a mock tone of shock.

Rusty and Goldie had mounted and were waiting nearby. Rusty caught Jack's eye and grinned from ear to ear.

"We'll make a first-class cowpuncher out of her yet," he said.

Jack chuckled. Abe was staying near the home place today. He didn't want to be a mile away and out of sight of the house if Randolph's cousin showed up. Maybe it was best to take Rachel with them. She could hone her riding and herding skills, and overall she was probably safer with Jack.

But his heart was safe. He would make sure of that.

He tried not to pay too much attention to her as they rode out, but Rachel cut a figure that drew a man's gaze. Besides, she kept Patch even with his horse until they reached a place where the trail narrowed. She plied him with questions about the coming roundup and how they would decide which steers to sell.

They rode along at a leisurely pace until they came to the first group Jack wanted to take in. He yelled to Rusty and Goldie, "Get them moving in. We'll go get that other bunch that's down on the flat by the river."

Goldie waved in reply, and he and Rusty headed toward the bunch of twenty or so cattle.

"There's some up ahead," Jack said to Rachel. "A mixed lot—about a dozen cows with calves and twenty or thirty steers."

"Do you want to separate them?" Rachel asked.

"No, let's take them all in closer to home. I want to check them over, and then I'll let the cows and the young'uns go."

When they came in sight of the herd, it was larger than he'd thought. He did a quick estimate and came up with sixty head.

"That's plenty," he said to Rachel. "Let's get behind 'em and start 'em moving slow."

They guided their horses smoothly until he was slightly beyond the cattle and Rachel was to the side away from the river, to keep any from running out in a different direction.

Jack took out his rope and swung it slowly. "Let's go! Up!"

The herd started moving languidly toward home, but then a yearling got excited and jostled an old cow, who took exception to his rudeness. She side-kicked the young steer, who bawled and took off running.

"Whoa," Jack called. "Easy now!" But it was too late. A steer slammed into Patch's hindquarters, and Rachel went flying.

Rachel grabbed at the saddle horn but too late. She flew over Patch's head. With a thud, she landed on the ground, facedown, her forearms and knees taking the brunt of the landing. She lay panting for a moment, until something hard and pointy stabbed her side.

Cattle. All around her, lowing, grunting cows jogged with their awkward gait. Most dodged her prone form, but one planted a hoof on her shoulder.

She scrambled to her feet. Aching all over, she turned to face the herd. What had Jack told her? Look big. Make noise. Her arms shot up, though pain shrieked through her left forearm. She could almost hear Jack's instructions now. *"Look 'em in the eye. Make yourself big and loud. And don't run."*

"Git on out of here, you mangy cows," she yelled, flapping her arms up and down. She took a quick glance around but couldn't spot Patch. When she looked back toward the oncoming cattle, they were mostly past her, but a crazed yearling steer thundered toward her. More than anything she wanted to run.

She stared right at it and screamed, "Don't you dare, you lumbering sack of stew meat!"

The steer swerved and hurtled by in a spray of dirt.

Rachel bent over coughing as the pounding hoofbeats receded. Jack rode Brownie toward her and pulled up three feet away.

"Are you all right?"

"I think so." She clutched her left wrist. "Got a real good look at the ground."

He smiled and swung down from the saddle.

"Don't we need to catch them?" She looked bleakly after the herd.

"They're heading in the right direction," Jack said. "They'll cool down after a while."

"Where's Patch? Is he hurt?"

Jack frowned, looking toward the dust cloud left by the cattle. "Can't be hurt too bad. He's running with them now."

Rachel felt tears coming on, the serious kind she couldn't blink back. "I'm sorry, Jack."

"Not your fault from what I could see. Come on. Brownie can carry us both."

He was in the saddle so fast, Rachel stood there staring. She'd expected him to boost her.

"What do I do?" she asked.

He kicked off the left stirrup and eased his boot forward of the leather. "Put your foot in there and jump up. I'll help you."

He bent down and reached for her hand, but Rachel grimaced. "My wrist hurts."

Concern flashed in Jack's eyes. "All right, easy does it then. Give it a try."

She managed to lift her foot high enough to get it into his stirrup and looked up at him helplessly. Jack stooped lower and got hold of her elbow.

"One, two, three," he said.

She jumped up on three, trying to ignore the tearing pains in her shoulder and her side. Somehow she made it to a precarious perch behind the saddle. She couldn't see past Jack's broad shoulders. He got hold of her right hand and pulled it around his middle.

"Since you're one-handed, you'll have to hang on tight with this one."

She tried to speak, but nothing came out. She cleared her throat. "Thanks."

Jack's plaid cotton shirt was warm, and she tried not to lean against him, but she was tempted. He started Brownie jogging quietly toward home in the wake of the herd, steering off to the side to avoid the dissipating cloud of dust. Rather than bounce to the side and down Brownie's flank, she clung shamelessly to Jack around his stomach. He held her hand firmly and didn't let go.

Rachel took it easy for a few days, babying her left arm. She'd decided it wasn't broken, but she'd probably sprained her wrist. With the mirror's aid, she could see some of the bruises on other parts of her body. They would take weeks to fade.

Abe wrapped her wrist for her, and she stayed out of the saddle and put off her shooting lessons. She tried to practice her roping, since that exercise mostly involved her right arm, but every muscle in her torso ached, and she tired quickly.

A week had passed when Abe drove Rachel into town for more groceries and supplies. She was a bit disappointed that Jack wasn't driving her, but he claimed that he, Goldie, and Rusty were needed to tend to some problem with the water pump and see the two new hands Jack had hired settled in.

Abe was good company. She had no quarrel with him, but he wasn't Jack. That thought surprised her and then annoyed her. She hadn't come here to find a man. In fact, she'd rejected Mr. Hill's proposal for that very reason. Sure, she hoped to marry one day, but she wasn't about to go after the first agreeable man who came into her sights.

"How's that wrist?" Abe looked pointedly at her arm. Rachel had left off the bandage for the first time, not wanting to cause comments in town.

"It's a lot better," she said. "Still a little sore but nothing like last week." She didn't mention the huge purple bruises that were finally starting to fade but still looked ugly.

"Well, don't you go carrying any heavy parcels today. You let me do that."

She and Abe were coming out of the post office when Mr. McClure hurried across the street toward their wagon.

"Miss Paxton! I thought I saw you drive by. Can you come into my office for a minute?"

Rachel looked to Abe, who nodded.

"Of course," she said. "Abe, I won't be long."

She crossed the street on the lawyer's arm and went inside with him. He showed her to the chair opposite his desk and sat down.

"Sorry to waylay you like that, but I thought you should know. In fact, I was thinking of riding out to the ranch this afternoon to tell you."

"Tell me what?" Rachel asked.

"Mr. Hill's cousin is in town."

"Oh." She gulped.

"He wants to contest the will."

"What does that mean?"

"It means he'll fight it. He believes he should get something from the estate." Mr. McClure made a distasteful face. "That is, he believes he should get it all. Of course, he was only bequeathed half in the event you didn't claim your own bequest. I set him straight on that."

Rachel's heart sank. Was her effort for nothing?

"He won't get it, of course," Mr. McClure said hastily. "I drew up that will, and it's tighter than a fat man's belt. But he might try."

"So what do I do?" Rachel asked.

"Just what you're doing. Continue to stay on the property and carry on the business of the ranch."

"Mr. Callen hired two more men," she said.

Mr. McClure nodded. "He told me. One's a man who's worked on the Hill ranch before, a good, steady hand. The other's new, but he comes with a good work record. And Callen said he'll probably hire two or three more in the next week so they can begin the roundup and get all the young stock branded."

Rachel breathed a little easier. Mr. McClure didn't seem worried. And Jack—she could count on Jack to handle anything complicated or unsuitable for a lady's attention.

"If he comes out to the ranch, you should probably stay indoors," Mr. McClure said.

Rachel's attention whipped back to the problem of Andrew Hill.

"Wh–why?"

McClure's gaze drifted away from hers. "He, uh, said some things. Wasn't very happy to learn someone else was inheriting."

"He didn't know?" she asked.

"As required by the law, I'd sent him a letter saying his name was mentioned in his cousin's will. I didn't want to put the particulars down until we'd located him for certain. Well, instead of letting me send a letter, he simply sent that telegram last week. I wrote another letter, but he'd left California before it arrived. He got here being none the wiser."

"And mad," Rachel said.

"You might say that." McClure extended a hand toward Rachel. "He wanted to know who you were, but I didn't give him much. I had to give him a copy of the will, but it only states your name, not your relationship to Mr. Hill. I didn't enlighten him. I only told him that you were the person Randolph had chosen to inherit his estate, and that you were now in residence on the ranch."

Rachel's pulse quickened and breathing became harder. "How much longer until it's legal?"

"You mean until the estate is settled and the property is in your name?"

"Yes."

"I make it eight more days. August third. You come into town that day, and we'll sign the papers."

She nodded slowly. "Thank you."

Mr. McClure walked with her to the door. When he opened it, Abe was coming up the steps.

"Abe," Rachel said, "it seems Mr. Hill's cousin is in town, and he's unhappy about the way the will is worded."

Abe lifted his hat and scratched his head. He looked at Mr. McClure. "Can you keep him away from the ranch until next week?"

Mr. McClure drew in a deep breath. "I don't see how. He may be out there now."

Abe frowned. "Well, he won't stay long. Jack will see to that."

"We might meet him on our way home," Rachel said. The thought frightened her.

"If you do, don't speak to him," McClure advised. "Just keep on driving and don't tell him who you are."

"We haven't done our shopping yet." Her head felt odd, as though it had lifted off her shoulders and was floating.

"Go and do your errands," Mr. McClure said. "Do just as you would on any other shopping day. You can stop back here before you leave for home if you like, and I'll tell you if I've heard anything more."

"Could Miss Paxton ask the sheriff to keep him away from the ranch?" Abe asked.

"Maybe, but I don't see a cause for that unless Hill makes some sort of disturbance."

"All right," Rachel said. "Abe, we'd better get going." She turned but felt so unsteady that she reached for the cowboy's arm. "Sorry, I . . ." She stood still and pulled in a deep breath.

Mr. McClure stepped forward and handed Abe a silver dollar. "Take Miss Paxton across to the hotel and get her some coffee and a piece of pie." He smiled at Rachel. "You'll feel better with something in your stomach, miss."

Rachel wasn't sure about that, but she let Abe escort her to the hotel dining room. It was only ten thirty. Breakfasters had left, and diners hadn't come in yet for lunch. Two old men sat at a table arguing about the price of beef. She sank into a chair, and an aproned man appeared almost at once with two mugs and a coffeepot.

"Thanks, Jim," Abe said. "Piece of apple pie for each of us." He arched his eyebrows at Rachel, and she nodded.

"Thank you, Abe," she said when she'd had her first sip of hot, strong coffee. "I hate to admit it, but I was feeling a little woozy."

"No shame," Abe replied. "We'll just take our time with the pie and then go get the stuff at the stores."

Abe had a long list for stocking up on extra groceries since the bunkhouse now had more hungry men to feed. Rachel decided to buy a few extra supplies for herself and prepare a surprise for the men.

"I thought I'd bake something for the bunkhouse tomorrow." She managed a weak smile. "Sort of a welcome for the new hands. Pies maybe. If you don't mind."

"Of course not," Abe said. "We'd all be tickled. So long as you don't hurt your arm none."

That was a consideration. Maybe rolling out piecrust wasn't the best idea. "A cake then. We'll see. But I'd also like to buy myself some boots."

"Oh yeah?" Abe grinned at her. "Sounds like you're planning to do more ridin'."

"My wrist is nearly healed. I think I will be riding a lot in the future."

He nodded. "You might just graduate from Patch to something a little spunkier."

"Not yet, please." She was just becoming comfortable in the saddle with the steady old gelding under her. She took another bite of pie. "This isn't as good as yours."

Abe smiled.

Mr. McClure was right. The short respite and food did wonders. She and Abe finished their shopping, which included a new hat that made her look like a true westerner. They stopped again at the lawyer's office, but he had nothing new to report. Abe turned the wagon toward home. Rachel sat beside him with her feet on the footboard in front of her so she could admire her new leather boots. The tooled leather looked nice now, but she knew she'd take more pride in those boots when they looked well worn. She was learning new skills, and the changes in her wardrobe showed it. But she was daunted by the thought of a struggle to keep her inheritance.

About halfway to the ranch, she sighed. "Maybe I should just go back to Boston and let the cousin have the ranch."

Abe looked at her sharply. "Don't you do it, missy. Mr. Hill wanted *you* to have his place."

"But why?" Tears pricked at her eyes. "I don't understand it, Abe. Mr. Hill proposed to me in a letter, and I gave it a great deal of thought. And then I declined his offer."

"Doesn't matter."

"Doesn't it?" She studied Abe's leathery face. "I felt as though I let him down badly."

"Well, maybe so, but he liked you. If he hadn't, he never would have popped the question. And when he saw that he was dying, you were the only person he could think of who he wanted to do something for."

"What about Jack?" she asked. "They were friends."

"Yes, and if you hadn't been in the picture, maybe he'd have left the ranch to Jack, I don't know. I wasn't as close to the boss as Jack was. I figure Mr. Hill knew you well enough to see that you'd keep Jack on."

"But I only wrote him four letters, and I disappointed him."

"Only in that one thing," Abe said. "I think that in everything else, he admired you. Could be he even admired you for turning down a proposal you didn't think was best for you."

She frowned and looked out over the rolling, brown plains.

She'd imagined that once she saw Texas, she would either love it or hate it. Why was this decision so difficult? Today she'd as good as told Mr. McClure she would accept the ranch and take ownership.

When had she become sure? And what had tipped the scales? Not the cattle, that was for sure. Maybe it was the land. No, she thought, it was the people. Abe, who had been so kind to her, and Rusty and Goldie, who worked so hard and were loyal to Mr. Hill, even though he was gone. And Jack. Mostly Jack. She couldn't deny that anymore.

Was she counting on Jack always being there for her? Because she might be fooling herself. After she became owner of the ranch, Jack might decide to go work somewhere else. She had no claim on him. Would she still want to stay if Jack wasn't part of the picture? She'd better make sure before she signed those papers. Was Jack the reason she still had doubts?

When the ranch house and the yard came in sight, Abe lifted his chin.

"Uh-oh."

Rachel looked ahead and saw a knot of men and a couple of horses outside the corral fence. One man sat on his horse, while the rest were clustered around him.

✤ Chapter 6 ✤

Do you think it's him?" Rachel asked.

"Got to be—the one in the saddle. But I think the other two are the men Jack hired." Abe guided the team at a leisurely pace into the barnyard. He nodded at one of the newcomers. "Howdy, Joe."

A middle-aged man who looked as though he'd seen many days on the range nodded back.

Jack walked a few steps to meet them. He stood beside the wagon, nodded at Abe, and focused on Rachel.

"It's Hill. I suggest you pull up closer to the house, Abe, and start unloading Miss Rachel's things. Ma'am, if you'll just get inside and keep out of—"

"You're the one!"

Rachel jumped at the roar. She wouldn't have thought the medium-sized man capable of producing such a loud yell. He dismounted and marched toward the wagon. She clutched the edge of the seat, every muscle tense.

"Wha'd you do, beguile my cousin?" he shouted, glaring up at her.

Jack stepped up beside him. "Take it easy, Mr. Hill. This is Miss Paxton, but she didn't do anything. She never even met your cousin before he died."

"That makes it even worse," Hill said. "Writin' him sweet-talk letters and makin' out like you wanted to marry him."

"I—" Rachel pressed her mouth shut as Abe's hand clamped around her forearm.

"Best do like Jack said and get inside," Abe murmured.

"Of course. Thank you."

Abe climbed down on the far side of the wagon and reached up his hand to help her. By the time Andrew Hill had walked around the team's heads and approached, Abe had her at the side of the house and was opening the kitchen door for her.

"Just a minute," Hill shouted.

Abe turned to face him. "Miss Paxton don't have to stay out here and take your abuse. And if you've got notions about going in the house, forget it. It ain't your place, and it never will be."

"Why, you—" Hill tensed but broke off as Jack grabbed his arm.

Rachel ducked inside, carrying her purse and the bag of cherries she'd bought at the mercantile. She shut the door firmly and threw the dead bolt. One of the ranch hands could bring in the rest of her supplies later.

She hurried to her room at the back of the house and shut that door too, and stood trembling, leaning against the wall. Her pulse hammered so hard in her ears that she couldn't hear anything from outside, but what had she expected? The noise of brawling? Gunshots? That thought stabbed her. Randolph's men were putting themselves in danger for her sake. She opened the bedroom door a crack.

Listening intently, she heard fading hoofbeats. Half a minute later someone knocked on the front door.

"Miss Rachel?"

Jack!

She hurried out into the great room, unlocked the door, and all but pulled him inside.

"Is he gone?"

"Yes, ma'am."

"Thank you so much."

She tried to steady her breathing.

"Are you all right?" Jack asked.

"Yes. The question is, are you and Abe?"

"We're fine."

"Thank God no one was hurt." She puffed out a breath. "Won't you sit down for a minute, Jack, and have some coffee? I'd like to tell you what Mr. McClure said this morning."

"I'd be happy to," Jack said, "but I think you should know Hill was making threats."

"What kind of threats?"

"He says he'll have you off this land before time runs out."

She sobered and thought about that. "Eight more days, according to Mr. McClure."

"That's what I calculate too." Jack eyed her closely. "You've decided then?"

"I told Mr. McClure I'll sign the papers August third."

Jack smiled. "Well now, that's good news."

"I'm glad you think so." She led him to the kitchen and held out a hand over the stovetop. "Oh dear, the fire's out."

"Let me tend to it, ma'am."

Jack set to work raking up the buried coals so efficiently that Rachel decided she had nothing to do but remove her hat and look in the pie safe for leftover biscuits. She took the butter dish and a half jar of jam from the cupboard. As Jack added kindling to the firebox, a soft knock came at the kitchen door. She went over and opened it. Abe, Rusty, and Goldie all stood on the stoop, carrying her bundles.

"Come right in, gentlemen," she said cheerfully. "I want to thank you all for defending the property. Will you join Jack and me for some coffee?"

"I'd love to, ma'am," Goldie said, "but Jack thinks we ought to take turns keeping watch, and I'm having the first turn with our two new hands, Joe and Chris."

"Oh."

Jack turned his head toward her. "It seemed wise."

"All right. Well, Goldie, thanks again, and you and the others can get your coffee later."

Goldie left and they gathered around the table. Rusty gave her a shy smile as she placed a mug and spoon in front of him and the same in front of Abe.

While the coffee brewed, Rusty said, "Hill sounded like he'll come back. What do we do besides posting guards?"

Jack looked around at all of them. "Let's hope he tries to do this legally. Gets himself a lawyer to fight for him."

"But then Miss Paxton could lose the ranch," Rusty said.

Jack shook his head. "I don't think so."

Rachel patted Rusty's sleeve. "Mr. McClure assured me today that the will is sound."

"Are there other lawyers in town?" Abe asked.

"I imagine there are several," Jack said. "Fort Worth is growing fast. If not, he can surely get one in Dallas. It's not that far away."

"I'm more worried about him coming back with some hired guns," Rusty said.

Rachel looked at Jack, not trying to hide her alarm. "Do you think he'd do that?"

"It's not unheard of in these parts. But there are some things we can do."

"Like what?" Abe asked eagerly.

Jack glanced toward the stove. "Miss Rachel, whyn't you see if that coffee's ready?"

She brought the pot to the table and poured all their mugs full. Jack picked his up, blew on it, and took a sip. He set it down and looked at her as she resumed her seat.

"First, I think we should get your shooting lessons started. Have you ever handled a gun?"

Rachel stared at him. "No."

He nodded. "You'll be safer if you know how and carry one with you when you're outside the house."

She wasn't sure about that, but she had a feeling she'd be over-ruled if she protested.

"Second," Jack said, "the two men who started today are good, solid hands. I've worked with Joe a lot in the past, and he's worked with Chris for the past six months. They both had jobs at the

Bar-D, but when Joe heard I was hiring, he wanted to come back here, and Chris came with him. I trust them both."

"That's good to know," Rachel said.

Abe nodded. "I know Joe too. Can't vouch for Chris, but if Joe says he's good, then he's good."

"So that gives us six men," Jack went on. "If we divide up into four-hour watches with three men on each watch, we have a good chance of stopping any shenanigans."

"What do you mean?" Rachel asked.

"I mean, if Hill thinks he can sneak in here and do something, like set the hay on fire or something like that."

Rachel caught her breath. "You think he'd do something so wicked?"

"Worse, most likely. Now, we'll keep one man on the house, one watching the barn and corrals, and one rover that keeps an eye on the road and the fence lines nearest the home place."

Rachel had misgivings. "When will you sleep?"

"It won't kill us for a few days to take our sleep in short spells."

"We do it all the time on cattle drives," Abe said.

"That's right." Jack went on to lay out the particulars to Abe and Rusty. He told them the assets he considered most valuable and most vulnerable—Rachel herself, the house, the expensive bull, the remuda, the barn and stored feed, and the cattle.

"We should bring the whole herd in closer," Abe said.

"Maybe, but that would make it easier for him to target." Jack shook his head. "Right now we've got several small bunches scattered around in the hills. It would be harder for anyone to destroy or steal the herd if we left it that way than if they were all together."

"Harder to stampede 'em," Rusty said.

"That's right. If someone ran off a bunch or two, that would hurt, but it wouldn't devastate us. I think we need to concentrate right now on protecting Randolph's investment and Miss Rachel."

Abe rubbed his bristly jaw. "So, what else can we do along those lines?"

"You got any ideas?" Jack asked.

"What about Ol' Grumps?"

That was the nickname the men had bestowed on the new bull. Rachel's cheeks heated, but she knew they had to discuss it. The men had confined the bull to a small enclosure with a high fence to keep him from getting where they didn't want him yet. After the roundup, they would let him mingle with the cows so that they would drop calves next spring.

"Maybe we ought to reinforce the fence," Jack said. "And put a chain and lock on the gate."

Rachel pushed back her chair. "I think you gentlemen can make these decisions on your own. I have some cherries to pit."

"Right." Jack stood. "Abe, you come with me, and we'll figure out what's best to be done. Rusty, why don't you stay and pit a few cherries for Miss Rachel?"

"Glad to." Rusty smiled at her.

"Thank you," she said. "But let me get you an apron. That juice stains awfully."

Jack and Abe went out, and she settled down with Rusty, the bag of cherries, and a couple of paring knives.

"Likely Mr. Hill's cousin doesn't know about the Hereford bull," Rusty said.

Rachel let out a little sigh. "Really, Rusty, I hope you're right, but I'd like to hear as little as possible about Ol' Grumps."

"Oh. Yes, ma'am." Rusty went at the cherries with a determined frown.

Rachel worked in silence, thinking over what Jack had said. What would it mean to the ranch if Andrew Hill sneaked in and killed the prized bull? Randolph's investment would be wasted. Most likely she'd have to buy another bull somewhere. She'd have to talk to Jack about that, as distasteful as she found the topic. Still, they could live with the loss. But if the barn was burned? Or the house? She supposed either could be rebuilt. But any losses would cost money.

Rusty glanced over at her and offered a smile. "We're going to have us a pile of cherries, Miss Rachel."

"Yes, and you'll have your fill of cherry pie tomorrow," she said with a chuckle.

"Can't wait."

The mood was lighter as they continued their work. Rachel realized she had never felt close to a man before, other than her father. She wasn't close to her older brother and most of her business in Boston was done for women. She met men, of course, at church and in stores. But she could feel bonds forming with Rusty and Abe, and even Goldie. But the strongest tie was with Jack. Jack had her interests at heart. He was her employee, or he would be in eight days. He had cared about Randolph. Was he transferring that loyalty to her now? She thought so. And she hoped that with it would come the respect and even fondness he had felt for Randolph.

These men could be like brothers to her if she did not betray their trust. Well, perhaps Abe would be more like a beloved uncle. He had a lot of wisdom and a doggedness she'd never had the chance to observe closely in a man before. She could easily envision Rusty as a younger brother. It might even be fun letting him show her how to shoot a rifle. Goldie could teach her a lot too, she was sure. He'd already helped her with a lesson in harnessing horses and driving the wagon.

What did she expect from Jack? He'd helped her see a possible future that looked bright and productive and even happy here in Texas. But there was something about Jack that she didn't feel for the others. He was a mentor, yes. Did she dare hope for more than that?

Chapter 7

Jack leaned on the fence and watched Rachel fire his repeating rifle at the target he'd set up fifty yards away. When she'd emptied the gun, she turned toward him with her eyebrows raised.

"Looks pretty good," he yelled, knowing both the shock of the blasts and the cotton in her ears would deaden the sound of his voice. She'd hit the target with four of the six bullets he'd given her.

She smiled and walked over to him, holding out the rifle.

"Now I think you should learn to handle a revolver."

The smile drooped. "Do I have to?"

"I think it would be good for you to have one close by in the house."

She said nothing, looking down at the ground. She scuffed the dirt with the toe of her riding boot.

"What?" Jack asked.

"I just. . .I'm not really comfortable with it."

He cocked his head to one side. "Were you comfortable with riding the first time you got on Patch?"

"No."

"Same thing. You've shot the rifle twice now, and you're hitting more than you're missing. Seems like you have a good eye for it and a feel for the gun. But the rifle isn't much good if the enemy is up close. You need to be able to grab that revolver when you need it."

"You think he'd assault me personally?"

"Why wouldn't he? You're the big threat. Let's say he shoots Ol' Grumps. What good does that do him?"

"It would scare us," she said. "Well, me, anyway."

Jack nodded. "It might even drive you away, but I doubt it. What it would do for sure is decrease the value of the estate. You know his cousin spent a pile of money on that bull. That would be lost if the bull was destroyed. You, on the other hand. . . If you were out of the picture, he'd get half the estate. Period."

She stood very still. "You think he'd shoot me?"

Jack just looked at her for a long moment then said softly, "I'm not trying to scare you, Rachel. At least not more than I think is necessary. This man means business, and the surest way for him to get what he wants is for you to be unable to claim the ranch."

Rachel's hands shook as she loaded the revolver, following Jack's instructions carefully. She looked toward him, and he nodded then stepped back. She raised her arms, holding the gun with both hands and pointing it at the target. It was only ten yards away now, but her hands quivered more than they had with the rifle. When she hesitated, Jack stepped up behind her and laid a hand on her shoulder. That didn't help. If anything, his touch made her more nervous than ever.

"Steady now," he said.

She let off one round, but it missed the target. She lowered the revolver and sighed. "I'm just tired, I guess."

"All right. Let's leave it for now," Jack said. "Maybe Abe can come out with you after supper and you can try it again."

Why Abe? She tried to ignore the flicker of disappointment. Jack probably had other things to do, like taking the evening watch.

He took the handgun from her, and they walked slowly back toward the house. They'd set up an impromptu shooting range in a small dip in the ground, so that the land formed a natural backing for the targets.

"I bet you can hit it every time," she said. "Especially that close." She was a little disgusted with her poor showing.

"You'll be better next time, when you're fresh."

"Maybe. I hope so."

"You did great with the rifle."

She shrugged, having no explanation for that.

"Most of the ammunition is kept in the house, in the drawer under the gun rack," Jack said. "We keep a few boxes in the bunkhouse. If you don't mind, I'll take a few more to increase our stock out there."

"Sure," Rachel said.

He nodded. "We'll leave you plenty. But I'm putting it on the list for the next trip to town. Until this is settled, we want to make sure we have plenty of cartridges."

"Of course."

They passed the bull's enclosure on their way to the house. The men had reinforced the fence, and it was now nearly as tall as Rachel. She paused and stood on tiptoe to look over the barrier. Ol' Grumps stood in one corner munching on hay the men had thrown into his trough. He snorted and shook his head.

"Do you think Andrew Hill knows about him?" Rachel asked.

"No idea. He might have seen him, I suppose, when he rode out here. But I think he was more interested in having a word with you."

She thought about what the bull meant to the ranch.

"Would the whole place go downhill if we lost him?"

"No, but we'd have to keep on breeding with the bull we used before."

"We still have one?" she asked in surprise.

"Yup. He's pastured out in the hills right now. We didn't want him and Ol' Grumps to get wind of each other. But we didn't want to get rid of him either. Not until we're sure the new king of the hill will prove himself."

Rachel's face burned, but she managed to keep her voice steady. "Then we must go on protecting him."

Jack nodded. "If it works out the way Randolph planned, we'll have a better quality of beef to sell within two years. Our stock will bring higher prices at the stockyards. If he hadn't of gotten sick, Mr. Hill would have been one of the leading ranchers in the area. A lot of the others were eager to see how he made out with this venture. I'm sure a lot of the ranchmen would follow his lead if things went well."

Rachel was sure the area cattlemen wouldn't accept a woman rancher the way they had Randolph Hill. "They probably won't care, now that I'll be in charge."

"I wouldn't say that," Jack replied. "They still want to know how it turns out. And this ranch will still be a leader in the cross-breeding experiment."

"I certainly will need your expertise, Jack." She turned away from the fence. "This is something I just can't do myself. I doubt I'll ever be confident handling cattle."

"You just keep at it. Your riding's improved a whole lot, and Rusty said you did a good job helping bring in that bunch the other day. By this time next year, you'll be as good as any cowpuncher."

"I doubt that," Rachel said. *This time next year* she thought. Would she really still be here then? She would have to write to Rhoda and ask her to pack up the rest of her personal belongings at the boardinghouse. And perhaps Rhoda could place an advertisement for her in the newspaper so that she could sell the sewing equipment and supplies she had left in the shop.

They had reached the door, and Jack opened it for her. He followed her inside and walked over to the gun rack. Rachel took off her hat and hung it on a peg near the door.

Jack took two boxes of cartridges from the drawer. "I'll send Abe around after supper."

"All right. And thank you, Jack, for everything you've done— are doing—for me."

He nodded and turned away.

Rachel watched him as he strolled toward the barn. Abe wasn't a better shot than Jack, she was sure of that. Maybe he thought

Abe was a better teacher than he was.

Funny, she was beginning to feel strong. Independent. Capable. All the things she strove for in Boston but never quite reached. So why wasn't she happy? Had she underestimated the importance of companionship—no, of love? If she was going to be honest, she'd better call it what it was. She cared deeply for Jack, but she wasn't sure if what she felt was love. He had been extremely kind and helpful, but he hadn't indicated that he had stronger feelings for her than that. None of the men had showed any of the resentment she'd feared, which was a big relief, but it wasn't enough.

She now believed Jack would be as loyal to her as he had been to Randolph Hill. But would he ever consider her wife material? Maybe that idea was totally improper in Jack's world. Or maybe he was just shy. Or maybe he didn't think she was anything special. Just a city girl who would never really be at home out here. One who happened to be the new boss.

Maybe she was foolish to think of selling her business in Boston and moving here. If her heart was going to ache with disappointment, what was the point? Not for the first time, she thought Randolph might have been kinder to forget about her and leave his ranch to Jack.

She had barely put away her clean dishes after supper when a knock came at the kitchen door. She opened it to find Abe standing on the step.

"Hi, Abe. I guess it's time for my next shooting lesson."

"That's right, ma'am, if you're ready."

She sighed. "I guess so. No more signs of Mr. Hill today?"

"None at all. Jack's thinking of riding into town tomorrow to see if the lawyer's heard anything."

"Only seven more days," she said.

"That's right. And we don't figure he'll wait until the last minute to do whatever he's going to do."

She nodded grimly. "Let me get my jacket."

"Fine. I've got everything else we need."

The next morning Jack came to the house while she was still brewing her coffee and scrounging up breakfast. Rachel was surprised, since he hadn't mentioned his plans for the day to her.

"Hello, Jack. Have you eaten?"

"Yes, ma'am. Just wanted to let you know I'm going into town. Abe and Rusty and Chris will be on watch here, and Goldie will take Joe with him to ride the fence on the western boundary line."

"All right."

"I thought I'd ask around and see if I can come up with a couple more hands to help us out."

"That sounds good," Rachel said. "Hire whatever men you think we need, Jack."

He nodded. "We'll need 'em next week for sure. Thought I'd stop at McClure's too, and tell him. He thinks we need more men in case Hill comes around again."

"A show of force?"

"Yeah. That all right with you?"

"So long as they're good men, Jack. I trust your judgment on that."

He held her gaze for a moment. "Thank you."

Rachel's pulse surged. She'd been thinking for weeks about

the ownership of the ranch, but last night one option had solidified in her mind.

"Jack, I want to ask you something."

"What's that?"

"You were a very good friend to Mr. Hill—to Randolph. I've been thinking that perhaps you're the one he should have given the ranch to."

"Oh no, ma'am." Jack held up a hand in protest.

"Now, hear me out," Rachel said. "After I sign the papers next week, I can do whatever I want with this property. I thought maybe I'd offer it to you."

He shook his head. "I don't have the money to buy this place."

"I could give you a good price." She watched his face. He turned partly away from her, gazing out toward the corrals. "Jack, you wouldn't have to pay me right away. We could work out terms. You're the one who should have this ranch. You can make it into the place Randolph envisioned."

He pulled in a breath and gave her a half smile. "I don't think that's a good idea, Miss Paxton. Really."

"Why?"

"What would you do then?"

"Go back to Boston, I suppose." The plan seemed suddenly colorless and bleak.

"With all respect, ma'am, that wasn't what Randolph had in mind."

"He told you what he wanted. You're the one who knows. I don't."

"Yes, ma'am, he told me all that."

Jack looked into her eyes again, and Rachel's cheeks warmed.

Was he implying that Randolph's dream was to have her stay on the ranch?

Jack looked over his shoulder, toward where the men were saddling their horses. "Maybe we should discuss this another time."

"Yes. I'm keeping you from your errand. But think about it, Jack. Please."

He touched the brim of his hat. "Yes, ma'am, I'll think on it."

Rachel's heart almost melted as she watched him stride toward the barn. She was sure that many, many thoughts flew around in Jack's head. She wished she could see them.

Did he think she was crazy? Foolish? She already knew he thought she was green as grass—but he hadn't made fun of her inexperience. Instead, he'd taught her to ride and shoot and keep from getting trampled by cows and a dozen other things she'd never had to know in Boston. But what did he think of her as a person? As a woman?

He came out of the barn leading Brownie and hopped into the saddle. Before heading out for Fort Worth, he looked over at the house and focused on her for a moment. He touched his hat brim. Rachel's heart pounded. She lifted a hand to wave, and Jack rode out. She sighed and closed the door.

❧ Chapter 8 ❧

Jack sat in the chair opposite Donald McClure and sipped the coffee the lawyer had offered him.

"That's all I know at this point," McClure said. "I went over to the Cattlemen's Hotel last night, where Hill said he was going to stay. Made a point of having supper there, but I didn't see him. I asked at the front desk after, and they said he is registered there. The clerk checked Hill's room for me and said he wasn't in."

Jack grunted. He wished they had a handle on that guy. He could be anywhere, getting into mischief.

"Well, I'm taking on a couple more men, both with good recommendations. They'll start tomorrow. That'll give us eight men. We're getting ready to sell off a bunch of steers, but mostly I want to make sure Miss Paxton is safe until this legal stuff is over with."

"I appreciate that. I don't really have a reason to think Hill would do anything, but I admit I'll feel easier knowing you've got some steady men out there protecting her." McClure rubbed his jaw. "I've thought about suggesting she move into town until we settle this business with Hill, but he's in town, and she might be in more danger if she was here."

"Wouldn't that violate the terms of the will?" Jack asked.

"She'd have to start over with the thirty days, after we took care of Andrew Hill and made sure he understood he's getting no part of the estate."

Jack flipped his hat against his knee, thinking about it. "No, I don't think she'd want to do that. She's so close now."

"I think you're right. And she shouldn't have to change her plans."

"You don't expect him to hire men to go out there with him and menace her, do you?"

McClure's mouth tightened. "I certainly hope not. I've spoken to the marshal, and he said he'd look into it, but until Hill does something illegal, there's not much the law can do."

Jack didn't like it, but he figured McClure was right. He stood and put on his hat. "I'll move along. Thanks."

"Oh Mr. Callen," the lawyer called after him.

Jack turned. "Yes, sir?"

"I've put a lot of thought into this, and I think Miss Paxton ought to sign a will of her own when she takes possession. She can name any beneficiary she wants, but it would seem wise to get the document in place the minute she owns that ranch."

Jack thought about that, and it seemed smart to him as well. "I believe she has a brother back east."

McClure nodded. "She might want to name him as her heir. Or someone else. But if she should pass on without a will. . ."

"I get your drift. I'll try to get her to see to it without making it too morbid."

McClure smiled and clapped him on the shoulder. "I appreciate it. Young ladies often don't want to think about such things, but it's wise to do so. She can see me anytime she's in town and tell me her wishes so I've got it ready for her to sign the day we transfer the property."

Jack shook McClure's hand and strolled back toward where he'd left his horse tied in front of the post office. He wasn't far from the hotel where Andrew Hill was staying, according to McClure. He decided to pop in there and ask for him.

"Mr. Hill isn't in," the desk clerk told him. "He left a couple of hours ago."

Jack tried his best to sound friendly but casual. "Know where I can find him? There's something I wanted to discuss with him."

"No, but I think he was going to rent a horse." A livery stable was only a couple of blocks away, and the clerk mentioned it to Jack. "That's the one we usually tell our customers about when they ask where they can get transportation."

"Much obliged."

Jack left the hotel, collected his horse, and rode to the stable. The ostler was willing to stop working and shoot the breeze for a minute.

"Yeah, he hired a hoss this mornin'," he told Jack.

"Do you know where he's at? I was hoping to see him today."

"Nope. He didn't say. But he said he expected to be back before dark."

"Hmm. Thanks."

Jack had planned to fetch a few items for the bunkhouse pantry, but he decided that could wait another day. If all was well at the ranch, he could send Rusty and one of the new men in to-morrow with the wagon. He turned Brownie toward home, and as soon as he was beyond the crowded streets, he urged the gelding into a lope.

He thought he heard a hail from behind him, and he pulled Brownie up. One of the men he'd just hired, an eighteen-year-old kid named Wade Darnell, was riding up on him. Wade's father was a telegraph operator, but Wade aspired to be a rancher, and he'd gotten in a few months' experience the previous summer. Jack waited, and when Wade reached him, he saw that the kid had his bedroll and a rucksack tied to the back of his saddle.

"I decided to come out to the ranch today if that's all right with you," Wade said. "Then I can start bright and early with the rest of your crew."

"No problem," Jack told him. "Glad to have you along."

They started off side by side, their mounts jogging companionably.

"I told you about the ranch's new owner," Jack said after they'd gone half a mile.

Wade nodded. "You said. Woman owner."

"Yes, but that's not a problem. She's a smart lady, and she wants to run a tight outfit. I think once she gets used to things, she'll do a good job."

"Glad to hear that," Wade said.

"You knew the old owner, from when you helped us with our roundup and drive to the stockyards last summer," Jack went on.

"Yeah. Too bad what happened to Mr. Hill. Is this lady a relative?"

Jack ignored that question. "There's a possibility that one of his cousins, a man who did *not* inherit the land, might make some trouble."

"You said that earlier, when you took me on."

Jack had made sure to mention the possible problem to the men who expressed interest in working on the Hill ranch, but not in detail. He'd downplayed it so they wouldn't think they were getting into a range war. But now that Wade was actually moving to the ranch, he deserved to know there was a slim chance things could get ugly. And he was so young. Jack hoped he wouldn't regret hiring the kid.

"Well, I hope it doesn't come to anything," he said. "This fella came out to the ranch a couple days ago. We had to run him off, and he left pretty riled."

"What, he wants to claim the ranch?" Wade asked.

"Yup. Thinks he should have inherited it, not Miss Paxton. But I've seen Mr. Hill's will. It's clear and simple. Miss Paxton becomes the legal owner in six more days. If this cousin wants to try anything, he'll have to do it before then. I was going to wait a couple of weeks to hire men for the roundup, but we need to have plenty of manpower showing when strangers come around—for the next week anyhow."

"Sounds like a good idea," Wade said.

"Well, I wanted to make sure you understood. We've started bringing the herd in close and separating the ones we're going to sell. We'll keep on with that. I don't think lead's going to fly, but we just don't know right now."

Wade patted the Colt revolver strapped to his thigh. "I'm with you, Callen. Happy to stand up with you and your outfit."

"Good. We've got a hundred or so spring calves we'll be branding." As they rode along, Jack gave Wade a rundown on the ranch's routine for payday and days off.

They came within sight of the home place, and Jack pointed

out the cattle they had sorted into different pastures. He spotted a man on watch on the rise behind the well house and waved his hat. The man waved back, and he was sure it was Abe from the color of the horse he was riding. The compact dun gelding was Abe's personal mount.

A movement near one of the corrals, closer to the barn, caught his eye. He frowned at the figure that seemed intent on something near one of the gates. He was pretty sure the man was hidden from Abe's view by the roof of the ranch house.

"Heads up," Jack said to Wade.

"What is it?"

"That man by the corral with the high fence."

Wade squinted toward where Jack pointed. "I see him. What's he doing?"

"I don't know. That's the corral we built special for the new bull. Shouldn't nobody be fooling with that gate unless it's feed time or we're moving him someplace."

They rode a few more steps while Jack mulled it over.

"Hey, there's a horse down there." They'd topped a rise, and Wade pointed to a riderless horse tied to a fence post in the dip below them.

"That's bad." Jack was certain the rider had left his saddled horse out of sight of the house, where he could reach it in a hurry and light out for town. "Come on!"

He dug his heels into Brownie's sides, but the corral gate swung open. They were too far out to do much good. He pushed his horse toward the corral, and Wade's mount pounded along close behind him.

Rachel heard a shout outside and looked out the kitchen window. The huge bull tore out of its corral with a bellow and charged into the barnyard.

Her heart raced. What was happening? How could Ol' Grumps get loose? The men had been so careful.

She leaned to the side, hoping to catch a glimpse of one of the ranch hands. Near the bull's corral, she saw a man running along the fence away from the gate. She couldn't tell which man it was, but maybe it was Chris or Joe. In a flash, she registered that this man wasn't as tall as Chris, and Joe had gone with Goldie to ride fence. *Andrew Hill,* she thought.

She wiped flour from her hands on her red apron as she raced into the next room. Whatever was going on, it wasn't good. Where were Abe, Rusty, and Chris, the men who should be on guard?

She seized the revolver she'd used for practice, knowing it was loaded and ready for the next session. With a quick prayer, she yanked open the front door. Not knowing exactly what she could do to help, she stepped out onto the stoop.

The bull had run beyond the house, past the barn and bunkhouse, toward the pasture, and then came up against a barbed wire fence. Rachel thought it would stop, but the bull lowered its head and crashed into the fence, tearing down wire and posts for a stretch of fifty feet. As he roared his rage and plowed on, trying to disentangle himself, more posts pulled out of the ground. The cattle that had been grazing placidly scattered and ran for the far reaches of the pasture.

Abe and Rusty suddenly appeared on the sloped land behind

the well house, whooping and yelling as their horses ran toward the barnyard. The bull checked its stride, and Rusty whipped past him, getting between Ol' Grumps and the range, while Abe rode into the yard. Rachel ran out to meet them.

"Can I help?" she yelled.

Rusty scowled at her. "Get inside!"

Abe, however, glanced her way and shouted, "Open the gate."

She understood at once, laid the revolver on the step, and ran to the pasture gate. She fumbled with the chain that held it to a fence post and swung the eight-foot-long board gate on its hinges until it was wide open. Abe galloped through it, entering the big pasture quickly, without having to take his horse near the writhing, tangled fence the bull had pulled down. Rusty whirled his horse into position on the near side of the mess. He took his rope from the saddle and began twirling a loop over his head.

Rachel held her breath. What would Rusty do if he lassoed that bull? Surely his horse couldn't hold the angry animal at bay. Then she saw that Abe was also working a loop on his rope. If they could both catch the bull at the same time, she supposed they might control it. She balled up her apron in her clenched hands.

With a furious bellow, Ol' Grumps lunged against the wires that held him and broke free, plunging toward Abe. The cowboy yelled and swung his rope. The bull darted to the side, and Abe's loop slapped its near horn and fell as Ol' Grumps sprang away and darted toward the gate.

Rachel's heart leaped into her throat. She should have shut the wide gate after Abe rode through. No time now! She ducked to the side, at least putting a sturdy fence post between her and the bull. But she'd just seen what the enraged beast could do to fence posts. She cringed away as it charged through the opening and headed straight for Rusty.

Jack and a horseman she didn't recognize galloped into the barnyard, flanking Rusty and yelling at the bull. Ol' Grumps pulled up short. He stood for a moment, snorting and pawing the ground.

Rachel held her breath. She had no way to retreat to the house without endangering herself further, so she stuck near the gate, trying to remember the things Jack had taught her. If the bull ran this way, she could try to herd him through the gate, but she was on foot. And she knew the men didn't really want him in the pasture, but she supposed that would be better than being loose, where he might tear out for town or across the range.

What if he threatened her?

Make yourself look big, she thought. *Make noise. Don't run!* She crumpled her apron, and something else she'd heard flitted through her mind. Bulls hated red, didn't they? Would Ol' Grumps attack her because of her colorful apron? She reached behind her and tore at her apron strings.

Jack, Rusty, and the new man all had their ropes swinging. She looked over her shoulder as she balled up the apron and dropped it in the grass. Abe was hanging back. He probably didn't want to be smack in the gate when the others pushed the bull toward it.

In an instant, Ol' Grumps whirled and plunged toward Rachel. If only he would lumber through the gateway! But no, he put his head down and ran straight at her, like a locomotive on its track.

She let out a yell, trying to keep it from becoming a shriek.

"No! You awful thing, get away!" She threw up her hands and jumped up tall, as huge and fierce as she could make herself.

The bull hesitated for a fraction of a second. It was enough. Three ropes snaked out. Two settled over the mad creature's massive head, and as Ol' Grumps plunged on, the third one neatly circled his hind hoof.

The next thing she knew, the bull was stretched out between the horses, and Abe rode through the gate to join Jack, the heeler.

"Get inside, Rachel," Jack barked at her. "Now!"

He was angry with her. She sobbed as she ran for the kitchen door.

Jack wearily pulled his saddle off Brownie and carried it to the harness room. Every muscle ached from their effort at wrestling Ol' Grumps back into his enclosure. At least that despicable bull was back in his pen now, and Jack had ordered Abe to watch the corral constantly. He hung up his bridle and turned.

Rusty had followed him into the barn.

"What do we do now?" Rusty asked.

"Get that fence back up," Jack said.

"Chris is getting the tools."

Jack nodded. Chris had been the rover, checking things farther from the home place, but he'd ridden up as they finally got the bull into the pen. "You remember Wade from last summer. He's staying. Put him to helping, but all of you keep your eyes open. I've got to talk to Miss Paxton."

"You reckon Hill will come back?"

"I don't know. Maybe not today, but probably sometime."

"We could chase him."

Jack shook his head. "He's got too big a start. After we get the fence fixed, I'll send a couple of you into town to talk to the marshal. Let him handle it."

"Awright."

Rusty strode out into the sunlight, and Jack followed more slowly.

What could he say to Rachel? She could have been killed, running out there like that. Except for Joe and Goldie, who were still out somewhere riding fence, all the men were busy repairing the gap Ol' Grumps had torn in the wire near the yard. Jack turned toward the house. He felt wrung out like a dishrag.

Rachel opened the kitchen door before he could even knock. Her mouth was a tight line, and her eyes were huge. She stepped back to let him in. Jack walked over to the table and put his hands on the back of a chair, leaning on it a little.

"Everything's all right. I'll send a couple boys in to talk to the marshal. Maybe he can rout Hill out when he goes back to his hotel."

Unless he was mistaken, Rachel's lips were trembling. "I'm sorry, Jack."

"What for? No, don't answer that. I know what for. You almost got yourself gored and trampled."

She swallowed hard. "I didn't mean to."

"Of course not." Jack hauled off his hat and slapped it onto the table. "What were you thinking, running out into the middle of that?"

"Abe said to open the pasture gate, so I did."

He'd have something to say to Abe about that. He pulled in a deep breath.

She said, "When Ol' Grumps came my way, I didn't know what to do."

"You did just right."

"Really?" She didn't look as though she believed him. "I tried to do like you said—look big. Make noise."

"Yeah, well, I wasn't counting on you going head-to-head with a furious bull when I said that. They can be unpredictable." He sighed and shook his head. "You got coffee?"

Rachel blinked. "Yes. You want some?"

"I'm drier than the Mojave."

She hesitated. "Sit down." She went to the stove and gave the coffeepot a swift tap. "It's still hot." She brought him a mugful a moment later, then poured a cup for herself and sat down opposite him. "Maybe I need a lesson on how to face a bull."

"No. I told you, you did fine. What you did actually helped, but. . .well, if it happens again, just stay inside and don't go near him, no matter what Abe says."

"I had the revolver out, but when Abe said to open the gate, I left it on the steps."

Jack stared at her for a moment. If she'd fired at the bull, she probably would have just made the beast madder. He hated to think what the result would have been.

"A revolver isn't a good match for an angry bull."

She nodded. "I wasn't really thinking of shooting at him," she said. "I grabbed it because I saw another man out there. The one who opened the corral. I think it was Andrew Hill, and I didn't know what else he would do."

"It *was* Hill." Jack made himself take a sip of his coffee. "He didn't stick around to see what happened. Wade and I passed him coming in, and he was streaking it for town."

"Who's Wade? I mean, I saw him, but—"

"A new hand. And there'll be one more here tomorrow morning."

She nodded and took a drink of her coffee.

"Look, Miss Paxton—" He broke off, unsure of his ground. He didn't want her to think he was angry with her, but seeing her in danger had shaken him. It was one thing for him and the other men to face Ol' Grumps, or even that sidewinder, Hill. But Rachel. . . He took a gulp of coffee.

"You want to say something else, Jack?"

He set down his mug and brushed some dust off his cuff. "Yeah."

"I'm listening."

She sat there looking at him, her hands curled around her coffee mug. She looked beautiful and—not innocent exactly—vulnerable. His lungs squeezed.

"You gotta be careful, Miss Paxton."

She nodded, never shifting her gaze away from his.

"I'm serious," he said.

"I know. Thank you for—for caring about me. I'm sorry I upset you."

"Hill didn't come all the way from California just to do mischief."

"What do you mean?" she asked.

"I don't like to say it, but if you think on it, letting Ol' Grumps out wouldn't do him much good in itself."

Rachel frowned. "That's right. If he ran off or got killed, that wouldn't help Mr. Hill at all. You said yourself, Ol' Grumps is a valuable asset to the ranch."

"He is."

"So why did Andrew Hill let him loose?"

"I think it was just a distraction."

"From what?"

He hated to say it, but he wanted to keep her alive. "From you."

She breathed twice before she responded. "Because the only way he can get the ranch is if I walk away from it or else die before I sign those papers."

"That's right. I figure he rode out here this morning and looked around. Saw one or two of the men on watch and figured he needed to keep them busy. Had to get them worried about something else while he—"

Her eyes widened. "While he came after me."

"That's all I can figure. Wade and I surprised him when we came tearing down the road, and he knew he had to make tracks. Rode right past us because we were concentrating on that bull. But by then there were four of us—five when Chris heard the commotion and rode in. The odds of him getting you and living to tell about it were slim to none, so he lit out. And we let him get away."

"But you think he'll try again."

"I do," Jack said. "So, like I say, be careful. If there's a ruckus in the yard, don't go running outside. Don't show your face. Just sit tight until we handle it, whatever it is."

"All right."

They sat there a moment longer, staring at each other. She'd acted foolishly, running out of the house like that, but he couldn't be angry. Not with Rachel. The thought of losing her scared him, but he was mad at Andrew Hill, not at her.

A shock of guilt jolted him. Did he care too much for the woman Randolph had loved? But Randolph was gone. Still, it seemed a bit traitorous.

She'd turned down Randolph though, and he'd had a ranch and some money. Jack didn't have anything except a plug named Brownie and a beat-up saddle. He could never expect a woman like Rachel to care anything about him, except as an employee who could run things for her. Make money for her. Maybe protect her from her own impulsive actions.

He shook his head. "I'm not upset. I'm just glad you're all right. And I'd have been mighty sorry if you got hurt."

Seemed like a good time to leave, or he might give away how strongly he felt about her. He wasn't used to this jumpy feeling he got every time she was near, or the terror that had seized him when he'd seen her in the bull's path.

"Well, I'd best get out there and see how the boys are coming on that fence." He shoved back his chair. "Thanks for the coffee."

"Oh, you're welcome."

He got as far as the door before remembering McClure's message. He turned back toward her.

"Almost forgot. Mr. McClure wants you to make a will."

She blinked those mesmerizing eyes. "As in, a last will and testament?"

"Yeah. Just in case. He says if you tell him who you want to be your heir, he'll draw it up for you to sign when you get the deed to the ranch."

He left with her sitting there like a statue, staring at him.

❧ Chapter 9 ❧

Rachel hadn't ventured into town in the last week, but she sent a couple of letters in by Rusty when he went for supplies. One of them was to her brother, the other to Rhoda, telling her she definitely planned to stay in Texas. She also sent a note for Mr. McClure, telling him her choice of an heir.

Out of caution, Jack sent Wade with Rusty. They hadn't run into any problems on that trip, but the men were under his orders not to go anywhere alone until the legal papers were signed.

To keep herself busy, she read from the Bible and cooked mountains of cakes and pies for the men in the bunkhouse. There were eight now, with the addition of Tom Williams. They took their sentry duties seriously.

Jack told her not to ride out on the range that week and to stay under cover as much as she could, but the walls of the house began to feel tight. On the day before she would sign the ownership papers, Abe was shoeing a horse just outside the barn door, and she ran across the yard to watch him from the shelter of the wide barn doorway.

Three men appeared on the road from Fort Worth, jogging toward the ranch. Abe straightened and squinted at them.

"That's the marshal."

Jack was on watch near the corrals, and he walked into the barnyard to meet the lawman and the two men who rode with him. The marshal swung down off his horse and shook his hand.

Abe moved a little closer, and Rachel followed him, relying on the marshal's presence to keep her safe.

"I've been talking to Mr. McClure," the marshal told Jack, "and we both thought it would be a good idea for me to ride out here and make sure you're all on the alert."

"Something happen?" Jack asked.

"Simon Hastings at the livery said a fella came in and offered him some quick money. Wanted him to start a fire."

Rachel quailed at the thought. She had asked Rusty about a possible fire, but he'd seemed to think Hill wouldn't burn down the buildings. Still, if he had the house burned with her inside. . . That might be worth the inconvenience of having to rebuild.

"A fire?" Jack asked. "Here?"

The marshal nodded. "Simon told him he wanted no part of it, and as soon as the man left, he came and told me."

"Was it Andrew Hill?"

The marshal shrugged. "I think so. Simon didn't know his name, but he'd rented a horse from him once before, and from his description I'd say it was Hill." He looked over his shoulder and waved at the two mounted men. "I thought I'd bring you a couple of deputies to help keep an eye on things until tomorrow. Mc-Clure tells me that's when the new owner takes over." He darted a glance Rachel's way. "Ma'am."

"Thank you, Marshal," she said.

"They can stay the night." He looked at Jack. "If there's no room in the bunkhouse, they can sleep in the haymow."

"We've got plenty of room for them," Jack said.

"Good."

"It he tries to pull something like that," Abe said, "he couldn't inherit the ranch, could he?"

"Not if we could prove he did it."

"So he might try to make it look like an accident?" Jack said.

"Or just make sure nobody actually sees him do it."

Rachel felt a little sick.

"All right then, I'll get going," the marshal said. "Miss Paxton." He touched his hat brim.

"Abe, you show these two fellows to the bunkhouse," Jack said. He walked over to Rachel. "Come on, let's get you inside."

When they reached the door, she stepped into the kitchen and turned toward him.

"Jack, this won't be over, even after I sign the papers tomorrow, will it?"

He pulled in a deep breath and let it out. "The worst of it will be."

She shook her head. "He can still kill me after that."

"But he wouldn't get the ranch. Not ever, once you sign your will that would give the property to your brother."

"I'm not naming my brother as my beneficiary."

He blinked then gave a little shrug. "Doesn't matter, so long as you're not leaving it to Andrew Hill."

"No, I'm not." She couldn't hold his gaze, but looked past him. "Jack, have you thought about what I said? About you buying the ranch after I'm declared owner?"

"No."

She jerked her gaze up to his deep brown eyes. "Why not? It might be best."

He hesitated. "I thought you were beginning to like it here."

"I am. But you know so much more about it. . ."

He shook his head. "I can't buy it, Rachel. And besides, none of us want you to leave."

"Even if I cause trouble?"

"Hill would cause trouble no matter who was getting Randolph's property. He doesn't hate you. He hates the person standing between him and the ranch—whoever that is."

"So it's not personal."

Jack's lips twitched. "Not really. But it would be a shame if you let him drive you away."

She sighed, knowing he was right.

"This is a beautiful ranch," he said.

"Yes. And I do see now why Randolph loved it so."

He smiled then. "Rachel, stay."

He said it so softly she wasn't sure she'd heard him right. She looked up at him. "You really want me to?"

"I do. I think you've got the stuff to make a ranch woman. Me and the boys will make sure you learn to do things right."

"Thank you." Her heart raced, and she felt very daring as she reached out and laid her hand gently on his sleeve. "Jack, I asked Mr. McClure to make you my heir."

His jaw dropped. "No. You can't."

"Why not?"

"I. . . You should leave it to your brother."

"Another greenhorn?" She smiled at him.

"Someone far away," Jack said. "Someone Andrew Hill can't get at until the ownership is settled."

"I'm not putting any conditions in there. My heir won't have to live here thirty days or do anything else to inherit. Just. . .be. That's how I want it. And I want it to be you. You can't talk me out of it."

He was quiet for a long moment. "What if I decide someday I don't want to be here? While you're around, I mean. What if I decide to take a job somewhere else?"

She swallowed hard. "Then I will be sad. But that's up to you. For now I had to pick someone, and I picked the person I thought was best."

He nodded slowly. "All right. I can see I have my job cut out for me."

She arched her eyebrows, and he chuckled.

"I have to make sure you stick around a good long time," he said.

"Oh, I intend to."

"Good," Jack said. "That suits me just fine."

The night passed almost too quietly. Rachel woke to sunshine streaming in her window. She jumped out of bed and dressed quickly for the expedition to town. She would have to get to know the other ranch women in the area and get advice from them on her wardrobe choices. For today she dressed as she would have in Boston if she were going to the shop to meet with her wealthier customers.

In the kitchen she peeked into the pie safe. Four brown apple pies sat on the shelves. She'd put her energy into baking yesterday, after the excitement. It had kept her from going crazy in the confines of the ranch house. Well, the men would have a treat later, after her business in town was completed.

A soft knock came on the kitchen door while she was preparing her breakfast. She opened the door, and Jack stood on the step, his eyes alight.

Rachel's heart lurched, and she smiled. "Good morning."

"Good morning to you. You look like a fine landowner."

"Thank you. Have you eaten?"

"Yes, ma'am. Just wanted to check when you'd be ready to leave."

"Give me ten minutes to eat."

He nodded but didn't turn away.

"Would you join me for coffee?" she asked.

"That'd be good."

He came inside, and she shut the door.

"How many are going with us?" she asked as she took down an extra mug.

"Six of us will go along with you, counting the two deputies, and four men will stay here to guard the ranch."

"You think I need that much protection?" She slid fried potatoes and an egg onto her ironstone plate.

"I do," Jack said. "It would be more efficient for him to pick you off along the road than to do something destructive here at the ranch while you're in town signing the papers."

Her pulse pounded at the thought of being attacked on the road. "All right." She poured their coffee and set the pot back on the stove. "Excuse me just a minute."

She went into the sitting area and carefully put the loaded revolver into the handbag she would carry. When she returned to the table, Jack eyed her bag soberly but said nothing. He knew what was in it, she had no doubt.

The food was tasteless, but she forced herself to eat. When she'd finished, she gulped the last of her coffee and carried her dishes to the sideboard.

"I'm ready. I'll tend to the dishes when we come back." She was pleased that her voice didn't give away her nervousness.

"I'll go tell the boys. Don't come out until one of us comes back here for you."

He slipped out the door, and she put on her hat—a stylish one she'd brought from Boston, not her cowboy hat—and a light shawl, more to keep off the sun than for warmth. She hovered near the kitchen door, wondering if she should open it. No, she decided. Jack was working hard to ensure her safety. She waited.

His knock came within a minute.

"Wagon's ready."

"Let's go then."

He walked beside her across the barnyard, his eyes darting here and there, ever watchful.

A team of horses stood in harness, waiting for them to board the wagon. To Rachel's surprise, Goldie sat in the driver's seat. Four other men sat on their horses, waiting.

"We'll sit one on either side of you," Jack said. He gave her a hand up then climbed to sit close beside her.

"Good morning, Goldie," Rachel said.

"Morning, miss." He gave her a perfunctory smile, but all of the men wore somber expressions.

Jack nodded to Rusty, and he and Wade headed out ahead of them. Goldie clucked to the team, and they leaned into their collars. Behind came the two deputies.

"Where's Abe?" she asked.

"He's staying here with Tom, Chris, and Joe." Jack gave her an apologetic frown.

Goldie glanced her way. "Abe wanted to come, but we didn't want to leave the new men here alone, so we drew straws."

"It's fine," she said, touched that the men who'd been with her longest all wanted to be near her today. "Thank you, Goldie."

He nodded and focused his attention on the horses. Jack and the mounted men never relaxed but scanned the landscape as they rode. Most of them held rifles, and she knew they sought out places a gunman could lie in wait. The morning sun was already too warm. She tried not to think about Andrew Hill. It was hard to draw a deep breath.

They reached town without incident, and her tension lessened. Would Hill try to attack her here, among so many people? Maybe he'd given up and left Fort Worth.

At McClure's office building, Rusty dismounted and went to the door. The others moved their horses in close around the wagon while they waited, searching the nearby buildings for anything out of place. Mr. McClure opened the door at Rusty's knock. He spoke to Rusty, who turned and waved at Jack. Jack hopped down and extended his hand to her, while the riders circled and watched, their guns at the ready.

Jack and Rusty went inside with her, with Jack walking slightly behind her. Protecting her back. The rest of the men waited on the street. Rachel wondered if they encircled the building.

"Well, the day has arrived," Mr. McClure said with a reassuring smile. "Come right in, Miss Paxton." He led her and Jack into the inner room where his desk sat. Rusty remained in the outer room, watching out a front window.

"Won't you sit down?" the lawyer said. "I have the papers all ready, and here's a pen, all filled with ink." He indicated the fountain pen that lay on the desktop.

"Thank you." Rachel sat down and arranged her skirts. She picked up the pen.

McClure laid a paper before her. "This confirms that you have lived on the property for thirty days."

She scanned the document quickly and signed it.

"This is the deed to the ranch and gives you ownership of everything on it, as well as Mr. Hill's bank account."

She looked up at Jack. His eyebrows hiked up, but he was smiling. She smiled back and signed the paper.

McClure presented a third document. "And this is the will leaving your—"

"Hold it right there."

They all jerked their heads toward the doorway. Andrew Hill stood in the opening, pointing a revolver at Rachel.

"How did you get in here?" McClure sputtered.

And where was Rusty? Rachel looked at Jack, but his gaze was intent on Hill.

Hill stepped aside, his back to the wall, his gun still aimed at Rachel.

"How'd you get past Rusty?" Jack asked.

Hill smiled. "He was busy watching out the window. But I came in last night. Been in the storeroom for twelve hours, waitin' for this moment. Wasn't hard to put him out of the way." He focused on Rachel. "Say goodbye to your friends, Miss Paxton."

McClure straightened his shoulders. "She's already signed the papers. The ranch is hers."

"Not for long," Hill said.

Rachel still had the pen in her hand. She leaned over the desk and scrawled her name at the bottom of the final document. "Hey!" Hill waved the revolver back and forth. "Get away from the desk. Now."

Jack scowled at him. "You can't pick your relatives, Hill, but if you don't like 'em, the law says you can pick someone else to leave your stuff to."

"It doesn't matter that Randolph left her the ranch," Hill said. "If she dies now, I get it. Me and my aunt, but she probably won't live long either." His satisfied smile made Rachel wonder if he had plans to kill his aunt too.

"I've signed a will," she said. "If you kill me, the ranch goes to Jack Callen."

Hill's eyes narrowed and his sneer flicked to Jack. "Then it looks like I'll have to kill him too and burn that paper you signed."

"Listen, Hill," Jack said, "there's no way you can get away with shooting all three of us. And you can't run a ranch if you're swinging at the end of a rope."

"Besides, if you burn the will, my brother gets the ranch." Rachel tried to put steel in her voice. "He lives in Connecticut. Will you go there and kill him too?"

Hill hesitated, and Jack took advantage of the moment to draw his Colt. "Drop the gun, Hill."

They stared at each other for several seconds.

"You might hit me, but it's the last thing you'll do," Jack said.

Finally, Hill stooped and laid his revolver on the floor.

"Mr. McClure, would you please pick up that gun?" Jack never took his eyes off Hill. "Rachel, go get the other men. Tell them to get the marshal and a doctor. Then see if Rusty's going to be all right."

That evening the men enjoyed Rachel's apple pies and coffee. The house seemed tiny with all eight of them squeezed into her sitting room.

"Miss Paxton," Rusty said, "I prob'ly shouldn't say this, but your pie's better than Abe's."

"It's all right," Abe said. "It's true."

Rachel smiled at them. "Thank you both. Rusty, I'm extremely pleased that you're here to enjoy it."

Rusty reached up to rub the back of his head and winced.

Rachel stood. "I hope you're good for seconds and a refill on your coffee."

"Oh yes, ma'am." Rusty, along with Tom and Wade, held out their plates.

Goldie pushed back his chair. "Gentlemen, we should let Miss Paxton sit and enjoy herself." He looked at Rachel. "With your permission, I will serve the seconds."

She laughed. "Thank you, Goldie. I'll let you pamper me today, but tomorrow I expect you to treat me like a ranch hand—a rather green one who still needs some instruction."

Goldie gave her a little bow. "We will make sure you learn how to throw a calf."

Half an hour later the men thanked her and drifted out toward the bunkhouse. Jack lingered behind.

"Miss Paxton," he said when the door closed behind Abe, the last one out.

"Please call me Rachel. You did last night."

His cheeks flushed, and he ducked his head for a moment.

"I reckon I was forward."

"No, I didn't think so at the time."

He swallowed hard and raised his gaze to meet hers. "Rachel then."

She smiled. "What is it, Jack?"

"You shouldn't have put me in your will."

"We've been over this," she said firmly. "It was my choice. And none of the men know about it, if that's what has you worried."

"It's not. Your property should go to someone close to you. Your brother."

"My brother has property of his own." She studied his face. She didn't want to embarrass him, but she was suddenly unsure of where she stood with Jack, what her future would look like here on the ranch.

"I hoped. . ." She pulled in a deep breath. "Jack, you're closer to me than anyone else now. I may never go back to Boston."

He frowned. "Don't you have things there?"

"A friend is shipping a couple of boxes. I told her to keep the rest."

"But your brother. . ."

"He doesn't expect anything from me. He only wants me to be happy. And I'll be happy if I know someone who loves this place will care for it if I'm not able. But my life is here now."

He looked away and let out a deep sigh. "We're glad you're staying. All of us, but. . . Well, I'll just speak for myself. *I'm* glad."

"So am I." She stepped toward him. "Jack, you'll stay too, won't you, and help me run this place?"

"There's nothing I'd like more. Rachel. . ."

She gazed at him, sensing that he was struggling with something difficult.

"What is it?" she asked softly.

"Feels out of line, but. . ."

She reached out toward him. "Just say what you're thinking, Jack. Please."

He seized her hand and squeezed it gently. "When Randolph first told me about you, I couldn't imagine why he was so taken by a woman he'd never met. But I see it now. In fact, I think I've been allowed to see things, parts of you, that he never knew about. And. . .and they're all good things."

She stood still for a moment, a wave of warmth washing over her. "Thank you, Jack. That's the sweetest thing anyone's ever said to me."

"Well, I. . .I meant it to be."

She looked up into his eyes. "I care about you too, Jack."

His brow wrinkled. "Still doesn't seem right."

"What do you mean?"

He shrugged a little, but he didn't let go of her hand, and she was very conscious of his touch.

"First you were Randolph's girl. Then you weren't. Then you

were sort of a guest on the ranch. Now you're the boss."

"Oh please," Rachel said. "That sounds businesslike and cold."

"I want to do things proper," Jack said earnestly, "But I also want. . ."

"Tell me that, Jack. What do you want?"

"I don't want anyone to think I'm taking advantage, but—"

She couldn't help letting out a little laugh.

"What?" he asked.

"Nothing. Just—well, I didn't want people to think I had improper designs on the foreman."

"Well, I hope it can be more than business."

"I want that too."

Slowly, Jack released her hand and reached toward her. Rachel took one step into his embrace. Several impressions hit her at once. She'd never been kissed by a man before, but now a cowboy was kissing her. He smelled like the prairie, and she liked that. His arms were strong and warm around her. She was staying, no doubt about that. She didn't care if she never got on a train again. Everything she wanted was here. The best foreman in Texas would teach her everything she needed to know about ranching. And her new life here looked very bright. She sent up a silent prayer of thanks.

Susan Page Davis is the author of more than eighty Christian novels and novellas. Her historical novels have won numerous awards, including the Carol Award, two Will Rogers Medallions for Western Fiction, and two FHL Chapter Reader's Choice Awards. She lives in western Kentucky with her husband. They have six children and ten grandchildren. Visit her website at https://susanpagedavis.com.

Twice the Trouble

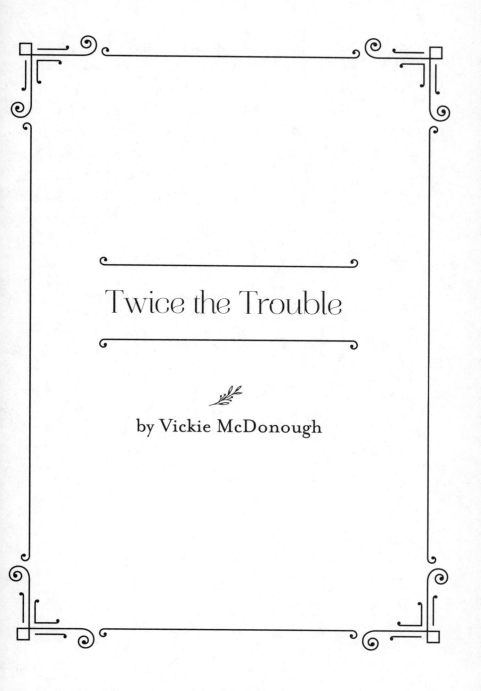

by Vickie McDonough

❧ Chapter 1 ❧

The road to Cactus Creek, Texas
Early May 1888

The stagecoach dipped into a rut in the road and back out, slamming Katie Quinn against the side once again. "Ouch. Slow down!"

"The faster the driver goes, the quicker we'll get there and out of this rough-riding contraption." Her sister, Keeley, shook her head and closed her book. "I much prefer the train. At least I could read on it."

"Aye, me too. And you could get up and walk around. As far as getting there quicker, I have mixed feelings. I'm both reluctant and eager to meet our future husbands."

"I know just how you feel."

Katie stared at her identical twin sister. Looking Keeley in the face was like gazing in a mirror. Wavy black hair pulled back in a loose bun, flashing dark brown eyes, a bit darker complexion than most Irish people had. Some people referred to them as Black Irish because they looked more Spanish than Irish. With matching forest-green dresses as they had on today, no one would be able to tell them apart, especially the people in the town they were traveling to—Cactus Creek, Texas.

"'Tis hard to believe we're in the grand state of Texas. 'Tis fierce warm here." Keeley turned from gazing out the window and looked at Katie. Concern filled her eyes. "Are you sure you want to do what we discussed last night? It doesn't seem quite fair to the men."

"I think we have ta. While we agreed to marry them, we never said when. 'Tis the wise thing to do."

"You do know Connor and Brian are expecting to marry us today." Keeley sighed. "But if you're certain about this plan, I'll go along. I just hope they don't change their minds, 'cause then we'll be in a dreadful predicament, for sure."

"That's true." The concern in her sister's eyes made Katie second-guess herself. But they had to make sure that Connor and Brian were honorable men before they agreed to marry, even if her plan made Keeley and her look less such in the beginning.

"I still wish we had prayed and sought God's will before agreeing to become mail-order brides."

"Don't fret yourself. We prayed He would show us a way to support ourselves, and He has, has He not?"

"Aye, you're right. M'belly is all ajitter though."

Katie nodded. "Mine too. But 'twill all work out, ye'll see."

Cactus Creek, Texas

"How do I look?" Connor McLoughlin stared at his cousin, who had also donned his Sunday suit for today's very special occasion.

Brian Barnett cocked his head and studied him. "Good. Except your tie is crooked."

"Well, fix it then."

"All right. Hold your horses while I tuck in my shirt."

Brian finished his task, straightened Connor's tie, then shrugged on his black frock coat. "I hope we don't have to wear these for long. It's blistering hot out today."

"If the stage is on time, we should be able to go straight to the church once the ladies arrive." Connor grinned. "Do you believe it? We're gettin' married on the same day and to sisters, no less."

Brian's mouth quirked up. "I never thought I'd see the day you got married, old man."

Connor chuckled at Brian's ongoing joke. His cousin liked poking fun at him for being eight months older. In truth, Brian was more like a brother than a cousin, since they'd grown up together.

"Did you remember to make the bed this morning?"

Connor puffed out his chest. "I did, and I even put on clean sheets."

"Glory be, there's hope for you yet."

"Ha-ha. Just because you like keeping things all neat and tidy doesn't mean everyone does."

Brian shrugged. "You have to be orderly when you own a mercantile. But I will confess that after sharing the house with you for so long, I miss having you there to talk to in the evenings. Although, I don't miss your mess or picking up after you."

"Yeah, me too. Adjusting to having a place of my own has been harder than I expected." He grinned. "Should be a whole lot easier once my wife joins me though."

"That's true." Brian bent down and wiped his hanky across the tops of his shiny boots.

Connor grimaced as he looked at his dusty Wellingtons. He swiped one across the back of his pant leg and then the other. They may not be shiny, but at least they were no longer dusty. Thinking of his soon-to-be-bride made his belly swirl. "I've got to admit I'm worried that I might not like Katie when I see her. What if she's as ugly as the back side of a mule?"

"I can't think of a single woman who's that unsightly. You liked the woman who wrote to you enough to ask her to marry you, so I think you'll be fine. All that matters to me is that Keeley is kindhearted and can count well."

"Count? What kind of criteria is that for a marriage?" Connor walked to the window and stared out at the main street of Cactus Creek. It was a quiet, sleepy town that didn't see much trouble. Katie should like that. Although, at the moment, there were quite a few folks out and about. Had word gotten out about the brides' arrival in spite of his and Brian's efforts to keep it a secret?

"My wife will need to help me with the store, thus she needs to be able to count well enough to make change and keep inventory. I already know Keeley can read and write, thanks to her letters."

"I reckon that makes sense." Connor scratched his neck. He hated wearing ties. His job as town marshal didn't require one, so every time he wore his suit and tie, he felt as if he was being strangled. "I just hope Katie can cook good. I'm tired of eatin' beans and corn bread."

"Are we still taking them to the café to eat after the weddings?"

"Probably be the nice thing to do. Don't seem right to make them cook after traveling so far. Besides, we want them rested up for other things." Connor waggled his brows.

Brian rolled his eyes. "You'd best treat Katie well. I don't want her to come running over to our house every time you upset her."

"Ah, c'mon. You know me better than that." He felt offended that his cousin would say such a thing. They'd both been raised to treat women well and with respect. "When was the last time I offended a lady?"

Rubbing his freshly shaven jaw, Brian stared at the ceiling then grinned. "I remember Mrs. Fennimore whacking you with her parasol a time or two."

"Crazy ol' woman. I was just trying to carry her packages for her, and there she was hollerin' for the marshal. She couldn't see well enough to know I was him."

Brian threw back his head and laughed. "That was the funniest thing I've seen in a coon's age." He checked his pocket watch and sobered. "Almost time. We should head on over to the stage office."

"There's a whole lot of folks outside for a weekday afternoon. Did you tell anyone what was happening today?"

"No. Did you?"

"Nope."

They stared at one another then snapped their fingers in unison and said, "Mrs. Davies."

Connor rubbed his neck. He hadn't wanted the sisters to be overwhelmed by the whole town showing up, so he hadn't told anyone that he and Brian were getting married except Pastor Rice, his wife, and Mrs. Davies, who was setting up a special table in the private dining room at her café for the four of them.

Brian cleared his throat. "I might have said something to Emily Willis."

"My landlady? Why?"

His cousin shrugged. "She cornered me and asked why you decided to get a place of your own. She wouldn't leave me alone until I mentioned you might be getting married, but I sure didn't tell her the date."

A cheer rang out, and quick footsteps raced down the boardwalk outside the jailhouse. Alfred French, owner of the livery, yanked open the door. "The stage is comin', Marshal. You two best get out here and meet your brides 'fore some other young bucks pretend to be y'all and runs off with 'em."

Connor and Brian stared one another in the eye for a second then raced for the door. As they neared the stage office, the crowd thinned and another cheer echoed through the streets. Several men slapped Connor on the back and shouted, "Congratulations, Marshal!"

Three of the towns' mamas who'd tried to match him up with their daughters stood together. They shook their heads at him, looking disappointed. At least he wouldn't have to suffer through any more uncomfortable meals with women he had no desire to marry. He avoided looking at the other ladies in the crowd and nodded his thanks to the men, even though this big commotion was exactly what he'd wanted to avoid.

"Here she comes!" Alfred hollered.

Connor stepped up in front of the stage office as the coach rounded the corner and slowed. His heart pounded like it did when he was chasing down a criminal and was close to apprehending him.

Brian gripped Connor's shoulder—a sure sign of his nervousness.

The stage stopped, and the crowd hushed. Mac, the shotgun driver, shinnied down and jogged around the back of the stage to the side. He reached up and opened the door.

Connor's heartbeat galloped as he saw the dark green of a dress and then the top of a frilly hat as a woman bent to exit the stage. A thin hand reached for Mac's, and the woman stepped down to the ground. When she glanced up, Brian's grip tightened on Connor's shoulder and a murmur echoed through the crowd.

"Whoa, Nelly, I sure hope that's Keeley. She's beautiful." Brian straightened his coat and wiped off an imaginary spot of dust.

So much for his cousin not caring how pretty his future mate was, but he couldn't fault him, because the woman was lovely. Young but very pretty. Her complexion was a shade darker than he'd expected with her being Irish, but it contrasted nicely with her dark hair and those near-black eyes, which reminded him of the center of a black-eyed Susan. His mouth went dry. He licked his lips and blurted, "I thought they had red hair."

"Me too." Brian shrugged.

And then a matching green skirt appeared. And a matching hat. Connor blinked. And a matching woman. He glanced at Brian, who had the same flummoxed expression he imagined was on his own face. "Did they ever mention they was twins?"

"No." Brian's hushed response held a tone of awe. "How will we ever tell them apart?"

"They'll just have to wear different colored dresses, that's all."

"They sure are magnificent."

"Hey, Marshal, if'n you don't want yers, I'll take 'er." Rawley Butler smiled widely, revealing his missing front teeth.

"We're keeping them, so the rest of you back off," Brian hollered. He elbowed Connor. "C'mon, cuz, before some yahoos steal them."

Connor swallowed the lump in his throat and stepped

forward. Not many things made him nervous—just big snakes, rabid critters, and gettin' married.

"Take off your hat," Brian whispered loudly.

Connor yanked it off and held it over his heart like a shield. What if Katie didn't like him? He'd never considered that. Brian was cleaner, smarter, and better looking. He might have Irish blood in him, but he was born and raised a Texan. He sure hoped he passed muster.

The women stared at them with questioning eyes.

Brian stepped up beside him. "I'm Brian, and this big galloot is my cousin, Connor. Which of you is Keeley?"

The twins glanced at each other, and the one on the left nodded. They straightened and looked back.

"We're Katie and Keeley Quinn. A pleasure to make your acquaintance," the one on the left said.

The gal on the right lifted her chin. "And we're not telling you who is who until we're certain you're upright, godly men. So the weddings are on hold."

Connor felt gutshot.

Brian looked about the same.

A gasp echoed through the crowd, and then raucous laughter erupted.

❦ Chapter 2 ❦

Now see here." Connor stepped forward.

Both women's eyes widened. They held hands and backed up until they ran into the stagecoach.

Brian reached out and grabbed his arm, pulling him back. "Let's hear them out."

Connor turned toward his cousin. "They made a promise, and you know how much a man—or woman—keeping their word means to me."

Brian motioned him closer. Half the crowd moved toward them, as if wanting to hear. "Look at it from their side," he whispered. "They don't know us from Adam."

Connor scratched his ear. "Adam who?"

Brian sighed. "Never mind. They're probably half scared out of their wits. It won't do any good to force them, so let's give them some time."

"They must be out of their minds to ask such a thing after we paid their way here." He shoved his hand to his hips and exhaled a loud breath. "Fine, I'll listen, but I put on this hot suit for nothing."

"That's not true. You look nice for your intended." Brian stepped forward. "Let's get you ladies out of the hot sun. I imagine you must be half starved after such a long trip."

The twins' posture relaxed. Both nodded.

"I'm fierce thirsty," one said.

"What shall we do with their luggage, Marshal?" Hank, the stagecoach driver, walked toward him.

"Throw it down, and we'll stick it in the jailhouse for now."

"All right." Hank climbed on top of the stage and Mac followed. In short order they tossed down four sad-looking satchels.

Connor caught a pair, and Brian grabbed the other two. It didn't seem like much for two women. Perhaps they were worse off than he realized. His ire at having to wait to get married melted like ice on a hot day.

"If you ladies will follow us, we'll secure your things at the jailhouse then go to the café."

At his office, Connor entered the cell room, put the four bags in the cage on the right, and locked it. When he entered his office again, he stared at two pretty pairs of surprised eyes.

"Why did you lock up our bags?" the twin on the right asked.

"It's just a precaution. I wouldn't want anyone slipping in and helping himself to your things."

The woman on the left lifted her hand to her chest. "Is it that dangerous here?"

Brian chuckled, drawing the twins' attention. "No. This town is quite safe, for the most part. Sometimes things get loud on the weekends when the local cowboys come to town for a good time, but that's usually about the worst of it."

Someone's stomach gurgled, and Connor surmised it was the twin closest to him by the way her cheeks reddened to a pleasing color. He held out his arm. "Shall we go eat? My stomach is rubbing up against my backbone."

Her eyes widened, and then she flashed him a grateful smile, revealing the most enticing pair of dimples he'd ever seen. His heart thumped—hard. He wanted to pull her into his arms and kiss her, but he had no idea if she was Katie or not. He'd quickly fallen in love with the enchanting letters they had exchanged. Too bad the gals wanted to wait. He'd been looking forward to being married.

At the café, Mrs. Davies ushered them away from staring eyes to the private dining room. The school board and town council often used this room, so Connor was familiar with it. But he'd never seen it quite as decked out as it was now with everything pushed to the side except for one table and four chairs. A stiff white cloth covered the table, and a bouquet of wildflowers sat in the center in an etched-glass vase.

"'Tis lovely." One twin moved forward and sniffed the flowers. "I have not seen these before. What are they?"

Connor flicked a glance at Brian since he knew more about flower names.

Brian cleared his throat. "The purple ones are larkspur, and the white with yellow centers are daisies." He pulled out a chair and offered it to the closest twin. He glanced at Connor.

Stepping forward, Connor smiled and tugged out the other chair. Once both ladies were seated, he and Brian dropped down on the other two chairs. Connor enjoyed having a pretty lady on each side, but he sure wished they didn't look so much alike. The next days were going to be taxing. How long would the twins make him and Brian wait before they could be married?

Though she was hungry, Keeley wasn't sure she could eat a thing. She'd been a bit nervous about marrying Brian, but she'd made her choice. When Katie suggested they wait to see what the men were like, she'd mulled over the plan and had agreed. Now she wasn't so sure. She'd watched the different expressions cross the men's faces when they'd told them they wouldn't be marrying them today—shock, anger, then reluctant acceptance.

They were doing the right thing. Still, they had taken the men's money and gotten their hopes up. But Katie's argument had been a good one. A man could say anything in a letter. Looking her in the eye and proving he meant what he said was something altogether different.

The woman with graying-brown hair who'd ushered them to the table returned with four glasses of water on a tray and single-page menus. "Welcome to Cactus Creek, ladies," she said as she passed out the glasses and menus. "I'll give you a few minutes to look those over. Would any of y'all care for coffee or tea?"

"I'd love a cup of tea with biscuits."

"I got the tea, but I don't got any fresh biscuits right now. Best I can do is corn bread."

Keeley shook her head. Why would the woman think she'd want corn bread when she asked for cookies? "I'll just take the tea then."

"Coffee for Brian and me." Connor flashed the woman a smile then glanced at her and Katie. "You two should eat a meal, even though it's in between lunch and supper now. That way you won't need to cook tonight. I reckon you're tired after coming all the way from Chicago."

"Perhaps a bowl of soup. We don't eat much, I promise." Katie smiled at the two men.

"I want you to eat your fill and not be embarrassed about it. We don't want you going hungry." Brian gave her and her sister a convincing stare.

Their aunt had fussed if they ate much, but then Aunt Colleen had complained about many things. Her constant nagging and trying to find them mates had driven them to become mail-order brides. At least she and Katie had been able to choose their own husbands that way. She could only hope they hadn't jumped out of the frying pan and into the fire.

Brian tapped the table. "Since you're unwilling to reveal your real names for now, we'll need to call you something. Twin A and B doesn't sound very nice."

"Neither does 1 or 2." Connor wrinkled his face.

Keeley reached out and fingered a velvety white daisy petal. She glanced at Katie. "What about Lark and Daisy? After all, Larkin is an Irish name."

Katie shrugged. "'Tis as good as any, I suppose. Which do you favor?"

Keeley tapped her lip. "Lark, I believe."

"Very well. I'll be Daisy then."

"We still can't tell you apart." Connor frowned.

Katie lifted her chin a wee bit. "Once we feel more comfortable around you, we'll reveal who is who. Until then, I suppose we'll simply have to tell you our temporary names each day."

Keeley could tell Connor didn't like the deception, but she imagined that was true with most lawmen. She hated fooling him and Brian, but she'd promised Katie to go along—and they always stuck together, no matter what. They'd never had anyone else they could depend on since their mum died.

Mrs. Davies entered with a tray of drinks. She placed the coffee near the men and two tall glasses of brown liquid in front of her and Katie. Keeley stared at the strange drink, wondering where her tea was. She glanced at Katie, who lifted one shoulder in a slight shrug.

Mrs. Davies glanced at each of them. "Now, what would y'all like to eat?"

"What types of soup do you have?" Katie handed the woman the menu. "I didn't see any listed."

Mrs. Davies gave her an odd stare. "Don't make soup when it's this hot. Nobody ever buys it. I got some beef stew or chicken and dumplings. Or I could fix you a sandwich."

Keeley looked at the men.

"The stew and dumplin's are both good. I can attest to that." Connor looked up at their hostess. "I think I'd like the latter today."

"And you, Brian?"

"The stew, please. And we'll want pie afterwards."

"Got apple or peach."

"You got a whole pie of either?" Brian asked.

Mrs. Davies nodded. "Got one peach and two apples that I made for suppertime, but I reckon I can crank out another one before then if you want a whole one."

Brian looked at her then Katie. "Which would you prefer?"

"Apple." Katie smiled.

Keeley didn't bother replying, since her sister knew her preference.

"We'll take the apple," Connor said. "I figure the gals might like to have some later in case they get hungry."

"And what about your meals?" Mrs. Davies stared at the twins.

Keeley tried not to squirm. "I'll try the dumplings, if you please."

"And I'll take the stew." Katie smiled at Keeley. "That way we can each sample both."

"All righty then." Mrs. Davies spun around and left the room.

Nobody said anything for a bit. Connor stared at the window on the back wall. Brian stirred sugar into his coffee.

"What is this?" Katie touched the glass of brown liquid that had a chunk of ice floating in it.

Connor wrinkled his brow. "That's tea—just what you asked for."

Katie's gaze shot to hers. "Tea?" they said in unison.

Connor nodded. "You've never seen iced tea before? That's how most folks drink it down here. We're fortunate that Mrs. Davies has an icehouse. She has the ice shipped all the way from up north somewhere. Folks that don't have an icehouse chill their tea in spring water."

Keeley shook her head at the same time Katie did. "We've only ever had hot tea. Not only did we live in an Irish community, but our aunt was Irish to the bone. Hot tea is all she served. She wouldn't allow us to attend social functions, so I have no idea if others in Chicago drank it."

Brian chuckled. "I guess there'll be a lot of things you'll have to become accustomed to now that you're living in the South."

Katie tilted the glass of tea a bit. "Why do you drink your

coffee hot then? Shouldn't it be cold also? It makes no sense."

Connor had just taken a sip, and he nearly dropped the cup. He coughed, and his eyes filled with tears. Finally, he laughed. "Cold coffee? Who ever heard of such a thing?"

Keeley stiffened. " 'Tis not funny. Cold tea is just as odd to us as cold coffee is to you."

Brian reached out and lightly touched her hand. "I can see your point. I have a solution. I actually have several teapots for sale in my store and a couple of varieties of tea. We'll stop by there and get one before we go to the house—" He looked at Connor. "Where are they going to stay?"

Connor blinked, looking confused. "Um. . .hadn't thought of that. I figured we'd be married and each go to our own place."

Keeley felt bad. They'd taken the men's money and gotten up their hopes of marrying, and now they had to find a place for them to stay. Brian, her intended, was the nicer of the two, but something about Connor's more rugged demeanor drew her. Oh dear. She mustn't allow herself to be attracted to her sister's future husband.

Brian rubbed his chin. "I think the best thing would be for the ladies to stay in your rented house, and you move back in with me."

Connor nodded. "I'll have to make sure it's all right with my landlady."

"Why don't you go ask her after we eat while I take the ladies to the mercantile to get a few things. I don't imagine you've got much food in the house."

He shook his head. "You know part of my salary is free breakfast here at the café, and I usually eat supper with you."

"All right then, that's what we'll do. You ladies can pick out some food items you like before we go to the house. I want to make sure you have all that you need."

Katie shook her head. "We cannot accept your charity."

Keeley wanted to pinch her. The thought of having food to eat whenever she wanted was a dream. Leave it to her sister to ruin it.

Connor squirmed in his seat. "It's our responsibility to care for you."

Katie's chin went up again. "Not yet. We are not married."

Katie was always the scrapper. Keeley could fight hard too, but she had no desire to reject an offer of food. Aye, she'd been reluctant to eat today because of her nervousness, but it made sense for them to have a stock of food. They sure didn't have the money to eat at the café.

"How about we make a trade." Brian eyed Keeley then Katie. "I need help in the store. I was hoping that my wife—whichever one of you is Keeley—would assist me. If you'd be willing to work in the store, I'll pay you in supplies until we marry. It would be a fair trade."

Keeley looked at Katie. She wasn't sure she'd like working in a store and hadn't considered Brian might expect her help, but they had to eat. They nodded at the same time, and then Keeley straightened. "That's more than fair. Perhaps I'll come tomorrow, and then Daisy can go the next day."

❧ Chapter 3 ❧

Katie wandered through Brian's orderly mercantile, fingering fabric, sniffing fragrant soaps, and simply enjoying the fact that she could linger there as long as she wanted. Life in New York had been such a struggle when they first came to America with their parents. Though she was only two when they first arrived, she could remember being cold in the winter and hot in the summer. But what clung to her memory the most was being hungry all the time and how her mother fretted over the lack of food. Whenever her mum tried to talk to Da about the lack of food, he would get angry and say he was working as hard as he could, and then he would leave and not return until after she and Keeley had gone to bed.

Sighing, she turned several cans of vegetables so that the labels faced forward. She glanced at Brian, where he stood tall at the counter, helping a customer look for a plow in a catalogue.

He was a handsome man with his dark hair and blue eyes. He was slim but strong, as he proved when he carried several heavy crates to Mrs. Davies's wagon earlier. He felt familiar somehow. Was it because Keeley had read all of the letters she received from him to her?

He glanced up and smiled, making her rebellious heart flutter. Thankfully, his gaze didn't linger. Keeley should have come today, since she was the one betrothed to Brian, but she had wanted to wash their clothing and clean the house. And besides, Katie had almost been beside herself to come to the store. Would Brian allow her to help once he knew she wasn't his betrothed?

She moved through the store again and noticed a supply of spices on a shelf. Ginger, cinnamon, mace, cloves, nutmeg, caraway seeds, and another half dozen spices she'd never heard of before. Brian was so tidy that she found it odd the spices weren't in alphabetical order. She glanced over her shoulder. He had moved around the counter and stood beside his customer with his back to her, bent over the catalogue. Her heartbeat tripled its normal pace as she quickly rearranged the small tin cans in alphabetical order. It only made sense, after all, and it would make shopping a bit quicker for his customers. When she was done, she opened the lid of a small metal box and peeked inside. It was a spice set with eight smaller tins and a nutmeg grater. With a sigh, she closed the lid, thinking of all the wonderful things she and her sister could bake if they owned such a set.

Aunt Colleen had a sweet tooth, but the only spices she kept on hand were cinnamon and ginger. She was quite stingy with her sugar and flour, except when it came to baking scones. To be truthful, her aunt was tightfisted with pretty much everything.

Did she miss them the least bit? Or was she angry with them for spoiling her plans to marry them off?

"What do you think. . .um. . .Daisy?" Brian walked up to her.

Katie spun around. "'Tis a grand store."

"You two didn't take very many items yesterday, and I know for a fact that Connor doesn't keep many groceries on hand. I want you to make a pile of supplies to take home with you when we close. Do you like ham?"

Katie nodded. "Aye, very much."

"Good. I just got several in on trade. I'll get one from the back for you to take home. Also, I would suggest you look through the ready-made dresses and see if there's any that will fit you. You're likely to faint in those wool dresses out here in the heat of Texas."

"Oh no, I couldn't."

"Once we're married—if you actually are Keeley, that is—you'll be able to choose whatever you need, so please, go ahead and take a couple."

Her sister was the lucky one, since she would be marrying Brian. "You're quite kind, but it doesn't seem right to help myself to anything I want."

"Need and want aren't the same. A person has basic needs, and those shouldn't be ignored. Come over here." He walked across the store to the ready-made section. "What's your favorite color?"

Her mind raced. She and Keeley had read one another the letters they'd written to the men before they mailed them, and they'd shared the four letters Connor and Brian wrote back, but she couldn't remember if her sister had ever told Brian what her favorite color was. "We like most colors except orange, although blue, lavender, and green are our favorites." She needed to remember to tell Keeley what she'd told Brian.

He frowned, as if disappointed his ploy hadn't worked. He tapped his lip with his index finger and pulled a calico dress off the rack that reminded Katie of the prairie violets that snuck into the yards of the well-manicured homes she'd worked at back in Chicago. "This light blue would look good on you." He handed it to her.

" 'Tis lovely." Katie held it up and looked in the long mirror in the clothing section of the store. She'd never worn a dress made from fabric that felt so thin. It would be like wearing her night-gown, except of course, she'd have on her petticoats and unmentionables. Her cheeks warmed at the thought.

"This soft green might look nice on you, but if you both want something that matches, we'll either have to order dresses from the catalogue, or you can pick out fabric and make something yourself. Do you have a preference?"

She couldn't remember ever having a new off-the-rack dress. Most of what they wore had been donations from the church, not that her aunt was all that poor, but she wasn't about to spend her money on them if she could avoid it. "I do like this blue one. I'll have to try it on to see if it fits though."

"Take it home with you. And if you see one that you think Lark would like, feel free to take it to her to try."

"You're a very generous man, Brian Barnett."

He flashed an embarrassed smile then shrugged. "Just looking out for my own."

"You're only marrying one of us, and yet you've offered two dresses."

"Family is important. Connor is the closest thing to a brother

I have. My mama had five babies, but I'm the only one that lived. One was stillborn, two died as infants, and another got sick and died just after his second birthday. Connor's folks died when he was only nine, so my ma took him in and mothered him too."

"I'm truly sorry that your mum lost nearly all of her babes, Brian. Where are your parents now?" She folded the dress then crossed to the counter and laid it down.

"Gone. Pa died when I was sixteen, and Ma got sick two years ago and passed."

"My mum died when I was only eight. I still miss her." She pursed her lips, dreading to mention her da.

"What about your father?" He walked over and leaned his hip against the counter.

Staring at the dress, she fingered the white button on one cuff. "Gone, but I don't know where. After mum died, Da took us to Chicago to live with our Aunt Colleen. He stayed a few weeks, but he and our aunt fought all the time. One day he went to work and never came back."

Brian reached out as if to touch her but drew his hand back. "I'm sorry. That must have been so difficult, especially after losing your mother. At least you had your aunt to care for you."

Katie shrugged. "She did not like us. Life there was almost as bad as when we lived in the New York tenements. After we got older, Aunt Colleen kept having men over, hoping we'd marry one of them."

Brian leaned back against the counter. "No wonder you became mail-order brides. And now it makes sense why you want to wait to marry until you know us better. You've had few people in your life whom you could trust."

Katie's heart soared. He understood.

He took her by the shoulders and stared into her eyes. "I can promise you that Connor and I are honorable men. We keep our word, and we've been raised to respect women. Connor might holler a bit when he's angry, but he's all steam, and it passes quickly—same for me on occasion. I can assure you that you two have nothing to fear from us."

Katie smiled, and her eyes stung with unshed tears. "I'm quite relieved to hear that, Brian. I hope you will be patient with us."

He released her and stepped back. "Take all the time you need."

The door jingled as a gray-haired woman walked in.

"How are you today, Mrs. Green?" Brian walked toward her.

"I'm quite fine, thank you. This must be your lovely assistant. I've heard a lot about her and her sister. Identical twins. That's a first for Cactus Creek."

The elderly woman smiled at Katie and walked toward her. "I'm Florence Green. Welcome to Cactus Creek."

Katie curtsied. "Thank you, ma'am. 'Tis a pleasure to make your acquaintance. You may call me Daisy, for now."

Mrs. Green smiled and placed her hand on Katie's. "You won't find any better men in our town than Brian and Connor, except for the pastor, but then, he's spoken for."

" 'Tis grand to know that, ma'am. Thank you."

Mrs. Green turned back to Brian. "Don't you adore her sing-song accent?"

Brian flashed Katie an apologetic look. "How can I help you today?"

Katie wandered over to the fabric stock and looked through

the colorful calicos, ginghams, and solids shades. She loved the cheery ginghams. She'd never had a checkered dress before. After thumbing through the cloth, she noticed the thread rack. The two dozen colors were haphazardly placed, in no order at all. She glanced over her shoulder. Brian was adding things to a pile for his customer.

Once again, her heartbeat took off as she contemplated organizing the thread. Ladies would appreciate having the various shades of the same color together when they were searching for a specific thread. She took a deep breath and plunged ahead. In short order, she had the colors looking good. Surely Brian wouldn't object to her help.

He tallied up Mrs. Green's order.

She handed him the money. "I don't suppose you could run these over to my house, could you? I was in the middle of my baking when I ran out of sugar. I'll need another five-pound bag, as well as several other items."

"Um. . .well, it's Daisy's first day here. I—"

Katie hurried to the counter. "Go! I'll be fine alone for a few moments."

"Are you sure?"

"Aye."

"Very well. I shouldn't be gone more than ten minutes at the most."

As soon as Brian left, Katie walked behind the counter. What a grand time she'd have if this were her store. She opened the lid of the big glass jar that held the peppermint sticks and took a whiff. She and Keeley had received one for Christmas from Da right before he left them. She put the lid back on before she was tempted to sneak one.

The door opened and two ladies walked in. They glanced around, obviously surprised not to see Brian. Katie surmised the two were mother and daughter, based on their blond hair, blue eyes, and features that closely resembled one another.

"I'm Elizabeth Sawyer, and this is my daughter, Anna."

Katie smiled at them. She guessed Anna to be fairly close to twenty, as she was. "You may call me Daisy for now. I'm sure you've heard it's not my real name but the one I'm going by at the moment."

Anna stepped forward, her blue eyes shining. "I think you are wise to wait to get married until you know the men better. I mean, how does any mail-order bride do that—just arrive in town and marry a complete stranger?"

"Anna, please." Her mother pursed her lips. "You promised not to run off at the mouth."

"I know, Mama, but just imagine—"

Mrs. Sawyer lifted her eyebrows.

"Oh, all right. I'll go look at the fabric."

"We're going to be making Anna a dress for the Independence Day celebration in July. I realize it's a bit early, but we wanted to select fabric before it's picked through."

Anna held up a navy-and-gray stripe and a red gingham. "What do you think about the blue stripe for the skirt and the gingham for the top?"

Her mother's eyes widened. "Oh no, that's far too gaudy."

Katie turned away, smiling at the thought of the dress Anna wanted. Maybe she and Keeley should consider the celebration when picking out a dress, although the garment would need to be practical enough for everyday use. Perhaps she could wear a blue dress with a red sash, and maybe Keeley could go with red fabric and a blue sash. She turned around the catalogue that still lay on the counter and paged through it to the fabric selection.

The bell above the door jingled, and she assumed Brian had returned. She scanned the page of fabrics for sale then turned to the next.

A shadow darkened the counter, and feet shuffled toward her. "Give me your cash box."

Katie glanced up and found herself face-to-face with a pistol.

Connor made his usual rounds through town, although he rarely encountered a problem, other than when the cowboys were in town on the weekends or when there was a case of cattle rustling. The sun shone bright, but the heat of summer hadn't yet settled in.

"Hey, Marshal, how's them gals doin'?" Alfred French jogged toward him. He stopped and hiked up his worn overalls.

Connor sighed. He was so sick of talking about how the twins had tricked him and Brian. Everyone in town wanted to jaw on about them. How was he supposed to uphold the law and earn folks' respect when the twins had made him the laughingstock of the town? "I reckon they're fine. Haven't seem 'em this morning." He'd thought he might run into the gals at the diner, but they must have cooked their own breakfast.

Alfred shook his head. "Don't seem right what they did, takin' yer money and gettin' yer hopes up. You shoulda sent 'em packin'. Then again, I reckon that's a mighty hard thing to do when they's prettier than a spring mornin'."

He'd actually thought about sending them back, but he'd grown to care for Katie through her letters, and he wasn't ready to let her go. Maybe he should stop by the house and see how she was faring. "I'm a patient man. I'll wait a bit and hope she grows used to me."

"Sounds like what I had to do with the last horse I broke." Alfred grinned then sobered. "Guess ya have ta be patient to be a lawman." He slapped Connor on the upper arm. "See ya around. Gotta see if my horse is shod yet."

Connor watched the bowlegged cowboy shuffle away. Alfred had to be seventy-five if he was a day. He smiled at how the man had compared the twins to a green-broke horse. Brian rounded the corner, saw him, and waved. Connor pushed his feet into motion and met him in the middle of the street.

"What are you doing outside?"

"Had to make a delivery."

"How's Lark working out at the store?"

Brian glanced toward the building that housed the mercantile. "Daisy showed up. Not sure why they traded—unless, of course, she's Keeley—but she's been helpful. She's a quick learner. In fact, I left her in charge of the store while I did my delivery. I should be getting back though."

Connor nodded. "I'll walk with you. You think that Daisy is Keeley, and that's why she decided to come today since she's the one you're marryin'?"

"Don't know. It's possible that Katie came today merely to throw us off, but then, she could be Keeley." Brian batted at a fly that was pestering him. "I wish they'd just told us who was who right off so we could woo our own gal. I don't like not knowing which of them I'm talking to. It's awkward, plus I'd hate to say something romantic and have her turn out to be your gal."

"I hadn't thought about that." Connor rubbed his hand down the side of his face, feeling the same frustration his cousin did. "How long you figure they'll make us wait?"

Brian kicked at a stone and sent it flying. "Daisy told me some things today. Sounds like they've had a very difficult life. We need to be patient and prove to them that we're men they can trust. When they were just little girls, their pa dumped them at their aunt's house shortly after their mother died, and he never returned."

"That's rough."

"Especially since the aunt resented having to care for them."

Connor stared at his cousin. "They never said a word about that in the letters."

"I'm sure it's what drove them to become mail-order brides."

Connor nodded.

Suddenly a woman's scream echoed down the street. Connor's gaze flicked from one building to the next as he started jogging in the direction of the scream. A man ran out of Brian's store, holding his arm. He raced around the corner into the alley.

"Go!" Brian swatted his hand in the air. "Get him. I'll check on Daisy."

Chapter 4

Connor raced down the alley and onto Pine Street. The flee-ing man had hopped onto a horse and was already galloping out of town. Connor fired a warning shot, but the man didn't stop. He had too big a head start for Connor to catch him on foot. He searched the area for a horse he could borrow, but oddly, there wasn't a single one nearby. Blowing out a frustrated breath, he hurried back to the store, hoping whichever gal was there hadn't been injured.

Brian stood over a woman who lay on the floor.

Daisy squatted next to her while Anna Sawyer bounced up and down. "Never saw anything like that. She whipped out a knife and flung it right into that thief's hand so fast that he dropped his gun and skedaddled out of the store. See, it's over there by the tools."

Connor strode to the gun and picked it up. He looked it over and found nothing noteworthy except for the initials JT carved in the handle. He removed the bullets and put the gun on the counter, and then he walked over to where Mrs. Sawyer lay on the floor.

Anna gazed up at him with excited blue eyes. "Mama fainted the moment she saw blood."

"Where'd the blood come from?" Connor asked.

"Oh, didn't you hear me? Miss Quinn was reaching for the cash box like the thief told her, but when she stood up, she flicked a knife right into the thief's hand. Pretty as you please. That's when Mama fainted, so maybe it was the knife and not the blood, although she usually faints whenever she sees blood. I sure wish I could do that—throw a knife, not faint, of course."

Connor looked at Daisy and motioned with his head for her to follow him. He wanted to get away from Anna and hear Daisy's side of the story. He turned and stared at her for a long moment. A pair of innocent chocolate-brown eyes gazed up at him. She didn't look the least frightened. "Tell me exactly what happened."

" 'Tis as Anna stated. I was behind the counter when a man came in and pointed his gun in my face. He demanded the cash box, but I wasn't about to give him Brian's hard-earned money. I merely pulled out my knife and let him have it in his gun hand."

Connor lifted one eyebrow. "*Your* knife?"

"Aye." She proudly pulled back her sleeve to reveal a small leather sheath.

He schooled his expression so she wouldn't see his surprise. "Do you know how dangerous what you did was? If you'd missed, that man could have killed you and the Sawyer women."

Daisy hiked up her chin. "I never miss."

"Everybody misses."

Her eyes flashed. "Would you care to test my skill?"

"No, because I'm confiscating your weapon as evidence in a crime."

Her pluck instantly disappeared. "But you can't. 'Tis the only thing I have that my father gave me."

He gazed up at the ceiling, thinking how sad that was. Why would a man give his daughter a knife? "I'll give it back, but for now, I want it."

"Promise?"

He looked into her pretty eyes and nodded. "I promise, and I always keep my word."

She gazed up at him for a long moment. Finally, she must have seen what she was looking for because she ducked her head, unfastened the sheath, then placed it in his hand. He shoved it into his pocket, noticing that she'd already cleaned the man's blood off the knife.

Connor walked over to where Mrs. Sawyer was sitting up. Her daughter waved a fancy ladies' fan in front of her face. "Are you all right, Mrs. Sawyer?"

"Yes, just give me a few more minutes before I stand. My head is still woozy."

"Can you tell me what you saw?"

"A man with a gun charged in and demanded the money box. Miss Quinn bent down as if she was getting it, then rose up and threw a knife at the man. She's a hero! Why that villain might well have taken my Anna with him."

Connor resisted rolling his eyes. The Sawyer women were well known for embellishing their stories. "Anything else you can think of?"

"He was dressed in dirty denim pants and a blue flannel shirt, but he had a kerchief over his mouth and nose, so I couldn't tell if I knew him or not."

"Um. . .Mama, I do believe it was red flannel."

Mrs. Sawyer frowned. "You may be right, dear. I can't think clearly yet."

"Thank you. Anything you want to add, Anna?"

"He was only about three or four inches taller than Miss Quinn."

Connor turned back to Daisy. "You agree with that?"

"Aye. His shirt was red-and-black plaid, and he had a brown bandanna wrapped around the lower part of his face, a single-pistol holster, and he had a scar running down from his right eye." She lifted her finger and drew a line down the right side of her face.

"Jim Thurman has a scar like that, and he generally wears checkered shirts like she described." Brian walked over next to Connor. "The Thurmans came upon hard times last winter. I extended him as much credit as I could, but I finally had to say no more."

Connor straightened. "That gives him motivation. I'll gather a couple of men and ride out to his place."

"I heard his wife's been sick. Try not to go barging in and frighten her. They have a youngster, you know."

"If I can avoid that, I will."

Connor started to walk away, but he turned back to Daisy. "Thank you for your excellent description of the man. I wouldn't know who he was if not for your keen observation."

Daisy smiled then ducked her head.

Connor strode out of the store feeling a bit bewildered. How had a petite woman who had faced down a gunman at point-blank range had the sense to get a detailed description of the man? Most women would have fainted or screamed their heads off like Mrs. Sawyer. He'd have to put an end to her knife throwing, but he had to admit she had gumption. Did her sister have the same talent and boldness?

Keeley walked around the tidy house. What a delight to have a place just for her and Katie—and such a nice cottage too. In New York her family shared one small room in a noisy tenement apartment. Once they moved to Chicago, she and her sister had shared a bedroom, even though her aunt's two-story gray-stone had five of them. Aunt Colleen's house was bigger than any place they'd lived, but it was dark and stuffy—scary for two girls who'd lost both parents. The draperies were never opened more than a foot, with the exception of the ones on the parlor window, which were fully open during the day. The house had always been cold, except for in the heat of the summer.

Walking through the parlor in Connor's house, Keeley enjoyed the light streaming in the windows and how the gentle breeze lifted and dropped the white curtains. No dark, heavy draperies were needed to keep the cold out in Texas. She walked to the front door, opened it, and stared out at the empty street. Now that she'd cleaned everything, prepared some Irish soda bread and baked it, as well as several dozen sugar cookies, she was bored. A stroll to Brian's store to see how Katie was faring was exactly what she needed.

After getting her handbag from her room, she moseyed over to Main Street and down to the mercantile. Before she arrived, she knew something had happened, based on the crowd out front. She pushed her way through, entered the store, and looked at her sister. "What's wrong?"

Katie smiled. "I'm fine. A man tried to rob Brian's store."

Keeley's heart flip-flopped. "Tried?"

Brian walked up beside her. "He would have gotten away with the cash box if not for your sister. She stuck him with her knife, and he dropped his gun and ran out of the store empty-handed."

She didn't miss the awe in Brian's voice. Then she realized what he said. "Gun?"

Katie nodded. "I was looking at fabric in the catalogue, saw a shadow, and glanced up to find a man holding a gun in my face."

Keeley gasped. She turned to Connor. "You said this was a peaceful town."

"It is—mostly. We haven't had a robbery in three years. We know who did it, and I'm fixin' to ride out to his place to apprehend him."

Keeley hurried over to Katie and hugged her. She knew her sister could defend herself—they both could, their da had made sure of it—but a gun made the odds uneven. She couldn't imagine life without Katie. "I'm so glad you weren't hurt."

"Everyone's making too much of a to-do over it."

"You could have been killed." Connor crossed his arms. "In a situation like that, it's best to comply with the outlaw's wishes and let the law catch him."

Keeley hiked her chin, ready to do battle for her sister. "When you've lived in the places we've lived, you learn early that if you don't fight back, you become a victim yourself."

Connor grunted a response then glanced at Brian, who looked a bit bewildered. Did they wish they'd chosen other women to marry?

"Since things are all right here, I need to round up a few

men and go after Thurman." Connor strode toward the door, and the people standing outside backed up, clearing a path for him.

Keeley watched him leave, so tall and confident. She shouldn't allow herself to be attracted to him, since he was her sister's intended, but there was something about the man that stirred her interest. She blew out a breath and turned back to see Katie staring at her with one eyebrow cocked and a humorous look on her face.

Brian walked over to the front door. "You folks are welcome to come in and shop, but if you're not of a mind to, I'd appreciate you not blocking the door." He stood there until the crowd began to scatter then walked over to where she and Katie stood. "All right, ladies, time to shop. What else do you need that you didn't pick up yesterday?"

"We can't take handouts." Keeley stared straight at him. Brian wasn't quite as tall as Connor, but he was a fine-looking man—and quite generous. He had pretty blue eyes. She frowned, remembering that Katie had said often she wanted to marry a man who had blue eyes.

"That is why Daisy is working here today. And besides, she saved me a world of trouble by not losing the cash box. But in the future, I would prefer you give the money to the thief rather than risk getting hurt."

"I didn't get injured." Katie sidestepped so that she was next to Keeley—a unified force—to get her point across better. "And like I said, we know how to protect ourselves."

Brian closed his eyes, shook his head, and sighed. "This isn't the streets of Chicago, ladies, where you encounter pickpockets and the like. The outlaws in Texas can be very vile men, and you sure don't want to provoke one of them. He wouldn't think twice about throwing one of you over his shoulder and riding off with you as his prisoner. Jim Thurman is a desperate, hurting man who has come upon hard times. Most likely he was merely trying to scare you. I can't see him hurting a woman, but there are men who would. Most Texas men would die to protect a woman, but not all of them. Just be cautious."

Keeley frowned at him. Had he and Connor been less than honest when they wrote in their letters that they lived in a quiet town with little crime?

"Is there anything else we need at the house?" Katie asked.

"Why don't you walk around, get what you need, and stack it on the counter. I'll get a crate from the back." Brian strode behind the curtain, not waiting for them to respond.

Keeley looked at her sister and shrugged. "We have the basics, but it would be nice to have a few extras. There are so many things I'd like to cook that we weren't able to at Aunt Colleen's."

"Very well." Katie walked straight to the spices and picked up cans of cinnamon, caraway seed, and nutmeg. Her hand hovered over the tin of thyme, but she didn't take it. She didn't want to appear greedy, even though the herb was used in many Irish recipes. "I'd like these."

Keeley smiled and strolled over to the canned goods. She picked out eight cans of vegetables and two of canned apples and placed them on the counter next to the spices. Keeley added a dozen potatoes, two onions, four ears of fresh corn, and five carrots.

"Brian wants us to pick out new dresses. He says ours are far too warm for this climate, and I can see that he's right." Katie walked up to her and looked around, even though no one else was in the store. "I'm sweating so much, my unmentionables are damp."

"Katie!"

"Well, 'tis true." She walked around the counter and pulled out the dress she was taking home to try on. "I like this one. See if there's anything that catches your fancy."

"I don't know."

"We have to have proper clothing. We can work to pay for them."

Keeley pursed her lips. While the idea of being around so many wonderful things intrigued her, she didn't like the idea of having to deal with people all day. Working as a nanny for a family was enough socializing for her. Perhaps she should ask around and see if anyone in Cactus Creek needed help with their children. She studied the supply of dresses and settled on a yellow calico.

Brian carried in a big crate. "You're going to have to choose a whole lot more to fill this thing."

After thirty minutes of shopping, the crate was still only half filled. Katie tossed in the blue dress and the yellow calico to make it look more so. "That's enough."

Brian looked as if he would object, but then he nodded. "Would you like me to run it over to the house now?"

"Why not wait until the store is closed, if that is fine with you," Katie said.

Keeley knew her sister wasn't very fearful, but she couldn't help wondering if the robbery had something to do with her reluctance for Brian to leave.

"That's fine. Daisy, why don't you head on home. You've had a bit of a rough day."

"Are you sure?"

"Of course. I'm used to running the store alone."

"Very well. I believe I will." Katie started to leave then turned back and took the dresses out of the crate and held them against her chest. "I'll go ahead and take these with me now."

"All right. I'll bring several catalogues with me when I deliver your groceries, and you can thumb through them tonight. Perhaps you'll find some dresses or fabric you like."

Katie smiled. "That's very kind of you."

As soon as they were out of the store, Keeley turned to her sister. "Tell me exactly what happened."

"You already know. I looked up to see a robber, and when he told me to get the cash box, I pulled out my knife instead, and threw it at his gun hand. He dropped the gun, yanked out the knife and tossed it down, then ran out the door."

"You put my heart crossways hearing that tale of you and the thief." Keeley took hold of her sister's arm. "Weren't you terrified?"

"Not really. It all happened so fast. One bully is about the same as another."

"You know that isn't true. Some are much fiercer."

"Aye, but as I said, it happened very quickly and I just reacted. Now, let's get home and try on these dresses."

Once inside the house, both shed their dresses and tried on the new ones.

Keeley frowned as she held the bodice together. " 'Tis too small. It must be an older girl's size."

"That's unfortunate. The blue could work if I hemmed it up two inches and took in the sides a wee bit. I don't know how I'll get used to this thin fabric though."

Keeley grinned as she shed the yellow dress. " 'Tis a bit like running around in your chemise, aye?"

Katie laughed out loud. "Not quite that bad, but for sure 'tis different."

Once they'd donned their own dresses again, Keeley turned to her twin. "How did you like working with Brian?"

They flopped down on the settee together. "He's quite kind and patient," Katie said. "Oh, and he's so helpful and polite to his customers. And mannerly. I did love working in the store, in spite of the robbery. Shall we trade tomorrow?"

Keeley watched her sister talk about Brian with a gleam in her eyes. Was Katie developing a fancy for the wrong man? She hoped that was the case, since she had gawked at Connor and felt a stirring inside whenever she looked at him. "I suppose I should go, although you know I don't look forward to being around so many people."

"There weren't all that many—only a dozen or so, not counting those who showed up after the robbery. Brian says most people come in on Saturday."

"I suppose that's not so bad." Keeley took a strengthening breath then grinned. "Now, tell me everything you learned about Brian."

❦ Chapter 5 ❦

Connor hid in a copse of trees about fifty yards from the back of Jim Thurman's cabin. He could hear a baby wailing. A light in the barn indicated Jim was probably there. He turned to the three men he had deputized—Steve Adams, Dan Hawthorne, and Luth Bradford. "Steve, you and Dan guard the house, and Luth and I will check the barn. I want to capture Jim alive and unharmed, if possible. Any one of us can fall on hard times like he has. That can make good people do dumb things."

The men nodded. They knew how hardship could sneak up on almost anyone.

Luth followed Connor, keeping quiet for such a big man. Luth had two inches and probably fifty more pounds on him than Connor had, and Connor was six feet tall. He motioned for Luth to cover the back of the barn, and then he crept toward the front door. Light spilled out, even though it wasn't completely dark out yet. He heard muttering then a crash. It sounded like Jim had thrown something.

"Stupid. I'm just plain stupid," Jim hollered.

"This is Marshal McLoughlin," Connor called. "C'mon out, Jim."

"I can't go to jail, Marshal. M'boy needs me. He ain't got nobody else."

Connor thought it odd Jim didn't mention his wife too. "C'mon, Jim. I merely want to talk."

Things were quiet inside for several minutes. Connor peeked through a thin crack in the wood, but all he could see was the wall on the north side. Toward the back of the building he heard a ruckus. Then a shout—and gunfire.

He spun and raced along the side of the barn. At the corner, he stopped and peered around. The back door was open and Jim lay on the ground, illuminated by the lantern in the barn.

"Sorry, Connor." Luth hung his head. He was a big man with a big heart. "Jim charged out the back, gun drawn, and shot at me. I fired back."

"It's all right, Luth. You had to defend yourself."

Connor hurried over to Jim and knelt beside him. The man was gutshot, and there was little chance he'd survive. "Why didn't you listen to me? It didn't have to come to this, Jim."

"My boy. What'll happen to him?" A trickle of blood crept down the side of his mouth.

"Your wife will care for him. We'll help her."

Jim grimaced and shook his head. "She's gone. Died two days ago."

Pain lanced Connor's heart. "Why didn't you tell anyone?

We could have helped."

"Pride, I reckon. . .shame that I couldn't afford. . .doctor." He moaned and pressed his hand against his stomach. "Robbed store to get money. . .to buy milk for m'boy."

"I'll see to your boy. What's his name?"

"James. . .Thurman, Junior. Call him. . .Jamie. Turned a year last Tuesday."

"Don't worry about him, Jim. I'll make sure he's well cared for."

"Thank. . ." Jim's eyes turned glassy, and he exhaled his last breath.

Connor pursed his lips and shook his head as the rise and fall of Jim's chest stilled. What a waste. The man could have spent a few days in jail and gone home to raise his son, but now he was dead, and his son wouldn't likely remember him. With a loud sigh, he pushed to his feet. "Luth, can you saddle Jim's horse, if it isn't already. I'll come back and help get him up on the horse after I check on the baby."

"Sure thing."

Connor walked toward the front of the house. "Steve. Dan. Come on out. Jim's dead."

The two men hurried toward him. "What happened?" Steve asked. "We heard shots."

"Jim charged out the back, shooting, and Luth got him in the gut. Could one of you check the barn for animals then douse the light and close it up? The other of you help Luth get Jim tied onto his horse. I need to see to Jim's kid."

"What about Mary?" Dan cast a concerned glance at the small shack. "My Laura and her were friends in school. She's been meaning to pay Mary a visit, but our youngest is teething and has been cranky the past few weeks. Laura is plumb wore out."

Connor shook his head. "Jim said she died two days ago."

"Died? How?" Dan stared at him in disbelief.

"He didn't say how. I need to see to the baby."

"My wife will be sad to learn that Mary is gone." Dan walked toward the barn, head down.

Connor braced himself as he entered the small one-room cabin. He realized then how blessed he'd been to have had a decent home all his life. His rented clapboard house seemed like a mansion compared to this.

Frantic cries pulled his gaze to a crib in the corner where a baby sat. He walked over, and the red-faced kid sucked in several breaths and stared at him. Connor wasn't sure what to do. He reached for Jamie, but the baby flopped down, buried his face in his blanket, and started wailing again. He wished one of the twins was here. Hadn't one of them mentioned caring for young'uns? Taking a steadying breath, he reached into the crib and lifted up the boy.

As he put Jamie to his shoulder, the boy reared back. Connor nearly dropped him and tightened his grip. The kid was stronger than he'd expected. The only other time he could remember holding a baby was when Mrs. Harding had thrust her infant into his hands for him to make a to-do over. "*Shhh. . .* You're all right. Settle down." He patted Jamie's back, and the boy slowly relaxed.

What was he going to do with the kid? He looked around and found a half-filled bottle on the small table, picked it up, noting it was lukewarm. He sniffed it then shifted Jamie to where the baby was lying in his right arm, but Jamie fussed and tried to sit up. When he held up the bottle, the boy relaxed and reached for it.

Connor felt something moist and glanced down. His shirt was soaked. "Well, that's just great."

Jamie ignored his sarcasm and sucked at the bottle, staring at him with a scowl. Connor laid the boy in his crib and searched for his clothing. Diapers hung on a line along one wall. He walked over and touched them, glad to see they were dry. He yanked them down. Three dirty feeding bottles sat on the table. He rinsed them out in a bucket of water and dumped the water on the dirt floor, then wrapped each bottle in a clean diaper and stuffed them in a burlap bag he found on a shelf. Several dirty baby gowns and diapers sat in a corner on the floor. He found another bag, and holding his nose closed, he placed the soiled items in it.

A knock sounded, and Dan walked in. "We're done. You need help with the baby?"

Connor glanced down at his soiled shirt, and Dan cracked a smile. "It happens when you have a baby. What do you think will happen to him?"

Connor rubbed his jaw. "I don't suppose you and Laura could take him in."

Dan shook his head. "Laura would probably agree, but we've got four under the age of six. She has her hands full already."

"You think you could change him before we head back to town?"

"That I can do. Where's a clean diaper?"

Connor pulled one from the bag and handed it to him. "He probably needs a dry gown too." He walked around the tiny room, noting the lack of food. There were several empty cans of milk on the stove but none that were unopened. No wonder Jim had been so desperate that he robbed the store. He should have had a cow, but he must not have had the money to buy one.

He turned to find Dan bent over the crib. "Let's head back to town when you're done. I'll return tomorrow with a wagon and get the crib and search through all of the Thurmans' belongings to see if there's anything Jamie might want when he's older. I'll have to hold an auction for the farm, and then I can put that money in an account for the boy. Sad thing that happened here."

"You're not likely to get much for this place, although Jim's horse is a good one and should fetch a decent price." Dan picked up the boy.

"Do you know how much land they owned?"

"I can't recollect Laura mentioning it, but I can ask her if she knows."

"Don't bother. I can get the info at the land office. You might as well give me the kid since I've already been doused."

Dan handed Jamie to Connor. His mouth quirked as he picked up the two bags. "You'd best get used to being wet if you plan to hold him much."

Connor decided then and there that he would hold the kid as little as possible.

Brian jumped when the front door rattled and suddenly flew open. He set aside the catalogue he'd been looking through and stood. His eyes widened when Connor stumbled in holding a sleeping baby in one arm and two burlap bags in the other. He set down the bags and kicked the door shut with his boot.

"Where did you get that baby?"

Connor's eyes darkened. "He's Jim Thurman's boy."

"Why is he with you?"

Connor walked over to the settee and sat. He looked plumb worn out.

All kinds of thoughts raced through Brian's mind. "What happened?"

"Jim tried to get away, and Luth shot him in self-defense. He's dead. So is the boy's mother, it turns out. Jim robbed the store to get money to buy milk—or perhaps he was going to buy a cow with it. There wasn't hardly any food in their house."

Brian rubbed his jaw and paced the parlor. "I feel awful. If I'd known things were so bad, I'd have given him some milk. He never told me."

"It ain't your fault. You do more than your fair share for the folks in Cactus Creek. You can't support everyone that's havin' troubles."

Brian dropped onto an armchair across the room from the settee. "What are you going to do with him?"

Connor shook his head. "Don't know."

"We can't keep him. We both have to work most of the time."

"I know that." Connor quirked his lips to one side. "I just need time to decide what to do."

"Probably the best thing for tonight is to take him to the twins. Keeley mentioned in her letters that she cared for someone's children."

Connor glanced down at the baby. "I did think of that, but I hate to ask with them being so new to town."

"I doubt they'd mind. Most women love youngsters."

"I reckon it would be fine for one night. I can ask around town tomorrow and see if anyone is willing to take him in. I don't like the idea of him going to an orphanage." Connor looked at Brian. "How did it go at the store with Daisy today—besides the robbery, I mean?"

Brian couldn't help pulling a face. "Fine, I guess, except that she rearranged the spices and thread."

Connor's lips puckered, and then he grinned. "Why that's positively awful."

Narrowing his eyes, Brian scowled at his cousin. "You know I have my own system. It will only confuse me and make extra work if she keeps doing that."

"Did you ask her *why* she did it?" Connor shifted the baby to his other arm.

"I only discovered it after she went home. I went by their place to drop off a crate of food, but I didn't want to ask her, with the robbery just having happened such a short time ago."

Connor pushed to his feet, looking awkward with the child in his arms. Brian couldn't remember ever seeing him holding one. "Could you walk with me and carry those bags? They've got the kid's stuff in them."

"Of course." Brian rose. "Once we deliver—that kid have a name?"

"Jamie." Connor reached for the doorknob.

"Once we deliver Jamie to the women, I'll run over to the store and get some milk and other things he might need."

Connor walked out onto the porch. "How do you know what a baby needs?"

Brian grunted as he shut the door. "I sell that kind of stuff to mothers all the time, that's how."

"Makes sense. You sure the twins won't mind taking him in?"

Brian tossed the bags over his shoulder. "Only one way to find out."

Katie tapped the page in the Montgomery Ward catalogue. "What do you think of that floral pattern? This says that it comes in blue, pink, or lavender."

" 'Tis a bit hard to tell from the picture. I wish we could see the samples in a color picture."

"I suppose we'll just have to order something and hope we like it. These heavy dresses are unbearable in this heat." Katie tugged at her bodice. "I didn't realize it would be so warm in Texas."

"Perhaps we should douse the lamps and run around in our chemises." Keeley chuckled.

A sharp knock on the door made them both jump.

Katie looked at her sister. "Who do you suppose it could be? It's rather late for someone to come calling."

"It's Connor. I need your help."

Katie jumped up at the same time as Keeley and hurried to the door. She'd been worried about Connor ever since he left to go capture the store thief, and was glad to know he was all right, but she had to see him to fully believe. She yanked open the door. Connor stood there with a sleeping baby on his shoulder. She stepped back to allow him to enter.

"Where did you find that wee one?" Keeley hurried up to him.

"He's Jim Thurman's son. Both of his parents are dead."

"Did you shoot them?" Stunned, Katie lifted her hand to her mouth.

Connor gave her an odd look. "I don't shoot women, and one of my men killed Jim in self-defense. It's a real shame. I wanted to take him alive and get him some help." He shook his head. "Turns out Mrs. Thurman died two days ago, but Jim never told anyone."

Connor plopped down on the settee, and Katie joined him. He lowered the boy so that he lay in his arms.

Katie touched the baby's fluff of dark hair. "Such a wee thing. And so sad his parents are gone. What will happen to him?"

"Well. . .I'm hopin' you two can watch over him for tonight. Brian and I know next to nothin' about babies."

Katie glanced at Keeley and saw her nod. "Sure, we can keep the babe, but we have no supplies. What if he gets hungry?"

"Brian is puttin' together the things you'll need. He said he's helped plenty of moms with those kinds of items, so he knows what to gather up. If you could take him, I'll grab the sacks of his belongings that I got at his cabin off your porch."

Katie nodded, and he passed the child to her. Heart swelling with love for the little orphan, she placed a kiss on his forehead. What would become of the wee laddie?

"He has a name, does he not?" Keeley bent down and took a closer look at the boy.

"It's Jamie." Connor rose and strode to the door, as if eager to be rid of the baby.

Katie cuddled the little boy. "Jamie. . .sounds as if the lad might have a bit of Irish in him."

Keeley reached out and lightly grasped Jamie's hand. "Where will he sleep? We can't leave him on a bed by himself, or he might fall off onto the hard floor."

"The chest of drawers in my room is larger than the one in

yours. I think we could pull out the big bottom drawer, add some bedding, and put him in it."

"He might climb out if he awakens before you do." Keeley leaned back on the settee. "I wonder if he's walking yet."

"I didn't think of that. He's pretty small, so my guess would be that he isn't, but he is most certainly crawling." Katie glanced around the room. "We'd better move the sewing basket to a place he can't reach and make sure there's nothing else he can get to that could hurt him." She walked over to where the basket sat on the floor next to the settee, picked it up, and put it on a shelf in the bookcase.

"Making the place safe should be an easy task since we don't have much of anything." Keeley rose and walked around the coffee table. "I'll go prepare the drawer."

Katie pushed up from the couch and followed her. Once in the bedroom, she watched her sister.

Keeley placed the drawer along a windowless wall. She hurried out of the room and returned with a blanket and towel. She folded the blanket to make several layers of padding and placed it in the drawer. Then she turned with the towel in her hand. "I thought we could use this for a covering since the weather is so warm."

Katie nodded then walked over and lowered Jamie into the bed. She placed the towel over him and tiptoed from the room.

Back in the parlor, Keeley looked at her with a serious expression. "I've been thinking, perhaps you should work at the store again tomorrow instead of me, if you don't mind, given the robbery and all. I've taken care of more children than you, and I'd like to watch the laddie."

Katie grinned. "I'd be delighted to, if you're sure you don't want to."

"You're much better suited to interact with so many people. I get the shivers just thinking of it."

Loud footsteps sounded outside, and then there was a sharp knock.

Keeley raced to the door and pulled it open.

Connor scowled at her. "You shouldn't ever open a door at night unless you know who's there first."

Katie frowned at him for reprimanding her sister. "You said you were only going to the porch."

"Someone needed to ask me a question, so I was delayed." He sighed as he stepped inside carrying two burlap bags. He set them on the coffee table. "Brian's coming."

Katie walked over to the table, opened one bag, and peeked inside. She jerked her head back, making a face. "Ai! That one's manky."

Connor looked at Keeley. *"Manky?"*

She smiled. "It means soiled."

"My apologies." He grimaced. "I should have warned you about that. The other bag holds the kid's clothes, as well as several feeding bottles that I wrapped up in clean diapers."

Katie headed to the kitchen door, opened it, and tossed the smelly burlap sack onto the back porch. One of them would need to do the wash soon.

As she returned to the parlor, Connor glanced at her then Keeley. "I imagine the boy will be hungry before long. I fed him about half a bottle at the house, but he hasn't had anything since then."

"I'm sure he'll let us know when he's hungry." Keeley nodded. "We made him a bed from a drawer, and he's sleeping there."

More footsteps indicated Brian had arrived. He stopped at the open door, holding a small crate, and stared at them.

"Come on in." Katie motioned to him.

He entered and walked straight to the kitchen, set the crate on the table, then dusted off his hands. "That should hold you for now. There's canned milk, several boxes of crackers, flannel for making diapers, a couple of gowns—I hope the size is correct—and a book on child-rearing that has some recipes for making food for a baby. Oh, and I tossed in a ball and a book of children's stories."

Katie gazed at Brian with adoration. "You're so generous, Brian. It's a wonder that you stay in business."

He shrugged and stared at the floor as if embarrassed.

Katie wondered if Keeley had noticed her attraction to Brian, since he was Keeley's intended. But then she'd caught her sister staring at Connor whenever he was in the room. What were they going to do?

"Well, I reckon we should head out. Morning comes early." Connor moved toward the door, and Brian followed.

Just before he walked onto the porch, Brian paused and turned back to face them. "If you both want to stay home to tend the boy tomorrow, I'll understand."

Keeley smiled. "One of us will be there, for sure."

He nodded and closed the door.

Katie walked into the kitchen, thinking how handsome Brian was. Though he worked in a store, his skin was tanned. He must spend time outdoors too. Most of the city men she'd encountered in Chicago were pale from being inside so much, and none were as manly as Brian. She liked how he treated his customers with kindness and respect, even those who were testy.

"Just look at all of this. Why do you suppose Brian gave us more potatoes and green beans?"

"Probably because they'll be easy for the wee laddie to eat, once they're cooked, that is."

Keeley thumbed through the children's book. "Jamie will enjoy looking at these pictures, but we'll have to be careful that he doesn't tear the pages."

Katie took the cans of milk and placed them on a shelf. "There are only eight cans of milk. That doesn't seem like much for a growing boy."

"Perhaps that's all Brian brought because he doesn't think we'll have Jamie for long."

Katie sighed. "I sure hope we don't get attached to him and then someone else comes to claim him."

Keeley unwrapped one of the feeding bottles. "Aye, this is manky too. We'll have to wash them." She finished unwrapping the others and carried them to the kitchen. "There's only one clean one, but we can use it tonight and leave the soiled ones soaking overnight."

Katie emptied the rest of the crate and set it in a corner.

Keeley scraped soap flakes into the basin of clean water she'd prepared then put the bottles in it. "I think we should move Jamie to my room so I can get up with him at night. If I get overly tired, I can take a nap when he's sleeping, but you can't since you'll be working at the store."

"That's a good idea." Katie looked through the book on

child-rearing, glad to see the recipes Brian had mentioned in the back. "I can prepare breakfast and watch Jamie so you can sleep a bit extra if he keeps you up."

Together they moved the drawer with the sleeping boy to Keeley's room, and then they tiptoed out into the hall.

"I grabbed my nightgown on my way out. I think I'll change in your room so I don't wake Jamie." Keeley yawned. "I sure hope the laddie sleeps all night."

" 'Twould be nice." Katie unbuttoned her sister's dress then turned around so Keeley could do the same. Excitement raced through her that she would get to be with Brian much of the day tomorrow. Had he discovered the changes she'd made?

Keeley slipped into her gown and gathered her clothing. "I'll see you in the morning."

"Sleep well." Katie hung her dress on a peg on the wall.

Keeley took one step toward the door, and Jamie let out a wail.

Chapter 6

Connor sat at his desk, thumbing through the latest batch of wanted posters he'd received in the mail. He was having a hard time focusing because he kept wondering how the twins were faring with Jamie. He'd seen one of them sweeping the walkway in front of the store, but he wasn't sure if it was Katie or Keeley. He didn't know if the same gal went to the store yesterday and today and was merely using the name Daisy one day and Lark the next, or if the gals were actually trading off. Wouldn't it be more likely that Keeley would be working with Brian since she was his intended?

He tapped his fingers on his desk. Connor didn't like a mystery he couldn't solve, like which twin was which. He and Brian needed more time with them. If he could study them for a bit in the sunshine, he felt certain there would be some distinguishing feature to help him tell one from the other. Of course, that still didn't tell him who was who, but first things first. It was time he and Brian took the gals on a picnic. Connor rose just as a ruckus sounded outside.

The door opened, and three of the town's busybodies attempted to squeeze through the doorway all at once. He pursed his lips to keep from grinning at the comical site. Mrs. Abernathy was big enough that she needed to turn sideways to get in.

"Stop it. You hear me? Quit your pushing," Mrs. Sherwood hollered. "This was my idea, so I should go first."

"Quit yanking on my arm," Mrs. Fennimore fussed. "It's so dark in there, I cain't see a thang."

Bertha Abernathy, the most respectable of the trio, backed up while the other two wrestled their way in. Connor leaned his hip against his desk, bracing himself to be lambasted for whatever offense he or someone else had committed. Whatever it was, it sure had ruffled their feathers.

Once inside, the ladies preened, shifting shawls, adjusting hats, and smoothing out their dresses. Finally, Mrs. Sherwood cleared her throat and looked straight at him. "We heard about poor Mrs. Thurman and her sweet babe." She eyeballed him and lifted her chin. "We think it's a travesty that you've left that innocent orphan—bless his heart—in the care of those two foreign women who are playing games with your emotions. Why, you don't even know their real names." As if to emphasize her words, she frowned, made a *tsk* sound with her tongue, and gave a single shake of her head.

He knew them as Daisy and Lark. "I do know their names, not that it's any of your business, and both women are perfectly capable of caring for Jamie for now."

"What do you mean by 'for now'?" Mrs. Abernathy was still winded from her march to his office.

"If I find a suitable family willing to adopt the boy, I'll give him to them, as long as no relatives show up asking for him."

"And in the meantime, who knows what them Irish gals are exposin' him to. Are they even Christian?" Mrs. Fennimore adjusted her spectacles, as if trying to see him better.

Annoyed with her attack on the twins' heritage and faith, he stood. All three women had to look up. He liked that fact. "I'm the law around here, and I see nothing wrong with leaving the boy with the Quinns."

"Well, I never." Mrs. Sherwood turned toward the door. "Let's go, ladies. He's not willing to listen to reason. We'll just have to show our disagreement with his choice at the ballot box, come next election."

Once the old hens had left, he shook his head. Every time he did something they didn't like they threatened not to vote for him. He might as well walk over to his rented house and see how Jamie was faring—not that he had any doubts, but it was his job to make certain the boy was all right. The twins were strangers to the child, after all. Everybody was. Poor little guy.

As he reached his rented house, he heard Jamie crying. Connor knocked on the door and waited a long minute before it opened. Whichever twin she was looked at him with a frazzled expression. "Oh Connor. I don't know what to do. He won't stop crying."

"Let me see him." She willingly handed over the baby, whose wails only increased. "When did you feed him last?"

"Several hours ago."

"Have you tried giving him a cracker or cookie?"

She shook her head. "I made some oatmeal, but he wouldn't eat it."

"Let's try a cookie. Perhaps his teeth are coming in and are hurting. I've seen plenty of babies gnawing on things around town. It seems to help."

"All right. We have a box of sugar wafers Brian gave us." She brushed her hands down her apron and hurried to the kitchen. She fumbled to open the box then pulled out a cookie and handed it to Connor.

He held the wafer in front of the boy, and Jamie's cries lessened. Connor pretended to take a bite then held the cookie near Jamie's mouth. Jamie shook his head and reached for the twin. "Which gal are you?"

She took the baby. "Kee—" She looked up at him with wide brown eyes.

He knew she was frazzled to have let her guard down. A slow, victorious grin pulled at his lips.

Her eyes turned defiant. "But you don't know if I'm Lark or Daisy."

"That's true." A quick trot over to the store could solve that mystery.

She sighed. "I'm already tired of this ruse. It's so awkward when we have to introduce ourselves to the people we meet. They're suspicious of us because we aren't using our real names."

"That will pass. They're more curious than anything. Brian and I grew up in this town, and many of the town mamas have tried to foist their daughters on us. It grew old years ago. That's why we looked into getting mail-order brides."

Her expression softened. "I'm sorry. Aunt Colleen had started inviting men she knew to dinner in hopes of us marrying one of them."

"Why didn't you?" He held up the wafer and waved it in front of Jamie. Finally, the boy reached out and snagged it. He put it in his mouth, sucked on it, then inhaled a shuddering breath through his nose.

She shrugged. "We didn't want men who'd marry us merely for our looks. And we'd never been able to make any choices concerning our own lives. Becoming mail-order brides was our decision. And we both wanted to live someplace where it wasn't cold and snowy. I just never realized how warm it was down here."

Connor didn't have the heart to tell her the heat of summer was yet to come. "It will help when you have some cooler clothing to wear."

Her cheeks turned a dusty rose. She walked over and sat on the settee and placed Jamie beside her.

"He seems to like that cookie." He took a seat in a chair angled to face the settee. "So, did you work in the store yesterday?"

"No. Katie is better suited for that. People make me nervous— at least when there's a bunch of them asking questions."

He leaned forward, elbows on his knees. "Won't that be a problem if you marry Brian?"

She gazed at him with wide eyes then stared out the window.

What was she not saying? "You are going to marry him, aren't you?"

Suddenly she jumped up and fled the room. Connor rose, unsure what to do or why she was so upset. He reached for the baby, and this time the kid let him pick him up. Connor walked partway across the room to where Keeley had disappeared. "I'm taking the boy with me for a while. It will give you a break and a chance for him to be outside."

When she didn't respond, Connor grabbed another cookie and headed out the door. He walked straight to the store, anxious to see Katie since he knew who she was. As he entered the mercantile, he was disappointed to find Katie helping a woman with some fabric. He located Brian in the storeroom.

His cousin looked up from the box of lanterns he was unpacking. "Hey, what brings you here, and how'd you get the baby?"

"Keeley was having a hard time. Guess he's been fussy. Understandable, since everybody he sees is a stranger."

"Aw, poor little fellow. I unpacked something today that he'd like." Brian turned and rummaged through a pile of things on the counter then suddenly spun back around. "Keeley?"

Connor grinned. "Took you long enough."

Brian moved closer, holding a shiny metal baby rattle. He shook it, and Jamie grinned and dropped his soggy cookie. He reached for the toy. "How did you learn her name?"

"Purely by accident. She was so frazzled because Jamie was crying that when I asked her name, she just plain said it."

"So Daisy is Katie." Brian frowned.

"Why does that upset you?" Jamie held the rattle up near Connor's face, and he shook the toy, receiving a grin from the kid.

Brian sighed and looked away.

Connor could tell he was troubled. They never kept secrets from one another, so he knew his cousin would tell him sooner or later.

Brian walked over to the storeroom door and peeked into the mercantile. Then he spun around. "Let's go outside."

Connor shifted Jamie to his other arm and followed his

cousin. He glanced down and grimaced at the cookie mess that slimed his shirt.

Brian sat down on the edge of the freight deck, and Connor joined him.

His cousin shook his head. "Daisy—uh Katie—does such a good job in the store, except for rearranging things. I thought for certain she was Keeley. Why would Katie come both days instead of her sister? You think Keeley is afraid of me?"

"Keeley told me she was more of an introvert, and that Katie was the outgoing one. Your customers intimidate Keeley."

"Well, that's a problem. Especially since. . ." He looked at Connor, eyes heavy with concern. "I seem to find myself attracted to Katie."

Connor's eyes widened for a second before he schooled his expression. "That could be a problem, except, well, I might be attracted to Keeley."

"You are?" Brian straightened. "What are we going to do?"

Connor smiled as Jamie whacked him in the chest with the rattle. "I have a plan."

Keeley tiptoed from the bedroom where she'd put Jamie down for a nap. She blew out a sigh as she entered the parlor. Today had been much easier than yesterday. Discovering that Jamie would eat some simple foods besides taking the bottle had been the main thing that helped to satisfy the little boy. And perhaps he was getting used to her.

She dropped onto the settee and fished out the diaper she'd been hemming from the basket. The boy went through them almost faster than she could wash them. Having another dozen or two would reduce the number of days she had to do laundry. She finished hemming the diaper and reached for the scissors. A knock sounded at the door.

Her heart leaped at the thought of seeing Connor again. She hurried to the door and opened it, peeking out with a smile on her face. An older woman she hadn't met stood at the door with a small basket on one arm. "Can I help you?"

The woman beamed a smile. "I'm Mrs. Evelyn Rice, wife of Pastor Rice. He leads the only church in Cactus Creek. I want to welcome you and your sister to town."

"How nice of you. I'm Keeley Quinn. Would you care to come in?" She stepped back and opened the door all the way.

"Thank you. I'd love to visit for a bit, but I'm sure you have your hands full caring for the Thurman boy."

"Please, have a seat. How did you know about Jamie?"

Mrs. Rice smiled again. "It's a small town, dear. There are few secrets. Although, I will say Connor and Brian did a good job keeping things quiet about you two almost until you got here. But word has a way of getting out. Two mail-order brides arriving at the same time was the talk of the town once it had. We've never had even one mail-order bride come to our small community, and we actually got two of you."

Keeley forced a smile. She didn't like knowing everyone was talking about them. Life in a big city like Chicago was so different. "Would you care for a cup of tea?"

"No, thank you, but I would like a glass of water, if it isn't too much trouble." She pushed the basket across the table. "I made you girls a batch of apple muffins."

"How kind of you!" Keeley took the basket to the kitchen, removed the muffins, then returned with the empty basket and a glass of water. She handed the glass to Mrs. Rice and set the basket on the coffee table. "In Chicago, where Katie and I are from, there were muffin men who'd travel the streets at teatime, ringing a bell and selling muffins."

"I've never heard of such a thing. With all the women in Cactus Creek who cook so well, I fear the poor man wouldn't be in business long should he ever decide to come here." Mrs. Rice chuckled.

"I think you're right." She liked the woman, whom she guessed was in her fifties, judging by her graying-brown hair. Her snowy-white shirtwaist had pretty lace down the front, but the navy skirt she wore was unadorned.

"Have you and your sister settled in?"

"Mostly. As I'm sure you know, we didn't marry Connor and Brian right off because we wanted some time to get to know them first."

"Some may disagree, but I think that is truly wise of you. I knew Thomas over a year before we wed. Marriage is quite difficult if the two people involved don't love one another, and it's mighty hard to fall in love if you've never even met face-to-face. Just beware, there are some ladies who think what you did was deceitful, but honestly, it's none of their concern. I only mention it so you can be aware in case a few women are not so hospitable."

"Oh." Keeley dropped onto a chair across from the settee. "I suppose we shouldn't be surprised. Connor and Brian weren't too happy at first either."

"I think they were mostly disappointed. I can assure you that both of them are decent, God-fearing men. Pastor Rice and I have known them since we first came here to pastor the church. They were barely in their teen years back then."

"I remember them saying they grew up in Cactus Creek. We were born in Ireland, but our parents came to America when we were only two. We lived in New York for several years, and then we moved to Chicago, where my aunt lives."

"Lots of people travel around. Thomas and I are originally from Michigan, but after we married, Thomas felt the call to preach. We've lived in Missouri, Louisiana, and now Texas."

"It must be hard picking up and moving so often."

"Not if you believe you're going to the place God wants you to be. Where is your sister today?"

"Katie is helping Brian at the store. He's been so generous to supply us with groceries and the things Jamie needed. We're working to pay him back, even though he insists it isn't necessary."

"Like I said, he's a kindhearted man." She took a sip of water. "I should go, but I want to invite you to come to church on Sunday."

Keeley smiled. "We will. We're looking forward to seeing how church here is different from the one we attended in Chicago."

"I'm sure there are many fine ministers in such a big town, but I do need to tell you that Thomas is a mild-mannered, soft-spoken man, so you won't hear him spewing fire and brimstone." She chuckled. "Before I go, there are a couple of things I want to tell you. On the first Sunday of the month, there's a potluck picnic after church. All the ladies cook a passel of food so that the single men and cowboys get plenty to eat. There will also be a big celebration on July Fourth. It's always a lot of fun. There are games, a talent show, lots of food, which the women bring, a hog roast, music, and then fireworks after dark."

Excitement flooded Keeley at the thought of spending the day with Connor, celebrating their country's independence. "It sounds delightful."

"It is, let me assure you. If you two weren't already promised to Connor and Brian, you'd probably have more invitations to attend than you could count. You might still get some."

Her heart thudded. She sure hoped that wasn't the case.

Mrs. Rice rose. "Thank you for such a nice visit. I look forward to getting to know you and Katie."

Keeley followed the kind woman to the door. "I do appreciate your stopping by, and thank you for the muffins."

"My pleasure. Oh, I almost forgot. There's a sewing circle that meets once a week on Thursday mornings at the church." She frowned. "I should have let you know sooner so you could have come today."

Keeley reached out and touched Mrs. Rice's arm. "'Tis fine. Since Jamie is still getting used to us, I wouldn't have come any-way. He has enough strangers in his life at the moment."

"You're right, poor boy. Connor asked me if I knew of a family who might want to adopt a child, but most of the mothers I know of have their hands full with their own youngsters."

Keeley couldn't help rejoicing inwardly. Perhaps she and Katie could keep Jamie for now, and then once she married, she hoped Connor—if she was fortunate enough to marry him—would agree to help her raise him. "Thank you again, and have a nice afternoon."

"You too." Mrs. Rice waved then walked down the stairs.

Keeley closed the door. It was kind of the woman to welcome her. She could only hope other women in town would be as nice. Her thoughts turned to Sunday. What could they wear? A small building filled with people would be stifling hot. The last thing she wanted was to faint the first day she attended the church service because she wore her cool-weather clothing. She thought of the dresses at the store. Katie had completed alterations to the blue calico, and she'd worn it today. As soon as Jamie awakened, she would walk to the store and take another look at the ready-made garments.

❧ Chapter 7 ❧

After Sunday's service Connor had thanked the pastor for his sermon, and then he and Brian ushered the twins to the covered surrey they'd rented and drove away from the crowd. Excitement like he rarely felt flooded Connor. Finally, they would get to spend the day alone with the twins.

He glanced to his right to see Keeley holding Jamie on her lap. The boy bounced and babbled. Connor wasn't sure if Jamie was happy to be outside or if he was enjoying the buggy ride. Either way, he was glad to see a smile on the little guy's face. Jamie seemed to be adjusting well to living with the twins after that first rough day. Connor still hadn't had any luck finding a couple to adopt the boy. No one wanted another mouth to feed.

Keeley looked at him and smiled. "I had a grand time at your Sunday service. 'Twas much different than what we've been to in the past. It felt lighter, if that makes a whit of sense."

"Aye, it does." Katie leaned forward on the back seat. 'Twas a fine, good time. People seemed happy, and Pastor Rice didn't frown or yell at us."

Connor had heard about churches where the minister preached hell and damnation messages, but he'd never attended one. Pastor Rice was a gentle man, and he got his point across without hollering.

"And could be that you feel lighter simply because you're wearing calico. Rather like wearing a chemise all day, is it not?" Katie snickered and sat back.

"Katie!" Keeley turned and scowled at her sister.

Connor looked over to see Keeley blushing. He knew well what Katie meant, as he was always glad to shed his Sunday-go-to-meetin' clothes for his normal denim pants and cotton shirt. He tugged at his string tie and loosened it a bit. The thing was too close to a noose for his liking.

Keeley shifted Jamie around so that he faced Connor. "There are so many wildflowers out here." She swiveled and pointed. "What is that big thing?"

"It's a prickly pear cactus. Down in southern Texas there are lots more than there are here."

"We need to keep Jamie away from them."

"That's true. I don't reckon he'll go far, since he isn't walking yet."

"Perhaps." Keeley kissed Jamie's head. "The wee laddie sure can crawl fast though." She pointed off toward the right. "Why are there so many trees over that way? That's one thing I miss about Chicago. There were some fierce big trees there."

"Those trees line Cactus Creek, which the town is named for.

Whenever you see a bunch of trees like that, you can almost bet there will be water nearby."

He guided the surrey off the road and headed for the shady area. After a few minutes, he reined the matching gray horses to a stop under a big oak tree. "Who's hungry besides me?"

"I sure am." Brian climbed out and lifted Katie down. "I could eat an elephant."

Katie giggled. "Sure now, there are none of those around here. We saw one at a zoo in Chicago when we were younger."

Connor took Jamie then helped Keeley descend. "Never seen one myself."

"They're bigger than the whole surrey." Keeley pulled the blanket from the trunk at the rear of the buggy. "My, what a lovely place."

Katie looked toward the creek. "I can hear the water."

"Connor owns this pretty piece of land," Brian said as he reached for the picnic basket.

Keeley hugged the blanket to her chest. "How nice. Why have you not built a house here?"

He shrugged. "For one, being the marshal, I have to live in town. That way if I'm needed, folks can get to me real quick."

"I suppose that makes sense." Katie helped her sister spread the blanket. "Do you plan to be marshal for a long time?"

"Not if the old busybodies have their way." Connor chuckled. "It all depends on if I win the next election."

"And if you don't?" Keeley stared at him.

"I'm not sure. I worked on a ranch before I became a deputy marshal. I've saved up some money, so I'll probably build a cabin and try my own hand at ranching."

Brian deposited the food basket on the blanket. The women both sat and started unpacking things.

"This looks delicious. We love fried chicken." Keeley set the chicken platter down then pulled a pie from the basket.

"You two certainly outdid yourselves." Katie handed Brian two plates.

Connor dropped down onto the corner across from Brian and winked at him. Brian set a plate next to Connor's leg. This day was going wonderfully. Connor stood Jamie up and held on to the boy's torso. Jamie bent his knees then stood again. The boy grinned and repeated the action.

"I bet he'll be walking before long." Keeley opened a jar of pickles Mrs. Davies had included and set it next to a tin can filled with flaky biscuits.

Katie set four apples on a plate along with a knife, and placed it on the far side of the basket where Jamie couldn't get to it.

"Oh look!" Keeley held up a small bowl. "Mrs. Davies sent Jamie some mashed potatoes, as well as cooked and smashed carrots. How thoughtful of her."

"I wonder if Jamie will like the carrots," Katie said. "We haven't given him any yet."

"Only one way to find out." Connor reached for the bowl.

Keeley pulled a tiny spoon from her handbag, wiped it off on a napkin, then handed it to him.

"Shall we pray?" Brian asked.

Everyone bowed their heads, except for Jamie, who reached for the spoon. Connor let him have it for the moment.

"Heavenly Father, we thank You for safely bringing the twins to town. We pray that we can quickly get to know one another and that You will bless our unions when that day comes. Thank You for this fine meal, and we ask that You bless the food and Mrs. Davies for preparing it for us. Amen."

Connor fed Jamie some potatoes while Brian and the women fixed their plates.

"Would you like me to prepare your food?" Keeley looked at Connor with those big, dark eyes. His heart kicked up several notches as he realized once again that this pretty woman might soon become his bride. All he could do was nod.

Keeley smiled. "How many pieces of chicken would you like?"

"Two, for starters."

She piled his plate with food then handed it to him.

While they ate, Connor told the twins about his childhood, how his parents died, and that he went to live with Brian's family.

In return, the twins talked about what little they remembered of life in New York and then Chicago. Neither of them remembered anything about Ireland or riding the ship across the ocean.

When he finished eating, Connor lifted Jamie into his arms and walked down to the creek to wash him off while the twins cleaned up the food items. "You liked those taters, didn't you? I wasn't sure you were going to eat the carrots, after that face you made." He blew on Jamie's stomach, making the boy giggle.

At the creek bed, he bent down and dipped Jamie's hands in the water and washed them. Jamie splashed and laughed. Connor raised him up a bit, and Jamie tried to stick his toes in the water.

"You like that, huh? I'll have to bring you back sometime and let you play, but today I have something really important to do."

"And what is that?"

Connor rose quickly with Jamie in his arms and turned to see

Keeley—he sure was glad the sisters has worn different-colored dresses—staring at him. He lifted Jamie in the air, needing a distraction. "This little dude is all clean, but I think he needs a diaper change."

"It's about time for his bottle and a nap."

As if the word *bottle* triggered something within him, Jamie yawned. Or maybe it was the word *nap*. Connor smiled at him and tried to lay Jamie in his arm, but the little dude wouldn't let him.

Back at the blanket, they sat again, and Keeley changed Jamie and fed him his bottle. " 'Tis so peaceful and shady here."

"I wish we had more trees in town too, but there isn't enough water there. And folks cut down the ones that were there to build their houses and businesses."

Connor reclined on one side and watched Keeley mother the baby. He could see the three of them as a family. He knew what it was like to lose his parents, as did Keeley. Who better to raise an orphan boy than them? But how did she feel? And Katie?

He glanced toward the creek where Brian and Katie were walking. There had been no objection at all from the women when Brian had ushered Katie to the back seat of the buggy and Connor had helped Keeley up front. He cleared his throat. "There's something I've been wondering."

"And what is that?" She glanced up with a peaceful expression on her pretty face.

He sat up. "Well, it's just that you and me seem to have hit it off together, as they have." He motioned to the walking couple. "Neither you nor your sister have objected to being with the man you weren't betrothed to. Can I ask why?"

A very pleasing blush rose up on her cheeks, and she looked away. "We both felt as if we knew you equally, because we read your letters out loud. I can't even remember how we decided who would marry who. But I can tell you that when I stepped off that stage, my eyes went first to Brian out of curiosity since he was my intended, but after that it was you I couldn't quit staring at."

A warm sensation heated Connor's chest. She'd been drawn to him from the start. The thought delighted him and made him want to brag to Brian, except he wouldn't. He'd never hurt his cousin like that. "But what about Katie? Does she know how you feel?"

Keeley nodded. "She was drawn to Brian as I was to you. Katie has always wanted to marry a man with blue eyes—and then there's the store. She loves working there, but it scares me. I'm much happier staying home and carrying for our wee laddie."

Connor smiled at the word "our" to describe Jamie. "So you have no objection to me courting you?"

She lifted her head and stared right at him. "None whatsoever."

He grinned back at her. "Makes me happy to hear that." He leaned closer, and her eyes widened a bit. "I'm hoping for a very short courtship."

Keeley sobered for a moment, but then he saw her fighting a grin. "Aye, that would make me happy too. But there is one thing I'd like—no, two."

Connor straightened, suddenly on guard. "And what is that?"

"I'd like for you to teach me to ride a horse and to shoot, if you don't mind."

A wide grin chased away his momentary wariness. "Now that's my kind of gal. It would be my pleasure to instruct you."

Connor looked over to where Brian and Katie were sitting near the creek. He scooted closer to Keeley. "Would you care to seal our deal with a kiss?"

Sitting beside Brian in the lovely setting, Katie felt at peace for the first time in a very long while. She could see herself spending the rest of her life with him, but she couldn't help wondering if he pined for Keeley. It had seemed as if he'd chosen to sit by her at church and in the back of the surrey instead of with her sister, but doubts still plagued her. She wasn't sure how to go about broaching the subject.

"Connor owns over four hundred acres of land, although most of it is on the other side of the creek."

" 'Tis a shame he doesn't live here."

"I think he will one day. His father left it to him. The house they lived in burned down with his parents in it while Connor was at school."

"What a difficult thing to bear—losing everything and everyone all at once."

"It was hard on him. I think that's the main reason he doesn't live here." Brian picked up a stone and tossed it into the creek, making a splash. "There's something I need to talk to you about."

Katie turned to face him. "Aye? What is it?"

Brian twisted his lips and stared at the water, as if the words were hard to say. Was he going to tell her that he still wanted to be with Keeley? Her hope plummeted.

Finally, after what seemed like hours, he looked at her. "We work quite well together. I'm even getting used to you changing things around." His mouth cocked up in an embarrassed grin. "I'm betrothed to Keeley, but the truth is. . .I'm attracted to you. I realize I haven't spent much time with you other than at work, but I wondered if perhaps you might feel the same." He shrugged and exhaled a long, slow breath, as if saying that was the hardest thing he'd ever done.

Katie's heart soared. She glanced at her sister and noticed Keeley and Connor sitting rather close together. When she looked back, Brian was frowning. She reached out and touched his arm. "Brian, I feel the same. I love working at the store with you. I know I was supposed to marry Connor, but look at them. I'd say they're quite happy the way things turned out. And the truth is, I'm attracted to you too. I was so hoping you felt the same."

Brian looked past her, and his eyes widened. Katie twisted around in time to see Connor kiss her sister. She grinned. "See, no objection on their part."

Brian grinned, his blue eyes shining. "I can't tell you how happy that makes me, to know you're attracted to me and not Connor. But could you see yourself married to me?"

Katie's cheeks warmed. "Aye, Brian. I can."

He moved closer and leaned in to kiss her then paused. "Do you mind. . .if I kiss you, that is."

"If you don't, I'll be kissing you."

His eyes danced with delight then he caught her mouth in a sweet, gentle kiss—her first. She breathed in his fresh, manly scent and returned his kiss, dreaming of the day they would be man and wife.

When he pulled back, he stared at her. "I thought Connor just might call off the weddings the day you arrived and said that you wanted to get to know us before we married." He reached up and tucked a lock of her hair behind her ear. "I'm so glad you two held your ground and wanted to wait. Just think, Connor and I might have married the wrong women. You seem far better suited to me, and Keeley is good for Connor. I think waiting was God's idea planted in your minds."

"I do believe you're right. I never thought about it that way. How dreadful it would be to have married the wrong man. I'm sure we would have gotten along, but it wouldn't be the same as marrying the man God had for me—and that is you."

He reached for her hand. "You don't have to worry anymore. So. . .uh. . .when do you suppose we could get married? Soon, I hope."

"I think we need to talk to the others and decide together."

"Agreed. Shall we?"

Katie nodded. Brian rose then helped her up. He looped her arm through his, and they strolled back toward her sister and Connor, joy flooding her heart. When she'd first considered waiting to marry, she thought she merely had cold feet, but now she could see it was God's hand at work. She glanced heavenward and said a silent prayer of thanksgiving.

❧ Chapter 8 ❧

Brian locked the back door of the stockroom with a frustrated sigh then returned to the store. It seemed as if everyone had been cranky and demanding today. Must be the full moon they'd had last night. He rubbed the bridge of his nose. Mr. Morrison had arrived just before closing time and had taken over an hour to decide on the suit he wanted to buy. While he was in back helping Mr. Morrison try on several, Katie had waited on their final two customers, and then she'd gone home without even saying good-bye. He'd hoped to walk her home and spend time with her, but this whole day had been one problem after another. He slammed his ledger book shut and set it on top of the food cans he was taking home.

A loud knock drew his gaze to the door. He crossed the room and opened it. He groaned when he saw who it was. Normally he could deal with Mrs. Sawyer just fine, but there were times her theatrics got on his nerves, and right now he wasn't in the mood to deal with her whining. "Mrs. Sawyer, what can I do for you?"

"I'm so sorry to bother you when you've already closed, but I saw a rose-colored dress in your store earlier today."

He nodded. "I know the one you mean. We just got it in yesterday."

She wrung her hands. "Well, the thing is. . .I was making Anna a dress for her birthday—it's tomorrow—but I can see now that I'm not going to finish it in time. And, well, I simply must have a gift for her. I would have come sooner, but then supper would have been late, and Mr. Sawyer doesn't like that." She glanced inside the store then back at him. "I wonder if I could bother you to sell me the dress now so I won't fret about it all night? I'm just sure I wouldn't get a wink of sleep worrying that someone would buy it before I could get over here in the morning."

With a grunt, Brian pulled the door all the way open. He hoped she was quick about it. He needed to get home to cook supper himself because it would be highly unlikely that Connor had. His stomach growled, reminding him supper was well overdue. While Mrs. Sawyer stepped inside, Brian walked to the counter and leaned against it.

"I don't know how to thank you." She made a beeline for the ready-made section. After a minute of searching through the gowns, she spun around, a frown on her face. "It's not here. You didn't sell it, did you?" She lifted a hand to her forehead. "Oh, what am I going to do? None of these others will fit my daughter."

"I'm sure I didn't sell it, but it's possible Katie may have. Let me check the ledger. We always write down clothing purchases so I know when to reorder." He walked to the counter and flipped open the ledger to the day's entries. The only clothing sales listed were the three-piece suit Mr. Morrison had bought and a gray skirt and shirtwaist that Mrs. Sherwood purchased. Katie had written in the skirt sale. He liked seeing her handwriting next to his. He checked yesterday's sales too. "I don't see it listed here."

Mrs. Sawyer held her hands in front of her as if she were praying. "I have to give my daughter a birthday gift. She'll be so disappointed if I don't."

"I have a nice assortment of bracelets and necklaces. Would you care to look at those?"

She frowned again. "Oh, I don't know. That's a bit of a luxury, but I suppose I don't have a choice."

Brian's stomach grumbled again. "Why don't you come and have a look. I'll check the storeroom and make sure Katie didn't put the dress back there for some reason." He strode into the stockroom again, but a quick search revealed the dress wasn't there. Had Katie taken it? Surely she wouldn't have done that without asking him.

"I guess I'll take this gold locket with the flowers on it. Perhaps Mr. Sawyer and I could have our pictures taken, and Anna could put them in it at a later date. It would be a nice keepsake for when we're gone."

"It's a lovely piece of jewelry. I'm sure your daughter will be quite delighted when she opens it."

Mrs. Sawyer straightened, a smile brightening her expression. "I do believe you're right. A dress is something you need, but this is quite special. I should have thought of it sooner."

Brian removed the locket from the jewelry case and put it in a small velvet-lined box. He listed the sale in his ledger and took the money from Mrs. Sawyer.

She beamed as she walked toward the door. "Thank you so much for letting me in, Mr. Barnett. I can't wait to see Anna's face."

Brian nodded, closed the door and locked it, then crossed the room to the clothing section. He riffled through the fourteen dresses hanging on the rod then checked the floor beneath them. What could have happened to the dress?

He still couldn't believe Katie would help herself to it without asking him. Especially since he'd give her anything she asked for. Hadn't he proven that? He didn't want to be upset with her, but he needed to find out the truth, and there was only one way to do that.

He locked up, leaving his box of food behind, and walked down Main Street. He was a block away from the turn to the twins' house when a woman darted out from the alley, nearly colliding with him. He stared at her. Blinked. She was wearing the missing dress. "Excuse me, but where did you get that dress?"

Her hazel eyes widened and a panicked expression engulfed her face. "I. . .um. . .it was a. . .gift."

"A gift? From whom?"

"That Katie lady who works in yer store."

Brian felt his ire rising.

The woman rushed away, looking half frightened to death.

Irritation stiffened Brian's spine. Why in the world would Katie give that woman a dress? He'd seen her around town begging—had even given her a couple of coins more than once—but he didn't know her name. Katie shouldn't be giving away his property. He thought she would have known that. It was one thing for him to give things to his future wife and her sister, but not to a near stranger. As much as he liked helping others, he had to draw a line, or he would be out of business by the end of the month. The weight of the troubling day pressed down on him. The more he thought about the dress, the angrier he got. He'd lost a good sale, and with all he'd given to the twins, he needed it.

He hurried down the last block and pounded on their front door.

It opened, and there stood Katie, wearing the same blue dress she'd had on earlier. She smiled. "Good evening, Brian. Did you need something?"

He glanced inside and saw Keeley holding Jamie on her hip while she set the table. She looked up and cast him a curious glance. "Could you step out here for a minute?"

"But—"

He reached for her and tugged her forward. She shut the door most of the way. Her forehead puckered as she looked up at him. "What's wrong?"

He drew in a breath and let it out, albeit a bit too loud. "Did you or did you not give a woman that rose-colored dress I got in yesterday?"

"Brian—"

He held up a hand. "I don't want excuses."

"But—"

He bent down. "Please be honest. Tell me."

She hiked her chin. "I did not."

Brian narrowed his gaze. "I just saw a woman wearing the missing dress, and she said you gave it to her."

"I didn't, but—"

Brian's anger soared. "I'd have given it to you, if you'd only asked. But as you well know, I'm not in the business of giving things to every John and Nancy who walks into the store. I'd go broke. I thought you were smart enough to realize that. Don't bother coming to the store tomorrow."

He turned and stormed off. How could he marry a woman who wasn't honest with him?

Keeley walked back into the house, worrying for her sister's sake.

"What was that about?" Katie met her in the middle of the parlor, holding Jamie on her hip. "Why was Brian upset?"

"He was so angry that he wouldn't give me a chance to tell him I wasn't you. He thinks you gave a dress to some lady."

Katie's face paled. "He must have confused us since we're both wearing blue dresses."

Keeley grabbed her sister's arm. "Did you actually do that?"

"No, not exactly."

Jamie reached out, and Keeley took him. "Well, what did you do?"

"Miss Pettigrew, a woman clothed in a shabby, patched dress came in and looked at some fabric, and then she spent a long time admiring the ready-made dresses. She was especially enamored with the rose one. I offered to help her, but she said she was merely looking. I felt bad for her because her dress was patched and the fabric was horribly thin."

Jamie reached for Keeley's hair comb, but she gently pulled down his hand and kissed it. "You know what it feels like to wear rags."

"You know I do, and I think that's why I wanted so badly to help her. I could tell by her red, chafed hands that she takes in laundry."

"And?"

Katie shrugged, looking at her with a guilty grin. "She didn't have enough money to buy the dress, so I helped her pick out some less expensive fabric because she said she knows how to sew. She was going to use the rose dress as a pattern then return it. She paid for half of the fabric and thread and will pay for the rest by bringing in eggs her hens lay and her earnings from doing laundry. We can sell the eggs to cover her debt. It may take awhile, so I went ahead and wrote the sale down under our tab." She lifted her chin. "If it turns out I was wrong about her character—and I must have been, since she was wearing the rose dress after promising she wouldn't—then I'll work off the cost of the garment and fabric myself."

"I'm sure Brian will be understanding when you explain, but you do know that you can't do that all the time. You'll never get him paid back if you give things away."

"I know." She walked over to the window and peered out. "What am I going to do? I'm miserable that Brian thinks he can't trust me. I can't go over to his house. It isn't proper. What if he no longer wants to marry me?"

"I doubt 'twill come to that. Brian seems like a forgiving man, but I can run over to the marshal's office and talk to Connor. He should be able to get Brian to see reason."

Katie nodded. "A grand idea. You want me to keep Jamie?"

Keeley shook her head. "I'll take him with me. He likes getting outside and seeing Connor. I can't help wondering if he realizes that Connor is the one who saved him."

"Don't be long. I'll finish getting supper on the table."

Keeley started for the door.

"Wait!" Katie hurried toward her and handed her half a roll. "For Jamie, in case he gets hungry."

"Thank you. This is all my fault. Brian wouldn't have confused us if we hadn't both worn blue on the same day."

"I'm truly sorry you're the one who got yelled at."

"Don't be concerned about that." Keeley hugged her sister then walked toward Connor's office, glad the sun was still high in the sky. With this being Friday evening, there was far more traffic in the streets than normal, and the saloon was already noisy. Several cowboys looked her way. She was thankful she'd brought Jamie with her, because they might surmise she was married.

Though the walk was short, she was relieved to finally reach Connor's office. She opened the door and stepped in.

He looked up from his desk then shot to his feet, a wide grin on his handsome face.

Keeley's heart flip-flopped. In a few weeks she might be married to this big man.

Jamie let out a screech and waved his roll at Connor.

"What brings you here? Not that I'm not happy to see you." He bent down and tickled Jamie under his chin. Jamie giggled and hid his face against Keeley's bodice.

When Connor straightened and looked at her again, his happy expression fled. "What's wrong?"

Keeley relayed what had happened with Brian.

Connor shook his head. "That sure doesn't sound like my cousin."

"I'll admit I was surprised too. I tried several times to tell him

I wasn't Katie, but he wouldn't let me get the words out."

"I'm sorry. I imagine that was awkward."

She shrugged. "He said for Katie not to come to the store tomorrow. She's worried he won't want to marry her now."

Connor placed a hand on her shoulder. "I doubt that's the case."

Jamie leaned over, nearly flying out of Keeley's arms, and Connor grabbed him. He chuckled. "Haven't your mamas taught you that you aren't a bird?"

Jamie babbled a response. He reached up and touched Connor's chin, where his whiskers had started growing again even though he'd shaved early this morning. Connor returned his focus to Keeley. Though she smiled at Jamie, pain remained in her eyes.

"Everything will be all right. Trust me."

Her gaze flicked to his. "I do trust you. That's why I'm here."

He stared at her for a long moment then pulled her close, hugging her. He kissed the top of her head, wishing they were already married. Soon. He just needed to be patient a bit longer.

With a sigh, Keeley stepped back. "Supper is nearly ready. I should get home."

Connor brushed his hand down her hair. "Try not to worry, all right?"

She nodded. "I will pray that God helps Brian not to be angry at Katie. She was only trying to help someone in need."

"I know." He stared at her for a long moment then bent down and gave her a quick kiss. When he straightened, her eyes were wide and her cheeks red. He grinned. "How about I keep the little dude for a while? That way you can enjoy your supper without having to feed him."

She looked at Jamie. "I suppose he'll be fine since he has the roll, although you should prepare for your shirt to get grimy."

Connor grimaced then grinned. "Guess I'll have to get used to it. Although, I may need to buy a couple more shirts."

Keeley smiled and waved. Connor followed her to the door. "I'll bring Jamie home in about twenty minutes, but let me walk you back. You shouldn't be out on the streets by yourself with the cowboys in town."

"That would be nice." She looped her arm through his, taking a moment to relish the fact that he wanted to protect her. How long had it been since she felt completely safe? Had she ever?

Connor escorted her down the street. At the door of his rented house, he bent and kissed her. "See you in a little while."

"Don't be too long. I need to feed him, and his bedtime is in an hour."

He winked and strode away. Her heart flooded with affection for the big man. With a wistful sigh, she entered the house. She sure hoped the weddings wouldn't be postponed because Brian was upset with Katie.

With Keeley safe at home, Connor tickled Jamie, eliciting a laugh from the boy. "What are we going to do about my cousin?"

He returned to his office, wondering if Brian had made supper or if he was stewing and had forgotten about it. His stomach grumbled. He needed to grab a quick meal and get back in case there was trouble tonight. He plucked his hat off his desk and set it on Jamie's head. The boy's face disappeared. Jamie squealed and kicked his feet.

When Connor removed the hat, Jamie reached up with grimy

hands, but Connor placed the slouch hat back on his own head, safely out of reach. "You're not touching my hat with those dirty hands, buster."

Quick footsteps sounded outside then the door flew open. Steve Adams rushed in. "There's a big fight at the Dirty Dog Saloon."

"All right. Let's go."

"You cain't take that baby in there. Fists are flying."

"Oh, you're right." He held out Jamie. "Here, you watch him."

"Huh-uh. I'm not a baby-holdin' man." He backed out onto the porch, turned, and ran.

Connor stared at the baby. He needed to get to the saloon fast. He spun around and strode to the cell he'd cleaned earlier. This would have to do. There was nothing in here that could hurt the boy. Connor set Jamie on the floor, and then he hurried back to his desk, grabbed his coffee cup, and pulled a spoon from his middle drawer. Back in the cell, he tapped the spoon against the cup. Jamie's eyes lit up and he reached for them. Connor put them on the floor, closed the door, then broke out into a run for the saloon as soon as he was outside. He sure hoped the kid would be all right.

❧ Chapter 9 ☙

Forty-five minutes had passed, supper was over and cleaned up, and Connor still hadn't returned Jamie. Keeley walked to the front door and looked out. No sign of the marshal.

Katie joined her. "I know the sun has set, but 'tisn't totally dark yet. Why don't we run over to Connor's office and see if he got tied up with something?"

"Aye, let's go. Jamie is sure to be hungry and getting tired."

Both women hurried down the street then turned onto Main Street. Several dozen saddled horses were hitched all along the street. There was little doubt where their owners were. Keeley was glad the saloon noise was barely noticeable at their house. Though it was at the far end of the street, the saloon sounded even louder than it had earlier. She opened the door to the marshal's office, stepped inside, and noticed Connor wasn't at his desk. She turned to face her sister. "Now what?"

Katie shrugged. "He left the lamp on, so he must be coming back. We could walk down Main Street a bit, but I don't want to get too close to the saloon."

"All right. I wonder if Connor went to see Brian and got tied up talking to him?"

A screech sounded from one of the cells in the back, and Keeley jumped the same time her sister did. They looked at one another. "Do you suppose Connor has a drunken man back there?"

"It sounded more like a bird." A wail echoed through the office. Keeley eyes widened as she glanced at her sister, who had the same flummoxed expression. "That sounds like Jamie!" She rushed to the door separating the two rooms, and there was the wee laddie, standing up in the cell, holding on to the bars, tears running down his cheeks. When he saw her he started sobbing.

She yanked open the door, relieved to find it unlocked, and lifted the baby into her arms, cuddling him. Scowling, she turned to her sister. "Connor must be an eejit. How could he leave Jamie alone? Why didn't he return the boy to us if he had to go somewhere?"

Katie rubbed her hand over Jamie's head. "Poor little laddie. Let's take him home, get him fed and into bed."

"Should I leave Connor a note?"

Katie shook her head. "'Twould serve him right to be worried about the boy after what he did."

Jamie had already stopped his crying and had laid his head on Keeley's shoulder. They hurried home, and by the time they got there, Jamie was asleep. "I'll change him and put him to bed."

"I'll prepare his bottle." Katie headed to the kitchen. "Perhaps he'll wake enough to drink it."

"Thank you." Keeley quickly changed Jamie and sat in the chair, patting his back. Her anger with Connor grew each moment. How could he have put an innocent baby in jail and left him alone? What kind of man did such a thing? How could she ever trust him to watch Jamie again?

The baby squirmed, as if he could sense her annoyance with Connor. She closed her eyes and took several steadying breaths, willing herself to relax. There would be time to deal with Connor later, but right now she needed to care for the little boy who'd so quickly stolen her heart.

Half an hour later Jamie had drunk a good bit of his bottle and was sound asleep. Keeley laid him in his bed and covered him with a lightweight blanket, and then she walked back to the kitchen. "I'll probably have to get up with him more tonight since he didn't have his supper."

"I can do it if you like. I'm not welcome at the store, it seems."

Keeley set the half-empty bottle on the coffee table and sat next to her sister. She tucked one leg under her and turned to face Katie. "What are we going to do?"

Katie shook her head. "I think Brian will come around. Once he gets over being angry, I'll go talk to him. Perhaps I'll wait a couple of days. At least that will give me time to finish this dress while he simmers down."

Keeley pulled her handkerchief from her sleeve and wadded it in her hand. "Do you think we've made a mistake coming here?"

Katie looked up from her sewing with wide eyes. "Do you?"

"I don't know. Everything seemed to be going so well, and then Brian got mad and Connor abandoned Jamie. I thought he would make a wonderful father from the way he's so attentive to

Jamie, but leaving a baby alone is inexcusable, especially since the laddie's father did the same thing to him. How will Jamie ever learn to trust people?"

"He trusts us." Katie laid her hand over Keeley's.

"But unless one of us marries, we probably won't be able to keep him. Connor told me how some ladies had come by his office, complaining about him leaving Jamie with us."

"You never told me that."

"I didn't want to worry you."

"My skin is thicker than you think."

Keeley smiled, even though her heart wasn't in it. "Did we do the right thing leaving Chicago?"

Surprise etched her sister's face. "Do you want to go back? You remember how hard life was with Aunt Colleen and how she was so often bringing men home who leered at us."

"There's nothing wrong with Chicago itself. There are many grand places to visit and beautiful sights to see, but I don't want to go back there. I never liked the cold winters, for one. Perhaps if Aunt Colleen had been kinder. I've been surprised by how much I enjoy living in Texas, even though 'tis hot here."

Hard footsteps hit the porch, and a pounding on the door brought both women to their feet. Katie was the closest and beat Keeley to the door. "Who's there?"

"It's Connor. Open up."

Keeley nibbled her lip. He sounded frantic. Even though she knew she should be forgiving, she wasn't quite ready to let him off the hook. Katie gave her a bracing look then opened the door.

Connor strode in. "Is Jamie here?"

Keeley hiked her chin. "I left him with you. Don't you have him?"

Connor's worried gaze searched the room. Then he walked over to the coffee table and picked up the half-empty bottle. "You've got him, don't you?"

"No thanks to you." She marched up to him and thumped him in the chest. "How could you lock a baby up in a cell? What if something had happened to him? The poor laddie was frightened and wailing when we found him. Jamie's own father left him alone. How could you do the same? What kind of man are you?"

His eyes widened, and then he scowled. "I'm a good man, and you well know it. I had an emergency to deal with, and I didn't have time to run Jamie home. I couldn't very well take him into a fistfight at the saloon. The cell was clean, and there was nothing to harm the boy. I thought he'd be fine until I returned. I had planned to send word to you, but the fight was worse than I expected, and it took awhile to get things settled." His chest rose and fell from his lengthy defense.

Keeley crossed her arms. "It would have taken only a minute to run Jamie home."

Connor's shoulders drooped. "Was he really crying?"

"Yes. And he was standing, holding on to the bars. What if he'd let go and had fallen backward and hit his head on the hard floor or the bed frame?"

Connor dropped onto the closest chair, his face pale.

Remorse flooded Keeley for being so hard on him, but something like that could never happen again. "Babies should never be left alone."

He set his hat on the table then forked his hands through his hair. Keeley felt sorry for him. She looked around and noticed her sister had left the room. She sat on the edge of the settee closest to him.

"I'm sorry, Keeley. It all happened so fast. . . . I really thought Jamie would be safe for a short while."

"I know, but you can never leave him alone again. I don't like the thought of him at the saloon, but I'm sure one of the girls who work there would have been happy to hold him."

"I've learned my lesson, and you can be sure it won't happen again." He looked up with pleading brown eyes that begged her to believe him.

"All right."

He reached out and took hold of her hands. "Was Jamie really upset?"

"He was crying, as I said, but I don't think he had been for long. His face hadn't yet turned splotchy."

"Good. I gave him a cup and spoon to play with, hoping that would keep him busy. Could I see him?"

"He's asleep in my room. I don't think that would be proper."

"Please? It's not that I don't trust you, because I do, but I need to see him for my own peace of mind. Otherwise, I fear I'll worry all night."

"Fine then, come on." She rose, and he followed. Keeley was glad to see Katie's bedroom door was closed. She entered her room and turned up the lamp.

Connor bent down and watched Jamie for a moment, then pulled up the blanket and gently patted the baby's back. As soon as he rose, Keeley backed into the hall and hurried to the parlor with him following.

He put on his hat and walked to the door. "I'm really sorry, Keeley. Please don't be angry with me."

"I forgive you."

A relieved smile brightened his countenance. "Thank you." He brushed his hand across her hair then slowly down the left side of her face, sending her heartbeat flying. He bent down and kissed her long and slow. Then he pulled her into his arms and deepened the kiss. When he stepped back, they were both breathing hard.

"Oh my."

He grinned. " 'Oh my' is right. Just wait until we're married." He frowned suddenly. "We're still gettin' wed, aren't we?"

Keeley nodded, unable to hold back her happy expression. She had hated being upset with Connor, and while she still disapproved of what he'd done, she understood why. If they could always work through their disagreements so quickly, they'd have a fine marriage.

He pulled down his hat and blew out a loud breath. "Now I've got to go talk to Brian."

He bent down and gave her another quick kiss. "Don't forget to lock the door."

She shut the door and secured it, once again warmed by his protectiveness. As she prepared for bed, she prayed that God would settle the situation between Brian and Katie as quickly as He had her and Connor.

Katie held up the lavender calico dress she'd just finished hemming. It would be nice to have another cool one to wear. She had already learned the value of donning the lighter-weight fabric, and a benefit she hadn't expected was how much easier it was to move around and do things without all that bulky clothing. She still needed to make some cotton petticoats, but that would have to wait until she made the navy skirt to go with the shirtwaist she'd gotten at the store.

She frowned at her reflection in the mirror. Two days had passed, and Brian hadn't yet come to talk to her. Was he still angry? Or was he merely busy? Of course, there was no reason she was aware of that he couldn't come by in the evening after work.

She hung the dress on a peg in her room. It still needed to be pressed, but she'd wait until tomorrow morning when the weather would be cooler. With a loud sigh, she left her room and walked into the empty parlor. Keeley had taken Jamie to have lunch with Connor. She looked around for something to do, but everything was tidy. Feeling bereft, she picked up her Bible, went out to the porch, and sat in a rocking chair.

Katie gazed up at the cloudless sky. Connor had told them about the terrible thunderstorms they often had in Texas. He'd mentioned the booming thunder that rivaled the sound of a stampede and warned them to be sure to stay indoors if there was lightning. But so far, not a drop of rain had fallen since they arrived. If she missed anything about her past life, it was the pretty flowers. A few brave wildflowers dared to stick up their heads along the sides of the streets, but sooner or later they'd get stomped or eaten by a passing horse.

Bemoaning the demise of the white daisies outside their house, she opened her Bible and continued reading in John 14. After several minutes, she read verse twenty-seven out loud. " 'Peace I leave with you, my peace I give unto you: not as the world giveth, give I unto you. Let not your heart be troubled, neither let it be afraid.' "

She gazed heavenward, mulling over the verse. On Sunday afternoon, when she and Brian had sat beside the water, she'd felt so peaceful. She didn't want him to be angry with her. Though she wanted him to come to her, she realized now that she had unwittingly wronged him. And then he thought she had lied to him. No wonder he was upset.

Katie sat there praying and asking God to repair things between her and Brian, and she prayed for peace—for both of them. Several minutes passed as she prayed, and then finally she felt the peace she'd longed for. Rising, she returned the Bible to the coffee table and hurried to her room to check her hair. She rearranged several pins then pinched her cheeks.

In the kitchen she took a plate off the shelf, placed a half dozen cookies on it, then covered it with a clean towel. With a steadying breath, she stepped outside and started toward the store.

As she rounded the corner of Main Street, she stopped suddenly. Brian strode toward her, holding a lovely bouquet of flowers. Where had he gotten them?

He paused in front of her, gazing at her with uncertainty. "Were you headed somewhere?"

"To see you." She held out the plate. "I brought you a treat."

A gentle smile lifted one side of his mouth, and then he looked around. "I'd prefer not to say what I need to say right here on Main Street." He motioned to the lane behind her. "Shall we?"

Katie nodded then followed him back to her porch. He indicated for her to have a seat, but she shook her head. "If you don't mind, I'd like to put those lovely flowers in some water before they perish."

"Of course." He held them out to her, and she took them.

"Now, if you'll take the plate and have a seat, I'll be right back."

Feeling more nervous than on the day she arrived in town, Katie hurried into the house, filled a glass with water and the flowers, then set them in the middle of the kitchen table. The bright purple, butter-yellow, pink, and white lit up the room. She prepared a glass of water for Brian, because if he'd eaten any of the sugar cookies, he was bound to be thirsty.

Outside, she took a seat and passed him the glass. Two of the six cookies were already gone.

"Thank you. Just what I needed. These are delicious, by the way."

She smiled her appreciation for his compliment. "Who's minding the store?"

"Nobody. I closed up."

"You did?"

Brian set the plate and glass on a small table on the far side of his rocking chair. "I had important business to see to." He cleared his throat. "I owe you an apology."

"No, 'tis I who owes you one."

"Let me go first, if you don't mind." He stared at her for a long moment. "On rare occasions, I have trouble with anger. When I was a kid, I was smaller than the other boys my age, and I was often picked on and knocked down. Once Connor started growing taller, he put an end to that, but it left its mark on me. Every so often when things pile up or I get overly stressed, I erupt. I generally get over it quickly, and I promise that it really doesn't happen very often. I'm sorry that I took out my anger on you and lashed out at Keeley. I hope you can forgive me."

"Of course I can. Everyone gets angry sooner or later.

I'm guessing Connor told you that it was actually Keeley you lambasted."

"He told me, and I feel awful. I need to apologize to her too."

"That's why she denied taking the dress. She had no idea what I'd done at the time." Katie ducked her head, wishing she had talked to Brian before she helped that woman, but he'd been busy in the stockroom with the man looking at suits. "I took pity on Miss Pettigrew. Her dress was in such sad shape, and her hands were red and chafed from doing laundry. She paid half of the money for enough yards of fabric to make a dress and is going to bring in eggs for us to sell until she works off the balance. I loaned her the rose-colored dress to use as a pattern. She promised she wouldn't wear it, but I'm guessing she did if you saw her in it."

Brian pursed his lips. "She did, but you'll be happy to know that she returned it this morning, freshly laundered and pressed."

"Oh good. I am relieved to hear that."

"I'm truly sorry for getting so upset. I honestly don't know why I did. I trust that you know we can't constantly be giving things away, or we'll soon go out of business."

She liked how he used *we* when talking about the store. "I do. Next time I want to help someone, I'll talk to you first."

He rose and moved closer then reached for her hand and tugged her up. "So we're both forgiven. Now what?"

Katie frowned. "What do you mean?"

Brian rubbed a hand across his jaw. "Are things all right between us? Can we proceed with our weddings plans?"

For the first time in two days, Katie smiled. "There's nothing I'd like more."

❧ Epilogue ❧

June 2, 1888

Just a few days shy of a month from the afternoon she and her sister rode the stage into Cactus Creek, Keeley sat next to her fiancé in church, anxiously waiting the end of the service. The double wedding would commence as soon as Pastor Rice finished his sermon. She reached over and stilled Katie's jiggling leg for what must have been the twentieth time in the past half hour. Katie mouthed, "*Sorry,*" then turned back to try to focus on the message.

Keeley glanced to her left, where Connor held Jamie, peacefully sleeping sprawled across his lap. She glanced up, and Connor cocked his head, sending her that special smile reserved only for her. Oh, how she'd grown to love this rough, strong lawman. At the sting of tears, she widened her eyes and blinked fast to keep them from spilling down her face. When she'd first left Chicago in the wee hours of the morning those few short weeks ago, she'd been unsure about becoming a mail-order bride in the unknown wilds of Texas, but she'd put her trust in God's direction. She couldn't be happier with the results.

Even when Katie had suggested not marrying right away and had come up with the plan to not reveal who was who, she'd been uncertain. But the plan had been a wise one, because otherwise she would have married Brian. She couldn't say what life would have been like had that happened, but now that she was so in love with Connor, she was very thankful for Katie's wise suggestion.

Tonight she and Connor would share the rented house with Jamie, and Katie would be at Brian's home. It would be her first night to be separated from her sister, but she would be all right, especially if she was wrapped in the arms of her beloved. Her insides spun like the dirt devil Connor had pointed out on one of their buggy rides. Paperwork to adopt Jamie was filled out and just waiting for her signature as Mrs. Connor McLoughlin. Soon she and Connor would be Jamie's legal parents. She peeked at the child again. They'd decided on James Thurman McLoughlin for his new name. James, she recently found out, just happened to be Connor's middle name. Only God could have worked that out so perfectly.

Soft organ playing jolted her out of her contemplations and back to the present. Sadly, she hadn't heard much of what Pastor Rice had to say today, but there would be plenty of other Sundays to enjoy his wise teaching. Her insides danced. The special moment was almost here.

"Let us pray, and then we will begin the day's exciting activities. This will be a first for Cactus Creek and for me also—two weddings at the same time." He smiled in their direction then bowed his head. "Heavenly Father, we thank You for this most unusual day. We ask Your blessing on our work this week and that You would send rain to help our crops grow and keep our livestock healthy. May those with businesses in town prosper. We ask a very special blessing on the two unions taking place today. Thank You, Lord. Amen."

As the parishioners stood, Katie squeezed Keeley's hand. "Are you ready?"

Grinning, Keeley nodded. "Aye, so much."

"Well, let's get this show started." Connor stood. Jamie had awakened. He rubbed his eyes then reached for Keeley. She took the wee lad she'd quickly come to love and kissed his cheek. Jamie grinned, leaned over, and slobbered on hers with an open-mouth kiss. Connor chuckled as he pulled his handkerchief from his pocket and wiped her cheek. "Looks like somebody loves you."

Keeley's heart stammered then kicked into high gear at Connor's subtle meaning. He'd told her he loved her several times, and each time it was precious to hear.

Emily Willis, Connor's landlady and a woman Keeley had met at the sewing circle, squeezed into the row in front of them, smiling. "Are you excited? It's a historic occasion." Her blue eyes twinkled.

"Aye, I am quite ready."

"So, you're getting married in a blue dress? It's quite lovely."

"I've heard that many American women are wearing white at their weddings these days, but blue is the traditional color for Irish matrimonial ceremonies."

Emily swatted her hand in the air. "Most women around here are happy if they can simply wear a new dress when they get married. Some even wear calico, but white—" She shook her head and made a clucking sound with her tongue. "White simply isn't practical for women like us."

Keeley smiled at being included as one of the town's women. "You're right. White gets dirty far too easily."

"Enough of me holding you up. I can see your man is ready to head outside. God's blessings on your marriage."

"Thank you."

Connor reached out from the aisle to her. "I'm glad to see you're making friends."

" 'Twas difficult at first, but once I started attending the sewing circle, I began meeting people."

Brian strode toward them. "What's taking you two so long? Katie sent me back in to get you."

Keeley hiked her chin. "I was talking with a friend."

"Were you now?" Brian smiled. "I suppose that's a good reason to be delayed."

Connor gave her a gentle nudge from behind. "We're not late. They can hardly start without us."

"That's true." Brian nodded. "Honestly, I think more people are eager to eat that fine potluck and roasted calf than to see our weddings."

Connor slapped his hat on as he neared the door. "Well, that's just too bad. They can't eat until we're married."

"True again. See you at the arbor." Brian trotted down the church steps.

Keeley squinted as she stepped out into the bright sunshine. Jamie sneezed twice, as he tended to do whenever they first went out on a sunny day. God had blessed them with the perfect day for a wedding. She gazed past the crowd to look at the lovely arbor that had been erected and decorated with flowers Brian had ordered from Dallas. What a delight to get married under the beautiful arbor.

"Let me have the boy while you finish getting ready."

She passed Jamie to Connor then looped her arm around Connor's free one and descended the steps. He escorted her to the tent that had been set up for the women to finish their wedding preparations. Connor bent down and kissed her. "See you in a few minutes, wife-to-be."

Inside the tent, Mrs. Rice was placing one of the floral wreaths that Keeley and Katie had made just before the service on her sister's head. Katie straightened and turned toward her, looking so pretty with her long, dark hair hanging freely past her waist. The lovely wreath of white flowers and greenery wrapped around her head, and in the back, blue ribbons that matched their dresses flowed down her back. Katie's headdress also had white ribbons, while Keeley's had medium blue ones as well as some that were a lighter shade, so that everyone could tell them apart.

"Your turn." Smiling, Mrs. Rice turned to Keeley, holding her headpiece.

Keeley pulled the pins from her hair, letting it cascade around her shoulders and back. In short order, she was ready. Katie held her bouquet of white, yellow, and purple flowers. Mrs. Rice handed Keeley hers. "Don't you two look lovely. Connor and Brian are blessed men, and you are fortunate as well, especially considering how things started with the four of you. I hear the music, but I would like to pray with you first, if that's all right."

"Of course," Katie said, although Keeley recognized her anxiousness by the way her sister nibbled her lip.

Mrs. Rice laid a hand on each of their shoulders. "Dear Lord, thank You for these lovely women You've brought to our small town. I ask that You knit each woman's heart together with her husband's, and that You establish solid marriages that will produce many godly children. Thank You for this beautiful day. Bless these women, we ask in Jesus' name. Amen."

Keeley opened her eyes to see Katie's moist brown eyes shining back.

"Come, sister. We have important business to attend to."

"You two line up at the back of the crowd, and I'll go get that sweet little boy from Connor." Mrs. Rice held open the tent flap, and Katie walked out first then Keeley followed. It looked like the whole town had showed up for the wedding, even some people who hadn't attended church. Keeley followed Katie as they walked behind the people. Murmurs of delight drifted through the crowd. The guests stood in two sections, leaving a wide aisle. Keeley stepped up next to her sister.

Smiling, Katie reached out and squeezed her hand. "I'll miss you tonight."

Keeley grinned widely and shook her head, unable to resist teasing her. "I seriously doubt it."

Katie chuckled, her eyes glistening. "You're probably right."

The violin and guitar music started, and Pastor Rice gestured for them to come forward. Her heart dancing a lively jig, Keeley walked alongside Katie, all the time staring into Connor's delighted face. Brian had the same excited expression as he gazed at Katie. Only God could have foreseen this day months ago when they'd chosen to answer Connor and Brian's ad in the matrimonial newspaper instead of one of the many other advertisements rom men looking for a woman to marry. Things may have started with a standoff, but God had truly answered their many prayers or a happy, secure life and a permanent home.

Vickie McDonough is an award-winning author of nearly fifty published books and novellas, with more than 1.5 million copies sold. A bestselling author, Vickie grew up wanting to marry a rancher, but instead, she married a computer geek who is scared of horses. She now lives out her dreams penning romance stories about ranchers, cowboys, lawmen, and others living in the Old West. Her novels include *End of the Trail,* winner of the OWFI 2013 Booksellers Best Fiction Novel Award. *Whispers on the Prairie* was a *Romantic Times* Recommended Inspirational Book for July 2013. *Song of the Prairie* won the 2015 Inspirational Readers' Choice Award. *Gabriel's Atonement*, book one in the Land Rush Dreams series, placed second in the 2016 Will Rogers Medallion Award. Vickie has recently stepped into independent publishing.

Vickie has been married for more than forty years to Robert. They have four grown sons, one daughter-in-law, and a precocious granddaughter. When she's not writing, Vickie enjoys reading, doing stained glass, watching movies, and traveling. To learn more about Vickie's books or to sign up for her newsletter, visit her website at www.vickiemcdonough.com.